MIDSUMMER MEETING

Petra joined the close village community of Mindon when she was unexpectedly left a cottage there by an old friend of her mother. Petra felt immediately at home and was made welcome by the local residents—in particular, by the members of the Mindon Amateur Dramatic Society. Presided over by the formidable Ursula, the ambitious decision had been made to put on *A Midsummer Night's Dream* as the next production. Petra, to her surprise and pleasure, was put in charge of the scenery. Rivalries, squabbles, love affairs and seething resentments threatened to scupper the production and all Ursula's management skills were needed to prevent disaster. But Petra had more pressing things on her mind than the set designs. A mystery from the past had begun to haunt her—and the answer to that mystery might solve the puzzle of why she had been left such a beautiful house by a total stranger.

MIDSUMMER MEETING

Elvi Rhodes

CHIVERS PRESS
BATH

First published 1999
by
Transworld Publishers Ltd
This Large Print edition published by
Chivers Press
by arrangement with
Transworld Publishers Ltd
2000

ISBN 0 7540 1474 6

British Library Cataloguing in Publication Data available

Printed and bound in Great Britain by
REDWOOD BOOKS, Trowbridge, Wiltshire

This is for Paul and Mary Scherer,
with love.

Acknowledgements

I thank my son, Stephen, in whose New York home part of *Midsummer Meeting* was written. He spent time reading every word of the book and made suggestions (and criticisms!), all of which were improvements.

CHAPTER ONE

'So there you are! We've read both plays. Priestley's *When We Are Married* and William Shakespeare's *A Midsummer Night's Dream*! We've read them together and each one of us has read them at home, on our own.'

Ursula glanced with some doubt around the group gathered in her sitting room. It was her sitting room partly because no other member had one quite as large or could offer a full complement of comfortable chairs, with no-one reduced to sitting on the floor or on a kitchen stool, but mostly because she was the producer of the Mindon Amateur Dramatic Society and as such had the power. As a sop, or out of the kindness of her heart, as she would have said, she never served anything other than good coffee. None of your nasty instant stuff with semi-skimmed, or worse still, powdered milk which tasted like whitewash. No, the finest filtered Colombian with cream, and it was this delicious smell that was now drifting from the kitchen into the room where they sat.

'At least I *hope* we've all read them at home?' She looked around the circle, not quite trusting one or two of them. 'Hattie and Joyce, would you be angels and serve the coffee?' She was happy to provide it; she was damned if she would hand it round. 'And you'll find a plate of chocolate biscuits on the dresser.'

'Certainly, Ursula!' Hattie and Joyce said in unison, scrambling to their feet.

'Dear ladies!' Ursula said before they were quite

1

out of earshot. 'What would we do without them?'

'Or without you, dear Ursula, and your hospitality,' a man said in a smooth, dark-brown actorish voice.

Ursula smiled at him. 'You know it's a pleasure, Giles! Anything I do for the MADS—I suppose anything any one of us does for the MADS—is a pleasure.'

There were murmurs of assent which lasted until Hattie and Joyce brought in the coffee on rather elegant trays, though not the best silver ones which would have been too heavy because they were both quite small ladies.

'So, while we're drinking our coffee,' Ursula said, 'if there's anything left to discuss about either of the plays, which I do doubt because I think it's all been said, we'll do that. And then we'll put it to the vote.'

She had no qualms about the outcome, and if it came to a pinch she, as producer, had the casting vote. She hoped not to have to use it. She did not like votes. Consensus—or if necessary coercion— was preferable. She was wrong, though, in thinking there was nothing left to say. That was a case of hope over experience. There was always more to be said in any MADS committee meeting, even if it went on until midnight, as it sometimes did.

'I still wonder whether Shakespeare isn't a bit too ambitious,' one man said. 'You know what I mean. All them characters. All that fancy talk! Will the people of Mindon understand it?'

'Oh come, Cyril!' Ursula protested. Really Cyril Parsons could be quite tiresome. He was what she called a professional Yorkshireman, and proud of it. But he was, inexplicably to her, well liked. 'You

2

underestimate Mindon. It's quite a cultured place.'

That was perhaps stretching it a bit far, but one could hope and strive, and to bring a modicum of culture to the village was one of the goals she had set herself. In any case she knew why Cyril wanted the Priestley. She could read him like a book. He wanted to play Alderman Helliwell.

'I think I could play Alderman Helliwell!' Cyril said. There was no point in beating about the bush. He knew he could do it and what was more, he'd bring a bit of authenticity to the role. 'I do really think I could do it!'

'I'm sure you're cut out for it,' Giles said.

Cyril turned a beaming smile on him. It was not often Mr la-di-da Giles Rowland gave him an approving word. 'Thank you, lad!' he said.

'But what about the rest of us?' Giles said. 'We don't have a Yorkshire accent between us.'

'Perhaps Cyril could teach us?' someone said.

Fay Holliday, Giles noted without surprise. She was known for making quite stupid suggestions. This one made him shudder. His voice had once been likened to that of Richard Burton. There was no way he would waste it on J. B. Priestley.

'I think not,' he said.

Giles was like the rest of them, Ursula thought. He viewed any production according to how it enhanced him. No doubt he had cast himself as Theseus . . . or perhaps Oberon . . . in the *Dream*. She was, she reckoned, the only one who considered what would be good for the MADS, good for the village. So as she was the producer, and as far as she knew there was no-one waiting to jump into her shoes, that was how it would be.

She had expressed these thoughts to her

3

husband more than once.

'You mean you like your own way, darling!' Eric had said.

Sipping her coffee, Ursula looked around. This was the stage at which they started talking to each other instead of through the chair (herself?. It had to happen and for a little while she would allow it, but when it had gone on long enough she would call the meeting to order. Ten minutes, she thought, looking at her watch, then back to whatever discussion she might decide was enough before actually choosing the play. That done, all those who were not on the Casting Committee, which meant at least half of those present, could depart, leaving the rest to get down to the nitty-gritty of sorting out the parts. There was no time to fix a separate meeting.

The allocating of the parts was an enormous responsibility which she would gladly have taken on single-handed had not the MADS insisted on committees for everything. They could hardly serve coffee in the interval of a performance, and wash up afterwards, without having a committee for it. Indeed, she was sure they must have one, though it was thankfully not in her field.

'There!' she called out after exactly ten minutes. 'Can we stop having six separate meetings and come back to one? Has everyone finished coffee?' (She never offered seconds.) 'Joyce, Hattie . . .'

'Shall we clear away?' they offered.

'Thank you so much,' Ursula said. 'Don't bother to wash up. I'll put them in the dishwasher later. I don't want you to miss any of the meeting.'

They scurried around like small bright mice, clearing away. She half expected to see them eat up

4

the biscuit crumbs.

'Now!' Ursula said. 'Have we any last-minute, *brief* points to make about either of the plays?'

'I think it's high time we tackled Shakespeare,' Giles said. 'We've been going a few years now and we've never done anything quite so ambitious. I reckon we're ready for it.'

'It won't be easy to stage. Several scene changes. Not one straightforward set like Priestley.'

The speaker was Norman Pritchard, usually and valuably stage manager.

'But I'm sure you'll cope with it, Norman,' Ursula said. 'You've never let us down yet!'

'And lots of props,' Doris, Norman's wife, said. 'And all period. I shall have to have a good look around the attic.'

The Pritchards' capacious attic was the repository for almost anything the Society had ever used or might possibly use in the future. It was access to the attic, and knowledge of just about everything in it, which automatically made Doris property mistress. Swords, stools, drapes, vases, small tables, jardinières, crockery, artificial flowers, a palm tree—anything, everything.

'I can't think of anything sixteenth century except perhaps the sword.' There was already a worried frown on Doris's face.

'There's sure to be a sword in Shakespeare!' Hattie said helpfully.

'I still reckon *When We Are Married* would be more suitable,' Cyril Parsons said. He was not ready to give up Alderman Helliwell without a bit of a fight. 'It's a rattling good play and we could do justice to it. It's a play performed all over the world. J. B. Priestley is one of our best living

5

playwrights!'

'He's dead,' Giles said.

'Not all that many years,' Cyril said.

'There'd be more parts in *A Midsummer Night's Dream*,' Jennie Austin said. 'All those lords and ladies, attendants, fairies.' She had been in the society eighteen months now with never a sniff of a part, possibly because she was a woman. Females were thick on the ground, men at a premium, and much sought after.

'The fairies could be played by St Peter's Brownies!' Amelia said cheerfully. 'They'd look awfully sweet!' She also happened to have two small daughters in the Brownies.

Over my dead body, Ursula thought, though she would not say so out loud. Who knew who might have to be dragged in when flu and broken legs and visits to one's grandmother had taken their toll?

'There's another thing,' Norman Pritchard said. 'Put to it I daresay I could manage the Shakespeare, but there's more to it than just somebody's living room, tables and chairs and a bookcase. There's complicated sets. A room in the duke's palace. A wood—trees, shrubs, animals— that sort of thing. Who's going to do all that?'

Ursula's smile was that of a conjurer about to bring the rabbit out of the hat.

'I think we can leave all that to Petra,' she said. 'Petra is an artist. She will design exactly what's wanted.'

'Ah, but who'll carry it out?' Chalky White demanded. He was a carpenter, both in real life and in the MADS. He'd be the one they'd call on every time they wanted a nail hammered in or two pieces of wood glued together.

6

'You will, Chalky dear,' Ursula said. 'With your usual skill which we couldn't do without! But we'll all help. We'll all muck in, as we usually do!'

She turned her smile from Chalky White and flashed it across to Petra, who was sitting on a low chair at the far side of the room. She was pleased about Petra Banbury. Petra had been in the village only a few weeks when they'd met at a wine and cheese do. She had lost no time in persuading her to join the MADS.

'Though not as an acting member,' Petra had stipulated. 'I could help with scenery—perhaps costumes—but not acting.'

'That', Ursula told her, 'is music to my ears. We have an absolute gaggle of females scratching around for acting parts. You don't know any men, do you?'

'Not yet,' Petra said. 'I haven't been here long enough.'

She had hardly had time to meet anyone. Uprooting herself from the North Yorkshire market town, where she had lived for all thirty-six years of her life, to this Surrey village—and it had been something done almost on a whim, a decision made on the spur of the moment—had absorbed her mind and her physical energy so that there was nothing left for meeting people. That she fully intended to do when the time was ripe. It was her intention, as far as her work allowed her, to join in the life of the village, but who knew how long that would have been delayed had not Cynthia Clarke, the wife of the local GP, invited her for a glass of wine?

Several of the people there, she had discovered, were members of the dramatic society. Both the

7

doctor and his wife were. 'Though Preston can take only the smallest parts,' Cynthia Clarke explained. 'He never knows where he's going to be. Called out in the middle of a rehearsal as like as not!'

'The MADS has by far the biggest membership of anything in the village,' Ursula had boasted.

'Except for the church, Ursula!' the vicar had said, joining the group just in time. 'Except for the church!'

So she had been happy to accept Ursula King's invitation to join the society, and therefore here she was, undertaking to do the scenery for *Midsummer Night's Dream* should it be chosen, which it seemed was highly likely.

This was not her first meeting. She had been to two playreading evenings. She had even been allowed to read a few lines—the reading was spread out so that no-one could say they hadn't had a turn—and had not done too badly though, as she had told Ursula, there was no way she wanted an acting part even in the unlikely event that she was offered one. She would stick to painting and designing, which had earned her a precarious living for several years now.

'Right then!' Ursula said, calling the meeting to order and frustrating at least two people who had been nerving themselves to give an opinion. 'I really don't think there's anything more to discuss. Now we must make a choice! Just a show of hands. Who would like *When We Are Married?*'

'Five! And who would choose *A Midsummer Night's Dream?*' Actually, it was in the bag.

Nine hands were raised, followed by three more, rather wavering. What shall I do? Cyril Parsons asked himself hastily. If he didn't vote for it he might not get a part. He raised his hand.

'Thirteen,' Ursula said. 'Let's consider it a lucky number, shall we?' She had noticed Cyril's tardy decision. She knew the reason why. He need not have worried, she had him marked for Bottom the Weaver. That rich Yorkshire voice, that particular brand of bossiness, made him a natural for the part.

'So the *Dream* it is,' Ursula said happily. 'Democratically chosen. And I'm sure those of you who perhaps *might* have preferred Priestley will rally round and give your support to the choice of the majority.'

'What does she mean, *might* have preferred Priestley?' Chalky White muttered to Norman Pritchard. 'Some of us voted for it, didn't we?'

Fortunately his words were lost in the small hubbub which had now broken out. Ursula gave it twenty seconds and then made herself heard over the top of it.

'Thank you all for coming. You all have homes to go to and I won't keep you any longer, except of course for the members of the Casting Committee. We will continue on your behalf and we'll let you know within the next few days who is to do what. Naturally there won't be acting parts for everyone, and some of you don't want them, but I expect you'll all help as usual and we couldn't do without you!'

Her smile swept around and enfolded Chalky and Norman, Doris, Hattie, Joyce, Angela Hatfield who would hopefully do the publicity and Amelia who was good on costumes. None of them would expect parts but that was no reason why they shouldn't receive encouragement.

9

'First rehearsal next Thursday, seven-thirty in the Parish Hall,' she said. 'That means everybody, whether you're acting or not.'

Then she left her place and crossed the room to Petra, who was already making for the door.

'I'm so glad you could come,' she said. 'You will be there on Thursday? I like to talk about things like scenery and props and so on right from the beginning.'

'Oh yes, I'll be there!' Petra assured her.

She went out by the front door at the same moment as Adam Benfield, and a group of others, all saying goodnight to each other, not a soul venturing a single word about hoped-for parts in the play. She had met Adam at a previous meeting. Someone had told her he was something in the new University of Southfield, which had once been Southfield Polytechnic. She didn't know exactly what he did. He seemed a pleasant man. Thirty-ish, she thought, or perhaps older. He was tall, with dark hair and a tanned skin, as if he spent a lot of time out of doors.

'Can I give you a lift home?' he asked her.

'Thank you,' Petra said. 'But it's no distance. I live right in the middle of the village. Not more than ten minutes' walk.'

'No matter,' Adam said. 'I have to go through the village. I live on the Southfield Road, a couple of miles out. I probably go right past your door.'

'Well,' she said, 'if you put it like that . . .'

'I managed to park quite close,' he said.

They walked down the broad drive, through the large, well-tended garden. Pinks, pansies, roses, all in orderly profusion, scented the dusk, reminding Petra that she really must get to work in her own garden, which showed serious signs of neglect.

'So are you enjoying living in Mindon?' Adam asked as he helped her into the car.

'Very much. People seem friendly.'

'Oh, they are!' he agreed. He wondered what had brought her here. He knew she had come from Yorkshire. But why to Mindon? It was nice enough, but why pick on it especially? There was no sign of any man around, whose job might have brought him here, whom she had to follow. She didn't wear a wedding ring, so presumably she was not a young widow. Did a divorced woman continue to wear a ring? He didn't know the etiquette of that.

'Have you lived here long?' Petra asked.

'Going on three years. I teach English in the university. Have you discovered the university yet?'

'I've driven past it, that's all. I hear they do some quite good courses in the neighbourhood.'

'That's right,' Adam said. 'Mostly in Southfield though, not Mindon.'

'Mindon seems quite lively,' Petra observed. 'Do you belong to many things?'

'Only the MADS. That takes up a lot of time.'

'I can imagine.'

They were at the door of her home, Plum Tree House. She had found out very little about him, only that his subject was English. He probably knew everything about *Midsummer Night's Dream*. Was he married? Was there a Mrs Benfield and one or two little Benfields waiting for him in his house in the Southfield Road?

He nipped out of the driver's seat and came around to open the passenger door. She added good manners to the little she knew about him. Should she ask him in for coffee, she wondered as

11

she got out of the car. She decided not. A move best made, if at all, when she knew him better.

'See you on Thursday,' he said.

He waited, and watched her as she walked between the stone gateposts—the iron gates which had swung between them had been commandeered more than fifty years earlier, supposedly to be made into a piece of a Spitfire—walked up the path and inserted her key in the door. For a moment she was silhouetted in the light from the porch as she turned around to wave to him, and then she was in the house and he drove away.

The house welcomed her as it had on that first day when, accompanied by Mr Craig the solicitor, she had stepped into the wide hall. When she'd boarded the train in Harrogate—it was still not quite daylight—she had left behind her a North Yorkshire in the throes of winter. In Mindon, stepping out of the taxi which had brought her from Southfield station, it was already early spring. The sun shone, daffodils were in bloom, blossom was bursting on the plum tree in the garden at the back of the house, from which the house presumably took its name. She had been a stranger to these parts. Surrey was a place she knew existed, but France, Italy, bits of Spain, were more familiar to her than the South of England. She was a stranger, yet she had felt herself welcomed.

She had stood side by side with Mr Craig in the hall, surveyed its black-and-white tiled floor, partly covered by a turkey rug in rich blues and reds. There was a door to the left and a matching one to the right, both of dark, heavy wood with large brass doorknobs. On the left a staircase rose, not overwhelming but of a generous width, dark wood, not carpeted. On the right the hall narrowed to a corridor, passing another door, then leading to the rear of the house.

'Oh! This looks nice!' Petra had said. 'Roomier than I'd imagined.' She had not been sure what to imagine. Perhaps a smallish cottage. There had been no clue, which was one reason why she had thought it best to make the journey to Mindon to take a look at it. There had been nothing in Mr Craig's letter to tell her what it was like. It might have been, in spite of its pretty name, a tumbledown shack. It was certainly not that.

'It's a good house,' Mr Craig had agreed, 'substantial without being over-large, though one might think it was for Miss Harden on her own.'

He had told her earlier that Dr and Mrs Harden had died within a fortnight of each other, both of influenza which had turned to pneumonia.

'But she never gave any sign of wanting to move,' he said. 'She was born here. She'd never known a time when her father wasn't the GP. Shall we look around?'

The door on the left of the hall led to what had been Dr Harden's waiting-room, and leading from that his consulting room. It was almost as if nothing had been done in the surgery rooms except to tidy things. The desk and tables were clear but in the area where the patients had waited chairs still stood close together around the room.

'Dr Harden was within weeks of retiring,' Mr Craig said. 'We now have Dr Clarke, who's chosen a more modern house on the edge of the village.'

The rest of the house, with the exception of the rather formal dining room and what had presumably been Dr and Mrs Harden's bedroom,

13

had a much more lived-in look. Partly, Petra supposed, because it had been left entirely as it had been on the day when its owner had so suddenly died. There were dented cushions on the sofa and chairs, magazines in the canterbury to the left of the fireplace, and on the low table by the fire some knitting and a knitting pattern, a long-sleeved sweater with a roll neck, the wool in a shade of moss green. The knitter had so far reached only to the armholes on the back, but, in a plastic carrier bag lying on the floor beside the table, was a supply of wool. Petra had put it all away in a cupboard though one day she knew she must finish it. Obviously Claire had started it, and because it was Claire who had changed her life she felt duty bound to complete it.

Not that she knew Claire. Not that she had ever met her. All she had known of Claire was an entry in her mother's address book, a great thick thing with entries going back for years, lots of them crossed out. Amongst those which weren't was Claire Harden's, Plum Tree House, Mindon. She had no idea who this woman might be, she had never heard her mentioned, but she had written to the address in Surrey, apprising Claire Harden of the date and time of her mother's funeral, just in case. Claire had replied at once, from a hospital bed. Two days earlier she had undergone a hysterectomy and was in no fit state to attend anything.

'I am truly sorry I can't be with you' she had written. 'Though I had not seen your mother for many years I shall never forget her kindness to me when we were at school together. I was new and frightened. She looked after me like an older sister.

14

At troubled times of my life she was always there for me . . .'

Petra had replied, thanking Claire for the nice things she had said about her mother, hoping, though vaguely, that one day they might meet. Nothing more until, much later, out of the blue a letter came addressed to her mother. This still happened from time to time and never failed to give Petra a shock, never failed to make her feel guilty as she opened an envelope addressed to someone else.

The correspondent was John Craig, of Craig, Craig and Butler, Solicitors, Mindon, Surrey, with the information that Miss Claire Harden, who had died suddenly of a heart attack, had in her will left her house and a sum of money to Marion Banbury, and would the said Marion please get in touch.

Letters flew back and forth between John Craig and Petra. Because Claire had specifically stated that, should Marion predecease her the legacy should go to *her* heir, Petra was now the rightful owner of Plum Tree House.

'But why?' Petra asked the solicitor, sitting across from his desk.

'I have no idea,' John Craig said. 'She told me nothing, except to agree, when asked, that your mother was not a relative.'

'Was she . . . well, eccentric?'

'Not quite eccentric. She was a very good headmistress of the village school here. She never married. She was unusual, perhaps. She gave money to unusual causes and people. The bulk of her estate has gone to a Home for Abused Women.'

'Abused women?'

'Yes. No reason given. One supposes just something which took her fancy. And she wasn't a lady who invited questions. At the time Miss Harden made the will, several years ago in fact, the residue wasn't much. The house only came into it after Dr and Mrs Harden died, and then since it became part of your mother's estate it was passed on to you.'

*   *   *

Petra hung her jacket in the hall, then went into the kitchen, filled the kettle. What she craved was a cup of Earl Grey tea with a slice of lemon floating in it. The coffee at Ursula's had left her thirsty. She would take the tea up to bed, have an early night. If she could keep awake long enough she might reread *Midsummer Night's Dream,* see if any ideas came to her for sets and scenery.

CHAPTER TWO

The Casting Committee consisted of four members, Tina Jackson, Nicola Pearce, George Shepherd and the producer herself. They were all, by common consent, non-acting members, so there would be no sound of gnashing teeth. It was the smallest casting committee Ursula had been able to get away with, though in fact she would much have preferred to do the whole casting on her own and, she reckoned, she was quite capable of so doing. But no matter, she thought as they arranged their chairs in a tighter group, she would get there in the

16

end, hopefully without too much time wasted.

'Now!' she said briskly. 'We have quite a job to do. More than thirty parts, not including Cobweb and that little lot of fairies or all those lords and ladies and attendants.'

'Thirty parts?' Tina Jackson said. 'We'll never do it!'

'Of course we will!'

Ursula's voice was firm, she would stand no nonsense. The trouble with Tina was that she would much have preferred them to do the Priestley. She was a nice woman but she had no vision, no get-up-and-go. She liked a play with a maximum of ten performers and one domestic set. It was a pity she was on the Casting Committee at all but George Shepherd had voted her on, without Ursula noticing, so that couldn't be helped now.

'It's all a challenge,' Ursula said. 'We must rise to it. The Bard himself! It's what Mindon has been waiting for!'

'You're right, Ursula,' Nicola Pearce said. 'As always!'

Smarmy devil, George Shepherd thought, though all he said was 'Shall we get on with it?' He had come straight from work, no time to call home for the supper which his wife would have left for him to heat up in the microwave before she went on night duty at Southfield Hospital.

'Quite right, George!' Ursula agreed. 'And I've already given some thought to it—'

'But we didn't know we were going to choose this one,' Tina interrupted.

'I gave thought to *both* plays,' Ursula said. It was not totally true. The only thought she had given to the Priestley was that it shouldn't be chosen.

17

'Well now,' she continued, 'let's start at the beginning. Theseus, Duke of Athens. I wonder if you agree with me that Giles is a natural for the part? He has the bearing, the dignity, and one can't deny that he has the voice for it.'

'I wondered about Oberon for Giles,' Tina said helpfully.

'I don't *quite* see him as Oberon,' Ursula said as if actually considering the possibility. 'A little bit lightweight for him.'

King of the fairies, George thought. Should suit him very well.

'And we must remember,' Ursula added, 'that Theseus is the very first person to speak in the play. Giles would grab the audience at once. "How this old moon wanes/She lingers my desires . . ."' She could hear him saying it. 'Yes, I really think Giles for Theseus, don't you?' She looked around the group as if it had been their suggestion and then, before they could reply, she put a firm tick against Theseus.

'Arabella for Hippolyta!' Nicola exclaimed, as if announcing a parliamentary candidate.

'She has the figure for it,' Tina agreed.

George nodded. 'Statuesque!'

'Right!' Ursula agreed, making the second tick. If she were to take an acting role, if it wasn't that she had more important things to do, she would quite like to play Hippolyta herself. Not that at five feet two with a 34A bust she could compete figure-wise, but in other ways . . . ' "Four days will quickly steep themselves in night,"' she quoted. ' "Four nights will quickly dream away the time".' But no, she had a duty to all of them to produce this play.

'Dr Clarke will do very well as Philostrate,' she

18

said. 'He doesn't have anything to do in the first act except stand around, and then leave when Theseus tells him—and in the last act no more than a dozen lines at most. And we all know that learning lines is *not* the doctor's forte, bless him! And then we come to the two pairs of lovers, Demetrius and Helena, Lysander and Hermia. I propose Adam Benfield for Lysander. I always think Lysander is much the nicer of the two men. Demetrius is a little mean. And Adam Benfield is a most attractive man and a good actor. He'll be a fine Lysander.'

'He certainly attracts me,' Nicola said. 'I wouldn't mind playing Hermia to his Lysander.'

Ursula suppressed a shudder at the thought of Nicola playing Hermia to anyone's Lysander. 'It's always been agreed,' she pointed out, 'that members of the Casting Committee took only the smallest roles, and then only when everyone else had been fitted in.'

'I know,' Nicola sighed. 'It was wishful thinking!'

And would remain so, Ursula thought. Nicola, alas, had a voice like a corncrake and an accent which was a rich and unusual mixture of Birmingham and Scouse. There was seldom a role, unless non-speaking, which fitted these constraints. It was a pity because she was more than presentable to look at: tall, slender, red-haired and indeed a very nice woman.

'I am hoping,' Ursula said kindly, on a sudden flash of inspiration, 'that in addition to your valuable work on the Casting Committee you will head Hippolyta's train of attendants. You would lend dignity to it!'

'Why, thank you!' Nicola said. 'Thank you very much!'

19

'I suppose Lucinda will be Hermia?' Tina said.

Ursula frowned. 'Why?' she asked.

'Well, she usually plays the lead, doesn't she? So I thought. . .' Tina floundered.

'The fact that Lucinda has played the lead in several productions doesn't mean that she must do so forever,' Ursula said. 'On this occasion I happen to think she's not suitable.'

'Why?' Tina persisted. She hadn't realized before that Ursula didn't like Lucinda. 'Why isn't she suitable?'

'Because . . .' It was Ursula's turn to flounder, but not for long. 'Her appearance is wrong for a start. Lucinda is tall, with long blond hair—'

'And beautiful!'

Ursula ignored Tina's interruption.

'Who says Hermia is small?' George demanded.

'George dear,' Ursula said patiently, 'Shakespeare says so! "Though she be but little, she is fierce". It's in the script.'

'We don't have to do every little thing by the book,' George grumbled. He was fed up, tired and very hungry. He couldn't do with going without his food. It gave him a pain in the belly. He fished in his pocket for an indigestion tablet. 'Anyway, who says Hermia's the lead?'

'I agree with that,' Ursula said. 'I can't agree that we needn't do everything by the book. Shakespeare didn't write his immortal words for us to change them. But I do think that though Hermia cannot possibly be tall and blond, she is not necessarily the lead.'

'I find it all very confusing,' George said. 'All these people chasing each other around a wood!'

Ursula's face split into a beaming smile, which

20

she turned entirely upon George.

'Absolutely right, George, you've hit the nail on the head!'

In his astonishment—he seldom met with the approval of Madam Bossy Boots—he swallowed the indigestion tablet before he had sucked the goodness out of it.

'Right? I said I was *confused*!'

'But that's it! Confusion! That's exactly what the play is about. Confusion!'

George shrugged. Since he seemed to be on a winning streak he'd say no more—though it was beyond him why people would pay good money to be confused.

Nicola brought them back to the subject in hand.

'So who *will* play Hermia?'

'Oh, I think Victoria Cattermole would do that very well,' Ursula said. She had never had anyone else in mind. 'She'll work nicely with Adam. As for Lucinda,' she added, again feeling suddenly kind, it seemed to follow getting her own way, 'she is exactly right for Titania! And I suppose one could say that Titania is the female lead, so that should be all right.'

Added to which, she thought, making a firm tick against Titania's name, she will spend a fair amount of time asleep on the ground, during which she cannot indulge in her usual habit of upstaging everyone else.

'So we come to Helena and Demetrius,' she said. 'Why not take a chance on Jennie Austin for Helena, and as for Demetrius, I think I'll have to ask my poor Eric. He didn't want a part this time but I'm afraid needs must. As always we're short of men.'

21

'He'll do it well,' Nicola said.

George looked at his watch. As well as needing to eat, he wanted to give Tina a lift home. Time spent with Tina was the bright spot of any day.

'I'm afraid I'll have to go soon,' he said.

'Quite!' Ursula jumped in. 'So, if I may make a suggestion, since we've dealt with most of the main parts you might like to leave the rest to me and if I need to I'll discuss with you on the telephone before Thursday.'

'We haven't chosen Bottom the Weaver,' Tina pointed out. 'He's very important.'

'Of course he is,' Ursula agreed. 'But who could play Bottom better than Cyril? I'm sure no-one could disagree with that!'

As far as I am concerned, George thought, she can ask Prince Charles to play Bottom, I'm off!

'If you would like a lift, Tina, I'm going in your direction.'

'Thank you, I would!' Tina said, as if it hadn't all been fixed beforehand.

*   *   *

'I think that went well,' Ursula said, not looking up from plumping the cushions as Eric came back into the sitting room. He had taken refuge in his study for the duration of the meeting.

'All as you intended?' he asked.

'Don't be silly, darling. It was a democratic meeting.' She switched off two superfluous lamps before settling into her usual chair. 'You can pour me a drink, dear,' she said. 'I've been thinking we should give one last little dinner before we plunge into rehearsals. There'll be no time then. I thought

22

Petra Banbury. I want to get to know her better. And Adam Benfield. He doesn't seem to have gone about much since his divorce, poor man.'

'You're not matchmaking, are you?' Eric asked.

'Certainly not,' she said. 'By the way, you're Demetrius!'

*   *   *

'Did you notice,' Tina asked when they were in the car, 'that Ursula cast all the parts?'

'She always does,' George said.

'It's very kind of you to give me a lift.'

'It's a pleasure. You know that,' he said. She was a lovely woman, Tina.

*   *   *

On Saturday morning, waiting in the baker's to be served, Petra found herself standing behind Adam Benfield. He was buying a small wholemeal loaf and two jam doughnuts, which did not seem like catering for a family, though perhaps the second doughnut was for Mrs B. He picked up his purchases, then turned around and saw her.

'Good morning!' he said. 'I didn't expect to see you here, which is a silly thing to say because you live here!'

'And you don't,' Petra pointed out.

She was pleasantly surprised when she left the shop to find him waiting outside.

'I sometimes go for a coffee after the baker's,' he said. 'I wondered if you'd like to join me?'

'Thank you. I would. Where do you go?' Petra said.

'Ye Old Tudor Tearoom. Built in the 1930s. Totally pseudo, but they serve the best coffee, not to mention shortbreads.'

The place was busy but they found a table by the window from which they looked out on to the street.

'You have a sweet tooth,' Petra observed, watching him stir a heaped spoonful of sugar into his coffee and bite into a shortbread finger. 'And you bought two jam doughnuts in the baker's. Does your wife have a sweet tooth also?'

'I hate to disillusion you,' he said. 'They're both for me. I don't have a wife. I did once. We had an amicable divorce about a year ago. We married too young, both of us still in university. My wife—my former wife—has remarried, and gone to live in Suffolk.'

'I see.'

'And you? Is there a Mr Banbury?' Or was there, he meant. He knew she lived alone.

'No,' Petra said. 'I never married. Not that . . . well, he was already married. He couldn't make up his mind between his wife and me.'

'I'm sorry.'

She took another sip of coffee and changed the subject.

'I didn't expect to see you shopping in Mindon. I thought you'd go to Southfield.'

'I do mostly. There's a good Sainsbury's in Southfield, but I come here for bread. No-one beats Mr Vickers as a baker. We're lucky to have him.'

'I know. And a village store, a butcher, a bank . . .'

'And at least four gift shops!' Adam said.

24

Eventually—there seemed no reason to hurry—they ordered a second pot of coffee. 'But no more shortbreads,' Adam told the waitress. 'I shall get as fat as a pig!'

He showed no signs of that, Petra thought. He was slender without being thin, and, though seated he looked no more than average height, when he stood up he was tall. His length was in his legs. She wondered again how old he was and put his age at two or three years below her own. He was one of those men who would look the same whatever age he reached. It was there in the bony structure of his face, the bright intelligence in his eyes.

'What brought you to Mindon?' he asked as Petra poured more coffee. 'It seems a strange step from North Yorkshire. And a long one.'

'It is,' Petra agreed. 'I'm still surprised, almost every day, at finding myself here. I wake in the morning and wonder what's happened to me. The fact is, I inherited Plum Tree House, though in the strangest way.'

Her mother and father, she told him, had been involved in a car accident. Presumably her father had lost control and the car had veered across the road and then plunged down a steep bank.

'My father was killed instantly,' she said. 'My mother died of her injuries two weeks later.'

'How terrible!' Adam said.

'It was. I don't know which was worse, my father's sudden death or waiting every day for my mother to die. I adored both my parents. I'm an only child.'

'Don't go on if you'd rather not,' Adam said.

'I don't mind,' Petra said, which she recognized as strange because she had never talked to anyone about all this, except the solicitor, and then only the barest facts.

She told Adam now about the entry in the address book, and how she had written to Claire Harden.

'So you met her at the funeral?' he said.

'No. I never met her at all. She was ill. But she told me what I hadn't known, that she and my mother had been friends from schooldays. It must have been at the same convent school in Bedfordshire. I know my mother was a boarder there. She paid great tribute to the way my mother had looked after her then, how close they'd been.'

'So how come you'd never heard of her?'

'I don't know. My mother never spoke of her and Claire didn't explain why they lost touch. At any rate that was the only letter I ever had. I'm still mostly in the dark about her, apart from small details the solicitor gave me.'

'So how did she come to leave you the house?'

'She didn't, not directly—'

She was interrupted by a sharp tapping on the window. Peering in, her faced fixed in a cheerful smile, was Ursula. She made signs that she was about to enter.

'I'll tell you the rest later,' Petra said quickly as Ursula opened the door and marched across to join them.

She sat down, distributed various shopping bags around, then raised the lid of the coffee pot and examined the contents.

'Is there enough left in the pot for little me?' she said. 'I could just ask for a clean cup and saucer!'

'It will be cold,' Adam protested. 'Let me order you some fresh.'

'How kind!' Ursula said. 'And do you think I might have one of their almond slices? They're quite delicious. Have you tried them?'

'Don't tempt me!' Adam said.

'Or me!' Petra added. 'In any case I must be going.'

'Oh, please don't!' Ursula begged. 'You can't leave me on my own. And I wanted to see you. Such a coincidence, finding you both here together!'

'We met in the baker's,' Adam said.

'And you decided to come in here for a coffee? How very nice! Such a cosy little place, I always think.'

'Why did you want to see us?' Petra prompted.

'Oh! Surprise! I thought I would give a little dinner party—quite small, nothing formal. Just the two of you, Eric and myself, the vicar and Grace. I'll make a date and let you know. Have you met the vicar, Petra?'

'Apart from MADS, only fleetingly,' Petra said. 'He always seems to be in a hurry.'

Ursula sighed.

'I'm sure he is, poor man! It's a busy parish and he has no curate. I myself have had a word with the bishop about that, but so far to no avail, though I shall keep at it. Apart from that, the vicar has two small children who seem to keep him occupied. Fathers do so much for their children these days, don't they? Eric would have left home if I'd asked him to change a nappy. Still, they say it's progress. So will you both come when I fix the date?'

'Thank you,' Petra said. 'I look forward to it.'

'Me too,' Adam agreed.

'Good! And we shall all get to know Petra

27

better!' A sudden look of apprehension swept over her face. Her eyebrows went up. 'You're not vegetarians by any chance?'

'I'm not,' Petra assured her.

'Nor me,' Adam said. 'I eat anything.'

'Thank heaven,' Ursula said. 'My vegetarian cuisine is limited. And now, Adam, I have news for you!'

'News for me?'

Petra hid a smile at the wariness in Adam's voice.

'Yes! I—that is to say "we"—' Ursula corrected herself, 'have cast the play. Well, most of it. All the important parts. And you,' she paused dramatically, '*you* are to be Lysander! What do you think of that?' She spoke as if she had just announced a knighthood.

'Marvellous!' Adam said in an unconvincing voice. 'I mean . . . wonderful! Thank you very much. I just hope I can do it, I hope I can live up to it. I've never tackled Shakespeare before.' He had not been one of those who had voted for it. He had too great a regard for Shakespeare.

Ursula leaned across the table and laid a kindly hand on his lapel.

'Of course you can do it, dear! You are a university lecturer in English. A PhD! Oh! Ah! Here comes my almond slice!' She withdrew her hand and, eschewing the pastry fork, picked up the slice and took a large bite. 'You'll do it beautifully,' she answered him through a mouthful, scattering a few crumbs here and there.

'Congratulations, Adam,' Petra said solemnly.

'Now I daresay, Adam, being you,' Ursula said, 'you already possess a copy of the play. But I'm

28

going to ask you a favour. Don't dash home and start learning lines. I like to have a preliminary read-through so that I can be quite sure everyone has understood their lines clearly, knows how to say them. Not that there's much hope of that, I'm afraid. Except of course in your case and one or two others. But I'm here to guide and help!'

'I promise faithfully not to learn my lines between now and Thursday,' Adam said.

'Now you're teasing me, dear,' Ursula reproved. 'But one thing you *will* like to know is that Victoria Cattermole is to be your Hermia. I'm sure *that* will please you!'

'Vicky will be fine,' Adam admitted. 'She'll do it well.'

Ursula ate the last of the crumbs from her plate then licked her fingers.

'You'll be very good together,' she said.

'I really must go,' Petra said.

Adam rose to his feet, picked up the bill. 'Me too!'

'I'll see you on Thursday, then,' Ursula said. 'And if you should see Victoria in the village, please don't tell her she's Hermia. I want the pleasure of telling her myself. I intend to call in on my way home.'

'Vicky works in the library,' Adam explained.

'I didn't know that,' Petra admitted. 'I saw her at the play readings, of course. I thought she read well.'

'She always does,' Ursula said. 'By the way, Adam, do you know any spare men? I mean, surely there are some in the university. I don't know how I'm going to cast all the male parts. There's Egeus, and most of the Mechanicals—and of course Puck.

29

All I can think of for Puck is Melvin Fairclough, and he's quite inexperienced.'

'I'll try,' Adam promised. 'I can't think of anyone offhand.'

'Well, do your best,' Ursula urged.

Petra and Adam left, walking together in the direction of Plum Tree House, since Adam said he had parked his car not far from there.

Shall I invite him in? Petra wondered. But they had had coffee and now it was almost lunchtime. She didn't know him quite well enough to ask him in to lunch, especially an extempore one. She wasn't sure that either her larder or her expertise could stand the strain.

'Well, here we are then!' she said. 'Thank you for the coffee.'

'A pleasure!' Adam said. 'Perhaps we'll meet up in the baker's another Saturday?' He thought she might have asked him in. Clearly she wasn't going to. She seemed an interesting woman.

Petra put down her packages on the table in the hall, took off her suede jacket and dropped it on the nearest chair. Sometimes nowadays when she did this she was reminded of her mother, so sharply reminded that she could almost hear her mother's voice. 'Petra, do hang up your coat. You come in from school, you throw your coat on a chair, your satchel on the floor. Why can't you learn to be tidy?' But there was no sting in the memory, just as there had been no sting in her mother's words. Theirs had been a loving relationship, as indeed had been her relationship with her father. She had grown up in a home of which love was the cornerstone. As an only child she had basked in their affection, and had returned it. It had never bothered her then that she had no siblings and it was something her parents never spoke about. She was made to feel that she was all they had ever wanted. They were a happy threesome.

She had made friends at school and they had always been made welcome in her home, indeed she was encouraged to invite them. It had been the same when she had gone to the local art college—instead of the university—to study painting. She could bring anyone home knowing they would be treated with friendliness and courtesy. Sometimes, for a fleeting second, she had thought that just possibly her parents' hospitality to her friends was given so that both she and her friends would prefer it to having Petra visit them in their homes. But the thought quickly vanished. She was happy as things were; she was cocooned in love.

Which was all very well, she thought now, standing in the hall of a house which was really too big for her, but their sudden deaths had left her marooned. Telling Adam Benfield about her parents had brought it back to her too vividly. She wasn't sure why she had done that.

She went through to her studio which was what had been Dr Harden's waiting-room and surgery. In fact, she thought, the house was not really too large for her because it allowed her space for her work, and she planned, when she could raise the money, to have the wall between the waiting-room and the study knocked down to give her even more work space. It wouldn't be a difficult thing to do. The wall had obviously been built to separate Dr Harden from the waiting patients.

Her easel stood in the window. The painting on it—on a smaller scale than she usually worked in—

31

was no more than half finished, and was of the garden and the view beyond, seen from the window.

She examined the painting with critical eyes. It needed a lot doing to it and today the light was not good. Perhaps she would get up early in the morning and work on it. For now she would go and make some lunch, and after that she might go along and join the library. She turned away from the window, then stopped in front of a shelf, picking up a photograph in a narrow silver frame.

When, after her first visit to Mindon and her first sight of Plum Tree House, she had returned to Yorkshire, it was with the half-formed idea that perhaps she would live in Mindon, pull herself up by her Yorkshire roots and leave the place where she had always lived. The death of her parents had left her restless, unsettled.

On the train journey back she had thought of little else. There was nothing to stop her doing whatever she wanted to do. She hadn't sought this freedom, hadn't really wanted it, but now that she had it why not use it? It was a small thing which decided her. When she'd left Mindon it had been on a bright spring morning. When she left the train in Harrogate the sky was dark, the wind was cold, and it was raining cats and dogs.

The next day she put her parents' house—now hers—on the market, and started at once to clear out the accumulation of years. She would take very little with her, only a few things to which she was attached. Plum Tree House was well furnished.

It was in the attic, in a drawer in an old chest, that she had discovered the photograph she was now holding in her hand. It had not been framed then. She had bought the frame later. It showed two young women, in their late teens or early twenties, standing in front of an ornate doorway, and between them, his arms around both girls, was a young man: dark, handsome, smiling.

One of the girls was clearly her mother. She hadn't altered all that much. There was no clue to the other girl, though Petra suspected it might possibly be Claire, which was why she had brought it with her to Mindon. When she got to Mindon there might just be someone who remembered Claire as a girl. Surprisingly, when she did arrive, there were no photographs around except of Dr Harden and his wife. As to the young man, there was no clue whatever to him.

What had been a more startling find, in the same drawer, had been three sketches of her mother, reclining on cushions on a sofa, wearing very little clothing. They revealed her as a young and physically sensuous woman. They were exquisitely drawn, by the hand of an expert. Petra recognized that at once. She had brought them with her to Mindon and put them away in a cupboard. She would like to have displayed them for the beauty of the drawing, but she could not quite bring herself to do so.

She took a long look at the photograph, as she often did, and went to the kitchen to scramble some eggs.

CHAPTER THREE

The Parish Hall had been built shortly after the Second World War, almost entirely by the munificence of John Henry Taylor and as a thanks offering for the deliverance of Mindon from the hands of the enemy. Not that Mindon had ever been in the hands of the enemy, or could even claim a bomb of its own. The nearest it had come to that had been a stray bomb jettisoned over Southfield by an enemy pilot on his way home. Even then he had considerately dropped it over a turnip field on the outskirts of the town.

Still, the inhabitants of Mindon said they had heard the blast, it had shaken them, and if the turnip field had been two miles closer—well, then!

They had also, along with those who were blitzed elsewhere in the land, undergone the blackout, fuel shortages, rationing (with only a small, though quite efficient, Black Market operating from the Queen's Head), double summer time and the removal of their iron railings.

Peace had restored all things to them (except the railings). It had also brought John Henry Taylor a contract from the county for the building of a small estate of council houses on the edge of the village. A council estate was not what the Mindonites would have chosen as a victory prize but it was manna from heaven for John Henry Taylor, and from the kindness of his heart, and the materials left over from the estate, he had built the Parish Hall. It was his hope that it would be named the John Henry Taylor Hall and moves were made (though never ostensibly by him) to accomplish this. At least one regular and two extraordinary meetings of the Parish Council had been given up to the choice of a name.

St Peter's had been the obvious choice until it had been pointed out that there was also a Methodist Church in the village and what about them? They had fought for their country too. There was a contingent who thought a saint's name would be nice, led by Lady Findon who had served as a major in the ATS. She suggested—demanded—that a female saint should be chosen. 'St Joan for Mindon!' she said in a strongly worded letter to the *Southfield Gazette*.

In the end, because the Parish Council met less often in the summer months, and its most vociferous members were on holiday, the naming of the hall fell from the agenda. Everyone was already calling it the Parish Hall.

It was on this hall, almost adjacent to the church, that the MADS converged on the appointed Thursday evening in July. It was raining heavily, a sudden, sharp shower which had started only minutes ago but had already formed pools on the uneven surface of the path to the hall door and soaked to the skin those members, which was most of them, who had been foolish enough to leave home on a fine, warm July evening wearing summer clothes.

In twos and threes they crowded into the entrance hall, shaking themselves like terriers, ineffectually trying to dry themselves on pocket handkerchiefs and chiffon scarves, while complaining loudly.

'This is really too bad,' Ursula said, looking

around for someone to blame. 'It's the flower show on Saturday and all the petals will be off my roses.' It was well known that she always won a prize for her roses.

'You're not the only one,' Dr Clarke said. 'What about my sweet peas?'

'Why can't we go in?' Betty James asked.

'Because the Brownies haven't finished,' someone replied.

To prove it the swing doors to the main hall opened a few inches and the irate face of Brown Owl showed itself.

'Do you *mind*?' she said. 'The Brownie meeting is still going on. We have the hall for five minutes more and we happen to have reached a point where I particularly like a bit of peace and quiet! You're making a frightful racket!'

'Sorry!' Ursula said. 'We're all rather squashed together and wet.'

'You can hardly blame me for the weather!' Brown Owl said, closing the door firmly.

Save for a few whispers, silence fell in the entrance hall. Brown Owl was a person to be reckoned with. Indeed, one or two of the women were still young enough to have experienced her rule when they themselves had been Brownies.

Ursula peered through the narrow glass panels of the door. There was a toadstool in the middle of the hall, and the Brownies in their sixes were standing in a ring around it. Brown Owl stood in the centre of the ring. What she was saying to the little girls could only be interpreted by anyone viewing it through the glass by someone able to lip-read, which was one of the things at which Ursula was not accomplished.

Ursula saw no signal given, but with one accord the children raised their hands in the Brownie salute, to which Brown Owl responded.

Really, Ursula thought, they did look rather sweet in their yellow and brown uniforms, baseball caps on their heads. Possibly three or four of them might have enough drama in them to be fairies? She must keep an open mind.

It was all over in no time at all. The Brownies rushed out of the hall, barged through the entrance hall and out into the open air, where the rain had mercifully ceased, and the MADS went in.

'Well,' Ursula said, taking her place at the front of the hall, back to the stage, with the members grouped around her, 'in the words of the Bard himself "Is all our Company here?"'

'"You were best to call them generally, man by man",' Cyril Parsons said. She needn't think she was the only one who could quote Shakespeare. He had by now read all the bits which included Bottom the Weaver.

'Quite so, Cyril,' Ursula said. 'And so I shall. I,' she addressed the gathering, 'that is to say your Casting Committee, have cast most of the roles and I shall do the rest as quickly as I can, perhaps even this evening. So please, when I give you your part, stand aside so that I can be sure who's left. And save your questions or comments for later. Right?'

She took a deep breath and composed herself. She liked to do the next bit without showing any emotion. There would be enough of that from the rest of them: pleasure, disappointment, surprise, disbelief. She took no sides in that.

'Theseus:' she announced, 'Giles Rowland.'

Giles moved aside, took a seat by the wall,

smiling with quiet satisfaction. It was what he expected and, he reckoned, deserved.

'Egeus: Sam Worth.'

She had come around in the end to casting Sam Worth as Egeus because, frankly, there was no-one else. She would have preferred someone with a little more fire. Sam was a recently retired teacher. He was conscientious, so he would learn his lines, but he lacked passion. Perhaps he would find it as rehearsals progressed, but she had no high hopes. Still, it was not a large part; he was only in at the beginning and the end of the play.

Sam gave a stolid nod and joined Giles.

'Hermia: Victoria; Helena: Jennie Austin.'

Victoria smiled, she already knew, but from Jennie Austin there was an unconcealed squeal of delight. Her very first part! And Helena!

Ursula watched her as she joined the others by the wall. Did I do the right thing? she asked herself. She's untried. But she had seen something in the girl, something in her bearing, and also she had a good clear voice which would reach to the back of the hall. And whatever is in her, Ursula thought, I will bring it out! Who knows, I might make her a star!

'Lysander: Adam; Demetrius: Eric,' she continued.

Petra, who had been standing next to Adam, smiled at him as he left her to join Hermia.

Within fifteen minutes, brooking no interruption, Ursula had gone through the list, including wardrobes, properties, stage manager (Norman again), front of house and sundry others. It was a good idea to give people titles, and if the title was grander than the job, what did it matter?

'And that's almost it,' Ursula said, 'except that you'll have noticed we haven't cast Starveling, Snout or Flute.' She turned to George Shepherd. 'George dear, I know you're Casting Committee but will you be an angel and take Starveling, the tailor, who plays Moonshine? It's not a large part. You'll do it well.'

'I don't mind,' George Shepherd said truthfully. 'Anything as long as you don't ask me to play a fairy.' Being six feet two with a heavy moustache he got the laugh he had hoped for.

'Thank you, George. Ah, yes! Now Flute, the bellows mender, who plays Thisbe, I've given to you, Grace,' Ursula said, turning to the vicar's wife. 'Thisbe should be a man who plays a woman. You will have to be a woman playing a man who plays a woman!'

'It sounds very complicated,' Grace Helmet said nervously.

'Don't worry, dear! I'll direct you,' Ursula promised. 'But I still have to have a Snout, so please, everyone, rack your brains as to who we could ask. It's a small part, but important. There *must* be a man for it somewhere, otherwise someone will have to double up.'

She looked at each male member of the company in turn, until her eyes fell on the stage manager and the carpenter, standing side by side.

'Or else,' she said thoughtfully, 'I shall have to ask either Norman or Chalky to step in.'

'Not me!' Norman said firmly.

'Not me!' Chalky White echoed. 'I'm no actor.'

'Nor was Snout,' Ursula said. 'In fact, in a way the worse it's acted the better. I'm sure you'd fit in well, Chalky!' He was also, though a world-class grumbler, more amenable in the end than Norman.

'What about all those attendants, all those fairies?' Lucinda alias Titania demanded. 'I'm supposed to have loads of them in my train.'

'Tina for your chief attendant and I shall do the best I can about the others,' Ursula said firmly. She would stand no nonsense from a temperamental Titania.

'*And* a real live little Indian baby!' Lucinda said. 'Perhaps we could borrow one?'

'My help has a nice little baby,' Fay Holliday volunteered. 'Not Indian, of course. She's Irish. But with a little make-up—'

'Thank you, Fay!' Ursula interrupted. 'We'll sort that out later.' She had done well to cast Fay as Moth. She would flutter her way through anything. And did any of them realize how a real live baby would upstage the whole cast?

'So there we are,' she said. 'I hope you'll be happy with your various roles, whether they're small or large and including those of you who have non-acting roles. You are every bit as important as the leading players!' Not that Lucinda Rockwell would ever subscribe to *that*, she thought. But it was important to say it. Treat little people well and they would do almost anything for one.

'Now,' she said, 'why don't we all sit down and be comfortable and I'll go through my thinking on the various scenes!'

They pulled chairs together and grouped around her. Stage manager Norman motioned Petra to a seat between himself and Doris, with wardrobes, publicity and the like nearby. Adam sat with Hermia at the opposite side of the group, in the company also of Titania, Oberon and the other

40

Thespians. George sat with Tina. Ursula, Petra thought, might like to present them as one big happy family, but there was clearly a separation of the sheep from the goats.

'Good!' Ursula said, somehow enveloping them all in a benign smile. 'Now to work! For convenience in rehearsing I've broken the whole play down into nine scenes. That doesn't mean', she said, looking at Petra and Norman, 'that we need nine scene *changes*!'

'I can't guarantee to do nine scene changes,' Norman said firmly. 'One person can only do so much!'

Ursula took a deep breath.

'You won't have to, Norman dear.' She turned to Petra. 'And that goes for you, Petra dear. Basically there are two locations—the Duke's palace and the wood. So that won't be too bad, will it?'

'Not at all,' Petra said.

'Not if you stick to that,' Norman said doubtfully.

'Of course I will,' Ursula assured him. 'In any case that would be true to Shakespeare himself. In his day very little scenery was used. It all took place on the stage with not much attempt at fancy scenery.'

In which case, Petra thought, why am I here? She already had several ideas of what she would do but for the moment, between Ursula and Norman, she would keep them to herself.

'We *must* have a fitting scene for Theseus, Duke of Athens,' Giles said testily. 'His home was a palace. A bare stage would *not* be the thing. Before we know where we are you'll be telling us we'll do it in jeans and sweatshirts!'

41

'I will do no such thing,' Ursula contradicted. 'You can be assured that Theseus's palace will be a place of splendour.'

She turned to Petra. 'Will you note that, dear?'

'I don't need to,' Petra said. 'I already have it in mind. In fact I've done some preliminary sketches if you'd like to see them.'

'Does that have to be now?' Giles objected. 'Shouldn't we just get on with the play?'

'Of course!' Ursula affirmed. Dear boy, he had such an artistic temperament—but wasn't that what made him such a good actor? Good actors of the male sex were as gold, she reminded herself. And mustn't be upset.

'Theseus, Hippolyta and Egeus are needed at the beginning and ending of the play,' she said. 'So for the first few weeks, until we begin to put the whole thing together, I suggest they need rehearse only one day a week, and the other two evenings we'll do the scenes in the woods. Monday, I suggest.' She looked hopefully at Theseus, Hippolyta and Egeus.

'Impossible for me, I'm afraid,' Hippolyta said. 'I go to Keep Fit on a Monday.'

'Friday, then?'

Theseus shuddered.

'Friday is *right* out! I'm *shattered* by Friday! I'm an early in the week person myself.'

Silently, Ursula counted to ten. Getting people to rehearsals, in spite of the fact that they had hankered after the parts, was the most difficult part of every production. She wondered, not for the first time, why she should go on with it. Why not stay at home and watch television, all those soaps which other people saw all the time and she never did.

But no, she told herself, she had a duty to the village and carry it out she would, never mind the sacrifice to herself.

She turned to Sam Worth.

'And what about you, Egeus?'

Sam shrugged.

'I can come any evening.'

The truth was, he was glad to get out of the house. His marriage wasn't much fun, especially since his retirement. He had married Olive a long time ago because she was pregnant, and once the baby, a boy, was born she had focused everything on him until the day, which was the moment he was old enough, he had left home to join the army. Now, Sam and Olive lived a dull, placid life, not even enlivened by the occasional quarrel. It was why he had joined MADS, to get away from those long, tedious evenings, their silence punctuated only by tclcvision, until they went upstairs after the ten-o'clock news and slept back to back in their double bed.

'Then Theseus and Hippolyta, you must decide between you, but I have to know. There are other people's rehearsals to fix.'

She herself would unselfishly be available five nights a week if that seemed necessary—and nearer the time on Sunday afternoons also.

'Why do you need to go to Keep Fit classes, Arabella dear?' Giles treated her to his most beguiling smile. 'You always look wonderful to me!'

She will fall for it, Ursula thought. Who could resist?

'Oh very well!' Arabella conceded. 'Monday it is. I won't be very popular with the class, though. If the numbers drop too far they have to give it up.'

'Right! Then the rest of you Tuesdays and Thursdays, seven-thirty!'

Interesting how Giles is the only one who has a choice, Petra thought—though it didn't matter to her, she was not yet far enough into Mindon society to have a full diary.

Chalky White voiced what Petra was thinking.

'Don't the rest of us get a choice on which nights we rehearse? Tuesdays and Thursdays might not be convenient.'

'Are they inconvenient to you, Chalky?' Ursula asked sweetly.

'Well . . . I don't suppose so,' he conceded. In fact they suited him quite well. Monday was the Snooker Club, Wednesday his favourite night for television, and Friday they usually had a turn on at the Queen's Head. Karaoke or something.

'Good! Then let's make a start! Get yourselves together in the necessary groups, starting act one, scene one. You've all read the play, you know where you fit in. We'll read straight through—no pauses for questions at the moment.'

She knew it would be otherwise. It always was. Someone—it could be any one of them but the leads were always the worst—would want to hold up the entire scene while they discussed exactly how they should speak a single phrase. Should I say *this*, or should I say *that*? And where should I stand? Preferably, in every case, upstage.

She shooed them around until they were standing in their groups. 'Act one, scene one! And I want you to mark the scenes in your scripts because I might not do them *exactly* as Shakespeare did. So—Theseus, Hippolyta, Philostrate and Attendant—I know you don't have a line, Nicola,

44

but stand there all the same. Look attentive. Are you all ready?'

I am considerably more than ready, Giles thought. In fact, gambling on the fact that he would be given Theseus—who else could do it?—he had learnt the first scene by heart, his own role, that was. His mother, who had once trod the boards herself, had painstakingly taken him through it. And if Madam Producer wanted to put a different interpretation on it he would fight her tooth and nail.

He took a deep breath, pitched his voice low but resonant.

'"Now, fair Hippolyta, our nuptial hour
Draws on apace . . ."'

Petra listened. Yes, Giles had a good voice. Mellifluous. And he knew how to use it. He had the authority for Theseus, both in his voice and in his appearance, being medium tall, and broad shouldered. His hair, while all around were into fashionable close-to-the-scalp crops, remained well down over his collar, dark and luxuriant. No way would he need a wig, she thought.

Her thoughts then wandered to the design she had made for this scene, and since Ursula was intent on Theseus and company she surreptitiously extracted her drawings from the folder and began to study them. All quite simple. A solid rectangular table for which she would find a rich, heavy cloth; a couple of leatherbound books, a few flagons. She would have to look around for high-backed, carved chairs, otherwise they would sit on benches which would be out of sight. She would rely on whatever hangings she could find or borrow to give richness to the scene.

Her thoughts were deflected again when Hermia, standing close to Adam in the role of Lysander, spoke up. Victoria was a pretty girl. Her voice was pleasant but breathy, though no doubt Ursula would see to that.

'Very nice, everyone!' Ursula said. 'Now we'll have Lysander's and Hermia's scene together. Plenty of passion, dears, even though it is only a read-through! Begin as we mean to go on!'

Petra was surprised at the passion Adam put into his part. She had judged him to be a rather calm, equable man, not in the least given to tempestuous feelings. That was not how he appeared now. Either she had misjudged him or he was quite a good actor. Or perhaps it was Victoria who inspired him, gazing up at him with what Petra had noticed earlier were the most beautiful eyes. They were deep violet, and as velvety as pansies, thickly lashed with silky black and set below finely arched eyebrows. For a moment it seemed to Petra that Adam and Victoria were the only two people in the room. Anyone else was an intrusion. And then she reminded herself that they were not Adam and Victoria. They were Lysander and Hermia, playing their parts. Playing them surprisingly well.

It was half-past ten before a nervous Puck read the last lines of the play.

I shall have to work on Puck, Ursula told herself. She had in the end chosen Melvin Fairclough because he was small and slight and moved quickly, and because there was no-one else.

Out loud she said again, 'Well done, everyone!' Encouragement was everything at this stage, otherwise some of them would drop out, and where she would find replacements she had no idea.

'Capital!' she said for extra encouragement. 'Capital! So Tuesday at seven-thirty for all except scene one, though we'll need the four lovers, of course. I'm afraid you four are going to have to put in a lot of time, but you do have very important parts.'

'I do hope we're going to concentrate somewhat on Titania tomorrow!' Lucinda said. 'It's a demanding part.'

'Of course it is, Lucinda dear. But I'm sure you'll meet the demands,' Ursula said. 'And if you need extra coaching . . .'

'I don't expect to require extra coaching,' Lucinda said coldly. It was not what she meant at all. What she meant was that the role of Titania needed *attention*.

'Do you need me tomorrow?' Petra asked Ursula.

'Oh, most certainly dear! It's all the scenes in the wood. Titania and Oberon. Bottom and his cronies, and of course the lovers. I'm sure you'll get inspiration from watching them.'

Will I? Petra wondered. 'I suppose I will,' she agreed. 'I'll be here.'

Did she detect a lack of enthusiasm in Petra's voice, Ursula asked herself. And so early in the production.

'I'm sorry I haven't had time for a word with you all evening, or to look at your designs,' she said. 'But you can see how it is, first rehearsal and so on. They need all my attention, poor dears!'

'I quite understand,' Petra assured her.

'Why don't I pop in and see you?' Ursula suggested. 'I'm in the village most days. One thing and another, you know!'

'Please do,' Petra said.

People were beginning to leave. Adam, Victoria beside him, stood by the door. He was looking towards Petra, clearly waiting for her to join them, which she did.

'I'm giving Vicky a lift home,' he said. 'She lives in my direction. Would you like us to see you home first?'

'Good heavens, no!' Petra said briskly. 'I reckon I must live closer to the Parish Hall than anyone in the company. A matter of minutes.'

'If you're sure,' Adam said. 'How did you think it went—the rehearsal?'

'Quite well. Lysander is a good part.'

'I know. And I have a lovely Hermia!' He smiled at Victoria.

'You have indeed,' Petra agreed.

As they moved away from the hall Jennie Austin caught up with them.

'You were very good as Helena,' Victoria told her generously.

'Thank you,' Jennie said. 'So were you—as Hermia, I mean.'

Petra, who had never before been a member of a dramatic society, even though they were rife in North Yorkshire, was to discover that a fair amount of time was spent by every member after rehearsals heaping fulsome praise on every other member while deprecating his or her own performance. With notable exceptions.

'We're rather late,' Jennie spoke anxiously. 'My mother will wonder what's happened to me. Will you excuse me if I rush?' She was away, half running down the road. Petra looked at the others.

'We usually go for a drink in the Queen's Head

48

after rehearsals—if we're not too late that is—but never Jennie. Her mother's an invalid,' Victoria said. 'No-one knows quite what's wrong with her but she rules Jennie with a rod of iron.'

'So how does she manage to come to rehearsals?' Petra asked.

'It's her one and only act of defiance,' Victoria said. 'The one thing she won't let go, though this is actually her first part. But she always has to rush home. Actually,' she added thoughtfully, 'I think quite a few people come to MADS to get away from home!'

'She seemed so . . . spirited . . . when she was reading Helena,' Petra said. 'Not at all meek and mild.'

Victoria nodded.

'I know. As if everything she feels comes out in her acting.'

'Well, goodnight,' Petra said. 'I'll see you both next time.'

She did not hurry in the direction of Plum Tree House. The night was warm, the fragrance of night-scented stocks in the cottage gardens filled the air. She had no demanding mother to rush home to. Her mother, bless her, had not been at all like that, though she had had an anxious streak, always over-careful where her daughter was concerned. Perhaps it would have been different if I'd had brothers and sisters, Petra thought. She wished now she had.

Turning the key in the lock, letting herself into her house, she wished she had just one relative in the entire world.

49

CHAPTER FOUR

Petra made herself a cup of coffee and took it upstairs with her. Sitting up in bed, an extra pillow behind her neck, she sipped the hot liquid and found it comforting.

What a spinsterish thing to do, she chided herself, sitting up alone in a double bed with a hot drink. But at least it was black coffee, not malted milk. Anyway, wasn't she a spinster? Thirty-six years old and not married, marriage not on the horizon. What *else* was she? All she needed to complete the picture was a bed-jacket to cover her silk nightgown with its low-cut neckline and spaghetti straps, and a large, fluffy cat, preferably one trained to sit on her shoulder.

She drained the mug and put it on the bedside table. She supposed she would now have to go and brush her teeth again. Did coffee rot the teeth? And why did the sudden thought of spinsterhood cause this ache in whichever region of her body the emotions were seated, which at this moment seemed more like the pit of her stomach than her heart.

It was not something which had ever bothered her before, or at least not the *state* of singleness. She had wanted to marry because she loved Malcolm. He was not the first love of her life, but he was *the* one. Beside him, all others paled. She had loved him deeply, faithfully, truly, for five years. She wanted to be with him all the time, have his children, even to grow old with him, though that had seemed a long way off. She had, she realized, been besotted by him.

He had loved her. He said he did and she believed him. He was not happy in his marriage, there was no longer anything left between himself and his wife, it was all over. He wanted out and he would get out, and then he and Petra would be married.

It was just that there was always something in the way, something quite reasonable. Violet was ill, she would have to have an operation and he must see her through it. He was up for promotion and that was important. When he left Violet he would still have to pay money to her. His promotion was by no means in the bag, he'd have to watch his step. His boss was a straightlaced, suspicious bastard, hot on family values.

She had asked herself many times why she had put up with it for so long, but the answer was simple. She loved him. He was also a wonderful lover.

She put out a hand, touching the empty side of the bed, and wished with all her heart that he was there.

But if he was she would send him away again. She had reached the end when she'd learnt—by accident, he had not meant to tell her—that Violet was pregnant.

Petra flung back the bedclothes, went swiftly to the bathroom and brushed her teeth long and vigorously. Back in bed she picked up the new Inspector Morse she had started the previous night. Now there was a man for whom the path of true love never ran smooth!

It was two in the morning before she closed her book and put out the light. Inspector Morse had solved the crimes but, once again, he had not won the girl. She felt sorry for Morse. She felt that if only *she* had met him . . . but since she was incapable of solving her own love life why should she think she could solve his?

Her last waking thought was that one day soon, perhaps even tomorrow, she would sort out the attics in Plum Tree House. They were still exactly as they had been—highly cluttered—on Claire's sudden death. What a mess we leave behind us when we die without warning, she thought. She supposed she would be the same. She had had rather too much of sorting out belongings. First there'd been her own flat when, after her parents' death, she had sold it and moved into their house. Then there had been her parents' house when she'd decided to come south to Mindon. The most interesting part of that had been the old photographs.

She fell asleep and dreamt that Adam Benfield and Victoria were lost in Harrogate, searching the streets for Demetrius and Helena while she, who could have told them where the latter were to be found, was rooted to the spot in a place she did not recognize, unable to move.

She wakened early next morning. It was difficult not to. Her bedroom window faced east and the sun was streaming in. Last night had been hot and stuffy and before getting into bed she had drawn the curtains back and opened the window wide, letting in what air there was. Now the light dazzled her eyes and the day promised to be hotter than ever.

She recalled her dream. It was still quite vivid, or rather, the feelings it had engendered were vivid:

52

the confusion of the lovers as they chased around the town, her own sense of being alone, separated, wanting to join in but unable to do so. It was stupid of course, and quite easily explained. Her head was full of the play, and she had felt apart because she was apart. She had not been here long enough to belong. Mindon was a village, and villages, however kind, and this one was, did not admit anyone to their inner circle all that quickly. It would happen in time, she was sure of it, but she would have to serve her apprenticeship. So why, she wondered, since she could explain it so rationally, did she have this lingering ache?

She flung back the bedclothes, went along to the bathroom and stood under a cool shower after which, invigorated, she put on old jeans and a cotton tee-shirt. Old jeans because she would spend the day either rooting around in the attics, which were probably covered with the dust of ages, or painting. Painting was what she wanted to do, attics were where duty called her.

Putting off the decision, she washed the breakfast dishes, tidied the kitchen, vacuumed and dusted the sitting room, cleaned the bathroom. She had no love for housework but she liked a modicum of order so it had to be done. She couldn't afford paid help even if there was any to be found.

Next, she hung a picture in the hall, a watercolour she had brought with her from Yorkshire. She knew full well that the hanging of the painting was another ploy to postpone the moment when she must go up to the attic and set to work. The painting had been leaning against the wall for weeks now, awaiting her decision as to where it should go. Suddenly, this morning, it seemed imperative that she should deal with it. When she had done that she would put duty before pleasure and mount the stairs.

She had taken a step backwards, checking to see that it hung straight, when the doorbell rang. A long, imperious ring, as if someone was leaning on the bell-push. Perhaps the parcel post—not that she was expecting anything.

It was not the parcel post, it was Ursula King, holding aloft a bottle of milk.

'Good morning, Petra dear!' she said. 'Did you realize you'd not taken in your milk? It was in the full sun. Quite the quickest way to lose all its vitamins!' She stepped inside, handing the milk to Petra. 'Perhaps you should put it in the fridge right away.'

'I will in a minute. I was just hanging this picture.'

'You haven't got it quite straight,' Ursula said. 'It's down on the left I'd say. Actually, I am the possessor of a very straight eye.'

'You're quite right,' Petra agreed. She adjusted it. 'Is that better?'

'Spot on! It's quite a pretty picture. Where is it?'

'Langstrothdale, in North Yorkshire. I know the artist.'

She also knew the very spot where he had stood to paint it. Whenever she looked at the picture she felt that she could step into it. If, in the future, she went back to Yorkshire at all—for which she had no plans—this narrow bridge across the infant Wharfe would be where she would make for.

'Would you like some coffee?' she asked.

'I would indeed,' Ursula said.

54

'Then come into the kitchen while I make it.'

She put the milk into the fridge, took the jar of beans out of the freezer and measured them into the grinder.

'Ah! I see you're a serious coffee maker!' Ursula approved. 'You keep your beans in the freezer.'

'Always. Do you like your coffee strong?'

'I do. And black.'

Petra ground the beans, put them in the machine, switched it on.

Ursula's eyes swept around the room, taking in the old dresser, the crockery displayed on its shelves—rather too bright, too colourful for her taste—the pine table, the collection of jugs on the wide windowsill, the calendar on the wall. Her gaze was frank and open, missing nothing. I'm glad I tidied up, Petra thought.

'I see you cook by gas,' Ursula remarked.

'Gas hob, electric oven.'

'Electricity is cleaner,' Ursula stated, 'but gas is instantly obedient.'

'Then I have the best of both worlds,' Petra said. 'Not that I cook much. One doesn't on one's own.'

'Oh, but you should! You must!' Ursula was vehement. 'We owe it to ourselves and others to keep fit and healthy, and food is the very first thing. I shall lend you a book about it!'

Which I might or might not read, Petra thought. She didn't dislike Ursula, not at all. She was friendly and forthright, probably caring and a lot of other good things, but she had to be watched or she would take over. One could easily become Ursula's good cause.

She poured coffee, seated herself at the table opposite Ursula. She wouldn't *offer her* usual sinful

55

chocolate-finger biscuits. From Ursula's extremely spare figure and bony face, not a centimetre of flesh anywhere to be gripped between two fingers, it was unlikely that chocolate ever passed her lips.

'I haven't been in this kitchen before,' Ursula said. 'Claire Harden wasn't a person who invited one into the kitchen. She was rather too formal for that.'

'You knew her?'

'Oh yes! That's to say, I doubt if anyone knew her well. She kept herself to herself, though she was highly respected as a teacher and the children loved her. She was headmistress of the village school, you know.'

'The solicitor told me that. What did she look like? There are no photographs around, except one I take to be of her father and mother, and one which might or might not—'

'That doesn't surprise me,' Ursula interrupted. 'She wasn't the kind of person to have photographs of herself around. And she was devoted to her parents. Dr Harden was a very popular GP in Mindon. As to what she looked like . . . well, she was small, grey-haired, quite pretty once, I would think.'

She didn't sound at all like a woman who would leave her money to a home for abused women, Petra thought. A children's charity, yes. Or even cats or dogs.

'So what did you think of your first rehearsal?' Ursula asked.

'I thought it went well.' She would hardly have described it as *her* rehearsal. She had not said more than a dozen words.

'It wasn't too bad,' Ursula agreed. 'Of course

56

everyone needs licking into shape, but that will come.'

'Adam and Victoria did their parts well,' Petra observed. 'Have they acted together before?'

'Yes. That's one reason why I cast them as I did. When they're acting together the chemistry is right.'

'Are they . . . long-time friends, or perhaps more than friends?' Petra was fishing, and she knew it.

'Oh, I don't think so! Perhaps Hermia (in the course of a production Ursula referred to everyone by the name of the character they were playing) might like to think so, but then there's more than one person in the MADS who would like to be on closer terms with Lysander. But since his divorce he's hard to get.'

'He seems quite friendly,' Petra said.

'Oh he is friendly. And quite charming. The trouble is, people mistake that for something more. Hermia, poor girl, will have to remember that she's only playing a part.'

'And so is he.'

'I'm sorry there wasn't time to look at your designs,' Ursula said. 'That's partly why I'm here this morning.'

'It doesn't matter. I'll show them to you in a minute. More coffee?' Petra asked.

'I'd love it. It's very good. But I shouldn't really. The other reason I'm here is because I'm on my way to a coffee morning and I wondered if you'd like to come with me? It's in aid of the organ fund—not that that matters especially, I try to support them all equally, though sometimes it gets a bit much. One way and another there's something every week. Coffee mornings, bring-and-buys, beetle drives, jumble sales. But one must pull one's weight.'

'It sounds an exciting life,' Petra said.

Ursula gave her a sharp glance. Was she serious or was she taking the mickey? She had not quite got the measure of this newcomer, though she seemed nice enough and would no doubt be very useful.

'So why not come with me?' she asked. 'It's at the vicarage.'

'I'd like to.' In fact that was true, Petra thought, surprising herself. It might be interesting. 'But I can't, not today. I've faithfully promised myself that this is the day I'll turn out the attics. I just keep putting it off, and I can't any longer.'

'Very well,' Ursula said. 'And remember when you're sorting things out that the Scouts have their jumble sale next Saturday, though if you find anything *really* good that you're willing to part with, please save it for the MADS's sale later on. I always have a special table there for things too good to be classed as jumble. You never know what you'll find in an attic, do you? Especially someone else's attic! And now, dear, shall I take a quick peek at your designs?'

'Yes,' Petra agreed. 'They're in my studio.' She rose to her feet and led the way.

'Oh! This was the waiting-room,' Ursula said as Petra showed her into the studio. 'I remember it. Not that I often sat in the waiting-room, only if there was some emergency with someone's children. You know how they're always cutting themselves, or falling over and breaking something, but aside from that Dr Harden came to the house. He always did, with certain patients.'

58

And you would be one of those, Petra thought.

Ursula looked around the room, taking everything in.

'It certainly looks different now,' she said.

'And will do more so when I've knocked down the wall between this room and the surgery. I like lots of space. I usually work on quite large subjects.'

'Of course you've done theatre designs before.'

'Yes, in the North of England. I used to get quite a lot of work, but now there are so many talented amateurs around, and money is tight, so quite often they do their own.'

'We're lucky to have you,' Ursula said.

Petra crossed to a table where a large sketch book lay open.

'Reserve your judgement until you see what I've done so far. You might not like it. I've only done one or two scenes as yet, Theseus's palace, and then some ideas for the wood. I don't know whether you'll agree but I like everything to be simple. Simple but, where necessary, bold. Easy to set up, easy to change the scene, with an impact which makes its own statement but is never louder than the play itself.'

'I do agree!' Ursula said, looking at the drawings. 'And this is the first scene, Theseus's palace. Yes, I like this.'

'It has to be rather grand,' Petra said. 'He was a nobleman. But I've tried to convey that with rich-looking materials—and colour—and not much furniture. Mainly a large table, any old table, which can be disguised with a suitable covering. And just a few props, which we can discuss. The costumes should be elegant, but not as grand as the last scene when we come to the wedding feast.'

'Quite!'

'And by the way,' Petra said, 'who does the costumes?'

Ursula looked dubious.

'Amelia. At least, she's wardrobe mistress. But she doesn't actually *design* anything. Dear Amelia, she's good at sewing, she's wonderful at keeping everything clean and pressed and looked after but she does lack imagination. Actually we've never done a costume production before—though I believe they once did *Barretts of Wimpole Street,* though that was before Amelia's time.'

'If you wanted me to . . .' Petra was hesitant. 'But I wouldn't want to tread on Amelia's toes!'

'Oh, you wouldn't do that,' Ursula assured her. 'I'm sure she'd welcome you with open arms. Especially if you could let her feel that she was *helping* you—you an artist and all that. She's a nice little woman.'

'I'll sound her out,' Petra suggested. 'And of course we'll have to discuss it at length. We're talking about dressing the whole cast.'

Ursula nodded agreement.

'Quite so. And there's no time at the moment. I *must* get to the vicarage or they'll be sending out a search party. They expect me to be present, you see. But if I could take a very quick peek at the woodland scene . . .'

She did so, declared herself enchanted, and was away in less than ten minutes.

Does this mean, Petra asked herself, standing in the doorway waving Ursula off, that she will leave things to me, not interfere? It had better, because there was no way she would allow anyone, even

60

Ursula, to dictate to her about her designs, either of sets or costumes. Suggest, yes. Dictate, no.

Ursula hadn't mentioned the dinner-party date, she thought as she closed the door. Now that rehearsals had started perhaps it was off. She looked at her watch. It was ten minutes to twelve, too late to make a start on the attics. She would have an early lunch, leaving herself a long afternoon for the dreaded task. And in the meantime, since the day was fine and sunny, she would eat her lunch in the garden.

She buttered a piece of French bread, cut a piece of St Paulin cheese, poured a glass of Chardonnay and took the tray out to the dark green, wrought-iron table which stood on the paved area in front of the window. There were four chairs around the table. Did Claire, then, entertain friends in her garden or had the furniture been bought as a set? She wished she knew. There was so little in the house or garden which gave any idea of what Claire was like, how she occupied her life. That she was interested in cooking was evident from the collection of pans and dishes, a shelf of cookery books and the fact that there was a small cupboard given over entirely to herbs and spices. Did she cook for friends or did she, unlike me, Petra wondered, cook decent food for herself?

There were herbs in the garden, too. Thyme, rosemary, chives, tarragon, two kinds of parsley in earthenware pots.

It was a pretty garden, not large, but well-designed; a lawn more circular than rectangular, a few decent-sized beds, a pergola thickly covered with clematis, though the flowers were over, and climbing the front of the pergola a passiflora heavy

61

with blooms and buds of more to come. Petra had never been able to grow passion flowers in North Yorkshire and now she took pleasure each day in seeing new flowers, with their spectacular markings, open to the sun.

She lingered over her meal, sipped the wine slowly, did not even attempt to read the book she had brought with her. She was, she acknowledged, happy here, yet she still asked herself, every day, how it could be that she was here at all. On the face of it, of course, the reasons she was here were simple, and had been easily explained in less than fifteen minutes by Mr Craig in his office. It was just that sometimes she still felt she was living in a dream.

A black-and-white cat came through what must have been a gap in the fence and strolled leisurely across the top of the garden, picking its way delicately. She had never seen it before. It was rather handsome. She called out to it and for a second or two it stopped and stared at her, haughtily, before continuing on its purposeful way and disappearing over the opposite fence. Perhaps I will get a cat, she thought. Or even a dog.

She drained her glass, then carried the tray back into the kitchen. Dream or not, it was time to waken, to set about what she had to do. She collected a dustpan and brush, dusters and two large black plastic refuse bags, one for jumble-sale material, the other for rubbish. One thing was certain, if Claire's attic was at all like anyone else's there would be loads of rubbish.

The stairs to the attic were behind a door at the far end of the first-floor landing. They were steep and narrow, walled in. At the top a square landing gave on to two doors, one on the left, one on the right. Which attic should she choose today? There was no way she could attack them both, she was unlikely to finish even one in an afternoon. Of course she had been into both attics before, though briefly, and there seemed nothing to choose between them. Both were equally packed, both—as far as the eye could see—with similar contents: chests of drawers, chairs, rolled-up rugs, boxes, suitcases, lamps, a Christmas tree and a variety of other objects which had probably been placed there temporarily and never moved again.

For no reason whatsoever she opened the left-hand door and went into the attic which occupied the roof space at the front of the house and whose high dormer window, should one climb up to look out of it, which Petra did, gave a bird's-eye view of the village green. Small pre-school children played there while their mothers, guarding even smaller children, and babies in prams, sat on nearby benches. A pleasing scene, but Petra tore herself away from it, stepped down and set to work.

It was difficult to know where to start. She pushed, pulled and dragged as much as she could towards the perimeter of the room, trying to clear the centre of the floor and, as she moved, she popped into a plastic bag anything which seemed remotely suitable for a jumble sale. In the end, exhausted by the sheer physical effort, she pulled out one of the several odd chairs and seated herself in front of a bureau desk. It was oak, heavily carved, a bit scratched but some use might well be made of it. At the very least it would find a place in her studio, the drawers would house her materials: paints, brushes, crayons, paper and so on. All the things which needed space and would be better for organizing.

She pulled open the middle drawer, which ran smoothly. Its contents were largely photographs, many of them, though by no means all, dating back to the war, or even earlier. There was no way she would ever know who these people were. This eager-looking soldier, stiff as a ramrod in his new uniform, had he ever returned? This man and woman, an older generation, were they his parents? They were not unlike Dr Harden in the photograph she had of him. They must be relatives.

She picked up the photograph of the soldier again and put it back in the drawer. How could she bear to consign even his likeness to the rubbish bag? She picked up another photograph, and gasped!

It was an exact copy of the photograph which she had found in her parents' house. The handsome young man in the centre, dark hair, smiling eyes, his arms around two pretty women on either side of him. One clearly her mother, the other . . . ?

She turned the photograph over. It was too much to hope for—but no, it was not! There it was, in neat sloping handwriting.

'Marian, Eliot, Claire. 1960'.

CHAPTER FIVE

Petra, wrapped in a dressing-gown, towelling her wet hair, jumped when the telephone rang. One of the things she had not yet become used to since coming to Mindon was the infrequency with which the phone rang, especially in the evenings. Back home—did she still think of Yorkshire as back home?—she supposed she must as that was the place which came to mind as she rushed to answer the ringing—that had seldom been the case. Now the only person she could think of who might be calling her was Ursula or, even more likely, someone selling car insurance.

'Petra Banbury.'

'Adam Benfield.'

'Oh!'

'Is this an inconvenient moment?' She sounded flustered.

'No. Not at all. I didn't expect . . . I thought it might be Ursula. She was here this morning. How are you?'

'I'm fine. And you?'

'I'm fine too. I spent all afternoon poking around in the front attic. I've just been washing the dust out of my hair.'

'Then I mustn't keep you if you're standing with dripping wet hair.'

'I'm not,' she assured him. 'It's already towel-dry. No problem.'

'Actually,' Adam said, 'I was wondering if you'd be out and about in the village in the morning. If so—'

'Do you want me to get something for you?' Petra interrupted. 'Of course I will!'

'No,' Adam said. 'I just wondered if you'd have coffee with me?'

She felt a small stab of pleasure.

'Oh, how nice. Yes, I'd love to.'

'Around eleven then. I have a few things to do first.'

'Don't worry if you're late,' Petra said. 'I'll grab a table.' A thought came to her suddenly. Her immediate impulse was to reject it, and then, just as swiftly, she decided not to.

'Yes?'

'I wondered if you'd like to come back here and have lunch with me. It's rather short notice because I only just thought of it. I expect you're doing something else, but never mind, I'll ask you another time.' She was gabbling.

'I'm not doing anything else,' Adam said. 'And aside from that I'd like to come. Thank you.'

'It won't be anything fancy. I'm not the world's best cook. But if you'd like to risk it . . .'

'Live dangerously,' he said. 'Why not. And you can tell me all about your discoveries in the attic.'

'Mostly jumble sale stuff,' Petra said. 'You can have first pick if you like.'

In fact, she thought after he had rung off, she wanted to tell him about the photograph, not that it would be wildly exciting to him but *she* would enjoy it. One of the disadvantages of living alone—to be weighed against the many advantages—was that you had no-one to tell when something good happened. She had told Malcolm everything, good and bad. And both before and since Malcolm there had been her mother, always eager to hear and to console or rejoice, whichever was appropriate.

And the discovery of the photograph was good. It was one more link in the chain. She now knew what Claire looked like, or had when she was young, and had confirmation that she and her mother had been friends. The man was a mystery, but probably unimportant. Certainly she had never heard her mother speak of him.

She supposed, if she faced the truth, that now she missed her mother more than Malcolm. There was this gap when she wanted to discuss something, seek advice, or even wanted just to telephone and pass the time of day, to hear her mother's voice. More than once recently when the telephone had rung she had immediately thought that it might be her mother—and had then remembered. She missed her father of course, but not quite in the same way. He had been the best of fathers, but not as close as her mother. Losing them both, so near together, had been a bitter blow.

She allowed herself, now, a few moments to think deliberately about that awful time. It was only recently that she had been able to do this, not to push every thought of it away the second it came into her head. She supposed she was, in a way, allowing her mother and father back into her life, having banished them because to do otherwise had been unbearable. And somehow that was a healing process. Gradually, then, though without undue haste, she turned her thoughts away from them to what she would give Adam for lunch.

She went into the kitchen and on an impulse took down one of Claire's cookery books from the shelf rather than one of her own. Seeking inspiration, she thumbed through it. She could choose something which would be easy to cook at the last minute, in which case Adam would be present and she would have to entertain him at the same time. Or, if she went out early, did a quick shop—the butcher, she knew, opened at eight-thirty—she might get something which would cook itself in a slow oven while she was out on her second trip. Drinking coffee.

Claire's cookery book was interesting. Not so much for the content, which was comprehensive but more or less standard, with few flights of fancy, but because against many of the recipes, which were mostly for four people, sometimes for six or eight, she had in the margins scaled down the proportions to one person, and occasionally to two. A vignette of her life, Petra thought. A woman who habitually ate alone but occasionally had a guest.

Chicken, she thought! A casserole. Or better still, why not coq au vin? A little more trouble but well worth it. She looked it up in the index and turned to the page. To her pleasure she found all the quantities adjusted to suit two people, with added notes in what must be Claire's handwriting, since she remembered it from the one and only letter she had received from her. So Claire had entertained a friend to coq au vin? A man friend? A woman colleague? Had it been a celebration? She would never know. Whatever it had been it felt like a good omen.

She listed the things she would need to buy. Chicken portions, since a whole chicken would be too much. Vegetables, a decent red wine. The herbs she would need were already either growing in the garden or were stored in the cupboard. She would buy something for pudding at the baker's, or perhaps have cheese and fruit.

She went to bed in a happy frame of mind, looking forward, though not totally without apprehension, to the next day. She set the alarm for seven o'clock. When morning came she would need to scurry around, laying the table and so on, before going out to shop.

She did not fall asleep quickly. Her thoughts got

in the way, which was absurd because they were not unhappy ones. On the contrary, she was looking forward to the next day with interest, even with excitement. Which was also ridiculous, she chided herself. What was so madly exciting about a friend coming to lunch? Besides, she wasn't a person who got into a flap about things. She was level-headed, she was cool. Everyone knew she was cool. No, the explanation was simply that it would be the first time she had invited anyone to a meal since she'd arrived in Mindon. That was all there was to it. She turned over on to her other side, closed her eyes and began to count sheep. She counted them as they jumped over the low broken wall in her painting of Langstrothdale. As was the way with sheep, they did not jump in an orderly fashion, but crowded together, jostled one another, exactly like her thoughts.

After a long time she fell asleep, and then was awakened what seemed no more than ten minutes later by the alarm. Unexpectedly refreshed considering how little sleep she had had —she must have slept deeply—she got out of bed with alacrity and drew back the curtains. Her bedroom, at the back of the house, overlooked the garden. The first thing she did every morning was to stand for a few minutes by the window and look out. The garden was bordered by a mixed hedge so that working or sitting in it she was completely private, but from the vantage point of the bedroom she could see beyond the hedge and past the small estate of quite pleasant, middle-class houses which had been built in the middle fifties also by John Henry Taylor, though by no means to be confused with his council estate. Bronwen Close, Bronwen Crescent,

Bronwen Avenue, named as a tribute to John Henry Taylor's wife, were altogether superior houses, with their mock-Tudor gables and their front doors in heavy oak, studded with iron nails and hinges.

She looked beyond the tiled roofs of the Bronwens to the high, green Surrey hills which marched across the horizon. It was going to be a beautiful day. She was learning to tell the weather by looking at the hills, and already, so early in the day, they were lit by a slightly hazy sun. It would be hot. Should we perhaps eat in the garden? she wondered. Would coq au vin lend itself to being eaten in the garden? Or should she change the menu to one more suitable for alfresco eating?

No you will *not*, she admonished herself, turning away from the window. You will eat sensibly in the dining room. You will lay a decent table, cut some flowers from the garden, and get on with things or there will *be* no meal. There was a score of jobs to be done.

She would use, for the first time, Claire's china, which was rather pretty: creamy-white with delicately painted wild flowers. Almost certainly, Petra thought, Claire must have inherited it from her parents. She knew little about ceramics but this service, though in perfect condition, had the look of another age about it.

She laid the table, arranged a centrepiece of pansies in a small shallow dish, cut roses for the sitting room. She recalled, quite calmly, welcoming the thought, that her father had loved growing roses but had hated to see them cut. It had been the cause of regular mild arguments between her parents. Her mother's idea of a garden was one

70

which would supply fruit, flowers and vegetables in season for the house. She arranged the roses in a silver bowl which had also been Claire's. At moments like this she felt as if she was living in Claire's life.

She was at the butcher's as Mr Enfield was unlocking the door.

'Two chicken breasts,' he said. 'Are we having company, Miss Banbury?'

'Yes,' Petra said.

He waited for her to tell him who, but she did not oblige.

'And what are you going to do with the chicken?' he asked. He took a keen interest in what happened to his stock after it had left his shop. It was generally agreed that he recited a recipe with every piece of meat he served, which resulted in long, slow-moving queues inside his small premises.

'I'm making a coq au vin,' Petra said.

'Oh, really? Now myself I always use legs for coq au vin,' he said. 'More flavour! But a little of what you fancy! The thing is to cook it slow and use a good red wine. People think any old wine will do for cooking, but they're wrong.'

'I'll remember that,' Petra promised.

'You do! You'll not be disappointed—nor your guest. Will there be anything else?'

He watched her as she left, crossed the road outside his shop. She was a good-looker, but a bit quiet. Didn't give anything away. He'd take a bet her guest was a man. She had that look about her this morning. Well, he reckoned, they'd know sooner or later, though he preferred to be first with news.

Nosey old devil, Petra thought. But he was a

good butcher—and the only one. He had probably known Claire. One day she might ask him, unless in return for his information he wanted *her* life story.

If I'd had any sense, she thought later as she stood at the kitchen table peeling onions, scraping carrots, I'd have excused myself from coffee and had Adam just to lunch. But she hadn't had the sense, and in any case she quite liked the coffee business.

The vegetables were finished, and since there was no more she could do now, she washed her hands. To her mind they still smelled faintly of onion, so she rubbed cream into them. She tweaked at her hair in the hall mirror, and left, hurrying all the way, arriving at the coffee shop quite breathless. Adam was not there.

She sat at the only empty table. Luckily, once again, it was by the window. The room was full, everyone twittering and chattering like birds in an aviary, the sound breaking like waves against the shingle. She appeared to be the only person in the café on her own. Even so, the waitress was by her side within two minutes.

'I'm meeting a friend,' Petra said. It was nice to say 'meeting a friend'.

The girl did not answer, but her face said it all. You can't take up a table, not eating, not drinking, not when we're so busy. This isn't a waiting-room! Moreover, she conveyed her thoughts without moving a muscle of her thin, pale face. Only her eyes showed any life, looking out on the world, and on Petra in particular, with deep dissatisfaction.

'Perhaps I'll have my coffee while I'm waiting,' Petra said, allowing herself to be browbeaten.

'Something to eat?' Obviously the girl *could*

72

speak, if pushed.

'Nothing at the moment. Just coffee.'

The waitress left, sighing audibly. Perhaps her feet are killing her, Petra thought, though it was early in the day for that. How would she get through light lunches and afternoon teas?

She looked out of the window, hoping for a sign of Adam, but her coffee arrived and she was halfway through it before he rushed in.

'I'm terribly sorry,' he said. 'A long queue in the post office. I can't think why. I'm sure Saturday isn't pension day. Have you been waiting long? Don't say you haven't because I can see you've almost finished your coffee. I'll order fresh.'

'Hello, Millie!' he said, when the waitress appeared. He gave her a kind smile and she permitted the corners of her mouth to twitch in recognition.

'We'll both have coffee. I'll have shortbread.' He turned to Petra. 'What about you?'

She shook her head. She hoped he wasn't going to stuff himself with shortbread and spoil his coq au vin.

'You know the waitress?' she asked when Millie had departed. 'She doesn't seem a happy girl!'

'She isn't happy. A bad case of unrequited love. She works in the university bar in the evenings and she's madly in love with a post-graduate student who doesn't know she exists even when she's serving him a pint of beer.'

'How sad!' Comfortable in Adam's presence Petra felt immediately more charitable towards Millie.

'It is actually. She's badly in need of someone. The thing is, she already has a fatherless baby.

73

Well, that's to say the father was a student and he's left. Canada, I think. I doubt he even knew she was pregnant.'

He changed the subject as Millie reappeared with the coffee.

'I half wondered if Ursula might be here,' he said. 'I've seen her here a few times. I usually try to hide behind a curtain.'

'I'm beginning to know the feeling,' Petra said. 'But I imagine she's a good producer?'

'Oh, she is! No doubt about it. She knows what she wants from everyone and it's always that bit more than they think they can deliver, but in the end they do. She's a bit of a bully, really. But I suppose she has to be to get the result.'

'Do you know everyone in the MADS?'

'Most,' Adam admitted. 'Some more than others, of course.'

'Victoria seems nice.'

She was fishing, and she knew it. It had surprised her that Adam had phoned her. She had thought, after watching them act together, and then noting after the rehearsal that he was taking her home, that there might be something going on between them. In which case . . .

'She is nice,' Adam agreed. 'I'm fond of Victoria.'

'And really pretty. Beautiful eyes!'

Adam nodded. 'Beautiful!'

He should know, Petra thought, having gazed into them with such passion.

'A distinct look of the young Elizabeth Taylor.' She was sticking pins in herself now.

'I think you're right,' Adam said. 'Actually, Vicky's away this weekend.'

74

So that was it!

'More coffee?'

'No thank you,' Petra said. 'Actually, I should be getting back. I have one or two things to see to. But you don't have to hurry. Come whenever you're ready.'

'I'm ready now,' Adam said. 'Unless you'd actually rather I came later. Would I be a nuisance now?'

'Of course not!' They were being so tediously polite. Really, it would be more sensible if she were to go back on her own, finish off the meal, tidy the kitchen, tidy herself, swallow a quick G and T, and be ready to answer the door, suave, smiling and serene. It would have made even more sense never to have invited him at all, but it was too late now.

'Then we'll be on our way,' Adam said. He signalled to Millie who, her pale skin flushed now with the heat and bustle but her eyes as troubled as ever, brought him the bill. Her tight mouth relaxed a little as she pocketed the generous tip he gave her. He saw Petra's eyes on him and the surprise on her face.

'She'll spend it on clothes for the baby,' he said apologetically. 'If there's no father around then at least she'll have the best dressed baby in Mindon. It gives her a purpose to her life. Though I wish for her sake there *was* a man.'

'You think a man gives purpose to a woman's life?' Petra asked.

'I think so,' Adam said equably, gathering up his shopping. 'Shall we go?'

So where does that leave me? Petra wondered, following him out into the sunshine. No man, no aim, no purpose. But she didn't have to believe

75

him. It was not true, at least not for her. She would not let it be. What she *would* do, she thought as she fell into step with Adam, was define her aim. I will not drift, she decided, but nor will I be pushed.

They were at Plum Tree House in no time at all. She unlocked the door and led Adam in.

He looked around him.

'What a good, spacious hall!' he said. 'Oh, I like this!'

'So do I,' Petra agreed. 'Sometimes I think it's perhaps a waste of space, but it does give a pleasant feel to the house. Now what would you like to do? I have a few things to attend to in the kitchen, so would you like to sit in the garden with a drink? It's quite pleasant out there. Or would you . . .'

'I'd much rather sit in the kitchen,' Adam said. 'If it won't put you off. Unless, like me, you don't have a kitchen big enough to sit in.'

'Oh, but I do!' Petra said. 'Come and see.'

'Now this is what I call a kitchen,' Adam said a minute later, standing in the middle of it. He glanced around, taking in the ample cupboards, the big double sink, the two ovens, and best of all the large, pine-topped table. 'It's a real family kitchen.'

With just one person using it, Petra thought. It called out for a family. A grandmother making herself useful, parents, children rushing in from school, the whole family seated around the table, the pleasant smell of cooking in the air. Well, at least it had the last-named. The rich, satisfying smell of coq au vin filled the room.

'It is,' Petra said. 'Though whether a sizeable family has ever lived here I don't know. If so, it must have been a long time ago. Dr Harden and his wife lived here many years, and Claire was their only child.'

'It calls out for a family,' Adam said.

'Yes. Well, since all it's got is me,' Petra said, a bit sharpish, 'it will have to keep on calling. Do sit down and I'll pour a drink. Do you like sherry, or gin—or would you rather have a beer?' A six-pack of beer was one of the things she'd picked up in her rush around the village this morning. 'Or a glass of wine?'

'Wine, please,' Adam said. 'Can I do anything to help?'

'You can open the wine.' She handed him a Screwpull, took two glasses from a cupboard; Adam opened and poured.

'Shall we drink to something?' he asked. 'Or just drink?'

'Why don't we drink to the MADS?' Petra suggested.

'A good idea! I don't know what I'd have done without the MADS this last year or two.'

And already they've done something for me, Petra thought.

They raised their glasses.

'The MADS and the *Dream*,' Petra said. 'Did you hear any more about Ursula's dinner?'

'Nothing. I think we can rule it out, don't you?'

She wondered why Adam had needed a very mixed bunch of amateur actors to see him through his personal trouble. He worked in a lively university. He was a professional among professionals, surrounded by like-minded people, and stimulated (presumably) by his students. What had MADS, or Mindon itself for that matter, offered him?

77

'Is there something else I can do?' Adam offered. 'Vegetables? I'm reasonably domesticated.'

'All done. I just have to make a quick starter.' She washed and dried salad, tossed it in the dressing, cut open the avocado pear—she'd chosen that well, it was the exactly right degree of ripeness—and removed the smooth, large stone, putting it aside with the vague idea that she'd plant it and watch something grow.

'I've laid the table in the dining room,' she said. 'But if you prefer it we can carry everything out into the garden.'

'The dining room is fine,' Adam said.

In fact, he would like to have stayed at the kitchen table. She would perhaps be a little less stiff, a little less reserved in her kitchen, a little less tight, with the main dish between them on the bare table, the vegetables served straight from the pans. He followed her into the dining room; observing the well-laid table, the flowers in the centre, the linen napkins, he realized she had taken trouble, and since he was the only guest she had clearly done it for him.

'This looks wonderful,' he said.

To Petra's relief the lunch went well, but then who could go wrong with coq au vin? All one had to do was to follow the recipe. When it was over Petra suggested they should have coffee in the garden.

Adam carried the tray outside, placed it on the table.

'This is very pleasant,' he said. 'Do you like gardening?'

'I neither like it nor dislike it,' Petra said. 'I know

so little about it. My father was the gardener in our family. I never did a thing. But I shall have to learn because I can't afford a gardener. I wish I had Dad here to advise me. There's so much to be done.'

'You miss your father?'

It was several seconds before Petra answered. Her gaze seemed fixed on the far right-hand corner of the garden, beyond the lawn, where a small statue of a boy was half-hidden behind an overgrown evergreen. She looked hard at him, in his marble whiteness, as if she was seeking inspiration.

'Yes, I do miss him,' she acknowledged. 'But I miss my mother even more. Perhaps because I spent more time with her I suppose, and isn't almost everyone's mother the best in the world? I certainly thought mine was.'

And yet, hadn't it been Malcolm, when he'd ditched her, who at the time she'd missed even more desperately? It had seemed then as though the world would never be the same again.

She gave a sudden, sharp twist of her shoulders, as if she was physically throwing off her thoughts of Malcolm. They were totally out of place on this pleasant summer's afternoon. There was no way she wanted Malcolm back in her life. If he rang the front doorbell at this moment she wouldn't so much as ask him in.

'I've something I want to show you,' she said to Adam. 'Though of course you might not be interested. It's a photograph of my mother and Claire.'

'Oh but I would be,' Adam assured her.

'Then wait here.'

She was back within the minute.

79

'There are two photographs, actually. The first one I found,' she said, handing it to him, 'amongst my mother's belongings, after her death. It had never been on display in the house, but then my mother was never one for framed photographs on every piece of furniture. She must have been quite young when it was taken, don't you think? It's not as I knew her, of course. She's pretty, isn't she?'

'Charming! And the other girl?'

'I didn't know. I had no idea, nor who the man was, not until I found an identical snapshot in the attic here yesterday.' She handed over the second photograph. 'Turn it over. Look on the back!'

He read the names out loud.

'Marian, Eliot, Claire.'

'I was so pleased to find a likeness of Claire. Here I am, living in her house, surrounded by so many of her things, though I'd never even heard of her until after my mother's death. And all she told me then was that she and my mother had been at boarding school together and that my mother had been kind to her. Now at least I know what she looked like, or once did.'

'And who is Eliot?'

'I haven't the faintest idea,' Petra admitted. 'I don't suppose I ever shall have, but that doesn't matter.'

He handed back the photographs. The two of them sat for a while without speaking. With the sun warm on his face, Adam closed his eyes and fell asleep. Petra watched him as he slept. His head fell back, his mouth opened a little and he gave a gentle snore. He looked so vulnerable, she thought, and younger than when he was awake. His head leaned against the ironwork of the chair and she wanted to put a cushion behind him but there was no way she would do so. She doubted that he'd be pleased he'd fallen asleep in her presence. They didn't know one another well enough for that.

Ten minutes later he wakened with a start, and looked around him, not knowing for a moment where he was.

'I'm sorry!' he said. 'How rude of me! Have I been asleep long?'

Petra smiled at him.

'Not more than a few minutes,' she assured him. 'It doesn't matter a bit!'

'I must go,' he said. 'I don't want to outstay my welcome. I've really enjoyed myself, even if I did fall asleep on you.'

'So have I,' Petra said. 'What are you going to do next?'

'Start learning my lines, I guess. I can't act, holding a script.'

'Well,' Petra offered, 'if you want me to hear them any time, I'll gladly do so.'

'Thank you,' Adam said. 'I might take you up on that, and I'll see you on Monday then. You'll be at the rehearsal?'

'Oh yes!' Petra said.

CHAPTER SIX

'Right!' Ursula said. 'You all have your scripts, I hope. And by the way don't forget that you have to pay for them. Two pounds ninety-nine. It's a large cast and the society doesn't have the funds, but I'm sure none of you will mind. Now, let's make a start.'

She took her place in the middle of the hall, several yards back from the stage, clutching a large, loose-leaf folder in which she had made copious notes, and would add many more as the weeks went by. No detail of place, speech, exits, entrances, moves, nuances, gestures, reminders, faults to be corrected, was too small or unimportant to be noted.

'Now to begin with,' she said in her loud, clear, play-producing voice, 'I want Theseus, Hippolyta, Philostrate and the Attendants at the ready in the wings. For the moment "Attendants" just means you, Nicola dear. We shall have to look around for more, though goodness knows where!' (She scribbled a note.)

'Philostrate isn't here,' Theseus said.

'I know,' Ursula said grimly. 'The good doctor has been called out on a case.' Some inconsiderate woman having a difficult labour, she supposed.

'But at least my husband doesn't have any lines in this scene,' the doctor's wife said. 'So it doesn't really matter, does it?'

'I can't quite agree with that, Cynthia,' Ursula said firmly. 'If any member of the cast is missing it unbalances the scene. It is no longer as Shakespeare intended it.'

'I'm sure I'm very sorry . . .' Cynthia Clarke began.

'But in this case,' Ursula said with what graciousness she could command, 'I do understand. Let us hope it doesn't happen when he has his little speech later on. Let us particularly hope that he will have no awkward patients on the nights of the production.'

82

'I don't suppose I need to be here for every rehearsal,' Nicola broke in. 'Seeing that I don't have any lines at all.' She had half hoped that Ursula might have written in a line or two for her, in the manner of Shakespeare.

'Of course you do!' Ursula's voice, meant at all times to be encouraging, even to the least, was verging on the sharpish. 'You are there to *be*, if not to *speak*. You watch with interest when the others speak. You listen to what they say. You must have the *look* of an Attendant.'

'Whatever that is,' Nicola muttered.

'It means you *attend*!' Ursula said fiercely. 'And now shall we get on? We're wasting valuable time. Theseus, you and Hippolyta enter first on to an empty stage and you take your seats at the table. Then Egeus, Hermia—'

'Except,' Hippolyta piped up, 'we haven't got a table, or any chairs for that matter!'

Ursula gave a deep sigh. This was *not* a good beginning. It was not her job, of course, to set the stage but she should have noticed. It was no use thinking she could leave anything to anyone else without supervision. From now on, for every rehearsal and every performance she would blame herself for everything that went wrong. It was the best way. It was better than losing her temper with the rest of them. And after all she was the leader, she held them together. The weight was on her shoulders and she would bear it.

At least she would while she was on the spot. Eric would have the benefit of her true feelings when she got home.

'Where is Norman?' she demanded.

Even as she spoke he rushed into the hall as if

83

blown by a hurricane.

'Ursula, I'm sorry!' He was breathless with anxiety. 'A phone call, just as I was leaving!'

'Norman—and this goes for the rest of you—' she said looking around, 'we do *not* answer the phone when we are due at rehearsal!'

'I've said I'm sorry!'

'Well will you just get on with it now, if you please. You of all people should be here early to see to it that the stage is set. Now put two of the small tables that the Darby and Joan Club use for their whist drives—no I do not know where they keep them—with four chairs around. Any chairs. Someone please give Norman a hand!'

While the tables were being set into place—they were quite awkward folding tables with strong metal catches which snapped back and trapped one's fingers—she made more notes.

'Right!' she said eventually. 'Can we actually make a start now? We've wasted at least twenty minutes.'

Theseus, impatient to give voice, needed no second bidding. He strode on to the stage two steps ahead of Hippolyta and took his place at the head of the table. And began:

' "Now, fair Hippolyta, our nuptial hour
Draws on apace—" '

He stopped. Ursula stared at him.

'This table is much too far back,' he said. 'Surely it should be further upstage. I take it the principal characters at least are here to be seen and heard?'

'Norman,' Ursula ordered, 'Giles is quite right. Would you kindly move the tables? We must get everything right from the beginning.'

She was not going to chance upsetting Giles at

84

this early stage. In fact, they were all being a bit bolshy, even Nicola who was usually most co-operative. Nerves, no doubt, but she would let them settle down for a rehearsal or two and then she would have to show them who was boss.

'Shall we go out and come in again?' Hippolyta asked.

'I think you'd better.'

Scripts in hand they re-entered, except that Theseus scarcely needed to look at his. He was always the first to learn his lines and already he was speaking them well. Of course, Ursula thought, the part suited him. Important, pompous, full of words—but would that some of the others were like him. Hippolyta for instance. She would have to work on Arabella to get her to deepen her voice, project it. She was far too light. It was not a voice which went with her tall, rather plump, full-bosomed figure. One expected a deep voice from that chest. But time and tuition would change that. It was a conscientious producer's task to see that it did.

Ursula took them through their opening speeches twice more, nodding approval, encouraging, gently correcting—then let it go. One had to know when to stop. Actually, she could never understand why people thought she was difficult. Really, she was a pussy cat!

'Well done!' she said. 'And now Egeus and the four lovers, are you ready in the wings? Your cue is "with pomp, with triumph and with revelling". Please all of you, underline your cues. Since you are paying for your scripts you may do so freely.'

' "Happy be Theseus, our renowned Duke!" ' Sam Worth said in his usual measured tones.

85

'Yes, Egeus, dear, but do remember you are *not* a happy man. "Full of vexation come I with complaint." You are very very, angry!'

'Sorry,' Egeus said.

Oh dear, Ursula thought as he repeated the line with no difference whatsoever. She had not been happy in giving him the part, but needs must. He was a nice man, willing to devote all the time in the world to the MADS, but he was no actor, and certainly no Egeus. He was too placid. In a word, he was dull. She would have to think of something to arouse his anger.

*   *   *

Petra crept into the hall on tiptoe, opening and closing the door behind her as quietly as possible. She had not intended to be late, even though she saw no urgent reason for her presence, but she had been caught up in her work. The light had seemed right to continue with her painting of the garden and, as always when she was painting, the time had slipped by unnoticed.

Still, no matter, she thought as she sat on the nearest chair, which happened to be next to Norman Pritchard, no harm done. No-one had seen her, not a head had been turned in her direction, not even Ursula's.

Petra smiled at Norman, then turned her attention to the play. Giles was holding stage, with Adam, Victoria, Jennie, Eric and Sam Worth clustered around him. Or, as she must learn to think of them, Theseus, Lysander, Hermia, Helena, Demetrius and Egeus.

Theseus was in full spate. With everything he

86

had to offer—resonant voice, good looks, acting ability—it was easy for him to dominate, which he did. Petra watched the scene with interest. Mostly they were better than she had expected them to be, though poor Sam Worth was miscast and surely Eric, though he delivered his lines well, was too old for Demetrius? A slightly receding hairline and the beginnings of a beer belly did not go well with an impatient young lover. But now Theseus was leaving, and taking everyone except Lysander and Hermia with him. Petra sat forward in her seat and with extra concentration watched the scene between the two of them.

' "For all that I could ever read," ' Lysander said, ' "The course of true love never did run smooth." '

Petra nodded in agreement. You could say that again.

'STOP!'

Ursula's voice rang out. Everyone, the two on the stage as well as those around the perimeter of the room were immediately silenced, as if struck by lightning. Lysander, about to carry on speaking, stopped with his mouth open. Hermia stood rooted to the floor like a statue in stone. Norman jumped in his seat and Doris gave a short, quickly stifled gasp. Such was the power of Ursula's voice when she chose to use it so.

'It won't do!' she said. 'You are both very nice, very charming, but has what Theseus said rolled off you like water off a duck's back? "Death" he said. "Or a single life"! Why aren't you terrified, Hermia? Why aren't you distraught, Lysander? You are passionately in love with each other. So can we have some fear, some passion, some anguish? I'm not sure that you shouldn't be clinging to each other, not standing three yards apart. Try it. Start again from Theseus's exit.'

They moved closer. Lysander held Hermia protectively by the shoulders, she raised her hand and touched his neck. They looked into each other's eyes.

'That's *much* better!' Ursula said. 'Just remember all the time how much in love you are.'

They're certainly carrying out Ursula's orders, Petra thought, watching them as the scene proceeded. They were certainly throwing themselves into their parts.

'Don't they make a lovely couple!' Doris Pritchard whispered.

'Right!' Ursula said presently. 'We'll take a break.'

She said it just as Jennie Austin, in the person of Helena, entered in a state of high nervous excitement. For the last three evenings she had shut herself in her bedroom learning her part, ignoring her mother's commands to come downstairs and keep her company. In front of the wardrobe mirror she had practised and practised and practised. She knew at least her first speech by heart. She would be *the* Helena. She would slay them. She would show Ursula that her faith in giving her the part was totally justified.

In the wings she took a deep breath from the bottom of her lungs, then walked on.

'We'll take no more than fifteen minutes,' Ursula said. 'Has anyone made any coffee?'

Petra watched Jennie crumple, deflate like a balloon going down. She felt sure Ursula had not done it intentionally. She did not come over as a cruel woman.

'Hattie Cumber will have made coffee in the kitchen,' Doris Pritchard said. 'She usually does.'

Petra joined the group of people going in that direction and found herself standing at the table next to Adam and Victoria. She felt curiously—not embarrassed, but awkward—as if she was intruding on something.

'Hello, Petra!' Adam said cheerfully. 'I didn't know you were here. I didn't see you come in.'

'I was late,' Petra said. 'You were otherwise engaged.' She smiled at Victoria, who in close-fitting jeans and a white tee-shirt looked younger and prettier than ever. Ursula came up behind them.

'Didn't these two do well?' she said with approval.

'Very well,' Petra agreed. 'Most convincing!'

Ursula put a hand on Petra's arm.

'I'm going to take you away,' she said. 'I want to discuss Theseus's palace for a minute. The sooner we get some sort of furnishings—props—the better I think, don't you? I mean, if it's only a cloth on the table, some tankards, a book or two. It helps the cast to feel in the scene. Don't you agree?' She set off to walk back into the hall.

'I do,' Petra said, following her. 'In fact I found a huge chenille curtain when I was clearing out the attic. Crimson.'

'That sounds perfect.'

'I'll have a word with Doris Pritchard about it,' Petra said. 'She's props isn't she?'

'How tactful you are,' Ursula replied. 'But then one has to be, I make a point of it.'

She called across the room.

'Time's up everyone! Back in the hall except

89

those who are washing-up. And please do it quietly, Hattie, and whoever's helping you.'

Naturally everyone did as they were told. Lysander, Hermia and Helena walked past Ursula as she stood with Petra.

'This is your big moment, Jennie dear,' she said kindly. 'Are you ready for it?'

Jennie Austin turned an expressionless face towards her.

'I was,' she said.

'She seems a little tense,' Ursula observed. 'I expect she's nervous!'

'I'll go and have a word with Doris,' Petra said.

Ursula nodded. 'Do that dear, but keep your voices down. I don't like to hear any other sounds when I'm directing. I'm sure you understand.'

But Petra had already gone. Ursula turned her attention to the stage.

'Now, Helena,' she said, 'the first thing is to come in promptly on your cue. No dear, you do *not* wait offstage until Hermia has said, "Here comes Helena". You must be visible by then. Your cue is "Tomorrow truly will I meet with thee".'

'Sorry,' Jennie said.

'Go out and come in again, dear. And remember you are a most unhappy lady. Distraught.' Had she done the right thing in choosing Jennie? Was her goose not going to turn out to be a swan?

*   *   *

'Thank you everyone! We'll call it a day!' Ursula said eventually. She was quite exhausted. It had not been easy, but was it ever?

'I can give a lift if anyone is going my way,' she

said.

'I am!' Eric said in a loud voice—and raised the laugh he had hoped for.

'Very well, Eric,' Ursula said. She was too exhausted to laugh. 'I'll take you to your own front door.'

They didn't speak on the short drive home. Back in the house, Ursula brewed herself a cup of camomile tea to calm her down—not that she had much hope that it would. Eric poured himself a brandy and they carried their drinks up to the bedroom. In no time at all Ursula was leaning against her pillows, reading a book. Eric, undressing, stood looking in the mirror, not liking one little bit what he saw.

'I'm not cut out for it,' he announced. He waited for his wife's reply, and when it didn't come he repeated himself, this time more insistently. 'I tell you, Ursula, I'm not cut out for it!'

'What?' Ursula asked reluctantly, not taking her eyes from her book.

'Demetrius. I'm not cut out for Demetrius!'

'Of course you are! Why not? What are you talking about?'

'Look at me!' He viewed his reflection with distaste. 'Demetrius is a young, passionate lover. I've got a face full of sags and wrinkles, and a paunch.' The paunch was very definite. His body from above where his waist ought to be, to where the elasticated top of his underpants cut into his flesh flowed in a more-than-generous curve. How had he got like this? How had it crept up on him? He put aside the thought of how unreasonably and increasingly tight everything had seemed over the last few months, how he had had to let out two or three notches in his belt. 'I tell you, I'm not fit to play Demetrius! I'll be a laughing stock!'

Ursula lowered her book. This sounded serious.

'Of course you are, darling! Of course you won't be! You don't have to be thin to be sexy. You look fine to me!'

'That's because you're used to me,' Eric said testily. 'And because you're not young yourself!'

'Thank you!' Ursula said. 'Anyway, you're wrong. Once you get into the part you'll be fine. For that matter . . .' she paused '. . . who else could we get?' It was the crux of the matter; it was the bottom line.

'That's what it boils down to, isn't it?' Eric said. 'I'm highly unsuitable, but I'll have to do, fat or not fat!'

Ursula sighed.

'Perhaps you have a paunch, dear,' she conceded. 'A little one. But you could get rid of it. I'll work out a diet for you. You could be as thin as a reed by the time we get to the production.'

'Thank you for nothing! I'm not going to starve for the MADS.' He turned away from the offensive sight in the mirror and put on his pyjamas.

'That's where we differ,' Ursula said. 'I'd do anything for the MADS!'

'Oh, I know that! You'd give blood if necessary. Well not me!'

'You could wear a corset,' Ursula suggested helpfully. 'An elastic one. I'm sure they do them for men. That would hold you in.'

'I am *not* going to wear a corset.'

'Oh Eric, you are being tiresome. Come to bed. You'll see things quite differently in the morning.'

'No I won't,' he persisted, climbing into bed. 'My

92

sodding belly won't be any different. I'm bloody fat now and I'll be bloody fat in the morning! And what about the rest?' he demanded. 'What about my hair, and having a face like a ploughed field? What can you do about that?'

'Oh, that's easy!' Ursula said cheerfully. 'Make-up and a bit of false hair will see to that! It's easier to make an older person look younger than a young one look older. And think of all the famous actors, older and . . .' She hesitated, looking for the right word. '. . . plumper than you who've played juvenile leads well after your age—'

'More fool them!' he interrupted, thumping his pillow into submission.

'Laurence Olivier, Sean Connery . . .' She searched for names and found none.

'I am no Olivier, *or* Connery!' Eric said. 'Anyway, I reckon you've got the wrong play. If you'd chosen better I could have been Falstaff.'

'Now there you *are* wrong,' Ursula said. 'For you to play Falstaff you'd have had to have miles of padding. So let that be a comfort to you!'

At the moment, he thought, nothing could be a comfort. Not even Ursula.

'Can we put the light out?' he said.

'Oh darling, must we? Just yet?' Ursula pleaded. 'You know how I am after a rehearsal! I have to read or I'd never sleep. It soothes me.'

'Very well,' he said. 'But please not half the night. What are you reading?'

'It's called *Blood on her Hands.* I don't think you'd like it.'

'I doubt I would,' he agreed, turning his back on her, pulling the duvet over his eyes to shut out the light.

                      *   *   *

As the members of MADS had left the Parish Hall, Ursula, stepping into her BMW, had called out 'Don't forget to lock up, Norman, or we shall be in trouble,' before she switched on the engine and zoomed away, bearing Eric, but no-one else. It seemed no-one was going her way. She had left them standing in a group, debating whether they would or would not go into the Queen's Head for a quick one. Quick it would have to be. There was only thirty minutes drinking time left and half of that was likely to be taken up in waiting at the bar to be served.

For Jennie Austin there had been no debate. No way could she prolong her absence from home, even for half an hour. She was already later than she'd meant to be. The rehearsal had gone on longer than expected partly, she had to admit, because Ursula had spent so much time in helping her to understand her part, not just the words, which were difficult, but the allusions to things in Helena's character which meant nothing at all to her. By now, however, she felt herself in some ways quite close to Helena. They had things in common. Life did not go easily for Helena, nor did it for Jennie. Helena was not beautiful, as Hermia was; nor am I, she thought, as Victoria is. Most of all, Helena loved Demetrius, who spurned her. As my love spurns me, Jennie thought. Well it was not so much that he spurned her as that he never so much as noticed her.

Jennie was in love with Giles Rowland, had been since she had sat in the audience in the Parish Hall

94

watching Giles playing Robert Browning in *The Barretts of Wimpole Street.* So handsome, so romantic, so . . . in charge. She had deeply envied Lucinda Rockwell, playing Elizabeth Barrett, pale and invalidish on her chaise longue for most of the play, her dog Flush by her side, until, in the end, she was carried away by her lover to foreign parts. What more wonderful could happen to anyone? Watching, she had not even been thrown by the fact that the dog Flush (real name Bonny), who had not been stage trained, had chosen the middle of an impassioned speech by Robert to his love to jump down from the bed and pee on the stage. Giles had been magnificent. With true professionalism he had carried on regardless in spite of the pool spreading across the floor. She thought that was probably the moment when she had fallen in love with him.

The very next week she had applied to join the MADS. It was only when she became a member that she discovered Giles's and Lucinda's deep loathing of each other, and the fact that Bonny/Flush was Lucinda's dog in real life.

Jennie knew it was hopeless, of course. She accepted that fact. All she lived for was that one day Giles would notice her, would say 'Why, hello, Jennie!'

So, before the group had finally made up their minds to eschew the Queen's Head on this evening, she had scurried home.

'You're very late!' Mrs Austin said. 'I've been dying for a cup of tea and my tablets are nearly an hour overdue. You know how it is if I don't get my tablets.'

'I couldn't get away,' Jennie said. 'I'll put the

95

kettle on at once. Or would you rather have your tablets first?'

'I don't know,' her mother said testily. 'Don't ask me to decide everything for you. What do you mean, you couldn't get away? You're a free woman, aren't you?'

Would that I were, Jennie thought as she went to fill the kettle. She had not been free since two months before she was due to leave school. She was to train as a children's nanny, she already had a place on the course. After which, she had thought, she would find a job with a lovely family and, as like as not, travel the world with them.

She had travelled no further than 62 Burnham Road, the house where she had been born. In her last term at school her father had taken a plane to Australia, never to return; never, according to the short note he left behind, with any intention of returning.

There had never been any question after that of Jennie taking up her training. Her mother's need was desperate. She had gone to pieces. Jennie was allowed to leave school before the term ended in order to look after her mother, and that she had been doing ever since. In the five years since then she had not been allowed to take a job. Her mother grew weaker and more dependent all the time, though neither her own doctor nor any of the others she had seen from time to time could find a physical cause and Mrs Austin stoutly brushed aside any suggestion of a mental one. 'I am not mad!' she said. 'What is mad about needing my own daughter to look after me?'

The only rebellion Jennie, at times deeply sorry for her mother, had shown was in joining the

96

MADS. Nothing, she had vowed to herself, would ever make her give up the MADS.

While the kettle boiled she gave her mother her tablets, and then her cup of tea, strong and milky, and the two Bourbon biscuits she liked to have with it.

'Are you sure you want a hot-water bottle tonight?' she asked. 'It's quite a warm evening.'

'Of course I do!' Mrs Austin said. 'It won't be warm in the middle of the night when you're asleep and I'm awake. I expect you mean you're too tired to do it. You've worn yourself out with that silly play-acting.'

'No I'm not. I'll do it at once, then I'll see you to bed as soon as you're ready.' She would never take up any of her mother's references to what she always called 'play-acting'. She didn't want her to know about it, she wished to keep it to herself, something that was not to be shared.

When she had seen her mother to bed she came downstairs again. She never went to bed early now. This time was her own. She settled in her chair and took out her script. She would learn a few more lines. She thought Ursula had been quite pleased with her, in spite of having had to give her so much help. She would be even more pleased if I were to learn my lines, Jennie thought.

*   *   *

Sam Worth was a bit disappointed that they decided not to go into the Queen's Head. He was not yet ready to go home, nevertheless he did so.

His wife, Olive, was as usual sitting in her armchair when he went in, and as usual knitting. As

97

was also usual, they did not exchange greetings but his cat, Flossie, whom he loved with all his heart, came at once and rubbed herself against him, weaving in and out around his legs. When he picked up the evening paper and sat in his chair, facing Olive, Flossie jumped on to his lap.

'That cat has fleas!' his wife said. 'If you ask me, all cats have fleas.' Her tone was amiable even if her words were not. It usually was.

'Other cats might have, Flossie doesn't,' Sam answered. He saw to that, brushing her assiduously every day.

Even so, he put his newspaper aside and began to part her silky black hair with his fingers, causing her to purr ecstatically.

'You should take her to the vet,' his wife said. 'Get her seen to.

Take her to the vet and leave her there, Sam knew she meant.

'No need,' he pronounced. 'She's as clean as a whistle!'

Olive finished her row, she was knitting a long green thing of no discernible shape, then stuck the needles through the ball of wool and put the whole thing away in the dresser cupboard.

'I'm going up,' she said. 'Goodnight.'

'Goodnight,' Sam replied.

It was curious that though they never greeted each other at any other time they never failed to say goodnight. They were not at loggerheads, just bored to death with each other.

Sam took Flossie into the garden, waited for her to come in, gave her a saucer of milk, then went back into the living room where he picked up his script. He knew Ursula wanted him to show more life as Egeus, to be more angry. He would try, he really would. He read aloud a line or two, quietly in case Olive was still awake.

' "With cunning hast thou filched my daughter's heart,
Turning her obedience, which is due to me
To stubborn harshness." '

Frankly, it was difficult enough to say, let alone to get anger into it. The trouble was, he had forgotten how to feel anger—if he had ever known. He didn't feel much of anything, except of course for Flossie.

He put down the script. He would work at it again tomorrow when Olive had gone to the shops. Upstairs the bedroom light was out. He undressed in the dark and climbed into bed.

*   *   *

'Well then,' said Adam to Victoria, 'as we're not going to the pub, I'll give you a lift home.'

'Thank you,' Victoria said. She had hoped he would suggest the two of them going for a drink, even if the others didn't, but five minutes later he dropped her at her gate, then drove home.

*   *   *

'Was it a good rehearsal?' Mrs Cattermole asked Victoria.

'Very good,' Victoria answered. 'But I'm quite tired. I think I'll go straight to bed if you don't mind.'

In front of her mirror she looked at her reflection. It was very different from Eric King's, probably being viewed by him at around the same time. Nevertheless she frowned at herself, then picked up a jar of cream, guaranteed to work miracles she didn't need.

She was a long time falling asleep but when she did *her* midsummer night's dream was of Adam—or, rather, of Lysander.

*   *   *

Norman Pritchard, fast asleep and snoring gently, was wakened by sounds overhead. Footsteps! In the attic! Burglars!

He turned to alert his wife, but Doris was not there. Gone to the toilet, no doubt. He left his bed and tiptoed stealthily up the attic stairs. Doris came forward to greet him.

'What in the world . . .! I thought we had burglars!' Norman said.

'It's only me,' Doris said placidly. 'I suddenly remembered where I thought we had three pewter tankards. You know Petra wants pewter tankards. We mustn't let her think we don't know how to do things in Mindon!'

CHAPTER SEVEN

Petra dropped her purse into her shopping bag, closed the door behind her, and set off for the village store, owned by Mr Handford. Less than ten minutes later she stepped from the brightness of the afternoon into its empty dimness.

'All on your own, Mr Handford?' she said

cheerfully. 'Where is everyone?'

'No doubt where they usually are when they want to shop,' he said. 'Gone to Southfield to the supermarkets. Anyway, Miss Banbury, what can I do for you?'

'I want a few things,' Petra said. 'I'll take a look around.'

Several years ago Mr Handford had made his shop a self-service store but it had not worked out. The aisles were too narrow, it was murder trying to pass anyone, and there was no room for trolleys, so that the most people bought was what would fit into a wire basket. Petra filled hers and took it to the counter.

'I'll bring this lot round to you after I've closed,' Mr Handford offered.

'Thank you,' Petra said. 'In that case I'll have five pounds of potatoes and a bag of self-raising flour.'

As she left the shop the children were streaming out of St Peter's church primary school while parents—mostly mothers but with a light sprinkling of fathers—waited to collect them. The little girls, in their red and white cotton dresses, looked like summer flowers; the small boys wore dark blue shorts and red tee-shirts. Almost without exception all the children were bowed down by backpacks, which they immediately handed over to an available parent.

Freed now from all constraints the children crossed the road and spread on to the green. Petra walked along the path which bordered it and thought how attractive the whole picture was: the children, the wide expanse of grass (fresh and green when she had first arrived in Mindon but

101

now turning yellowish from the dry summer), the two horse chestnuts, heavy with summer foliage, the benches at intervals around the perimeter.

She walked a little way, then stopped and sat down on an empty bench. She was in no hurry and it was all so pleasant.

Five minutes later she saw a young woman coming towards her, pushing a toddler in a buggy, with two little girls in tow. The mother was Amelia, wardrobes, Petra thought. She was falling into Ursula's habit of ticketing everyone by what they did in MADS. She looked up and smiled as Amelia and her family drew near.

'Hello!' Amelia said.

'Hello! Are these your children?'

'Yes! All three of them! Teresa and Emma, and this is Bobby.'

'And how old are you two?' Petra asked the girls.

'I'm eight and a half,' the taller one said. 'Emma is seven and a quarter.' She turned to Amelia. 'Can we go and play, Mummy?'

'I suppose so,' Amelia said. 'Don't go too far away. And don't play on the middle bit of the green!

'Not that they'll take any notice,' she said to Petra. 'Well not of the last bit. None of the kids ever do.' She sat down beside Petra.

'The middle bit is sacred to cricket. At least that's what the cricket team likes to believe. But you can't stop the children. No-one's ever been able to. And after all it's *their* green, I mean the children's. It doesn't belong to the cricketers, does it?'

'I don't suppose so. Who does it belong to?'

Amelia frowned.

'I'm not sure. The county council, I expect. Anyway, we all pay our council tax, don't we, so it should be fair do's all round!'

Two or three ball games were already in progress in the centre of the green, and they were playing on what, to Petra's eyes, must be the crease. Her father had been a keen amateur cricketer. She knew how dear to them was the ground on which they played, every blade of grass sacred.

'Quite often,' Amelia informed her, 'they have someone from the cricket club around when the children come out of school. He shoos them away. But nobody's turned up today so they've a free run. Good luck to them, I say.'

'I think Bobby's falling asleep,' Petra said.

'Oh dear!' Amelia said. 'If he sleeps now he'll not go off quickly this evening and I want to go to the rehearsal. I don't go to them all because of the children, but I go as often as I can.'

'Me too,' Petra said. 'And since I'm doing the sets for the production, and, really, scenery and dress are part of the same visual thing, do you think it would be a good idea if we got together?'

'That would be great,' Amelia said. 'I don't know anything about clothes for Shakespeare, but I can sew, or alter things. I usually do whatever Ursula tells me—don't we all! But between you and me *she* hasn't ever produced Shakespeare before, so she can't know it all, can she?'

'I suppose not,' Petra said.

'I'm hoping she'll use some of the Brownies as attendants to Titania,' Amelia confided. 'Teresa and Emma are both in the Brownies. They'd just love it. I think they'd be quite good.' A thought struck her. 'I wonder if she *will* try to use a real live

103

baby? You know Lucinda wants her to? I wonder if she'd consider Bobby for the part? He'd be no trouble.'

Privately, Petra reckoned Bobby, or indeed any other baby, would be the last thing Ursula would consider. She was saved from making a reply by the sight of Tina Jackson walking towards them.

Ah, Amelia thought, I can guess which member of the cricket team should have been watching the children today! George Shepherd! There was something going between George and Tina. Everyone in MADS knew that, though not just what, and no-one said much, or asked questions. It was as if people's lives within MADS were quite apart from what went on elsewhere, which quite a bit of the time they were because they were acting parts anyway.

Tina Jackson, Amelia knew, didn't have an easy time of it with a boy of twelve and no husband. As far as she knew, Tina had never had a husband. But none of this did Amelia pass on to Petra. Live and let live. And it would have been impossible anyway because Tina had reached them.

'A meeting of the MADS,' Tina said. 'You can't go far around Mindon without seeing one or another of us.' She sat down on the other side of Petra.

'I was just saying,' Amelia began, 'I was just wondering if Ursula was going to let Titania have a real live baby. I wondered about Bobby.'

Tina tried not to show the horror which arose in her. A real baby! She had nothing against Bobby, now angelically asleep in his buggy, but the prospect filled her with dismay. Also, she knew exactly what Lucinda Rockwell would do. She

104

would have the baby for the few moments when it was convenient, when it was cooing and smiling and behaving itself, and the rest of the time, when it was sick or dribbled or worse, she would hand it to her attendant. Which means to *me*, Tina thought.

'I don't honestly think Ursula *will* have a real baby,' she said. 'They can be very awkward. We all know—you especially since you've had three—how they can do the wrong thing at the wrong time. Very embarrassing! You know what they say, never act with children or animals!'

'Well it was just an idea,' Amelia said. 'Of course when I think about it I realize that Bobby could take everybody's attention away from the play. Babies *do* attract attention, don't they?'

A totally new thought came into Tina's mind, a thought foreign to her nature, for she was at heart a nice woman, but when it came to Madam Almighty Lucinda Titania she was no more charitable than the rest. Amelia was right, a baby could upstage them all, especially if given the right incentive at the right time, which was to say, when she was in the Chief Attendant's arms. She must think further about this, not dismiss it too hastily.

'I must be going!' Amelia said. 'See you both at rehearsal!'

She called to the girls who did not hear her, or if they did took no notice, so she gathered her things together and set off across the green.

'She has no business to wheel that buggy on the grass!' Tina said. 'She knows that perfectly well. George will be furious!'

'George?'

'George Shepherd. He's not just in MADS. He's

105

also chair of the cricket club. I know he *had* promised to keep an eye on the children this afternoon. There's an important match on Saturday, against Featherwell. It's vital for the crease to be in good nick, *and* the outfield.'

She sounds just like my father, Petra thought.

'You haven't seen him around, have you?' Tina asked.

'No,' Petra said. 'Wouldn't he be at work?'

'He would if he wasn't taking a week's holiday,' Tina agreed. 'Which is what I'm doing or I wouldn't be here either. We both work in Southfield Town Hall. George is in Environment, I'm in Housing.'

'And he's taking a week of his holiday to look after the cricket pitch? How noble!'

'Well . . . more or less. He can't get away for a proper holiday.'

She stopped short. The truth was that he couldn't get away for a week because his wife wouldn't let him. The selfish cow didn't want him for herself, nor did she want anyone else to have him. He was a meal ticket, pure and simple.

Nor, of course, if it came to that, could *she* ever get away from Mindon, not for so much as one night. There was Daniel to think of. One fine day, Tina told herself, when Daniel had flown the nest and George had plucked up the courage to walk out on Moira—she would never give him a divorce—the two of them would take off. They didn't want much. Just each other. But until that day dawned at least they could take their stay-at-home holidays at the same time.

Petra watched Tina, saw the downward curve of her lips, the deep frown lines between her eyes, and

106

then, quite suddenly, Tina's face changed. Her brow cleared, her eyes opened wide—she had rather beautiful grey eyes—and her lips curved upwards in the beginnings of a smile. Petra followed Tina's look and saw, coming towards them, several children who were clearly being driven off the green, and driving them, like a well-trained sheepdog, was George Shepherd.

Petra and Tina watched. It was not a moment to interrupt. Tina nodded her head in approval, her face glowing with pride.

'Now be off, the lot of you,' George shouted in his deep loud voice as he drove the last of them off the green. 'Get home where you belong! And if I see any of you on the middle of the green again I'll report you!'

It was an idle threat. He knew it, and so did they because their parents had told them. There was no law against them being on any part of the green. For years now Mindon Cricket Club had sought permission to rope off the cricket pitch, but it had never been granted. Something to do with common land. But in any case, he thought, the little buggers would go under the rope.

He walked over and joined the ladies.

'Well done, love!' Tina said. 'You saw them off well and truly!'

He shrugged.

'I haven't any doubt they'll be back tomorrow,' he said. 'I blame the parents. What do they teach them?'

'I must go,' Petra said. 'Mr Handford promised to deliver my groceries. I must be in when he calls.' It was not totally true. If Mr Handford was coming after he'd closed his shop he'd be at least another hour and a half. What she sensed was that George and Tina would prefer her room to her company.

When Petra walked away George moved closer to Tina on the bench and took her hand in his.

'You shouldn't, George,' Tina protested. 'Someone will notice. It'll be all around the village.' It probably already was. Nevertheless she did not withdraw her hand.

'Tina, you do love me, don't you?' George asked.

'Of course I do. You know I do!'

'And I love you. I don't care if it's shouted from the housetops. I just don't give a damn any longer. I want to tell everyone. All that lot at the Town Hall. Everybody in Mindon, including Moira. Especially Moira.'

'You know we can't,' Tina said quietly. It was not the first time they had had this conversation. 'Anyway, I expect Moira knows.'

'I reckon she does. She doesn't know who, though.'

'Someone's sure to have told her.'

'Tell me who?' he demanded. 'She has no friends, doesn't speak to the neighbours. She never goes out except to work. Doesn't even do her own shopping. Just gives me a list and I have to do it every day in my lunch hour—well, I don't have to tell you that, do I?' He was bitter about that. He knew his colleagues in the office laughed at him.

'No, you don't!' Tina said. She had lost count of the times she had accompanied George, doing the shopping for the other woman in his life. Sometimes it was the small, domestic details, like knowing what they were going to have for supper, or what kind of soap they used in the shared bathroom, which hurt most.

108

'She says the Church won't let her divorce me,' George said. 'But how can that be? She never goes near the church, hasn't for years. I hate her! I tell you, I hate her! I wish she was dead!'

'Hush, love! You mustn't talk like that,' Tina said. Nevertheless she knew what he meant.

*   *   *

'Act one, scene two!' Ursula called out. 'The Mechanicals, Quince, Snug, Bottom, Flute, Snout and Starveling! Are you all ready?'

' "Ready!" ' Cyril Parsons quoted. ' "Name what part I am for, and proceed!" '

He knew every line, every word of his part. Each evening, after supper, his wife had tested him on it. He really liked the role. He had some really comical lines as Bottom, and of course he knew exactly how to deliver them. Whatever the rest of them were like *he* wouldn't disappoint his audience!

'Thank you, Cyril,' Ursula said. 'I'm glad you've been learning your lines. And as the Bard says: "You, Nick Bottom, are set down for Pyramus." '

Cyril came in quickly.

' "What is Pyramus? A lover or—" '

'Thank you again, Cyril,' Ursula said firmly. Who was producing this play, anyway? 'And now can we go back to the beginning of the scene? Just come on to the stage and stand or sit around. Quite casual. A group of workmates come to discuss something. All that happens is that Quince gives out the parts to the men who will later on play them before Theseus and Hippolyta. Quite clever of Shakespeare really. Tempting us with what's to

109

come.'

'I haven't yet learnt all my part,' Ralph Helmet interrupted. 'Quince has quite a lot to say and I've been rather busy.'

'Well do try to learn it before the next rehearsal, Vicar,' Ursula said. She could never understand why parish priests always said they were busy. What did they do from Monday to Saturday?

'I'll do my best,' the vicar said. 'Unfortunately we have the Archdeacon's visitation next week! That's always a time of trial!'

'I'm going to feel very strange playing Thisbe—I mean Flute,' Grace Helmet broke in anxiously. 'Am I a man or a woman, or what?'

'You are not going to feel strange,' Ursula ordered. 'You will do it perfectly well, and I will be here to guide you!' She had no intention of giving in to nerves at this stage. 'And now can we start? Quince!'

' "Is all our company here?" ' Ralph Helmet asked in his mellifluous pulpit voice.

Ursula swallowed hard and said nothing. It would not be easy to roughen the vicar. He was a perfect product of public school and Cambridge.

She heard them through to the end without interruption. The only sign she gave of the tension inside her—for those who happened to be watching—was the quiet tattoo her red-varnished nails tapped out on the table at which she sat. They were awful! How could they be so bad with such wonderful lines to deliver, such comic parts to play? All except Bottom, of course. Cyril was perfection, and the trouble was he knew it. By the time of the performance he would be overacting, milking his lines for all they were worth, stealing the show. Why did his competence irritate her more than the shortcomings of all the others?

'"Enough: hold,"' Bottom said, starting to exit with his merry band.

'Hold indeed!' Ursula said, raising her right hand, though she had no intention at this moment of stopping to tell them what she thought of them. 'While you're on stage, and as this is such a short scene, we'll move forward to your next one. Act three, scene one.'

While they thumbed through their scripts she glanced around the hall. No-one, as far as she could see, was taking any notice of what was going on on the stage. They were engaged in their own pursuits, knitting, reading the *Southfield Gazette,* gossiping in muted tones. It was typical. All that mattered to any of them was their own part in the play. It seemed not to occur to them that they could learn (if only what not to do) from watching the others. And in particular, of course, listening to and profiting from the advice she gave without stint to everyone.

She turned her attention to the stage again. Incredibly they were still searching through their scripts.

'Page seventy-three,' she said impatiently.

They went through the scene; they went through it twice more. With great restraint she forebore to tell them exactly what she thought. After all—she summoned up every last vestige of charity—aside from Cyril she had known when she cast them that they were not the cream of the acting world. She would simply have to work at it. Firm yet gentle, as one would with children. And, in a way, bad acting was what was called for in the last scene—still to be

111

rehearsed. But the problem was, did it take a really good actor to deliberately act badly? She was not certain. There was a fine line to be drawn and she was not quite sure where.

'Thank you,' she said at last. 'That's all we'll do with the Mechanicals this evening. If you could learn your parts by the next rehearsal I'd be grateful. Some of them aren't more than a few lines. And don't forget—those of you who haven't done much acting—*learn the cues* as well as the lines. No use having the words pat if you don't know when to say them!

'Now for act two, scene one. Puck and the Fairy first. Are you both ready?'

'Puck's not here!' someone said.

'*Not here!* Why not? And where is he?'

'I think he went to the loo,' someone else said.

'Then go and get him out!' Ursula said sharply. 'This is not the time to be going to the loo!'

'I don't know!' she said to Eric later, as they lay in bed. 'They're just not *dedicated*! One has to be dedicated, don't you agree?'

'Of course, dear,' Eric said. He felt dead beat.

'What am I to do about it?' she demanded.

'I'm sure you'll think of something,' Eric said, 'you always do. Can we have the light out?'

She switched it off. She was far too worried to read.

'There's just one thing, darling,' Eric said, a few minutes later.

'What's that?'

'I'm still not happy about Demetrius. I don't think I can do it, love! I just don't look the part, and if I don't look it I can't act it.'

She switched the light on again, and sat upright.

112

She could tell this was serious.

'Of course you can, Eric! You must pull yourself together!'

'All the pulling together in the world won't make me into a young lover,' Eric said firmly. 'You must think of something—or someone. I mean it!'

He switched off the light again. 'Now can we get some sleep,' he said.

Ursula slid down under the duvet, but not to sleep. Oh no! She lay with eyes wide open. What was she to do? There was no way, no way at all, she could get anyone else to play Demetrius. It was a total impossibility. 'You'll think of something, you always do,' Eric had said, but this time she was stymied.

She lay awake a long time, her thoughts going round in circles, before the idea came to her. It was simple, yet it would be difficult to carry out. Eric felt he was not suitable for Demetrius. He was not young enough, he was not attractive enough. (In her innermost heart she conceded he had a point, though she would never admit it to him.) To find anyone else in the whole of Mindon was impossible. The part of Demetrius could not be changed, she could not rewrite Shakespeare. Therefore Eric must change. He would not change of his own volition, therefore she must do it for him, and if possible so that he would hardly know it was happening.

On Saturday she would take him shopping. She would see to it that he bought some new clothes—trendy yet casual, young-looking, colourful. He had got into a bit of a rut with his clothes. She would persuade him to have his hair not only cut, but restyled; it was too long for the present fashion.

Something quite short, close to the head, and that alone would take years off him. She would suggest joining a health club—yes, even if it meant taking part herself, a thought which horrified her, but it was all for the good of the cause; they would go to the gym together. They would work out.

She would also revise his diet, cut out the rubbish, put vitamins and minerals into him. He would lose weight, be healthy and feel on top of the world. It was all bound to make him not only look younger, but feel younger.

And last *but not least*, she decided, I will be more loving. She would woo him. Everyone knew sex was a great rejuvenator, and it must be admitted they had rather let it slide.

Yes, she would make him over!

She closed her eyes and at last composed herself for sleep. The things she did for MADS!

*   *   *

'It's a nice, bright day again,' Ursula remarked to Eric as they sat at breakfast next morning. 'Why don't we go into Southfield, do a bit of shopping?'

'Shopping?' Eric said, doing the giant crossword in the *Weekend Times*. 'I thought you'd done all that on Thursday?'

'I did the food shopping then,' Ursula said. 'I was thinking of something more interesting.'

Eric grunted. 'There can't be another thing we need in this house. It's chock-a-block.'

Ursula took a knifeful of Cooper's Oxford marmalade and spread it thickly on her wholemeal toast, then bit into it with pleasure. How nice if the rest of life was as uncomplicated as toast and

114

marmalade.

'I'm not thinking of household things,' she said. 'I'm thinking about you and me and whether we shouldn't treat ourselves, to some new clothes for instance.' She spoke as inconsequentially as she could, as if the idea, instead of keeping her awake half the night, had suddenly come to her.

Eric lowered his newspaper.

'What in the world do you want with new clothes? You've got wardrobes full of them! There's hardly room for me to get a thing in.'

'Don't be silly, dear,' Ursula said. 'One should keep up one's interest in one's appearance. It helps to keep one young.'

Actually, he needed the reminder. Even allowing for the fact that he was not yet dressed for the day, he looked pretty awful. His dressing-gown had seen better days, though those must have been a long time ago. His hair fell over his ears and around his neck; his shaggy, greying moustache drooped. Yes, quite apart from the Demetrius thing he needed taking in hand. Had she, among her myriad responsibilities, been neglecting him? Looking after everyone else, forgetting her husband? Well, she would change that. And him.

'I'm thinking of you, dear,' she said. 'You hardly ever buy yourself a thing. So I've quite decided, I'm going to treat you!'

He looked at her in astonishment.

'It's not my birthday,' he said.

'I know. I just feel like treating you! Let's get ready and go!'

She rose from the table, walked around to his side, dropped a light kiss on the top of his head (he definitely had a bald patch), and went off to dress.

CHAPTER EIGHT

Adam left his flat, pulling the door to behind him, and ran down the three flights of stairs to the forecourt where his car was parked. He had moved in six months ago and he had not yet settled, or at any rate not enough to think of it as home. It was no more than a place to eat and to sleep. Not so much to eat, either. He took a great many of his meals in the university, alternating between the senior common room and the bar, where in both places the food was adequate, cheap and boringly repetitive. Sometimes he told himself he must learn to cook. Whenever he turned on the television someone—almost always a man—was demonstrating how to knock up a delicious meal in thirty minutes flat. Dorothy, his one-time wife, used to tell him that anyone who could read could cook. You only had to follow the recipes.

Occasionally he missed Dorothy's cooking along with one or two other things about her, but fewer and fewer and less and less, and life was certainly more tranquil than their final years together had been.

There was nothing of Dorothy in the flat. When they'd split up they'd put the house they'd bought (were still buying) on the market and he had stayed on alone there while waiting for a buyer. It had seemed to take for ever, they had hit a lull in the housing market. After that, finding a small flat for himself had not been difficult, and he had brought with him only the things which were his alone: a few bits of furniture, his computer, his books, music centre and his CDs.

He drove towards Southfield. It being Saturday morning he might well have gone to Mindon, indeed he had been tempted to phone Petra and suggest coffee, but there were things he had to do in Southfield. Also, on the way back, he intended to drop in on the university and do some work in the library. It was a good place to work. He often stayed on after his students and colleagues had gone home, researching into the English essayists about whom he proposed to write a book. Of course there were fewer spare evenings now that rehearsals had started.

It was a fine morning, he enjoyed driving, and when he reached Southfield he was lucky in finding the last remaining space in Sainsbury's car-park.

The first two people he met, when he walked into the fruit and vegetable area, were George Shepherd and Tina Jackson.

He knew neither of them well, only that they were fellow members of MADS, nor had he realized that they were particular friends. Now, standing side by side in front of the apples, there was an indefinable closeness which made it clear that that was so. Something about them spoke louder than words. It was nothing overt, they were not even touching but it was as if they were two parts which, put together, would make a complete whole: two pieces of a jigsaw made to fit each other. He was minded to walk past without interrupting, but at that moment Tina turned and saw him.

'Hello, Adam!' she said.

'Hello, Tina,' he said. 'Hello, George!'

'I was looking for Cox's apples,' George said,

'but Tina says I won't find them because they're not in season. I thought everything was in season all the year round these days.' He waved an arm in the direction of various exotic and unusual fruits.

'Not Cox's apples, silly!' She called him silly, but there was tenderness in it.

'You're obviously right, love,' George said reluctantly. 'There's none here! What are you after?' he asked Adam.

'This and that. The usual. I'll leave you to it then.' He smiled, and walked away. They looked so right together. Why had he never noticed it before? Did he perhaps walk around with his eyes half-closed, his mind elsewhere?

When he had finished his shopping, he packed his purchases in the boot of his car and, leaving it where it was, made his way to Marks & Spencer. Not what Sainsbury's had in mind, but parking in Southfield was tricky, you took what opportunities you could.

Thus it was that shortly afterwards he found himself pushing open the door of Marks & Spencer immediately behind Ursula and Eric.

'MADS are everywhere this morning!' he said.

'Good gracious!' Ursula said, doing a swift turnabout.

'I met George Shepherd and Tina in Sainsbury's,' he began—and then noticed the look on Ursula's face.

'A nice man George!' Eric said quickly. 'A great asset to the cricket club. A good all-rounder. Very useful in the field!'

'He's a nice enough man,' Ursula agreed. 'And I do feel sorry for him.'

'Sorry?' But do I want to know why? Adam

118

asked himself, too late. Clearly, Ursula intended to tell him.

'Yes.' She shook her head with a slightly avid look of sorrow on her face. 'He doesn't have the happiest home life, though none of us know his wife; I for one have never even seen her. They say that apart from going to work she's a bit of a recluse. You know, she's never been to any of our productions! Not a single one. Ever!'

'Really?'

'Really. So no wonder George looks elsewhere, though one has to wonder if Tina Jackson is the right direction! In my opinion—'

'Well, I must get on,' Adam interrupted. 'I'm about to stock my freezer with delicious meals for one.'

'They have even better ones for two,' Ursula informed him. 'You could invite Petra—or would it be Victoria?'

She ignored Eric's disapproving glance. She wouldn't mind being in the shoes of either of those women. Adam was a dish. In fact *he* was a younger version of how she would like Eric to look when she had made him over.

Adam laughed. 'I'll think about it!'

'Adam,' Ursula said suddenly, 'do you mind if I ask you where you buy your clothes? You always look so *right*. And Eric and I are in Southfield to do a bit of clothes shopping.'

'Really, Ursula,' Eric remonstrated, 'must you?'

'I'm sure Adam doesn't mind,' Ursula said. 'It's a compliment.'

'Mostly small places,' Adam said. 'I just look around until I find what I like.'

Ursula would not have chosen Marks & Spencer

119

for Eric's new look. Irreproachable though they were, and icon of the great British public, they did not have quite the image she had in mind for him. She was after something more akin to the ads in the Sunday supplements but he was being stubborn. Of course she wasn't stupid enough to think that, however hard she worked on him, he would look exactly like those gorgeous models. He was, for a start, twenty years older and at least twenty pounds heavier. She would also have to do something about the latter.

'And your hair?' she enquired of Adam. 'Where do you get your hair cut?'

'In West Street,' Adam said. 'A place called Cutting Edge.'

She had seen it. It gleamed with black marble, was awash with lean hairdressers of both sexes dressed in tight white trouser suits. It was also unisex. How could she ever get Eric in there?

'Well, they certainly do a good job!' she said.

'Thank you,' Adam said. 'I really must move on.' He picked up a basket and fled.

'You've embarrassed him,' Eric said. 'You are the end!'

'Of course I haven't embarrassed him! He recognizes a compliment when he hears one. Everyone likes compliments!'

'No they don't,' Eric contradicted.

She began to lead the way to men's underwear. She supposed they couldn't go far wrong with men's underwear.

'Anyway,' Eric said, 'what are we here for?'

Ursula sighed.

'Because this is where you chose to come,' she reminded him. 'I'm sure we'd do far better, just this once, in one of those men's boutiques.' And it was, she decided, time to change her strategy, soften her approach, or she would get nowhere.

'You know, darling, you'd look really good in something stylish!' she said. 'You are an attractive man, Eric. You have . . .' she sought for the right word, '. . . you have *charisma*! Don't ever think you haven't!'

She opened her eyes wide and looked up at him. Being almost a foot shorter than her husband she had long ago discovered what an upward glance from her sparkling dark eyes could accomplish.

'Oh very well!' Eric conceded. 'Have it your own way!'

They were out of the store before he could pick up so much as a pair of Y-fronts. Possibly, Ursula reckoned, it was the first time she had ever left Marks & Spencer not festooned by green plastic bags.

It was amazing to find, walking around Southfield with a precise goal in mind, just how many shops were devoted to men's fashions. Man at the Top, Male Box, His and His, Blokes, Guys, Royal Male and the rest.

'Wonderful!' Ursula said. 'I never knew they existed!'

'Why should you?' Eric asked. 'What would you be doing, roaming around men's clothes shops?'

She had never been one of those wives who bought every item of her husband's apparel. Nor had he wanted that. He had always preferred to make a short, sharp foray on his own, returning with the mixture as before, so that nothing actually looked new, which suited him down to the ground.

In any case these shops, boutiques, whatever

they called themselves, towards which he was now being dragged were not to his taste. Their garments were, well, if not exactly flamboyant, then noticeable.

'I think we should try Blokes,' Ursula said, as they came out of Male Box having discarded yet another jacket. 'They've got a wide selection there, and everything under one roof.'

'Not my thing,' Eric grumbled.

'How do you know, dear?' Ursula's voice was long-suffering yet patient. 'We've not yet set foot in Blokes. But for my sake! And if we don't find anything you fancy, well then we'll go home! I promise.'

But this time, she decided, there would be no shenanigans, no messing around. They would not leave Blokes without at least a basic new outfit.

'What are you doing this for?' Eric said testily. 'What's got into you?'

'I told you, darling,' she said soothingly, 'I just looked at you this morning and thought what potential you had! How attractive you'd look, just a little differently dressed. And I wanted to do it to please you, to please us both!' She also wanted a willing and happy Demetrius.

What devious routes we take with men, she thought. It was the same in MADS. If she had to make the slightest criticism of one of the men she had to wrap it up in smooth talk. With the women she could get straight to the point.

Entering Blokes they were met at once by an exquisite saleswoman: smiling, slender, blond, almost as tall as Eric himself. Oh dear! Ursula thought. This is no good! Eric would never consent to be fitted by a young woman, no way would she be allowed to take his inside-leg measurement. A sober-suited man with a tape-measure around his neck was Eric's line.

'I'm Eileen,' the assistant said in a deep, husky voice. 'May I help you, sir, madam?'

It was probably the voice, Ursula decided. Her husband had an ear for a voice, and this one was seductive. Whatever, like a lamb to the slaughter he allowed himself to be led farther inside and comfortably seated while Eileen fetched and carried, plying him with garments all of which, he was assured, would suit him beautifully. Trousers, jackets, silk shirts, a fancy waistcoat, ties the like of which he would never have thought of in a thousand years. Mesmerized, he went behind the curtain to try things on. This young lady, Ursula thought, must be worth her weight in gold to Blokes.

'My husband doesn't like buying clothes,' she confided. At least he never had before.

'But he looks so good in them,' Eileen said.

'Perhaps you'll tell him that when he reappears,' Ursula suggested. 'And in the meantime will you pack up three pairs of the Calvin Klein boxer shorts and the Armani polo shirt we looked at. Don't tell him.'

Meanwhile, in the confined space of the fitting-room—he was rather pleased that there was not enough room for Ursula to accompany him—he tried on the creamy silk shirt and then tried to keep his balance while pulling on a pair of trousers. They were a sort of palish blue-green—totally unsuitable of course. He breathed in deeply, sucking in his stomach as far as he could while doing up the zip, relieved when it actually reached

123

the top.

He surveyed himself in the mirror, then put on the jacket—brownish, with a hint of terracotta. He had to admit that the ensemble was pleasing, and that something in the cut disguised his less-than-flat stomach, which he now patted with a new-found approval.

When he stepped out from the fitting-room Ursula's mouth dropped open.

'You look *wonderful*, darling!' she cooed.

'You certainly do, sir!' Eileen gave him the warmest of smiles.

'Thank you,' he said modestly. 'I'm not sure which shirt. I tried this one on but actually I like them both.'

'Then you must have both!' Ursula cried. 'Let's not stint!' Her credit card would take a bashing, but what the hell!

'And now,' she said, as Eileen packed the garments into exceedingly smart bags, 'we're off to the hairdresser.' Her eyes narrowed as she looked critically at Eric's hair. It really would spoil the whole picture.

'I think you should have a Claudius,' she announced.

'I think you mean a Caesar, madam!' Eileen said.

'Do I? I know it's some Roman Emperor or another.' She was fairly certain it was what Adam Benfield sported.

Eric had not bargained for having his hair cut. He liked it—if ever he thought about it—as it was. He had gone to Mindon's village barber for years, through short hair and long hair and something-for-the-weekend, sir? He was contented with things

124

as they were, but Ursula had been unbelievably generous—he couldn't think what had come over her—so he would be generous in his turn and give in. After all, it would grow again.

If only, Ursula thought, he would have his moustache off! It was a far from luxurious moustache and it was going grey. But it was too great a sacrifice to demand of him, perhaps ever.

They reached Cutting Edge. Ursula stepped boldly in and marched up to the reception desk, Eric bringing up the rear.

'My husband,' she announced, 'would like a Caesar!' The word rolled off her tongue with total familiarity. 'Who is your very best stylist for that particular cut?'

'All our stylists are skilled in it, madam,' the receptionist said, 'though we call it an Imperial, not a Caesar.' She studied the appointments book in front of her, a perplexed frown on her face as though ready to tell them that there was no possibility of an appointment for at least three months. Eric's spirits rose. He was about to be saved from the scissors.

'Ah!' the receptionist said at last, looking up at Eric. 'You are *very, very* lucky, sir! Deidre has a cancellation.'

'*Deidre?*'

'That's right, sir. Please take a seat. She won't be long.'

'I'll wait here until you're through, darling,' Ursula said.

'I feel like Samson,' Eric grumbled. 'About to be shorn of my strength! Deidre! Can I be sure her name's not Delilah?'

Within a few minutes he was borne away, and

forty minutes after that he was back again. At the sight of him Ursula let out a cry. The second transformation of the day!

'Oh, Eric!'

It was not the Imperial cut which caused her to cry out. That suited him well enough, but she gave it in the circumstances no more than a glance. It was the fact that his moustache was gone, his upper lip was as smooth as a schoolboy's. It was the first time, ever, she had seen him clean-shaven.

'She *was* a Delilah!' Eric said. 'I didn't have a chance against her!'

But a rather smug smile played around his hair-free lips.

*   *   *

Leaving Sainsbury's, George and Tina crossed the road to the Magic Lantern coffee shop. In a previous life it had been Maisie's, with Formica-topped tables and neon strip lights. Now it was all dark oak, with high-backed booths dimly lit by lanterns. And for George and Tina the name was right. It was magic to them. They found a booth in the farthest corner, spreading their shopping around so that no-one would be tempted to join them.

'The last day of our holiday,' Tina said. 'Have you enjoyed it, love?'

'Of course I have! Every minute. I only wish . . .'

'I know!'

'I just wish we could have gone farther afield. Somewhere for the whole week. Just you and me, away from everyone.'

'What would we have done about rehearsals?'

Tina asked.

'Bugger rehearsals!'

Tina laughed. 'Ursula wouldn't like that! Anyway, if it wasn't for MADS we might never have met.'

George reached across the table and covered her hand with his. He had large, practical-looking hands, short nails, stubby fingers.

'Oh yes we would, sweetheart! We were meant for each other. It was written in the stars!'

He was so romantic; poetic even, though you would never have thought it to look at him. He was not a pin-up, though he was *her* pin-up. She loved him so much.

And to think that if she hadn't plucked up her courage and joined MADS, she would never have met him. It was Daniel, too, who had encouraged her to go along. 'I'll be all right,' he'd said, and he had been. His friend Gerry came in, she made them a nice supper and they did their homework together and then watched videos.

'We haven't really known each other long,' she said to George. 'Have we?'

'It didn't take long. I knew the minute you walked in on that Tuesday evening.' He paused, and looked at her intently.

'Do you know what I want? Do you know what I'd really like, more than anything?'

'Tell me!'

'I'd like to take you to Paris! That's what! Imagine it! You and me, in Paris!'

'Yes, I'd like that,' Tina said.

'And one day I will!'

'Do you know what I'd like?' Tina asked.

'Tell me!'

127

'I'd like, when we went home from MADS, or all this week when we've been coming back from our trips out, I'd like you to have been coming home with me. I'd like to cook meals for you, do things for you . . .' She felt the tears coming. She couldn't go on.

'I know, love!' George said. 'I know. But it's been a good week, hasn't it?'

She nodded.

In fact, they hadn't done too badly. On Wednesday they'd caught the train in the morning and spent a few hours in Brighton, and yesterday, Daniel being off on a school trip, they'd spent the whole day in London, strolling in St James's Park, lingering for a while outside Buckingham Palace before walking up to Hyde Park Corner and all the way up Park Lane to Oxford Street where they'd had tea in John Lewis. Afterwards they'd been to a movie, sitting close together in the dark, isolated from the world, only the two of them existing. It had been quite late when they'd arrived back in Mindon. Tina had been worried for George's sake.

'What will you tell Moira?' she'd asked.

'She's on nights this week,' he'd reminded her. 'I'll not need to tell her anything. And she wouldn't ask. She's no more interested in me than I am in her. Believe me, you're not taking me away from Moira! I left her in spirit a long time ago!'

Tina, sipping her coffee now in the Magic Lantern, thought back to what George had said. Though she'd also been attracted to him from the beginning, if he'd been happily married she would have allowed none of this to happen. She was not a home-breaker and never would be.

She drained the last of her coffee.

'There'll be other times,' George said. 'We'll make sure of that, won't we?'

'Yes we will,' Tina said.

'We'll have to get back to Mindon fairly soon,' George said. 'It's the match this afternoon, you will be there, watching, won't you?'

'Of course I will! I think Daniel's coming too. He's off swimming with his pals this morning but he'll be back for his dinner.'

George checked the bill and left a substantial tip. He was never mean on things like that.

'He's a nice lad, Daniel!' he said. 'You've done a good job there.'

Tina nodded.

'Yes, he is. I wish you could get to know him better. He's at the age when he could do with a man around.'

She didn't know how that could be accomplished, not unless she and George came right out into the open, but what would that do to Daniel? She had to put Daniel first.

'Come on then, love. We'd better be off,' George said. Then he leaned across and kissed her, not caring if anyone saw.

*   *   *

Adam stopped in front of yet another tempting range of meals for two, this time Italian, and wondered whether he would or would not take up Ursula's idea. Would it work? Would he be welcome?

Give it a try, he decided, picking up the carton, dropping it in his trolley before going off in search of wine to go with it. And on the way out of the

129

store, passing a flower display, he stopped and bought a bunch of carnations. Exquisite deep red roses were to be had but perhaps that would be over the top.

He picked up his car and left Southfield. The traffic was heavy until he turned off the main road and drove up the hill to the university, where he worked until late afternoon. He liked the place at the weekend. It was quiet; for a newish campus it was pleasant to look at—the architects had insisted on keeping many of the great trees which had been mature long before the university had been thought of—and there were few students around.

That done, he called back at his flat briefly, had a quick shower, gave the carnations, beginning to wilt in the heat, a drink of water. Should he telephone and make sure it was all right? No, he would not. He would turn up on the doorstep and hope for the best. She might of course be out, she might have a date—he sensed that she was popular—but he would chance it.

He walked up the path and rang the bell. There was no reply. He ought to have known better. Now he would have to go back home and eat his meal for two all by himself. In which case, he decided, he would also drink the whole bottle of wine.

He rang once more, for luck, and was already turning away when the door opened and Petra stood there. Her jeans were paint-stained, her tee-shirt had seen better and cleaner days. Her red hair was wild.

'Oh dear!' he said. 'I can see I've arrived at an inconvenient time. I'd begun to think you were out.'

'I was in the back attic,' Petra said. 'I wasn't

certain I'd heard the bell. Do come in!' She was pleased to see him, of course she was, but she wished he had given her some warning. She caught sight of herself in the hall mirror and realized what a fright she looked.

'I've come to supper,' Adam announced.

'Supper?' Surely she couldn't have invited him and forgotten all about it?

'I know I wasn't asked. It's a colossal cheek. I was in Marks & Spencers and I just happened to spy this Italian meal for two, and I thought . . .'

He ran out of words. He shouldn't have listened to Ursula, but that was the trouble, everyone did.

'How nice!' Petra said, trying to hide her surprise. 'You're welcome!' She glanced at the flowers in his hand.

'For you. I hope you like carnations?'

'My favourites!' Petra told him. It was not quite true, and besides the garden was full of them. 'Thank you. I'll get a vase.'

Adam followed her into the kitchen.

'What were you doing in the attic?' he asked.

'I've finished the painting I was doing, the one of the garden. I thought I might find a frame for it. I imagine, from the few cursory glances I've given it, there's anything and everything in that attic.'

'And did you find a frame?'

'I think there are some propped against the wall behind a tallboy. In fact, I'm pleased you're here because I can't quite get at them. Perhaps you'd give me a hand? It shouldn't take long. After which I'll clean myself up and make the supper.'

She picked up the food carton again and studied the details.

'This looks delicious! What a bright idea!' She

131

felt a sudden surge of happiness. 'How much better than eating alone!'

'Absolutely!' Adam said. 'So shall we go up to the attic?'

Petra hesitated. On second thoughts he looked rather clean and tidy to be rummaging in the attic.

'We can do it another day if you like. The frame isn't desperately urgent.'

'No! Let's do it now,' Adam decided.

She took a torch from a drawer. 'The lighting's a bit dim up there,' she said.

He followed her out of the kitchen and up the two flights of stairs to the back attic.

CHAPTER NINE

As they walked up the main staircase, squares and crescents of coloured light flooded in from a long stained-glass window set at the turn of the stairs. When they came to the second flight it was different; the only light now was from a single bulb hanging over the landing at the top.

'I suppose this was considered adequate for servants when the house was built,' Petra remarked, leading the way.

'Or even for children if there was a large family,' Adam said.

'I suppose so. I don't know the history of the house, but it must have had an owner or two before Claire's parents came to live here. She was an only child, so there'd be no need for her to sleep in an attic.'

At the top of the stairs Petra opened the door on

132

the left.

'This is the front attic,' she said. 'I've more or less tidied this up, though not totally.'

The walls sloped, the ceiling in parts was so low that Adam, moving to stand beside Petra, had to stoop.

'It's better than the back attic because it has a dormer window and the back only has a skylight, as you will see.'

Two strides across the landing brought them to the back attic. The door creaked as Petra opened it.

'I shall have to attend to that,' she said. 'I hate creaking doors.'

'Wow!' Adam said, following her into the room. 'You've certainly got your work cut out here. You won't sort this lot out in one afternoon!'

'If ever I do at all,' Petra said. 'It's certainly not top of my list of things to be done. But there might be some useful finds in here, things which would do for MADS for instance.'

'Why don't I come in one day and give you a hand?' Adam suggested. 'I reckon there's a lot of heaving around to be done. I'm free most weekends.'

'Would you really?' Petra said. 'That would be great.'

'Right, we'll fix it.'

Adam looked around the room. There were chairs, a large folding screen, a towel rail, countless boxes, ewers and basins from an earlier age, and a hundred other things, all higgledy-piggledy, in no sort of order.

'This was how the front attic looked when I first walked into it,' Petra said.

133

'Do you suppose all this stuff was Claire's?' Adam asked.

'I've no idea,' Petra admitted. 'I suppose some of it could have been her parents'. Actually, you see, I don't know much about any of them. I suppose I could find out more if I asked around but I don't want to appear too nosey.'

'I would say it wasn't a room anyone came into much,' Adam observed. 'Some of these things look as though they've been undisturbed for ever. Anyway, let's try to get at the frames. I suppose this is the tallboy?' He was looking at a heavy walnut chest of six drawers standing against the wall, not far inside the room. 'It's rather a nice piece of furniture, isn't it? You wouldn't expect it to be shoved away in the attic.'

'That's what I thought,' Petra agreed. 'I get the feeling it hasn't been up here all that long. And it's quite near the door, isn't it? As if it was one of the last things to come into the room.'

Adam pushed against it, testing it.

'It's pretty weighty,' he said. 'What's more, I don't think it's all that secure on its feet. I reckon we'll have to take the drawers out before we attempt to move it. Or at least the bottom two, they're the deeper ones.'

He knelt in front of the bottom drawer and pulled on it. It was reluctant to move, and when it finally did give way to him the reason was obvious. It was filled to the top: manila files, exercise books, envelopes, sheets of ruled paper covered in fine, sloping writing and held in clips.

'Claire's things!' Petra exclaimed. 'I recognize that writing. I told you she sent me a letter once, when she was in hospital.'

She opened one or two files and gave the contents a cursory glance. 'It looks as though it's all school stuff,' she said. 'I'll go through it later.'

'Hang on!' Adam said. 'There's something else here!' He thrust his hand into the space where the drawer had been and brought out an envelope. 'It must have fallen down the back.'

It was a stiff, white envelope, about eight inches by five inches, and sealed. Nothing at all was written on it. He handed it to Petra.

Petra looked at it.

'Why would it be sealed, and nothing written on it?'

'Because whoever sealed it, presumably Claire, knew what was in it and didn't need to be reminded. Simple!'

'But why seal it at all?'

'If you open it you might find out,' Adam said.

Petra held the envelope in her hand. She had a strange feeling about opening it, as though she was prying into something not meant for her eyes—or anyone else's. Nevertheless she *would* open it.

She extracted two sheets of thick, creamy-white drawing paper. From the appearance of one rough edge on each sheet it was obvious they had been torn from a pad. A sketch pad. And here in her hands were the sketches, two beautifully executed pencil drawings. Some instinct made her move a step away from Adam as she examined them.

In the first one she looked at a young woman lying on a bed, her back to the artist. The bedclothes were ruffled, the top sheet clear of her shoulders; her back was bare almost to the waist. Though her face was not visible she was, by her relaxed pose, which the artist had caught with great

135

accuracy, asleep. In the bottom, right-hand corner were the initials E.F.

In the second sketch she had turned over and now faced the artist. One arm was raised, curled around her head, partly—but not entirely—obscuring her features. Again she was asleep. What was visible of her body where the sheet did not cover it showed a young, nubile woman: a slender waist, the curve of a hip, full rounded breasts. There was a close intimacy about the drawings, great sensuality, but although they were erotic they were not in any way prurient. There was a feeling that the artist had drawn them for himself, not for others to see. And here I am, Petra thought, looking at them.

One thing she knew immediately, she was expert enough to recognize it at once, was that these drawings were done by the same hand as those which she had found in her parents' house.

She continued to look at them for a moment, then she replaced them in the envelope which she put down on a small table nearby. Adam had noticed her move away from him. Now, as she raised her head and met his look, his eyes held questions, though he refrained from voicing them.

'They are drawings of my mother,' she said quietly. 'I can't show them to you at the moment.'

'OK,' he said. 'I understand.'

No you don't, Petra thought. How could you possibly?

'I think I can ease the tallboy away from the wall now,' he said in a matter-of-fact voice. 'Get at the frames.'

Carefully, he moved it until there was enough space to insert his arm and draw out the frames,

136

one by one. There were four of them, one of which—gilt, but rather dull, not at all fancy—Petra reckoned would suit the painting very well.

'Shall I put the others back in the same place, or not?' Adam asked.

'Definitely not. We'll leave them where I can get at them if I want to,' Petra said. 'Then we can push the tallboy flat against the wall.'

She found a place for the frames while Adam dealt with the tallboy, replacing the bottom two drawers with their contents as they had found them. I shall want to go through those, Petra thought, but not now, only when I'm on my own.

'Thank you,' she said in a steady voice. 'Now let's go down and I'll see to the meal.' She picked up the envelope from the table, and led the way. Adam followed her, carrying the chosen frame.

When they reached the bottom of the attic stairs Petra said, 'Do you mind if I stop off here and tidy myself up? I feel filthy. You go down and pour yourself a drink. I won't be long.'

She went into her bedroom and he continued down the stairs.

She sat on the bed and opened the envelope again, took out the drawings. Did she actually want to see them again? Whether she did or did not there was a compulsion which made her do so. With her artist's eye she could not but help admiring the skill of the drawings. But there was more in them than skill, much more. What did they say about her mother, and did she want to know? She did not. Most of all, she wished she had never found them. She wished they were still hidden away behind the back of the drawer, never to be discovered.

137

And yet, she admonished herself, what was it that her mother had done which had been so terrible? Presumably it had all taken place before her parents had been married to each other. Hadn't she herself been there, done precisely the same thing again and again? What about Malcolm? And he had not been the first. But the point is, she thought, it isn't about me. It isn't about any other woman. It's my mother. One's mother was entirely apart.

She dismissed at once the idea that the artist might simply have been drawing a paid, professional model. The intimacy of the drawings went far deeper than that. There was something in the deep sleeping posture of the woman which was redolent of what had gone before it.

I am making a mountain out of a molehill, she chided herself. And this is my mother's secret, not mine. Mine are prying eyes. Yet what she disliked as much as anything was the fact that she would never know.

She returned the drawings to the envelope and put it away in a drawer of her dressing table.

She stripped off her soiled clothes and took the quickest possible shower, luxuriating in the hot water swilling away the dust and dirt. She towel-dried her hair and combed it away from her face, catching it in an amber slide at the nape of her neck. There was no time to use the hairdryer. She dressed in a long, summery skirt and a black, sleeveless silk top, which showed off her arms, long, smooth and rounded, tanned and slightly freckled from the hours she had spent in the garden.

Downstairs, Adam had opened the wine but had

138

not started to drink it.

'I'm sorry if I was a long time,' Petra said. 'You shouldn't have waited.'

'You weren't a long time,' he said. 'I preferred to wait.'

He poured two glasses and handed one to her. She took a sip, then picked up the packet and began to read the directions for cooking it.

Adam watched her—and was suddenly conscious that what he most wanted to do at that very moment was to take hold of her, to kiss her down the length of her arms, to kiss away the frown line between her eyes as she concentrated on what she was reading, to trace with his fingers the curve of her neck, from her chin until it met the hollow between her breasts.

He took a deep drink from his glass. He was shaking.

Petra looked up, her grey eyes meeting his.

'It all sounds quite easy,' she said. 'It shouldn't take long!' She paused. 'I'm glad you thought of it. I'm glad you came!'

Less than an hour later they sat at the table, eating the meal—which surprisingly was as good as it looked on the packet. To Adam's pleasure Petra had served the meal at the kitchen table, using the colourful peasant earthenware and apparently with no thought of the dining room. Does this mark a step forward in our relationship? Adam asked himself. He hoped it did, but strangely she seemed a little more aloof, a mite withdrawn.

That her demeanour had to do with the envelope she had found in the attic he was fairly certain. She had no doubt put it away somewhere and it was not to be mentioned. He was to be admitted so far into her life and no further. A week ago this would not have mattered, but now his feelings towards her had changed. Was it as sudden as it felt? He wanted to know everything about her, he wanted to share. But did they have anything which could be called a relationship? Was he leaping ahead?

Perhaps, he thought, it was that the sight or mention of anything to do with her mother brought back the grief, and she couldn't deal with it. But he didn't think that could be the whole of it. She had talked quite openly about the deaths of her parents; she had, without any need to do so, or any prompting, showed him the photograph she had found previously. So what was different? Clearly the contents of the envelope was the barrier between them, and one which he felt he had no right to break down.

'Shall we have our coffee in the garden?' Petra asked. 'It's cooler out there.'

Not only was it cooler, but the air was full of scents: stocks, pinks, roses. The light was fading, so that the paler flowers stood out boldly, coming into their own. She switched on the garden lights and from every corner pale-winged moths converged, and flew around the light bulbs.

'Inside the house I'm quite scared of moths,' Petra confessed. 'But never outside. It's the same with mice. If I saw one inside I'd jump on the table. If I spotted one now, playing around under that viburnum shrub, I'd watch it with interest.'

'It's a case of when they're outside, they're in their own territory, not invading yours,' Adam said. 'It's amazing how territorial we are, though we think it only applies to animals, birds.'

140

And she isn't going to let me invade her territory, he thought. Certainly not get far inside the borders. She has her defences ready.

'You're quite right, of course,' Petra acknowledged. 'It's fear isn't it? We might give away too much ground, and would we be able to get it back?'

'And if not,' Adam said, 'would we be willing to let it go?'

In the end the talk turned to MADS. There was always something to be said about MADS.

'I ran into Ursula and Eric in Southfield this morning,' Adam said. 'I think Ursula was taking Eric on a great big shopping spree. Poor Eric! He did *not* look a happy man!'

Petra laughed.

'Do you think she rules him with a rod of iron?'

'I think she tries,' Adam said. 'Whether she gets her way in the end I'm not so sure. My reading is that Eric would have to be persuaded rather than driven.'

'What were they shopping for?'

'Clothes. For Eric.'

'Then I suppose we shall see in the end who won,' Petra said.

'I also met up with George Shepherd and Tina,' Adam said. 'I hadn't realized about them, had you?'

'Not until the other day,' Petra said. 'I met them together on the green. They're dotty about each other. It's rather sad, really.'

It was sad, she thought. In only the few moments she had spent with them she had felt the depth of their love for each other—and where would it end? What sort of future did they have? And in the same

141

mood she felt sorry for herself. What have I done with my life? she asked herself. Any normal person of her age would be happily married, with a clutch of children and a stake in the future. And what about Adam? A failed marriage was not something to look back on happily.

'I suppose you could say that,' Adam agreed. 'Though they didn't look sad this morning. Quite the contrary.' There had been something about them that he had almost envied.

Petra gave an involuntary shiver. Without either of them noticing it, night had fallen and the air was cool. There was a narrow band of deep red sky to the west, with the lower branches of the plum tree silhouetted against it, but otherwise the only light left was from the four small lamps in the garden. Beyond the limits of the bright circles they shed there was nothing to be seen.

'You're cold!' Adam said.

'A little,' Petra admitted. 'What about you?'

'I'm not sleeveless,' he pointed out. 'I'm all right. Shall I fetch you a jacket?'

'Or shall we go in?' Petra suggested.

'Perhaps I should be leaving,' Adam said. 'I don't want to outstay my welcome—after all, I did come uninvited!'

'Please don't go,' Petra said quickly. 'It's not at all late. Why don't we go inside and I'll make some fresh coffee? Perhaps you'd like a brandy?' She sounded, she thought, as if she was persuading him, almost bribing him to stay. And it's true, I am, she thought. I don't want him to go.

She cleared the table and Adam carried the tray into the house. From the panel inside the kitchen porch she switched off the garden lights. The last few inches of the sunset had disappeared. Trees around the garden obscured the view of lights going on in nearby houses. Here it was inky black.

At Petra's suggestion, when she had made fresh coffee they took it into the sitting room. 'It's more comfortable in here,' she said, switching on a couple of lamps. That was true. There were armchairs, two deep sofas, small tables. She put the coffee on a table in front of one of the sofas and, sitting behind it, motioned Adam to an armchair.

'Ah,' she said, pouring the coffee, 'will you do me a favour and fetch the brandy from the sideboard cupboard in the dining room? You'll find glasses there, too.'

He did as he was bidden, but when he returned he sat down beside Petra on the sofa. She gave no sign that she had noticed and she hoped, as she poured the coffee, that he would not see that her hand shook slightly, or, if he did, that he would not put it down to his nearness, although it was.

He had sat down beside her not so much deliberately as instinctively. It was where he wanted to be. As he leaned back he was aware that she moved almost imperceptibly away from him.

'There you are!' she said. 'Black, no sugar!'

When she picked up her own coffee she moved herself another foot away from him, and this time there was no mistaking it, though the smile she gave him as she turned her head towards him was full of warmth, as she had been all evening.

'Will you help yourself to brandy?' she said.

'Thank you,' Adam said. 'Will you have some?'

'A little. I don't know much about brandy. Is this a reasonable one? It was in the house when I came. Something else I inherited!'

143

'It's very good,' Adam said.

'Somehow I can't imagine Claire being a brandy drinker,' Petra said. 'Though I don't know why I say that.'

'It's the headmistress bit,' Adam said. 'The two don't go together.'

'Well it certainly wouldn't have with the headmistress of my school,' Petra agreed. 'She was more for speaking against the evils of strong drink.' She twirled the brandy around, cupped the glass in her hands and inhaled the aroma. 'Wonderful!' she pronounced. 'On the rare occasions I have brandy I tend to think the smell is almost better than the taste. It's quite heady isn't it?'

'The taste is even more so,' Adam said. 'Didn't you like school, then?'

She took the smallest sip of brandy before setting the glass down on the table.

'I suppose it was all right. I neither liked it nor disliked it. Going to school was just something one did. I'd have been happier if we'd done more art, but it wasn't considered all that important. What about you?'

I know next to nothing about him, she thought. And she would like to know more.

'I went to grammar school,' Adam said. 'In Bedfordshire, where I was brought up. It did quite well, I enjoyed it. I suppose you could say I was a swot. I wasn't all that good at games—except cricket. I enjoyed cricket. Still do, though only watching now.'

'Is the Mindon team any good? You could join that.'

'Quite good,' Adam said. 'I suppose I could.'

'Did you know George Shepherd played?' Petra

144

asked.

'No, I didn't. May I help myself to more coffee?' He wasn't going to talk about MADS again. He wanted to know about *her*: what she liked, what she disliked, what she thought about, what cheered her, worried her.

Petra took his cup and refilled it. She also realized she didn't want to spend the evening talking about MADS, even though it was she who had introduced George Shepherd's name. She wanted to know more about Adam.

'Tell me about—'

'Tell me—'

They spoke simultaneously.

'You first!' Adam said.

'I was about to ask you, did you always enjoy English? Was it something you wanted to teach?'

'I don't know about teaching,' Adam said. 'I think that sort of happened. But yes, English was always my thing. As a matter of fact I . . .' He hesitated.

'Yes?'

'Actually, I dreamt about being a writer. But I've discovered it's something a lot of people dream about but don't actually do. It's easier to dream than to take the plunge. In fact, though, I *am* about to take the plunge. I'm about to start a book on English essayists—Addison, Steele, Lamb, Hazlitt. I suppose I'd like to be an essayist myself, but it wouldn't work. It seems to me the essay is quite out of fashion. My father, of course, would have said writing wasn't a proper job for a man.'

'*Would* have said?'

'He died in my first year at university. I suppose if he'd died while I was still at school, university would have been impossible. Somehow my mother managed.'

Petra leaned forward, picked up her glass and took another sip of brandy. When she settled back she was closer to him. It was inadvertent, he was sure, but at least she hadn't purposely kept the distance. He could smell the scent of shampoo on her newly washed hair. It smelled of apples, green apples, which was ridiculous for a shampoo, and surprisingly titillating.

'Does your mother still live in Bedfordshire?' Petra asked.

'No. She married again. She lives in the West of Ireland. County Clare.'

It had been surprising how quickly his mother had married again, and to a man totally unlike his father. Fergus Donnelly was a bluff, easy-going Irishman. He was a bit of a musician, a bit of this, a bit of that, but his mother seemed happy with him.

'I was a bit thrown by my mother's marriage, so soon after my father's death,' he said. 'It was as well for me I was at university. I'd made friends. They supported me.'

'And was that . . .' Petra hesitated, then went on. 'Was that where you met your wife? Really, I shouldn't be asking you all this!'

'You haven't been asking, I've been telling,' Adam said. 'Yes, it was. And Dorothy was my chief support then.'

He could never, even now, with everything that had since gone wrong between them, fault Dorothy for what she had been to him at that time, but they had not been many years into their hasty marriage before he had realized, and soon afterwards so had she, that what they had between them was not

146

enough. Support on one side and dependency on the other were not the best ingredients for marriage, especially when he eventually realized that he no longer wanted or needed support.

'I am not an advocate of early marriage,' he said, the words leaping out of his thoughts.

'Are you an advocate of marriage at all?' Petra asked.

He turned his head and looked at her very directly. 'I don't know,' he said. 'I'm not sure. I'm an advocate of love, and friendship. And we've talked enough about me. What about you?'

'I'm an advocate of friendship, that's certain. I mean real friendship, not just acquaintances. There's not enough of it around. As for love, I'm not sure. I've experienced it. In some ways it's brought me great happiness, but always fleeting, always at the moment. Perhaps I'm not good at choosing lovers. Yet when I think of my father and mother, I know it's all possible.

'I would like to have married,' she admitted. 'I would like to have had children. It didn't work out.'

There was a silence which Petra was the first to break.

'Do you have children?'

She didn't even know that much about him. He could be the father of a son or a daughter, or both, whom Dorothy had taken with her into her new life. He could be one of those fathers who took their children out for the day once a month and bought them birthday and Christmas presents. Though if that was the case surely someone in MADS would have said so.

'No, we never did,' Adam said. 'It just didn't happen.' It was strange that Dorothy, who had

147

cared for and supported him in his need had never seemed to feel the need for children. Perhaps she had found his needs sufficient?

'Well,' Petra said, 'I don't suppose we're untypical. Perhaps it's my parents who were that.'

She let out a deep sigh, and as she did so Adam took her hand and held it firmly in his. She made no move to disengage herself, but let her hand lie where it was. She felt, for the moment, safe and happy. Other feelings also stirred in her but those she would not dissect, not for the moment.

'I'd better go,' Adam said presently, looking at her. 'It's late. If I don't go now I won't want to go at all.'

'I know,' Petra said. 'You'd better go.' It was not the time.

He pulled her to her feet, took her in his arms and kissed her on the lips—then released her abruptly and made for the door.

CHAPTER TEN

Ursula had suggested, at the previous week's rehearsals, that as many members as possible should attend more, or even all, rehearsals in future.

'I don't want any of you to be stuck in just your own part in the play, whether your part is large or small. Together we make up the whole. That goes also for those who have non-acting parts. We must steep ourselves in the play! We must all pull together!' She opened her arms wide, smiled an expansive smile. She felt as if she was leading soldiers into battle, with, at the end, and if they stood shoulder to shoulder, victory.

Thus it was that when the remodelled Eric made his appearance, wearing his new clothes, his cropped hair falling in uneven bits of fringe over his forehead, his upper lip as clean as a whistle so that his rather well-shaped mouth was on view for the very first time, it was not to a select few of his fellow Thespians but to the biggest turnout MADS had witnessed since the last production. A three-line whip could hardly have brought a larger gathering.

With an actor's instinct for the right moment, or perhaps with a producer's skill supplied by his wife, he timed his entrance perfectly. The two of them were, unusually, a little late. Everyone was there, standing in small groups, thumbing scripts, catching up on gossip, when Ursula and Eric arrived. Also unusually, Ursula did not walk three paces ahead, with Eric bringing up the rear (as in the case of Her Majesty the Queen and Prince Philip). No, on this occasion as they opened the hall door Ursula gave her husband a firm push into first place while she herself dropped demurely behind.

Those facing the door were the first to fall silent, followed quickly by those who turned around to see what it was all about. Half-formed sentences hovered on the air for a few seconds, and then everyone, remembering their manners, went back to what they had been saying. Though no longer exactly what they had been saying.

'Good evening, everybody!' Ursula called out cheerily. 'Sorry we're a bit late! Anyway, I propose we start right at the beginning and see how far we can get—so no lagging about, and come in on cue, and I hope you've been learning your lines!'

She took her place at the table halfway down the hall, facing the stage. Petra, who was with Adam, Victoria and Jennie, watched Eric walk towards them. He really did look quite extraordinarily different. He even walked differently, more upright. If Ursula had achieved this, then all credit to her.

'Theseus, Hippolyta, Philostrate—do we have a Philostrate? We do!' Ursula beamed on the doctor. 'And attendants. All of you enter left. Egeus and the lovers be ready in the wings, if you please!' She looked around the hall. 'And no talking in the ranks! Everyone would benefit from watching and listening!'

The rehearsal proceeded. Not without difficulty Ursula held herself back from interrupting, instructing, criticizing. If she stopped to do that they would never get through. So she suffered a dull Egeus and a Philostrate whose impatience with a part which kept him less than five minutes on the stage, and gave him not a word to say before being sent off again, clearly showed in his manner. Was it for this that he had rushed his evening surgery?

The lovers were better. Lysander knew most of his words, Helena was coming on well. Demetrius . . . well, he seemed more confident but she knew she must continue to encourage him, both publicly and privately.

When Eric made his exit he went and sat beside Petra, and was quickly joined on his other side by Lucinda who was sitting impatiently through the Mechanicals, who would be followed by Melvin-alias-Puck, waiting for Titania's first entrance. Not that she had any intention of sitting here like a mute.

'You're looking very smart!' she whispered to Eric. 'Very cool!'

She had long ago perfected the art of the stage whisper. Without adding any sound to the words, every syllable she uttered on any stage could be heard clearly by the audience on the back row. So it was that Ursula heard her, and giving an angry glance sideways caught not only Lucinda's provocative smile but her husband's answering smirk. What he replied, which provoked a giggle from Lucinda, she could not hear. She took a deep breath, buttoned up her mouth, and concentrated on Quince.

Actually, the vicar would do well in this part. He had the authority. It came, she supposed, from his vocation, in which he was used to taking charge, telling people what to do and (except by his children) being obeyed. But his real-life manner, which he still adopted, was just too polite, too kind. She would have to make him rough it up.

Her concentration was broken again by the sound of another, not at all subdued, giggle from Lucinda. Ursula took her eyes off the stage and looked across the room. Lucinda's arm was on Eric's arm and she was looking into his eyes with undisguised admiration. Worse than that, he was lapping it up.

Ursula faced front again, held up her hand, and shouted, 'STOP!'

There was no stopping Bottom. He was in full flow and couldn't even stop himself. The rest of the cast waited in silence until he had finished his speech.

'Thank you, Bottom!' Ursula said. 'You have

151

done very well. All of you on the stage have done well to battle your way through the constant interruptions from the sidelines! On your behalf (not to mention on mine, she thought) I ask *everyone*', she turned and glared in Lucinda's direction, 'to keep quiet when other people are on the stage! If you are not interested in your fellow performers then I suggest you quietly get on with learning your own lines!'

'Silly cow!' Lucinda muttered, turning to Petra. But this was not a stage whisper, only a mutter. No-one except Petra, not even Eric, heard it.

Ursula turned back to the play.

'Quince, please. "Some of your French crowns . . ."'

She would deal with Eric when she got him home. But then again, will I? she thought quickly. Isn't this just what he needs, what I'd hoped for? Plenty of appreciation to boost his confidence. But not from Lucinda Rockwell.

Ursula was surprised to find in herself what was—she faced it—jealousy. And behind the jealousy there was fear. Jealousy is born of fear, she had once read—and it was true. So, in making over Eric was she going to be hoist by her own petard? She could not do without Eric, and she was not thinking here of Demetrius, but of real life. It was a frightening thought which had never come to her before.

She came to with a start, suddenly aware that the stage was empty. Bottom and his friends had exited and she had not noticed them going. Quickly, she found her place again in the script as the Fairy came in at one side and Puck at the other.

Jennie Austin, when she had left the stage, had

152

taken her seat at the side of the hall and from there she had watched every move, listened to every word said up there by her fellow members, and not least those scathing words from Ursula. She devoutly hoped that she would never do anything to upset Ursula, though this evening she had incurred praise. Ursula had said she was coming on very well.

And now, heavenly bliss, Giles Rowland had taken the seat beside her. True, it was the only one vacant, but he said, 'May I sit here?' in his beautiful voice, and smiled at her as he did so. It was the first time he had ever said a word to her. She could have swooned with pleasure.

His presence made it difficult for her to concentrate on Titania, who was now on stage with her train. It was not much of a train: Tina as first attendant and Hattie Cumber, who had been called away from coffee-making to fill in, plus Peasebottom and the other three fairies. They were an ill-assorted lot. Not one of them was the least bit fairylike. Nevertheless, Jennie thought, Lucinda was worth watching, she was very accomplished. She could make you feel that she was surrounded by people: small children, fairies, even a little Indian baby.

Surprisingly, Giles was not watching Titania. He was reading the *Southfield Gazette*, holding it in front of his face, entirely blocking out his view of the stage. But then, Jennie excused him, *he* has *nothing* to learn, not from Titania, not even from Ursula. His Thescus was perfection.

'She's good, isn't she?' Jennie said.

'Who?' His voice came from behind the newspaper.

'Lucinda! Titania.'

Giles lowered the newspaper and looked Jennie straight in the face.

'Not as good as she thinks she is,' he said. 'She's a conceited bitch!'

'Oh!'

'But you are far too nice to see that,' Giles said smoothly. He didn't know whether she was or not. He knew nothing about the girl. Of course he had seen her around in MADS; she was quite a pretty little thing but she wasn't memorable.

Jennie blushed deeply, not only at his words but because of the kindness in his voice.

'I don't know her very well,' she said. 'Really, I don't know anyone very well.'

'You don't join us when we go into the Queen's Head, do you? At least I've never seen you there.'

How wonderful, Jennie thought, that he had noticed her absence! She could hardly believe it.

'I have to hurry home,' she told him. And how stupid that sounded!

'Oh, but you should try it,' Giles said. 'You'd get to know people better. Why not come this evening?'

She could hardly believe her ears. Giles Rowland was asking her to go to the pub with him! She stifled a still-small voice which said, With him and a dozen others. He had not actually *asked* the others.

Before she could answer—and how was she to answer? How could she say 'yes' and how could she bear to say 'no'? Ursula turned in their direction and gave them a nasty look. Giles returned to his newspaper and Jennie fixed her eyes on the stage. Titania and Oberon were going on at each other

154

hammer and tongs, but she saw nothing of it. She saw in her mind's eye a different scene. She was in the Queen's Head, standing close to Giles as he raised his glass to her while looking deep into her eyes.

I *will* go, she said to herself. If her mother didn't like it she could lump it. In fact, there would be no need to say she had been in the pub, only that they had had an extra-long rehearsal.

So immersed was she that she never saw Titania leave the stage and neither saw nor heard Oberon's scene with Puck. When she surfaced from the ocean of her thoughts Titania was on stage again, having a first-class tantrum.

'This is ridiculous!' she shouted. 'I can't possibly do this scene! I have to have fairies! I am Queen of the Fairies! Where are all my little fairies who are supposed to sing me to sleep?' She looked with scorn at Tina and company. 'I don't think you could describe my so-called attendants as singing fairies!'

'There is no need for personal remarks about other players,' Ursula said sharply. 'I will not have it!'

But of course, maddeningly, the woman was right. The scene called out for little girls with wings on their shoulders. For a wild moment she wondered whether she could simply cut the scene, ignore Shakespeare, but no, she could not. Besides, anything which put Lucinda Rockwell to sleep was worth doing.

She took a deep breath.

'Very well,' she said. 'I shall consult Brown Owl and see if she can recommend a couple of Brownies.'

'Two won't be enough,' Titania said. 'It says "chorus of fairies".'

'Two will have to be enough,' Ursula said firmly. 'We don't have room on the stage for more. This is Mindon Parish Hall, not Stratford-upon-Avon!'

A voice came from the hall.

'Excuse me, Ursula,' Amelia called out. 'My two little girls are Brownies. I'm sure they'd be glad to help out. I could teach them the songs at home.'

'That,' said Ursula, 'is a very good idea.' Amelia was sensible and reliable. She was the kind of woman whose children were likely to be well-behaved. 'Do you think they'd like to do it?'

'They'd love it,' Amelia said. 'They're always play-acting.'

'Very well then. Bring them along to the next rehearsal. And now can we get on please? We'll cut the rest of the scene. Titania, you are asleep.'

Titania opened her mouth to speak but was thwarted by Oberon's quick entrance. He had been hanging about long enough.

At a quarter to ten—they had continued all evening without a break but had still not reached the end—Ursula called it a day. 'We'll leave the Mechanicals' play until next rehearsal,' she said. 'You've all worked very hard.' She had detected signs of restlessness in the ranks: conversations between those not on the stage, shuffling of chairs, trips to the loo and so on.

'Right!' Oberon said. 'Who's for the pub?'

Giles discarded his newspaper. 'Well,' he said, looking at Jennie, 'are you coming?'

Without the slightest hesitation she replied, 'Yes I am!' She would live for the moment and no doubt pay later, but it would be worth it.

'I'll buy you a drink,' Giles promised generously.

Almost everyone converged into a group. George and Tina, Oberon, Lucinda, Norman and his wife, Chalky and Cyril and the rest.

'Petra, you are coming, aren't you?' Adam asked.

'I'd like to,' Petra said.

Victoria, who had stayed close to Adam all evening, on stage and off, looked slightly peaked. Lysander had not asked his Hermia. It seemed now to be all Petra, who of course was nice enough but . . . well . . .

'And you, Vicky?' Adam asked.

She brightened up at once.

'Of course!'

It was Petra's turn to take slight umbrage. Of course Adam and Victoria were bound to be close, considering the parts they played, but she thought he was specifically asking *her*.

'Well, dears,' Ursula said, 'Eric and I will get along and leave you to it.'

'Oh!' Lucinda cried. 'Don't say you're not coming for a drink, Eric?'

'I think I will,' Eric said. He turned to his wife. 'You go on home if you like, darling. I know you're tired.'

'And how will you get home, dear?' Ursula asked.

'I'll walk of course. Do me good! I need the exercise!'

The trouble was, Ursula thought, she knew exactly who walked in his direction. No way would she leave him to be done good to by Lucinda Rockwell.

'On second thoughts,' she said pleasantly, 'why

don't I come too?'

Firmly, she took his arm and led the group which swam out of the hall and across the road to the Queen's Head like a shoal of fishes.

'Now, my dear, what would you like to drink?' Giles, first at the bar, asked Jennie.

She had no idea. What would be the proper thing? She wished someone else had chosen first. She did not want to show the depths of her unsophistication by asking for lemonade, which she actually liked, but alcohol played no part in the Austin home, except perhaps at Christmas.

'Could I have a sweet sherry?' she asked. It was the only thing she could think of except port, and that sounded a bit common.

'You could indeed,' Giles said. Dear little thing, he would have bet his last penny she would choose that.

Eric and Ursula were close behind, and George and Tina and several others.

'Now!' Eric said. 'This round is on me! What's everyone having?' He had not felt so chirpy for a long time.

Ursula was aghast. At least a dozen drinks!

'Eric!'

'Yes, darling? What would you like?'

It was a dilemma. If she chose what she liked, which was a gin and tonic, everyone would think they could demand shorts, but she loathed beer.

'Serve the others first,' she suggested.

It was always the same with the MADS, the publican thought, trying with the help of his barmaid, Elsie, to serve fifteen drinks at once. They all crowded in at the same moment, and because drinking time was short they had to be

158

served quickly, otherwise how would he sell them a second or a third drink? Not that he was grumbling. They were good for trade and they livened up the atmosphere.

George and Tina accepted their drinks from Eric, raised their glasses to him, and went off to the far corner of the lounge where they had spied two vacant seats together. They sat down, sipped their drinks, then George stretched out his hand and took hold of Tina's.

She drew away quickly.

'We mustn't,' she said. 'Not here. Someone might see us.'

'I've told you,' George said. 'I don't care.'

'But I do!' Tina protested. 'I have to. Oh, I don't care about Moira, not the least bit, but I do about Daniel. Supposing someone comes up to him and says, "My dad saw your mother holding hands in the pub?"' She looked around nervously, as though someone might already be plotting this.

'No-one would do that, love!' George said.

'Oh yes they would!' Tina contradicted him. 'People will say anything, do anything.'

'I'm sick of this,' George said, suddenly cross.

'But you're not sick of me, are you?' She didn't know what she'd do if he were.

'Of course not, love! How could I ever be sick of you? You don't have to worry about that. It's just all this hole-in-the-corner business I hate. And to be frank, Tina, just to hold your hand, give you a kiss in the car, isn't enough. I'm a man. I've got feelings. I want to make love to you, properly.'

'Don't think I don't know,' Tina said quietly. 'I'm a woman and I've got a woman's feelings. I don't suppose they're any different from yours except that I've got a mother's feelings as well.'

'So what are we going to do about it?' George demanded.

'I don't know. I really don't know.'

George jumped to his feet.

'I'll get some more drinks. At least we can drown our sorrows!' How awful, Tina thought as she watched him make for the bar, that what's between us he describes as a sorrow!

It was Melvin Fairclough who bought Victoria her second drink. She had been standing in some sort of no man's land in a group consisting, for most of the time, of Adam, Petra, Ursula, Eric and three or four others including Lucinda. She stood with them but because she was not with Adam, as she had expected to be, she felt curiously alone. Her expectations, she now realized, had been foolish. She had mistaken her closeness to him in the play for a similar closeness outside of it. She had mistaken Lysander and Hermia for Adam and Victoria, partly because he had given her lifts home since they lived in the same direction. But they were not the same at all, and she should have had the sense to realize that. She felt foolish.

She was pleased and relieved, therefore, when Melvin appeared, seemingly from nowhere, and stood directly facing her.

'Your glass is empty,' he said. 'Let me get you a drink. What is it?'

'Lemonade shandy,' Victoria said. 'Thank you.'

He hardly looked old enough to be allowed in the pub, let alone to be buying drinks, though she knew he was about the same age as she was. It was just that he was so slim and slight, as well as not very tall. But that, she thought, was what made him such a good choice for Puck.

'Are you enjoying playing Puck?' she asked him when he returned with the drinks—his an unlikely pint of bitter.

'I like the part,' Melvin said. 'It's great. Whether I'm up to it or not I'm not sure.' He took a long drink of his beer. 'I think you're a wonderful Hermia!'

'Thank you,' Victoria said. 'Any time now Ursula will start working on us—no-one will escape, except possibly Giles. He's the blue-eyed boy, he can do no wrong. It's awful at the time, I mean what Ursula says, but it works in the end. She knows what she's doing.'

The blue-eyed boy was still standing at the bar, Jennie perched on a high stool beside him, draining the last drops of her second sweet sherry. He was bored out of his mind. He simply had to get away.

'Well,' he said, looking around, 'I must love you all and leave you!' He turned to the barmaid. 'Give this young lady another sherry,' he ordered. 'Make it a schooner!'

'But I . . .'

He leaned across, gave Jennie a swift peck on the cheek, and was gone.

Jennie stared after him in disbelief. He couldn't. He couldn't do this to her. What had she *done*?

The barmaid put a glass of sherry in front of her. 'That will be one pound seventy.'

Before Jennie could look in her purse for the money—and she wasn't sure she had any—Adam Benfield was standing beside her.

'Allow me,' he said. 'I'm just getting last drinks for Petra and myself.'

She watched in a haze while Adam paid, then

161

she looked at the full glass of sherry.

'Don't drink it if you don't want to,' Petra said.

Jennie turned wide eyes to Petra.

'Why did he do that?' she said. 'Why did he go? Why did he rush off like that? He asked me to come. I thought he liked me!'

'Really, it's nothing to do with you,' Adam said gently. 'That's Giles. He doesn't like people. Not for long, anyway.'

'Especially he doesn't like women,' Petra said.

Jennie's eyes filled with angry tears.

'That doesn't mean he has to be rude.'

She picked up the glass of sherry and held it aloft. 'Damn and blast him!' she cried—and drank down half the sherry in one gulp, then choked, recovered, and downed the rest. 'Damn and blast him to hell!' she said, swaying a little on her high stool.

'We'll be leaving in a couple of minutes,' Adam said. 'Why don't we give you a lift home?'

'Why would I want to go home now?' Jennie said. 'I'll meet nothing but trouble. I should have gone home straight from rehearsal and I wish I had.'

They left a few minutes later, as inconspicuously as possible. Once outside, Jennie's steps faltered. Petra took her arm as they walked to the car.

'Would you like us to come in with you?' Petra asked when they reached Jennie's gate.

'You mean help me to face my mother?' Her words were a little slurred. 'No need. No need what-so-ever! Just let my mother say one word to me and I'll tell her what I think of her!'

She was full of anger, brimful and running over. She had never felt like this before.

'I'm afraid she's filled with the bravado of alcohol,' Adam said unhappily as they watched Jennie struggle to fit her key in the lock. 'Perhaps we should have gone in with her.'

Petra shook her head.

'I think better not. It would make things worse with her mother. Bad enough having your daughter come home drunk, worse still to have other people involved. But we'll wait a minute or two in case she comes running out again.'

They waited a while. Whatever was going on in the house, none of it was audible outside.

'Shall we go?' Petra said. 'I'm not going to offer you any more wine but I'll make you a cup of whatever you fancy if you'd like to come back with me. It's not all that late.'

Even if it were, she thought, what does it matter? We're not children. Nor do we have a nasty mother waiting up for us. Poor Jennie!

'I'd like that,' Adam said.

CHAPTER ELEVEN

Jennie turned her key in the lock—it seemed unusually stiff and stubborn—and pushed open the door of the bungalow. This she did as quietly as possible, hoping not to disturb her mother who, with luck, might have gone to bed and be fast asleep. Unfortunately, deciding not to switch on the light, in the darkness she tripped over the doormat, tottered a step or two, bumped into the hallstand, and was unable to stifle a small cry of pain as she barked her shin against it.

'Who's there? Is that you?'

Mrs Austin's voice came sharp and querulous, and not from her bedroom. A thin strip of light around the edge of the door showed she was still in the living room. There would be no avoiding her.

'Is that you?' Mrs Austin repeated. She didn't always bother to address Jennie by name. Who else would 'you' be, anyway?

'It's me!' Jennie answered. 'I'll go straight into the kitchen and make your cocoa, Mother!'

She would also splash her face with cold water, see if it would take away the dizziness. At the moment the chairs, the small table and a plant stand bearing a pink geranium at what seemed a strange angle, all seemed full of movement. She would have to negotiate her way between them.

She had taken one uncertain step when the door of the living room opened and her mother stood there. Her nightdress, yellow fluffy cotton with blue roses, ending well above her swollen ankles, drooped several inches below her pink towelling dressing-gown. Her small feet were encased in crimson felt slippers decorated with pink pompoms. Four blue plastic rollers took care of the hair on the top of her head. The rest fell lankly to her shoulders. She looked awful, Jennie thought— and why was she swaying as she stood in the doorway? Why was the door frame swaying?

The two women faced each other. Mrs Austin looked at her daughter in horror.

'Where have you been?'

'I've been to rehearsal!' Jennie said, speaking slowly and carefully.

'You're drunk!' Mrs Austin cried. 'You're drunk! How dare you come into this house intoxicated!'

164

She put her hand to her breast and staggered backwards into an armchair, as if she had received a mortal blow.

'I am perfectly sober,' Jennie said. 'I have had three sweet sherries and one of them was a schooner.' It was quite difficult to say.

'Some man's been buying you drink!' her mother accused her. 'Who is he? Don't lie to me!'

'All men,' Jennie said solemnly, grasping the back of the nearest chair to steady herself, 'are shits. And Giles whatever-his-name-is is the shittiest shit of them all! Did I tell you he bought me three sweet sherries, one of them a schooner? Make it a schooner, he said. But he's still a shit! All men are!' She nodded her head wisely.

'I could have told you that,' Mrs Austin said. 'I could have saved you the trouble of finding out!'

'I bet you never had three sherries!' Jennie boasted.

'I most certainly did not,' Mrs Austin said. 'I did not touch strong drink. Your father did enough of that for the whole street! And it seems to me you're following in his footsteps!'

'I wish I was!' Jennie said. 'If I knew where he was I'd follow him.'

She remembered almost nothing of her father, except that he was a big man, who would sometimes sweep her up in his strong arms and hold her tight, her face against his. He smelled of tobacco and of something else, a sort of warm, sweet smell, not unpleasant, on his breath. The way he swung her effortlessly through the air, she must have been quite small.

'And much good that would do you!' her mother said. 'He'd not take responsibility for you, the way

165

I've done all these years. He'd take no responsibility for wife or child, not the moment some floosie came on the scene. And now you'd better sit down before you fall down. Better still, get yourself off to bed. I'll deal with you in the morning, and don't think I won't, young lady!'

'Don't tell me what to do!' It was Jennie's turn to shout. Anger flared in her as if someone had put a match to paraffin. It was an unusual, almost unknown, emotion for her. Resignation was more in her line. .

'Don't you dare tell me what to do!' she repeated. 'I'm not a little girl. I'm a grown-up woman. And I hate you! Did you know that? I hate you! You're a shit as well!'

On Mrs Austin's cheekbones two bright blobs of crimson flared against her putty-coloured skin. Her mouth dropped open.

Then, as quickly as it had arisen, Jennie's anger died down. She was quite tired. Perhaps she *would* sit down.

'I'm an actress,' she announced conversationally. 'I'm Helena, and I'm in love with De . . . Demee . . . Excuse me, I can't quite say his name! I've had three sherries, you see! But he doesn't love me. He's a shit as well!'

Sadness filled her veins.

'Nobody loves me!' she said morosely. 'They all love Hermia! It's not fair, is it?' Tears filled her eyes. Perhaps she would go to bed after all. She attempted to rise from her chair but suddenly the room spun around and her mother with it, a conglomeration of pinks and blues and yellow and crimson framing an angry face.

Something like a tidal wave swept across her

stomach. Oh God, she thought, I'm going to be sick! She clapped a hand to her mouth and stumbled towards the bathroom.

*   *   *

Ursula observed, not without concern, a distressed Jennie being escorted from the Queen's Head by Petra and Adam. Of course she was concerned. Wasn't Jennie her latest protégé, and doing so well, but also was not Giles her star? Silly children, she thought indulgently. But right now she had troubles of her own, standing right beside her.

'Last orders!' the landlord called.

Eric turned to his wife.

'What will you have, Ursula?'

'Nothing more for me, thank you dear. I think . . .' We should be going, was what she intended to say, but he was already speaking to Lucinda.

'Same again?'

'Oh, Eric, you're spoiling me!' Lucinda said. 'But all right, I will. If you twist my arm!'

'Are you sure you won't?' Eric asked Ursula.

'Quite sure. And I don't think you . . .'

He was already on his way to the bar and she was left with Lucinda.

'Dear Eric!' Ursula said. 'He's such a generous man, my husband! He's the same with everyone! It doesn't matter who it is!'

In fact it wasn't true, she thought. He wasn't mean, of course, but he was careful. He didn't fling his money around. Nor did he drink three double gin and tonics in a row and buy the same for this or any other tart. The leopard was changing his spots before her very eyes, and all because of a bit of

167

flattery from a few members of the opposite sex. But deep inside her a small insistent voice said, Is this what he wants, and if it is, hadn't he better get it from you? And the answer was yes, and yes again. There was no way she would allow him to stray because—and this went even deeper, so that she could hardly face it herself—she was afraid to do so. She became aware of the fragility of her hold on him, and if on him, then on everything else.

Eric returned from the bar carrying two large drinks and two bags of cheese-and-onion crisps.

'Eric, dear,' Ursula said. 'You know potato crisps always give you indigestion!'

'No they don't!' he contradicted.

'Especially cheese-and-onion, dear!'

'Nonsense!' Eric said, handing a glass and a packet of crisps to Lucinda.

Lucinda opened her packet.

'Do have one, Ursula!' she offered.

Reluctantly, Ursula took one. If she didn't they would both think she was sulking, and she wasn't. Of course she wasn't, not the least little bit. She was thinking of Eric's stomach.

'I don't think we should linger,' she said. 'After all, we don't want actually to be *thrown out*, do we?' She did not see being thrown out of the pub, any pub, but particularly the Queen's Head in Mindon, as being in line with her image.

'Don't worry,' Eric assured her. 'We'll leave ahead of the mob.' It was a pity. He didn't want to go. He was enjoying himself.

'I expect you're tired, Ursula,' Lucinda said sweetly. 'You do look tired!'

Ursula took a deep breath, squared her shoulders. 'Not in the least!' she replied. 'But I expect you want to get home to your husband.'

Lucinda gave a squeaky cry of surprise.

'Oh, but I don't have a husband! I'm divorced! Footloose and fancy free! Didn't you know?'

Ursula was annoyed with herself that she didn't know. She liked to know the personal and domestic arrangements of her members. It gave her, she reckoned, a better understanding of each one of them. If called upon she could advise and guide in other matters than taking a role in a play. She had clearly slipped up on Lucinda Rockwell, perhaps because she had never liked her well enough to be interested. Not that the news surprised her.

They left, as Eric had promised, before the final exit.

'We'll take you home, Lucinda,' he said. 'We all go in the same direction.'

They crossed the road to where he had left the car. Eric was about to get into the driver's seat when Ursula stopped him.

'I think not, dear! I'll drive,' she said.

'I'm perfectly capable . . .'

'I will drive!' said Ursula.

They set off, Lucinda in the back.

'Where do you live, exactly?' Ursula called out as she drove.

'Birch Road,' Lucinda said. 'Number fourteen. About half way down.'

'Why don't you stop on this road, at the top of Birch Road?' Eric suggested to his wife. 'I'll walk Lucinda down to her gate. Save you having to do a turn in a narrow road.'

Oh no you don't, Ursula thought.

'Certainly not, dear,' she said graciously. 'I wouldn't dream of dropping Lucinda anywhere other than at her own gate!'

In Birch Road she drew up outside number fourteen. Eric jumped out of the car, gallantly helped Lucinda out, then opened her gate, accompanied her up the path to her front door, and waited until she fitted her key in the lock and pushed the door open. Lucinda gave him a slow smile.

'*Au revoir*,' she said softly.

She would have asked him in but for his cow of a wife sitting there in the car, no doubt watching them.

The rest of the journey home was passed in silence. On Eric's part it was a pleasantly dreamy, alcoholic-tinged silence; on the part of Ursula a thoughtful, sober and far from pleasant one. Eric dashed up the steps to the house—as far as there was any dash in him, but he was desperate to get to the loo, his G & Ts were telling on him—while Ursula carefully garaged the BMW and locked it up cosily for the night, giving it a little pat on its bonnet as she left it. She had a low opinion of people who didn't garage their cars at night.

In the house she made for the kitchen. Eric was already there, peering into the fridge.

'I'll make a nice pot of coffee,' she said. 'I think we could both do with it.'

In fact it was Eric who could do with it, black and strong, otherwise he would fall asleep the minute his head touched the pillow, lie on his back and snore all night. She had other plans for him. All the coffee would do for her was keep her awake, though for once she wouldn't mind that. She had a lot to think about. *I must sort out my life*, she thought, the words forming themselves in her mind like a line from a play.

'I'll do some sandwiches as well,' she said. 'Cheese-and-tomato or lamb?' There was a pack of garlic sausage at the back of the fridge, but that she did not intend to offer.

'Both!' Eric said. 'I've got quite an appetite!'

They sat at the kitchen table.

'I think,' Eric said between mouthfuls, 'on Saturday morning I'll nip into Southfield again. You were right about the clothes, Ursula. *And* the haircut. Just what I needed. I feel like a new man!'

'Oh! Good!'

'So I thought I'd splash out a bit more. A second jacket—you remember there was another one I liked? Shirt. Tie. Oh, and some trainers!'

'Trainers? Are you sure, dear? You've never worn trainers,' Ursula said.

'Never too late to start, eh?'

'I'll go with you!' Ursula said quickly. At least she might be able to stop his wilder excesses.

'Oh no! No need,' Eric said. 'I know you always have plenty to do. Why would you want to waste your time in Southfield? And I know where to go. I'll make straight for Blokes.'

I'll bet you will, Ursula thought. Out loud she said, 'But I'd like to go with you, darling!' Besides, who might he meet on a Saturday morning in Southfield? There was no telling. While pleasant and friendly to all, he had never shown any particular interest in other women. She could have trusted him to the ends of the earth. Now, if his behaviour this evening, both in MADS and in the pub, was anything to go by she couldn't trust him even when she could see him. So she would accompany him to Southfield and she would

171

certainly never let him get anywhere near Birch Road unaccompanied.

'These sandwiches are good,' Eric said, biting into his fourth.

'Thank you!'

'I thought the rehearsal went well.'

'Thank you again,' Ursula said. 'So I take it you're happier with Demetrius?'

'I really think I am,' said Eric.

Well at least she had achieved *that* objective. But she had done it for MADS, not for Eric. It was for MADS that she had caused Eric to be an object of admiration. It had been for Demetrius, not Eric, and now she had to deal with it.

She watched as he undid the top button of his trousers and let out a sigh of relief. It was interesting, and quite baffling, that the problem of his being overweight—about which none of her plans had as yet been put into action—seemed not to be a problem at all, image-wise. It was certainly not the first thing one noted about the new Eric. What was noticeable was the increase in his self-confidence, and the way he lapped up admiration, especially from that trollop Lucinda.

At least there was one thing she could be thankful for, that she had not cast Eric as Oberon, which she might well have done. Demetrius and Titania did not share a single line throughout the whole play. Too much hanging about off-stage, however.

Strange, she thought, that Eric should fall for admiration, approbation. She had never considered him a vain man, except that her experience in drama had led her to the conclusion that most men are vain. Look at dear Giles! Look at Cyril and at

Oberon! As yet, though, she had seen little vanity in Adam Benfield. And the vicar, outside his role as a man in charge of a parish, seemed not to be a vain man.

Eric interrupted her thoughts.

'I think Jennie is coming on well. She's a good Helena.'

Ursula nodded.

'Very good! I'm pleased with her.'

'So what did that louse Giles do to upset her, I mean in the pub?'

Ursula gave a dismissive wave of her hand.

'I expect she misunderstood him. Poor darling, she is rather naïve, personally I mean. But don't worry, I'm working on her. You'll see a big difference before we're through!' It was uncanny how she could have this effect on people. She saw them blossom, come out of themselves. Sometimes she felt quite humble in the face of her own talent. It was God-given, of course.

She brought her mind back to Eric, who was drinking a second cup of coffee and reading the paper. Eric was different from all the rest, of course he was, he was her husband and she loved him. She had somehow to bring him back. Not that he had strayed very far, *as yet*, but the signs were there.

She was herself, she knew, a person of great self-confidence, but what she also knew—she was no fool—was that her confidence arose from being in charge, from things going to plan. Her life, ever since she had met Eric when they had both been Young Conservatives, had moved along a straight road. They came from similar backgrounds. They supported good causes, they were moderate

173

churchgoers—nothing too excessive of course. Eric, like his father before him, was a Freemason, so there had always been ladies' nights where they had mingled exclusively with friends in the same set. They had never had children, not from choice, it had just not happened and it had not really bothered her. There were lots of worthy things in the world to work for. She didn't think it had bothered Eric.

She would have said, if she'd stopped to think of it, that all throughout their marriage she had seen herself leading the way down a straight road, Eric following behind without protest. Now, suddenly, she was less sure that he would follow her down that straight road, so she would have to apply her talents to her own situation.

Fortunately, she reminded herself as she put the dirty crockery in the dishwasher, she had the advantage that she was physically with Eric, *and* that she shared his bed. They had never been the world's greatest lovers but, on the other hand, the thought of single beds had never entered their heads.

'I think I'll go up,' she said. 'Don't be long, dear!'

Without looking up from the sports' page he gave a grunt which was probably assent.

In the bedroom she opened a drawer and took out her best nightdress, the one she took on holiday if they were booked into a five-star hotel. It was a pale mushroomy-beigy silk, with lace at the neck, and the thinnest possible shoulder straps. The success of a nightdress, she had read in some magazine or other, could be measured by the desire it caused in one's partner to take it off, fling it away. That was not quite Eric's style, but they would see. She sighed. She herself was not a woman of high sexual passion, and really, they were both out of practice.

She brushed her hair, fluffing it away from her face in a softer style. She had good hair, thick and dark, and she always immediately discouraged the least sign of greyness. She sprayed herself with perfume—Opium was very suitable—climbed into bed and lay back against the pillows, waiting.

And waiting, and waiting.

In the end she got out of bed and went to the top of the stairs.

'Eric,' she shouted, 'have you fallen asleep down there?'

'Just coming!' he called back.

In bed—he had not noticed her nightdress, she might as well have been wearing striped flannelette with a high neck—he said a polite 'Goodnight, dear!' and turned on his side, facing the wall.

Ursula turned so that she lay close into his back, like two spoons in a cutlery box. Then she put her arms around him and allowed—or, rather, directed—her hands to stray over his body, lightly at first, and then more insistently. She remembered all the right places.

Eric, having composed himself to fall into an immediate sleep, came to with a start. What the hell . . .'? (Though not out loud.) She pressed her body closer into his back, her hands strayed further. Wow! he thought. Is it my birthday, or what? He turned around to face her and, just as it had said in Ursula's magazine, slipped the straps of her nightdress off her shoulders.

*   *   *

George brought the drinks for Tina and himself back to the table. Waiting at the bar to be served, he had witnessed Giles's departure and Jennie's outburst. Indeed, he had made a move to pay for Jennie's sherry but Adam had beaten him to it.

'Who does he think he is?' he asked Tina, telling her about it. 'He's an ill-mannered conceited oaf!'

'No-one likes him,' Tina said. 'Except Ursula. If this was a crime novel instead of real life he'd be the one to get murdered and everyone in MADS would have a motive.'

'Except Ursula.'

'Except Ursula!'

George picked up his glass.

'Who shall we drink to?' he asked.

'Us, of course,' Tina said.

'You're right, love,' George said. 'Sometimes I feel as if it's you and me against the world. And I wouldn't mind that, I really wouldn't, if we *were* actually together.'

Tina found nothing to say.

'To us, then,' George said. 'And damn the rest. Especially Moira.'

'I don't think you should say that, love,' Tina reproved him, but half-heartedly.

'Well I do,' he said. 'She's ruined my life and now she's ruining everything for both of us.'

He was sick and tired of the way he and Tina had to conduct their lives, the small bit of their lives they managed to share. He gave her a lift to Southfield every morning; they popped in and out of each other's offices once or twice during the day if an excuse could be found. Shopped in

176

Sainsbury's with Moira's bloody list in hand at lunchtime or, when there was no shopping to be done, dry cleaning to be collected, or prescription to fill, they sat on a bench in the War Memorial Gardens, watching the time so they wouldn't be late back. Then, after work, he gave her a lift home again. If only they had been travelling home, together, instead of him giving Tina no more than a squeeze of the hand when she got out of the car, or a hasty kiss if there was no-one around.

They sipped their drinks slowly. It seemed as though neither of them had the heart to down them. We'll drown our sorrows, he'd said, but they both knew that a half of bitter and a port and lemon couldn't do that. All the drink in the Queen's Head couldn't do it.

'Shall we go?' George said.

'If you want to. It'll be closing time before long, anyway.' He was very down this evening, poor love. She wished she could cheer him up. In a way, it was worse for him than it was for her. At least she was happy in her home, with Daniel. Not fulfilled, of course, but she didn't go home to someone she hated.

They got into the car. Then George, instead of turning left along the Southfield Road in the direction of her house, turned right, through the village, and along the road which climbed up to the Downs.

'Where are we going, love?' she asked.

'Where we can be on our own for half an hour,' he said.

'I mustn't be late,' she told him. 'Daniel might worry!'

'Do you want to come, or don't you?' George

asked roughly.

'You know I do.'

At the top of the hill he turned off the road into a narrow lane, bordered on one side by beech trees and on the other by fields from which, Tina knew, in the daylight you could see half the county. George drew into the side and stopped the car, then he went around to Tina's side, took her by the hand and helped her out of the car. He led her across the grass verge to the low stone wall, and in silence they climbed the wall. Tina lay on her back on the summer grass, cropped short in the daytime by sheep, and opened her arms to George.

Less than an hour later—he had taken Tina home—George let himself into his house. It was no surprise to him that Moira was still up, sitting in her armchair, reading one of her interminable novels. Since she was more often than not on the night shift at work this was like the middle of the day to her. She did not look up from her book as George came in and his first instinct was to walk past her and straight up the stairs to his own bedroom. It would have been the natural thing to do, and on this occasion more so than ever. He had no wish to speak to her but, perversely, it was the fact that she totally ignored him which made him shout out.

'Why won't you divorce me?'

'What's brought this on again?' Moira asked, her eyes still on her book. 'I suppose you've been with her?'

'What do you know about that?'

'You'd be surprised,' she said. 'You're not very discreet, are you?'

'You don't want me!' George cried. 'I don't want

178

you. Why do we have to go on with it?'

'I suppose she won't have you unless she can marry you?' Moira said. 'Well I suppose that shows a bit of morality, just a bit. Or does she want you to keep her? Is that it?'

'Leave her out of it,' George said. 'You and me were like this before ever she came on the scene.'

'And will be when she's gone! I won't divorce you.'

'Why?' he asked. 'Why, why?'

'I don't know why you're asking me,' Moira said calmly. One of the things that irritated George most was the way she kept her voice flat and even, as if she was talking to a backward child.

'You know why,' she said. 'It's against my religion.'

'What religion?' George demanded. 'You don't have a religion. You haven't been to church in years. You don't know the meaning of the word!'

'I know it means I won't divorce you,' Moira said. 'Once a Catholic, always a Catholic. Except in your case.'

She returned to her book. It was her final word. It always was. He asked himself yet again why he didn't just leave, and the answer was still the same. Where would he go? Tina wouldn't have him unless they could be properly married. It would be unfair to Daniel. He didn't want to leave Mindon, try his luck elsewhere, because he couldn't bear to leave Tina. She was what he lived for.

He went upstairs to bed, sat on the edge of the bed, his head in his hands. It had been wonderful up there, on the top of the Downs. He had never been so happy, but it wouldn't go on, he knew. Tina wouldn't countenance it. She would give him up,

179

she would find someone else.

He swerved around and thumped his fists against the headboard in a tattoo of anger and frustration.

CHAPTER TWELVE

Petra let herself into the house and walked through to the kitchen, Adam following her.

'Coffee or tea?' she asked. 'Since you have to drive home.'

How nice, she thought, if he didn't have to go home, if he stayed here, if he had a *right* to stay here. The thought was sudden, out of the blue, taking her completely by surprise but so strong that it seemed as if she must have said it out loud, but since she knew that she had not, that at least he must guess what she was thinking. Did it show in her face? She pushed the thought away and hid her face from Adam as she looked in the fridge for milk.

He noticed her nervousness. There was a coolness, a hesitation in her manner, a shortness in her conversation as she went about making the coffee, almost as if she regretted having invited him. Why was that? Why was she now aloof, after a pleasant evening in which, he had believed, friendship had flowed, even progressed, between them? Yet perversely, the fact that she had in spirit moved away from him made him want to seize her physically, to shake her, to bring her back from the distance she had so unaccountably placed between them.

180

She brought the coffee to the table and they sat down facing each other. She had a wary look about her.

'Come back!' Adam said.

'Come back?'

'You went away,' Adam said. 'Quite suddenly. What were you thinking of?'

'I've no idea,' Petra lied. 'Beyond making the coffee. Or I suppose . . .' She seized on the idea '. . . I was thinking about MADS. My head's usually full of MADS after a rehearsal. It was good in the pub, wasn't it?'

'Very good,' Adam agreed. 'Except for the obnoxious Giles. Vicky seemed to be getting on well with Melvin.'

'I noticed,' Petra said. 'I was a bit surprised. I thought Victoria was madly in love with you!' She spoke lightly, behind her words there was a pinprick of jealousy.

Adam laughed.

'Don't be silly! You're confusing the *Dream* with real life! We're not really Hermia and Lysander, you know! That's acting!'

'It's pretty convincing acting,' Petra said.

'Thanks for the compliment!'

'All the same,' Petra persisted, 'I still think she's potty about you!' She knew she was worrying at the subject like a dog with a bone, the trouble was she couldn't help herself.

'You're wrong,' Adam said. 'She's just a nice kid. Much too young!'

'Some girls like older men,' Petra said. 'Anyway, you're not too far apart in real life to play lovers in the *Dream*!'

'Ursula,' Adam pointed out, 'has to cast the play

181

with whoever she's got. Look at Demetrius and Helena—really, as far as age goes, they're quite mismatched!'

'As well as young women liking older men,' Petra said, 'it's well known that men prefer younger women. It's a fact of life!'

'Come on, Petra, that's too sweeping!' Adam said sharply. 'Some men prefer grown-up women, not girls. Maturity has its attractions.'

His words were music to Petra's ears, but she was being far from mature. She knew she was behaving like a schoolgirl and the sooner she changed the conversation the better.

'I hope Jennie's all right,' she said. 'I don't mean physically. She probably feels terrible. I mean with her mother. I believe she's a dragon.'

'Then it might be for the best!' Adam said. 'Dragons have to be fought! Though Jennie doesn't strike me as a slayer of dragons.'

'It's amazing how mothers vary,' Petra said. 'What was your mother like? I haven't heard you mention her.'

Adam thought for a moment.

'She was fair,' he said. 'She was competent. She was competent in most things, including motherhood. She looked after us.'

'Us?'

'I have a sister,' Adam said. 'She married an American, she lives in Washington.'

'So your mother looked after you . . .' Petra prompted him.

'Yes, very well. I suppose that's one way of being loving, but she wasn't demonstrative, she wasn't a woman for hugs and kisses. I always thought if I had children I'd make certain they knew I loved them.'

'I think I must have had one of the best mothers in the world,' Petra said. 'She was just . . . well, tops at everything. The thing is, I suppose I never saw her as being anything other than my mother. As far as I was concerned that was her role in life. My father's wife, of course, but that was just part and parcel. I never thought of her as having a life outside the three of us, or as having anything else in her life.'

'Perhaps she didn't,' Adam said.

But she did, Petra thought. In her mind's eye she saw the drawing. She had looked at it now so often that she felt she knew every line, every bit of shading, every curve and contour of that beautiful body.

'Oh yes, I think she did,' she spoke quietly, almost as if she was talking to herself.

Adam raised his head sharply—he had been pouring himself more coffee—but the look on her face, the way she spoke told him it was not for him to ask questions. She might or might not tell him what caused the troubled look in her eyes. He let the silence lie between them.

'I'm sorry,' she said eventually. 'You must think I'm very rude. It's just that . . .'

'You don't have to explain.'

'I'd like to.' She wanted to tell him. She wanted someone to share. 'You remember the drawings I found when we were looking for the frames in the attic?'

'The drawings of your mother? Yes, I remember.' It had been strange to him at the time that she had deliberately not allowed him to see them. He would have expected her to share what must have been a pleasant discovery with the nearest person to hand. Rejoicing.

'I'd like to show them to you,' Petra said. 'They're in my bedroom. I won't be a minute.'

She was down again a few minutes later, the drawings in her hand.

'I had a feeling you didn't want me to see them,' Adam said. 'In which case . . .'

'I've changed my mind.' She handed the drawings to him.

He looked at them—and caught his breath. They were exquisite, and they were, at the same time, as highly erotic as anything he had ever seen. This beautiful body, soundly asleep, was sated, drugged with sex. He could not begin to tell by what skill, what magic, the artist had conveyed this. It leapt out of the sheets of paper. He felt that he was present in the room, the smell of sex was in his nostrils. He didn't know what to say.

'They're quite beautiful!' He pronounced eventually. 'And immensely powerful.'

'Yes,' Petra said. 'But not how one would expect to see one's mother.'

He could find nothing to say to that.

'I know I'm being silly,' Petra said. 'It was all a long time ago. It must have been before my mother was married to my father, or why would I have found them in Claire's home? As far as I know, though I can't be sure, Claire and my mother hadn't met since they were girls.'

'Your father . . .'

'My father couldn't have known about this,' Petra said. 'He was . . . I suppose you'd call him an innocent man. Whoever made these drawings was my mother's lover.'

184

It would be idle to deny that, Adam thought, nevertheless, to comfort her, he tried.

'That's an assumption. Isn't it just possible that they weren't even drawn by a man?'

'Oh, but . . . !' Petra hesitated. 'The one thing I'm certain of is that they were drawn by the lover. It's there in every line. If that were not to be a man . . . I wouldn't like to think—'

'Definitely a man!' Adam interrupted. 'It shows.'

'I don't know why I'm so upset,' Petra said. 'It isn't something I haven't done in my time. I've had lovers. It's just that . . . well, one has certain ideas about one's mother. My mother was sweet, and pure.'

'Get rid of the drawings!' Adam said sharply. 'Don't keep them. Burn them! Give them to me and I'll do it for you!'

'Destroy them? Burn them? What are you saying?'

'If they upset you, why keep them?'

Petra shook her head.

'I could never destroy them. These are no ordinary drawings. No matter who the subject is they're works of art, near genius. I know enough to recognize that. I couldn't even contemplate destroying them. And if I did, do you suppose I'd ever forget them?'

'I'm sorry,' Adam said. 'It seemed to me they were of less importance than you. So what will you do?'

'I don't know,' Petra admitted. 'I'd like to know who the artist was, but if I did I might discover more than I wanted to know.'

She took the drawings from him and put them back into the envelope.

'Do you mind that I showed them to you?' she asked. 'Perhaps I shouldn't have?'

'I feel privileged,' Adam said.

They sat at the table for a minute or so without speaking.

'Would you like more coffee?' Petra said presently.

'No thank you.'

'Perhaps you want to be off? It's quite late. I forget you have to make an earlier start in the morning than I do!'

Adam stood up abruptly, then pulled her to her feet and took her in his arms, held her close, kissed her hungrily.

'I don't want to go at all,' he said. 'It's the last thing I want to do. I want to make love to you. Tell me I can stay!'

She drew away from him, shaking her head.

'Why not?' he said. She had been happy in his arms. She had responded to his kisses.

'I don't know,' she admitted. 'It's just that I'm mixed up. It's not the time.'

'When will it be the time?'

'Soon,' Petra said. 'Very soon. But not now.'

'You promise?'

'I promise!'

'Then if it's what you want, I'll go.'

He held her close again, kissed her gently. 'Will you be all right?' he asked.

'Yes.'

'Shall I see you tomorrow?'

'Of course!' Petra said. 'There's a rehearsal.'

'I'm not talking about the rehearsal,' Adam said. 'Can I come back with you afterwards?'

'Yes,' she said. 'I promise.'

'And there'll be no sending me home?'

'No.'

She saw him to the door. Standing in the porch, she watched him as he walked down the path, crossed the road and got into his car. He gave a wave of his hand as he drove away, quick off the mark. Only when distance and darkness had faded his rear lights did she go into the house, closing and locking the door behind her.

Why had she let him go—in fact, pushed him out? Now that he had gone she longed for him, her body craved him. She knew she would count the hours until she saw him tomorrow. Was she, she asked herself, falling in love? Did she even want to? The word 'love' had not been mentioned between them, nor did she know if it applied at all to Adam. What had passed between them had been sexual desire, and no worse for that. And how much of it had been generated by the atmosphere of those drawings? It was for that reason she had not been able to let him make love to her tonight.

She went into the kitchen and started to clear away. Adam, she reminded herself, was a free man, she had no rights over him. If they chose to make love with each other they were free to do so, with no complications. Except, she thought, that falling in love *was* a complication. But we are also friends, she consoled herself.

She washed the coffee pot and returned it to its place on the shelf, then looked around the kitchen. There was nothing else to be done. It was all as neat as a new pin. Too neat, too tidy, rather like her life. She would go to bed.

She picked up the drawings, switched off the downstairs lights, and went upstairs. In her bedroom, not even allowing herself one last look at the drawings, she put them in the bottom drawer of her bedside cupboard. She would leave them undisturbed, as they had been for so long in the attic. Adam, though admiring, had seemed quite unfazed by them, not shocked as she had been on first seeing them. But then, why should he be? It wasn't his mother, was it?

She undressed and, before getting into bed, she went to the window and drew back the curtains. It was a dark night, no moon. Rectangles of light showing from most of the houses, which she usually saw by day, now cut the darkness. She wondered, not for the first time, what was going on behind those lighted windows. She breathed in the perfume of night-scented stock and nicotiana which rose from the garden. Then she closed the curtains. She felt calmer now. Looking out of her window always had that effect on her. She thought about MADS. All was going well there, she thought, at least her part of it was. She had all but completed her designs for the *Dream* and Ursula had approved them.

*   *   *

Ursula was massaging night cream into her face and neck with a skill born of long practice. Firm yet gentle upward strokes, never downwards. Nature, allied to the force of gravity would, in the course of time, drag everything down. It was her job to fight nature, to thwart it for as long as she could. She peered into the magnifying mirror which held a prominent place on her dressing table, assessing which of them, she or time, was winning. There were fine feathery lines at the outer corners of her eyes—laughter lines she liked to call them, but more deeply etched was the vertical line just above the bridge of her nose and the rather more than faint tramlines across her forehead. Which meant, she supposed, that she spent more time frowning than smiling.

As if to confirm her findings she glared at herself in the mirror and then, in contrast, changed to a wide smile, stretching her mouth, showing her teeth! Thank goodness there was nothing wrong with her teeth! They would not, she thought complacently, have disgraced an American movie star. She raised her chin, stretching the slackness which was undoubtedly showing below it, applied more cream and beat a sharp tattoo to the area with the backs of her fingers.

'Are you *ever* coming to bed?' Eric grumbled.

'I won't be long, darling!' Her voice was distorted by the fierce beating of her fingers against her throat. 'I *am* doing this for you, dear! You wouldn't want me to let myself go, now would you?'

Eric grunted. All he wanted was that she should get into bed, turn out the light and let them both go to sleep, though there was no hope of the last until she had gone through her usual summary, out loud, of the day's events.

'I thought the rehearsal went well,' she remarked. 'Everyone seems to be pulling together at last.'

'Mmm!' It was all that was required of him, the acknowledgement that he was listening.

'Except for that drama queen, Titania!'

'I thought she was quite good,' Eric said, momentarily arousing himself in Lucinda's

189

defence.

'Oh no, dear! She plays to the gallery. All the time!'

'Isn't that what actors do? Play to the gallery, or possibly the stalls and dress circle. Or in the case of MADS to eighteen rows of uncomfortable wooden chairs, all on the same level!'

Ursula roused herself on one elbow and looked at him. That had been an unusually long speech for Eric on the verge of sleep.

'I'm not sure,' she said, 'that it's a good idea for you and me to go to the pub after rehearsals. We should let the others go, but desist ourselves. I am, after all the producer. I have to maintain discipline, which is not so easy if one becomes too familiar. Or allows others to become too familiar.'

'Rubbish!' Eric said. 'I thoroughly enjoyed it. They're a nice crowd.'

'I know they are. I'm just saying that in my position . . .'

'Which is not *my* position. I am a humble Thespian, playing a part for which I'm not suited. A little bit of fun to round it off doesn't come amiss.'

'You are the producer's husband!' Ursula said, as if conferring a knighthood on him.

Eric gave something between a snort and a grunt, turned his back on her and prepared for sleep. Ursula, who had by no means finished the day's summary, continued to talk.

'I've seen Petra's designs. They're really very good. And she tells me Amelia is being a great help with the costumes. She, I mean Petra, seems to be getting on rather well with Adam. Do you think there might be something in it? They would make a

190

nice pair. She's older than he, of course, but it doesn't seem to matter so much these days, does it?'

Eric's answer was much as she expected: a gentle snore, which rose quickly to a crescendo and, when it had reached its peak, dropped back to the beginning and started all over again.

He was well away. She could switch on the light and read her book and he wouldn't notice. His next awakening would be at three in the morning when he would, with sobs and sighs and the delicacy of movement of a bull elephant, heave himself out of bed, totter to the bathroom, relieve himself and totter back, falling fast asleep again within minutes while she, thoroughly wakened, turned to another chapter of her book.

There was much to be said for separate bedrooms. But not, she thought, while Lucinda Rockwell was on the scene.

*   *   *

When they left the Queen's Head George tucked his hand under Tina's elbow and guided her to where his car was parked, a minute or so away. They did not speak to each other until they were in the car. George turned on the engine, glanced in the mirror, and drove out into the road.

'It's very kind of you to give me a lift home,' Tina said.

'For heaven's sake!' George sounded slightly annoyed. 'What else would I do? Do you think I'd leave you to get the bus?'

But instead of driving her straight home he made a sudden left turn into a narrow, dark lane, pulled into the side, and switched off his engine, and the lights.

'What . . .' Tina began.

'I want to say goodnight to you properly,' George said gruffly. 'I'm sick of dropping you at your gate, watching while you walk up the path and open the door, then driving away. It's not enough! Nor is this for that matter. In fact I don't want to say goodnight to you at all. You know that.'

'Of course I do, love! And don't think I don't feel the same way,' Tina said. 'But what else is there for us?'

He stopped her words by taking her in his arms and kissing her.

'Oh, George,' she said. 'I do love you! You do know that don't you?'

'Of course I do!'

'And you won't ever forget it?'

'It's what keeps me going.'

After that there were no more words. His mouth fastened on hers. His hand explored her body, and her hands his. He wanted to have her naked, be done with fumbling through layers of clothing, but how could that be, cramped in a car, in a lane, where any moment another car might pass and flood them with its headlights? There was no prospect that it would ever be any different. Sometimes he felt like throwing in the sponge.

'I'll have to be going,' Tina said eventually. 'Daniel will be home. I gave him money to go to a movie but he'll be back by now.'

Damn Daniel, George wanted to say, but he wouldn't. That would be the last straw. Besides, the boy didn't deserve it. None of this was his fault, poor little bugger.

192

They put themselves to rights and George drove off. For some reason or other Tina thought about Lucinda Rockwell. Since her divorce had gone through, from all reports she had had a whale of a time ever since. But she didn't have a child, did she? And I wouldn't be without Daniel for the world, Tina thought. Anyway, she didn't hanker after a whale of a time. All she wanted was George. But oh, how badly she wanted him!

George drew up outside Tina's house. No more kisses, not even a peck, silhouetted as they were in the light of the street lamp.

'Goodnight, sweetheart,' he said.

'Goodnight, love! There's a light on. Daniel must be home.'

She walked away quickly and George drove off.

He drove slowly. He was reluctant to go home— if you could call it home. There would be no welcome, no spark of warmth, more than likely not a word spoken. Sooner than he wanted, even his slow driving brought him to his house. He garaged his car—he didn't believe in leaving cars out all night, summer weather or not. It was asking for trouble. Even Mindon had its share of vandals who would smash the windscreen or scratch the paintwork as soon as look at it. In fact, his attitude to the care of cars was exactly the same as Ursula's, though it was the only thing they had in common.

That done, he let himself in at the door in the corner of the garage which led straight into the kitchen. He would like to have walked straight up to bed, not seeing his wife, but entering via the garage meant that he must walk through the living room to reach the staircase which rose up not more than a couple of yards inside the front door. Before

193

he did that, he thought, he would make himself a cup of Ovaltine and carry it up to bed with him. Perhaps it would make him sleep.

Minutes later, mug in hand, he walked through the living room on his way to bed. She was sitting in the armchair, his so-called wife, snoring like a pig. Let her sleep, he thought. He had no intention of waking her, it would only mean a row. As far as he was concerned she could stay where she was until morning.

He paused to pick up the evening paper, which he would read in bed. As he did so he was aware that she had suddenly stopped snoring. Without thinking he glanced in her direction, and at once realized that this was no little catnap his wife was indulging in. She had slipped sideways in her chair and now half sat, half lay at a grotesque angle. Her face was flushed deep red, her mouth gaped open and a trickle of saliva ran down her chin.

He had never seen anyone suffering a stroke but he knew this was it. He put down his mug and his newspaper, reached for the telephone, and rang for the ambulance.

CHAPTER THIRTEEN

The ambulance came quickly, or as quickly as was possible, considering it had to cover the three miles from Southfield General Hospital. George switched on the light in the front porch to act as a beacon and then, with some reluctance because he didn't know what to do for the best, turned his attention to Moira.

194

She looked acutely uncomfortable, her body slumped at all the wrong angles. But being unconscious, he thought, would she be aware of discomfort, would it penetrate to whatever place she now inhabited? He was afraid to move her in case he did some damage, but he could hardly stand by and do nothing. 'Keep the patient warm.' How many times had he read that? From the redness of her face she looked far from cold, but at least he would give it a try.

He fetched a blanket from the spare bedroom and draped it over her, lifted her head and rested it on a cushion from the sofa. That done, he returned to feeling helpless. Should he make himself a hot drink while he waited? His Ovaltine had gone quite cold, a revolting skin forming on its surface. But no, because most likely the ambulance would be here any minute. He would have preferred to have waited in the kitchen, away from the sight of his wife, but he felt that this was not a moment he could desert her.

When the ambulance arrived the men were polite and competent, lifting Moira on to the stretcher and into the vehicle as if she were a doll.

'Do you want to ride in the ambulance, sir?' they asked. 'Or would you rather go in your own car? You do have a car, sir?'

'Yes,' George said. 'I think my own car would be best.'

By the time he had left Moira in the care of the hospital and returned to his own home it might well be the middle of the night. There'd be no buses from Southfield to Mindon.

He set off in the wake of the ambulance but, sirens wailing, blue light flashing, it was quickly out of sight and sound. There was no way he could keep up with it, though he drove at a speed which was far higher than his usual one. Long before they reached Southfield he had lost it. The hospital car-park was several levels up twisting ramps and, it seemed at first sight, chock-a-block full. It took him several minutes to find a space.

Standing at the admissions desk he gave his name and stated his business to an impassive-looking clerk. She listened without comment to his story—she had heard similar ones a hundred times before—and elicited the answers to several routine questions, which George answered impatiently. It seemed to him that it was all leading nowhere.

'Will you please take a seat?' the clerk said presently. 'I'll call you.'

There were plenty of seats to choose from at this time of night. He bought a cup of coffee from a machine and, shunning company, took his place on an empty bench. The last thing he wanted was to talk to strangers.

What will happen? he wondered. What would the consequences be? He doubted from the look of Moira whether what had happened could be described as a *slight* stroke, though of course he didn't know, did he? And if it wasn't, if it was more severe, what would that do to her? What would it do to her long term? Supposing it left her crippled, or half-paralysed, or without speech? It happened to people all the time. You heard the horror stories. And what would it do to him? How would he cope?

He would have to look after her. Hospitals these days didn't have long-term beds for stroke victims. He would have to wait on her hand and foot. She

196

would hate it, and so would he. It would involve the kind of intimacies they had not known for many years. But worse than any of this, it would mean the end of everything between himself and Tina. He had little enough to offer Tina as it was, but if this was to be his future he would have nothing.

It was interesting, he was to remember later, that in all of this it had never once occurred to him that he would not look after his wife.

He jerked himself out of his thoughts and looked around. Uniformed nurses, male and female, came and went; men and women in white coats and draped in stethoscopes appeared and disappeared. Porters pushed trolleys around. Everything was happening but none of it to him. He had clearly been forgotten.

In the end, tired of waiting, he went back to the desk.

'Have you any news?' he asked.

'I'm sorry, Mr Shepherd,' the clerk answered. 'I haven't. But you can be sure your wife's being well looked after. I expect there'll be something soon.'

He went back to his seat, picking up an out-of-date Sunday supplement from a table, and settled down again, trying to read but not making much sense of anything.

Eventually the clerk picked up her telephone, tapped in a string of numbers, and listened.

'He's here!' she said in the end.

She called out George's name and he went back to the desk.

'The doctor will see you now, Mr Shepherd,' she said. 'Room two-six-three, down the corridor and then first right and right again through the swing doors. You can't miss it. Dr Harper.'

Presumably, George thought, it was Dr Harper who sat behind a large desk and rose to his feet as George entered.

'Good evening, Mr Shepherd,' he said.

'Good evening,' George replied. 'How is my wife?' He spoke as calmly as he could, steeling himself against bad news.

'I'm sorry,' Dr Harper said. 'I'm afraid the news isn't good. I'm afraid I have to tell you your wife died just few minutes ago. I can assure you we did everything we could to save her, but it was not to be. She had suffered a massive stroke.'

George stared at the doctor. He couldn't believe it.

'I'm sorry,' the doctor repeated.

George had no idea what to say. He had prepared himself for bad news, indeed while he had waited on the bench he had, in his head, written whole new scenarios for his future life, but this had not been in them at all.

The doctor spoke again.

'Try to see it as for the best, Mr Shepherd. Death sometimes is, though it doesn't seem so at the time. Had your wife lived she would have had a difficult time, hard both for her and for you to bear. Perhaps that will be some consolation to you. I do hope so.'

Dr Harper stood up, held out his hand again. It was the end of the interview. George heard himself saying 'Thank you' as he left, making his way back to the desk clerk.

'I'll just need a few details from you,' she said, 'then you can come back in the morning and we'll settle the rest. Do you feel all right to drive your car?'

198

'What? Oh yes! Yes, I can drive my car.'

Back at home he didn't remember much of the drive back except that, being after two o'clock in the morning, the roads had been almost empty.

He must ring Tina, tell her he couldn't pick her up in the morning. He must let the office know, but not yet. It wasn't the time. He made himself a pot of tea and sat there drinking it, wondering whether he would go to bed or not. He wasn't at all sleepy.

With no motive at all, really no notion of what he was doing, he walked around the house, in and out of rooms. The whole place, except for his own bedroom, was full of the detritus of Moira's life: stockings and a pair of knickers drying over a rail in the bathroom, a pile of ironing in the kitchen, including a couple of his shirts—even though they hardly spoke to each other she had still ironed his shirts, and quite beautifully.

He opened the door of her wardrobe. Not much there. She'd never been dressy. Two sets of uniform, blue-and-white striped. Strange that she'd died in the very hospital where she'd worked. Would they know? Would they connect her? It was a large place. He supposed it might come out when he called there tomorrow. No, not tomorrow, come to think of it, later today.

He closed the wardrobe door and moved towards her dressing table. Would it tell him anything about the woman he'd once, a long time ago, loved and married, but whose bedroom had been no-go territory to him for years? It didn't. It revealed nothing except that she was neat and tidy and not much given to make-up. A box of tissues, hairbrush, manicure set, a length of pink beads, a cut-glass powder bowl empty of powder.

Perhaps he would go to bed. It would be a busy day tomorrow, several things to see to. He put the alarm on for seven o'clock so as to telephone Tina early. He wished she was here. He'd never wanted her more, not for anything in particular, not even to talk to, just to be there.

Surprisingly, he fell asleep almost as soon as his head touched the pillow, and didn't waken until the alarm went off at seven. He would ring Tina at once, he decided. She'd be up and doing. She had the boy to see to as well as herself.

'It's me!' he said.

'George! Whatever . . . ?'

'It's Moira! She's dead!'

Tina went cold from head to foot. It couldn't be true.

'She's dead!' George repeated.

Tina struggled to find words. What had he done? She knew the depth of his frustration, all his bitterness and it had been very near the surface last night. But what had caused him . . . ?

'Did you hear me?'

'Yes, George. Tell me exactly what happened, love.'

'She had a stroke. A massive stroke they said at the hospital. She died just after she got there.'

Tina felt shaky with relief.

'She's not old enough to have a stroke!' And that was a stupid thing to say. 'I mean . . . how did it happen?'

'I don't know. When I got home I thought she was asleep in the chair.' And if I hadn't, George asked himself, if I'd tumbled to it more quickly would she have died? He didn't know.

'Oh, George love, I am sorry! Would you like me

200

to come over?'

'Not at the moment.' Of course he wanted her, but somehow it didn't seem right, not just yet, not with his wife's things around. 'Will you pop in to see Mr Landseer? Tell him I can't be in today. I'll phone him when I know what the arrangements are. I daresay there'll have to be an inquest.'

'An inquest?'

'She hadn't been ill. She hadn't been under the doctor. And as you say, she was young for a stroke.'

'But there wasn't anything wrong, was there? They won't suspect anything wrong?'

'Why should they? It's all straightforward—if dying suddenly can be called straightforward.'

'Of course. Silly of me!' Tina said. 'Shall I give Ursula a ring, say you won't be at tonight's rehearsal?'

'You could,' George said. 'Phone me this afternoon, will you?'

Actually, he would be quite glad if Ursula was informed. It would save him having to announce it to everyone in MADS. She'd lose no time in doing that for him.

'I will, love,' Tina promised. 'And I'll see you as soon as ever you want me to.'

*   *   *

Eric and Ursula were still at the breakfast table when the telephone rang. By design rather than accident the cordless phone lay close to Ursula's right hand because it was she who always answered it. Eric didn't mind that, the call was usually for her anyway, but what did irritate him was that she deliberately let it ring ten times before answering,

201

even though her hand was hovering over the instrument. She had given him her reasons more than once.

'Never rush to answer,' she'd told him. 'People will think you've nothing better to do than sit beside it, waiting for someone to call. If they have to wait it establishes that you are a busy person!'

The only drawback to this habit, from Ursula's point of view, was when the caller grew impatient and rang off seconds too soon, in which case curiosity meant that she must ring 1471 to check who it had been and whether it was worthwhile ringing back. If it wasn't, she didn't.

Precisely on the tenth ring she picked up the phone.

'Ursula King!' Then a second later, 'Tina! What can I do for you?'

She looked across the table, pulled a face at Eric who was spreading marmalade on his last piece of toast.

'Oh, but how awful!' Ursula cried. 'Poor George! What a shock!' She paused long enough to allow Tina a word in edgeways.

'Yes, of course, Tina! But I'm not sure it would do him any good to miss rehearsals. I say that entirely for his own sake, of course. It would be better for him to throw himself into his part.' Though how he could throw himself into the part of Starveling-cum-Moonshine even she was not sure. He had a total of seven lines throughout the whole play.

'Well, give him my condolences, and Eric's of course, and we hope to see him as soon as possible. I trust *you* will be at rehearsal this evening? Good!'

She put down the telephone.

'What was that about?' Eric asked.

'George Shepherd. His wife has died. Quite suddenly. He found her unconscious. She had a stroke.'

'Poor George! Poor woman, of course. Do we know her?'

'I don't know anyone who did,' Ursula admitted. 'She kept herself to herself. But at least he doesn't have a big part in the *Dream* and I don't think he'll need to miss many rehearsals, so we'll manage.'

'Then let's hope George will also manage!' Eric said.

'Of course he will,' Ursula said firmly.

Her dread was always that someone playing a leading part in one of her productions would have something dire happen to them—anything from a broken leg to death itself.

'I'm thankful to Providence it's not someone with an important part,' she said. 'Though I'm not sure where I'd find even another Moonshine at this stage.'

'Perhaps you should insure the whole cast, especially the lead players!' Eric made the suggestion with a straight face.

'Do you think so?' Ursula said thoughtfully.

Eric opened his mouth to explain that he was joking. Jokes often had to be pointed out to Ursula, especially if MADS was involved.

'It might be a good idea,' she agreed, speaking before he could.

'You could grade the insurance according to the player's importance,' Eric said. 'But not just players. Don't underrate the scene shifters, the electrician and so on. Where would Theseus be without someone to put the spotlight on him?'

'You are quite right, dear. And the producer. Perhaps the producer needs the highest insurance of anyone. After all, what would anyone do without the producer?'

For one moment Eric thought she was having one of her rare flashes of wit. But no, he decided, looking at her closely. She was totally serious.

'Quite!' he said.

Ursula shook her head.

'The thing is, we couldn't afford it. MADS doesn't have the money, and I don't suppose people would pay their own premiums, do you?'

Eric appeared to give the matter great thought.

'I suppose you are right, as always, my love!' he said. 'Anyway, I must be off. Can't afford to miss my train. Got an early meeting this morning.'

'Don't be late home, dear. Rehearsal!' Ursula reminded him.

'As if I could forget!' Eric said, giving her a kiss on the cheek.

She stayed a little longer at the table, poured herself another cup of tea. That was an interesting idea Eric had had about insurance. She supposed it was done all the time in the West End theatres.

*　　　*　　　*

Just before lunchtime George telephoned Tina at the Town Hall. 'I've changed my mind about not wanting to see you just yet,' he said. 'Of course I want to. I don't know what to do with myself. Perhaps I should have gone into work?'

'Oh, no love,' Tina protested. 'You couldn't have done that. I daresay you're in shock.'

'Whatever it is, it feels awful,' George said. 'Did

you tell Mr Landseer?'

'Of course! He was very sorry. I told him you'd ring him yourself the minute you felt able.'

'Then I'll do that this afternoon. I've done everything else I can. The inquest's fixed for Friday morning. It'll be a few days more to wait for the funeral.'

Really, there had been little else to do. He had no family to inform and Moira only had an older sister in Dublin. He'd phoned her, of course, but she'd said she was very sorry, she couldn't possibly travel all that way, and in any case she and Moira had never been close, even as children. If George would like to send her a memento . . . She recalled her sister had had one or two nice pieces of jewellery.

'When can I see you, Tina?' he asked.

'As soon as you like, love. Where?'

'Will you come here? Would you mind?' He had already cleared away all visible signs of Moira, packed her few clothes in plastic bags to be taken to the Oxfam shop.

'Do you think that's all right?' Tina asked doubtfully.

'I don't know. I can't think straight.'

'Well, if it's what you want,' Tina said. Without a doubt the neighbours would talk, but never mind.

'I'll pop in home first and come on to you as soon as I can,' she promised.

He was watching out for her, standing at the open door as she walked up the path. She thought he looked terrible: lost. It stabbed her to the heart that he could look like this over the death of a wife he had not loved for years, and had wanted to divorce. How could that be?

205

She stepped inside quickly, and he closed the door. She took him in her arms, and held him close.

'Oh, love, I am sorry!' she said. 'What can I do?'

'Nothing,' George said. 'Just be here.'

'Of course I will, though I'll have to let Ursula know because I promised faithfully to be at rehearsal. Anyway, I'm going to make a meal and you're going to eat it. I daresay you haven't eaten all day.'

She cooked a passable meal of eggs and chips which they both ate.

'Now I'll phone Ursula, tell her neither of us will be there,' Tina said. 'I'm not leaving you on your own.'

'What about Daniel?'

'He has Scouts. I've explained it to him.'

They sat in near silence, not able to find anything to say. Everything had been said about Moira and they avoided talking about themselves. It was not the right time.

'I think I'll change my mind and go to the rehearsal,' George said, breaking the silence. He wanted to get out of the house. 'Would that be wrong?'

'If it's what you want, of course not,' Tina said. 'There's nothing more you can do for Moira, poor soul!' She heard her own words and thought how strange it was that Moira, who only a few hours ago had been a stumbling block, the implacable, obstinate cause of their unhappiness, in fact the enemy, had by the act of dying become nothing more than a poor soul.

'So will you ring Ursula?' George asked. 'Tell her I'm coming but we'll be a bit late and will she tell people before I get there.'

'Splendid!' Ursula said on hearing the decision. 'Quite the best thing he could do! It will take him out of himself!'

The rehearsal had not started when they walked into the hall. It was clear, by the sudden hush which descended, that everyone had heard. Ursula was the first to greet George, breaking the silence, after which to his astonishment he found himself the recipient of a care and compassion which he had never thought of as being part of the MADS' crowd. He was deeply moved. If he wasn't careful he might disgrace himself by breaking down.

'Right!' Ursula said presently. 'On with the show!'

But in spite of the atmosphere of goodwill towards George, it was not a happy rehearsal. Far from it. It seemed that the milk of human kindness had all been poured out on him and there was nothing left for each other.

Giles was the first to complain. At the end of his first speech he broke off, and moved to the front of the stage.

'I really must protest! This scene is not properly set. If I have to sit at the table, then the table should be up front. Otherwise when the others enter they will mask me!'

'I don't think so . . .' Ursula began.

'After all, Theseus Duke of Athens is the one who holds the play together—'

'With Hippolyta,' Arabella interrupted. 'Don't forget *I'm* in the play too.'

Giles ignored her.

'Theseus holds the play together. He is the beginning and the end!'

'But totally missing from the rest. Nothing at all in the middle!' Lucinda Rockwell spoke to Bottom, sitting beside her, but loudly enough for everyone to hear.

'Titania!' Ursula said sharply. 'Will you please keep quiet when someone else is on-stage!'

'Everyone knows,' said Lucinda, who was not the least bit afraid of Ursula, 'that what the audience really likes best are the bits between Titania and Bottom!'

Giles turned his attention to Titania.

'Since you spend a large part of your time asleep,' he said icily, 'it hardly calls for much acting!'

I hate him, Jennie Austin thought, listening on the sidelines. Pompous idiot! Yet actually, and she knew it, she owed him something. If he had not been so disgustingly rude to her in the pub, if he hadn't aroused her temper as he had, she'd never have gone home and defied her mother. It was something she should have done ages ago and had never thought possible. Now that it had happened she felt all the better for it. She would never be under her mother's thumb again. Life would be different. While Theseus declared his lines (having moved the table forward to centre front) she dreamt of what she would do.

'Splendid, Theseus!' Ursula said. 'And of course, Hippolyta, though I can think of no excuse for *you* not being word perfect, since you only have one speech! Now, we skip to page sixty-seven, "Enter Titania . . . with her train".'

'If you can call it a train!' Lucinda said.

'I have told you,' Ursula said with what patience she could muster, 'it will be all right on the night.

208

Start with your one speech before you fall asleep. I actually want to hear the fairies, and Oberon.'

And if I were writing the play, Ursula thought, she'd sleep through the rest of it. Lucinda, she had to admit, was clever. Asleep she might be but no way would this stop her attracting the attention of the audience whenever she was minded to do so. She had only to stir in her sleep, utter a faint moan, wave a languid hand or turn over for the attention of the audience to be on her and away from whoever else was speaking. And these tactics she was already employing.

Ursula threw her script to the floor, and shouted.

'STOP! Everyone stop.

'I will not have it, Titania!' she cried. 'You are being very naughty. From now on you will sleep quietly and keep still!'

'People don't kccp perfectly still when they're asleep,' Lucinda protested. 'They move around. They turn over. I'm doing what comes naturally!'

'In my production Titania does *not* move.'

'Anyway, it's very uncomfortable, lying on the hard floor,' Lucinda complained.

'No-one said acting was comfortable,' Ursula picked up her script and signalled to them to start again. 'Now, Oberon, please! "What thou seest when thou does wake".'

'I'm sorry,' Oberon croaked. 'I'm afraid I've got the most awful throat! I think it might be flu!'

'Then go *straight* home!' Ursula ordered. 'And don't go near *anyone* in the cast! Lysander and Hermia, please!'

Petra watched while Adam and Victoria played their love scene. ' "One heart, one bed, two bosoms

209

and one troth,"' Lysander said. They were both so convincing. She wished she was playing Hermia. But I will be, she told herself. When we go back to the house I will be his Hermia and no way would she say '"Lie further off. Do not lie so near".' She was filled with desire, yet as nervous as a schoolgirl. Would it be all right? Would she be all he wanted?

CHAPTER FOURTEEN

At the end of the rehearsal, most unusually, no-one seemed inclined to linger. There were none of the customary congratulations, no post-mortems, almost no chatter. Norman Pritchard cleared the stage, Doris Pritchard gathered up her props and locked them in the cupboard assigned to MADS and between them they tidied the place ready for next day's Darby and Joan Club. Long before they had completed this Giles had stamped off without a word to anyone, Ursula watching him anxiously. He was still really upset in spite of getting his way about the table. Supposing—the thought filled her with horror—he threw up the whole thing? She would, she decided, telephone him as soon as she reached home, try to soothe him, calm him down. She blamed Lucinda, of course. Lucinda was a disturbing influence, and not only to Giles.

Petra, putting her design drawings away in her folder, watched Melvin and Victoria slip away together quietly, not saying a word to anyone. Victoria's performance had evoked no criticism, indeed she and Adam were the only ones Ursula had found fit to praise, but Melvin had been at the

receiving end of several sharp comments from
Ursula. His Puck was not quick enough, not light
enough, it lacked fire and mischief. And, unless
Ursula wrought a miracle in him, it always would,
Petra thought. Except in appearance, he was no
Puck, poor lamb.

When she turned her attention away from the
two young ones Adam was by her side.

'Are you ready?' he asked.

There was more in the question than the three
words, delivered in a conversational tone. Are you
ready for what's to happen? Will you keep your
promise? Are you ready to be my lover, let me be
yours?

Petra fastened her folder, her fingers trembling
slightly as she tied the tapes.

'Yes,' she said. 'I'm ready.'

Adam took the folder from her, and held her
lightly by the arm as they left the hall, watched by a
benevolent Doris Pritchard whose hobby in life,
aside from props, was watching other people. Their
leaving was not noticed by a tight-lipped Ursula,
who seldom missed anything but was now
concentrating on Lucinda Rockwell who, in no
hurry to leave, was flirting with Eric.

'Are we going to the pub then?' Lucinda was
asking. 'I fancy a little drinkie, don't you?'

Eric opened his mouth to assent, but Ursula
moved in with the swiftness of an arrow from a
bow.

'I think not this evening, Eric dear! You've had a
long, hard day. Indeed we both have.'

She turned to Lucinda.

'So I'm going to take my old man home, give him
a nice hot toddy, and we shall have an early night.'

'Old man?' Lucinda said archly. 'He looks younger every time I see him! And you don't look the least bit ready for bed!' She paused, gave him a long, slow look. 'Or do you?' she queried.

The hussy! Eric thought. The cheeky little hussy! But the thought was pleasurable. It was quite a time since he'd had two women at daggers drawn over him.

'Well,' he said, 'why not? I think a little drink would do us all good. Relax us!'

Relax was the last thing some people needed, Ursula thought, but she knew Eric. She could push him so far and no further. 'Very well,' she agreed. 'One quick drink!'

She wished she had never started on this remake of Eric. It had been all too successful. But then, she reminded herself, she had done it for MADS. And if tonight's rehearsal was anything to go by, she had a great deal more to do for MADS.

George and Tina left the hall immediately behind Victoria and Melvin but the young ones, Tina could tell, were oblivious of anyone else. Once outside the building she saw Melvin take Victoria's hand in his, clasping it firmly, interlacing his fingers with hers. How wonderful, Tina thought, to be so young, and in love. There was nothing to hide. Unless you wanted to keep it as a delicious secret, you could show it to the whole world, and most of the world would approve, look upon you indulgently. It was different when you were older. Almost always there were complications, and even when there were not, people thought you were silly, old enough to know better. But what was better to know? she thought as she walked along with George towards his car, not taking his arm because they were in public though she longed to touch him, to bring him comfort—what was better to know at any age than that you loved someone and were loved in return?

'I can't go back with you,' she said as George held the door for her to get into the car. 'Daniel will be back from Scouts and I think I ought to be there before he goes off to bed.'

'I understand, love,' George said.

'But I'll tell you what,' Tina said, coming to a sudden decision, 'you could come in for a few minutes, have a cup of coffee or something.'

'Are you sure that would be all right? I mean . . . Daniel.'

'Yes, it would. He knows you're my friend, he knows you're in trouble. He's not unsympathetic.'

'Well, if you're sure. I wouldn't stay long.'

'Just long enough to have a cup of coffee,' Tina said. Where was the harm in that?

'It wasn't the best of rehearsals, was it?' she said. 'Really, Lucinda can be awful. I don't enjoy being her chief attendant one little bit. I can never do anything right—I can't even stand in the right place!'

'I didn't enjoy it,' George admitted. 'People were nice to me at the beginning, but after that it wasn't good. I suppose I shouldn't have gone.'

He hadn't been able to get himself into the mood, he couldn't concentrate. It wasn't that he forgot his lines—there were so few that that was hardly possible—but he forgot where they came in, missed his cues. If there was one thing Ursula couldn't stand it was people missing their cues.

Daniel was sitting at the table, doing his homework when Tina showed George into her home. He had never been there before, nor she to his before Moira's death. George had met Daniel two or three times, at the cricket matches, and once when Daniel had been shopping with his mother in Southfield, but that was all.

The room was bright and warm, cushions on the chairs and pictures on the walls, and on the table a bowl of sweet peas. In spite of the fact that George was nervous, not sure whether he should be there or not, he felt an air of welcome.

Daniel looked up as they entered, not able to hide his surprise.

'I brought George home for a cup of coffee,' Tina explained. 'I thought it might cheer him up.'

Daniel nodded, and smiled.

'You look busy,' George said to Daniel. 'I mustn't interrupt your homework.'

'That's all right,' Daniel said. 'Actually I've just finished.'

'What was it tonight?' Tina asked.

'English. An essay.'

'English was my favourite subject when I was at school,' George said. 'But that's a long time ago. I expect everything's changed.'

'Well, do sit down,' Tina invited. 'I'll go and make the coffee. You'd like a cup, wouldn't you, Daniel?'

'Yes please,' Daniel said. 'Would you like me to make it?'

'No, love. You talk to George.'

What about? George thought anxiously. What have we to talk about? And then he remembered cricket.

'So what do you think's going to happen at Trent Bridge?' he asked. 'Are we going to beat the South

214

Africans or not?'

'I don't know,' Daniel said. 'They've got some good players to choose from. Shaun Pollock, Gary Kirsten—and Hansie Cronje's a great all-rounder.'

'You're right, of course,' George agreed. 'But we can look to Alec Stewart—and Darren Gough should take a few wickets.'

'I wish I could be there,' Daniel said. 'I've never been to a test match.'

An idea sprang at once into George's mind. I'll take him, he thought. One of these days we'll go together. They might even manage the Oval this year.

After that they were well away. Tina had to interrupt them to serve coffee.

Half an hour later George said, 'Well I'll be going. Thank you for your hospitality!' He had no intention of outstaying his welcome, and Tina, sensible woman that she was, he thought, made no move to detain him.

'Goodnight, Daniel,' he said. 'And since neither of us can be at Trent Bridge, remember Mindon should make a good showing on Saturday against Reigate, if you have time to spare from your homework, that is!'

'Oh, I daresay I will,' Daniel said.

Tina saw George to the door. They parted without so much as a handshake, but there was a quiet smile of satisfaction on Tina's face. It had gone well.

*   *   *

Petra's and Adam's short journey from the Parish Hall to Plum Tree House was a silent one. Small talk was impossible and the emotions which hung in the air between them were not to be put into words, though Adam's showed in the way he drove, fast and furious, careless of everything else on the road. He parked his car as always, in the small bay immediately opposite the house, while Petra went and unlocked the door. She was already in the hall when Adam caught up with her. He grabbed her from behind, twisting her around, almost roughly, so that she was facing him, and was in his arms, and he was kissing her, so hard, so long, that in the end she broke away from him, breathless and trembling.

'I'm sorry!' he said. 'It's just that, well, I seem to have been waiting for ever. All through that wretched rehearsal. I thought it would never end, and all I could think of was you and me.'

'I know!' Petra acknowledged. 'It was the same for me.'

Yet even so, now that they were alone, and he had held her close and kissed her until her lips felt bruised, and she had returned his kisses, she felt strangely shy, as if not knowing what the next move was to be.

How can I feel like this? she asked herself. It was ridiculous, as if it was the very first time, as if she was a young girl, a virgin, who had never been down this road before.

'Would you . . .' she spoke hesitantly. 'Would you like something to eat? Shall I cook a meal?'

He stared at her, unbelieving—then burst into laughter, in which, in the end, she joined.

'Food, my darling, is the last thing on my mind! I'll show you what is.'

He took her by the hand and led her up the

stairs, into her bedroom. And closed the door.

He pushed her gently, so that she was sitting on the bed, then, slowly and deliberately, one garment at a time, he took off her clothes. When she tried to help him with a difficult bra fastening, he stopped her.

'No! I want to do it all! Let me!'

When she was completely naked she closed her eyes, knowing that he was looking at her. What would he think, what would he see in her? She was thirty-six, no longer young. She had always been too thin.

He ran his forefinger over parts of her body, the curve of her neck, her hip bone, a thigh, gently stroking her.

'You are beautiful!' he said quietly. 'And now open your eyes. It's your turn!'

She had never undressed a man before. It was something which had just not happened to her. She was a painter herself and for most of her life she had looked with pleasure at the work of great painters, so she knew that a man's body could be beautiful. And she had had lovers. But it had never happened like this, she thought as she looked at Adam lying there. His eyes were closed, as hers had been earlier. Even lying quite still, he was vibrant, he was strong. A small, steady pulse beat in his throat, there were beads of sweat on his upper lip, the hair on his chest was darker and curlier than that on his head. But it was all much more than that, and then she realized that she was looking at him with the eyes of love. Yes, she really did love him.

He opened his eyes.

'And you are beautiful,' Petra said, bending her

217

head to kiss him.

Then they lay together on the bed, their clothes in one heap on the bedroom floor, and made love.

When it was over, Petra lay close in Adam's arms, head on his chest while he stroked her hair.

'Are you all right?' he asked.

She raised herself up so that, propped on one elbow, she looked into his eyes.

'Much more than that,' she said. 'I feel . . . I don't know how to say how I feel. As if everything was suddenly new. I mean everything—the whole of life. As if I was in a new country.' It was an extraordinary sensation, too difficult to verbalize. 'Does that sound ridiculous?' she asked.

'No. It's exactly how I feel. As if I'd found something I didn't even know I'd lost, or I'd never had.'

Nothing, Petra thought, will ever be the same again.

Adam pulled her close and, without any further words, they made love again; as if it was inevitable, nothing else existing except each other, except their own needs and their need to give to the utmost, each to the other.

Afterwards, entwined, they fell asleep.

Petra was the first to waken. Daylight was showing through the curtains, though as yet no sun. Without looking at the clock she judged it to be about five. Adam was lying close, she could feel the heat from his body. As she moved to free her arm, which was trapped beneath his shoulder, bearing his weight, he stirred, and opened his eyes.

'Good morning!' he said.

'Good morning!'

'What time is it?' he asked.

218

Petra twisted around to look at the clock.

'Twenty to five.'

'I'd better go,' Adam said. 'Before the whole of Mindon wakes up.'

Petra shook her head.

'I don't want you to go!'

'People will talk. This is a village, my love. It's inevitable. And it's you they'll talk about.'

'I don't care,' Petra said. 'In fact, I'd be happy for everyone to know. I feel like standing in the middle of the village green and shouting it out loud!'

'What about MADS?'

'What about them?' Petra asked. 'What's it got to do with MADS? Anyway, they're all convinced you're in love with Hermia!'

'Well you know I'm not, and so does she.'

'Anyway, no sneaking away?' Petra said.

'All right! No sneaking away. I'll stay to breakfast. But first I shall make love to you again.'

After that it seemed the most natural thing in the world that they should shower together. It was something outside Petra's experience, but in the last twelve hours she felt she had shed any inhibitions she had ever had. As far as Adam was concerned, she thought, there was nothing that would not be right between them.

'And now I'm going to cook a proper breakfast,' she said. 'I'm hungry! Are you?'

'I am.'

She cooked eggs, bacon, tomatoes, fried up some cold potatoes. They ate steadily through everything, and moved on to toast and marmalade. The idea that love took away the appetite was quite wrong.

She heard the thud of the newspaper falling on the mat, and went to collect it. Back in the kitchen, she dropped it on the table.

'I get *The Times*,' she said. 'What do you usually read? That's another of the things I don't know about you. What newspaper you take, what books you read. Music? Films? So many things!'

'Which we'll have pleasure in finding out,' Adam said. 'I look forward to it, don't you? In fact, I usually read the *Guardian* but I like *The Times*. Its politics aren't mine but it has first-class journalists, so sometimes I buy it.'

'And are you willing to share your daily paper?' Petra asked. 'Or is every page sacred to you? I mean, are you possessive about it?'

'Since this is your paper, delivered to your address, ma'am, I shall be grateful for whatever part you hand over to me.'

'Then that's easy!' Petra said. 'I'm not the least bit interested in this.'

She extracted the sports section and handed it over to him.

'Ah ha! How well we fit together!' Adam said, smiling. 'Jack Sprat and his wife aren't in it.'

He took the sheets from her and was quickly absorbed in them. Petra was pleased that he was cheerful in the mornings—though how often would she have to test that? she wondered. She started on her preliminary skim through the paper, which was her usual way, stopping to read in more detail whenever something interested her. It was strange, considering how healthy she was, how much the medical page attracted her, and of course the arts section, to which she turned now. Her eye was caught at once by a headline: 'Thirty Years of

220

Portrait Drawings'.

She read on. 'This is a small, but interesting exhibition, including work by Judith Somers, John Carson and, in particular, Eliot Frobisher, whose skill in portraying exquisite and sensuous nudes is as great as ever.'

She stopped reading. Bells rang. Somewhere in her mind there was a connection. 'Sensuous nudes' was obvious, but where was the connection?

And then it came to her. The photograph she had found among her mother's things, the three young people and their names on the back, in her mother's writing: 'Marian, Claire and Eliot. 1960'.

Eliot? Could it possibly be . . .? Eliot, as a first name, was surely not common, certainly she had never come across it before. The name Frobisher rang no bells. It could be because, living her sheltered life in North Yorkshire, she had not bothered to follow the trends, indeed she had never set foot in a London gallery. Possibly, also, Eliot Frobisher had never penetrated the North. It was also possible, she faced the fact, that the man had nothing whatever to do with the drawings in her possession. But if she were to see his work, she would know. She was certain of that.

She looked across at Adam.

'Listen!' she said. 'There's something here I'd like to go to!' She handed the paper across to him. 'That bit there! "Thirty Years of Portrait Drawings".'

'Why?' Adam asked. 'I mean why this one? Why not the National Portrait Gallery, for instance?'

'Look at the names of the exhibitors. Eliot Frobisher.'

'Do you know him?'

'No, but read what it says. "Exquisite and sensuous nudes". It *could* be, it just *could* be, the man who made the drawings of my mother. The description certainly fits, and I have the initials E. F. on the back of the drawings. How many men do you know whose first name is "Eliot"?'

'None!' Adam admitted.

'I'd know as soon as I saw his drawings in the exhibition,' Petra said eagerly. 'I'd recognize the style. It's something . . . well, something special.'

'So you want to go?'

'I do!' Petra said. 'I *could* go on my own—and I will if I have to—but I'd like it if we could go together. I've never been to London, only passed through it on my way from King's Cross to Victoria.'

'I don't see why I shouldn't,' Adam agreed. 'I don't go to London often enough.'

'Wonderful!' Petra said. 'Let's fix a date. The exhibition starts next Thursday, so how about if we went on Saturday?'

'Suits me!' Adam said. 'We'll make a day of it. Go to the theatre if you like!'

*   *   *

Ursula waved off Eric to work with a sigh of relief. It had not been the happiest of breakfasts. His conversation had consisted of a series of grunts except when he stated emphatically that there was no way he could look a boiled egg in the face, thank you.

Come to that, she had not really known a happy moment since the start of yesterday evening's awful rehearsal. She was not inclined to blame anyone else for the quality of the rehearsal. She was the producer and in the end it was up to her, though she doubted if even God himself could make some of them learn their lines. All the same, she was worried. Was she losing her touch?

She shuddered at the memory of the Queen's Head. Far from having the one drink, and a quick getaway, as she had confidently planned, Eric had refused to move until the bell had rung for closing time and they had been turned out with the rest. The ignominy of it had made her hot with shame, though not as hot as Eric, flushed to the eyeballs with a succession of double whiskies and the close attention of that alley cat, Lucinda.

Lucinda herself, though gin and tonics had disappeared down her throat like bathwater down a plug hole, had remained relatively sober, except for a tendency to require someone (Eric) to lean on, and an ever-increasing flow of sexual innuendo which Eric had lapped up. Fortunately, Ursula thought, *I*, remembering my responsibilities, not to mention my standing in the community, stuck to tonic water—or how would we have got home?

Of course they had had to take Lucinda home first, there was no getting out of it, but Eric was 'sleepy'—a kind way of putting it—and had not demurred when Ursula had seen Lucinda swiftly out of the car and had driven off before she had so much as put her key in the lock.

Eric had walked—staggered?—straight upstairs to bed. Indeed, but for Ursula who had followed close behind him, he might not even have bothered to undress, but she had been adamant about that.

'If the Lady Lucinda could see you now,' Ursula had said, 'she might think differently! You would be about as much use as a wet sponge!' She doubted if he heard her. He was on the opening bars of a grand concerto of snoring.

She, on the other hand, had stayed awake well into the night, and had awakened early this morning. It was a situation she had to take seriously, she had to resolve it. The thought that she might actually lose her faithful old Eric was not to be borne. Even to lose him to a temporary fling would be humiliating. She could imagine the snide remarks, the giggles, how Lucinda would crow, how her own authority in MADS would be undermined, but the thought that she might lose him permanently—and she would not put anything past Lucinda—was devastating. When all was said and done, she loved Eric. He might not be everyone's cup of tea (though clearly he was Lucinda's) but he was *her's*.

Was all her care for Eric to go down the drain? Was she making a mountain out of a molehill? Whatever it was, she thought in a mixed metaphoric rush to the brain, she would prepare for battle and nip it in the bud!

So what does that tart have that I haven't? she asked herself. Well, certainly nothing in the brain department. Low cunning, certainly, but culture, intelligence, learning—no, none of that. But then, was any of that what Eric was looking for? Apparently not—which brought it down to the purely physical. And here, she determined, I will be quite ruthless with myself.

She took a shower and went back to the bedroom. There she studied herself critically in the full-length mirror. She could hardly remember when she had last seen herself in the nude.

224

She saw a short woman with quite good legs. Not long enough, but shapely, with slender ankles. Moving upwards, she was nowhere fat but she was undeniably saggy, especially around the stomach area, and her hips were beginning to spread. She took a deep breath and held her stomach taut. Yes, something could be done about that!

Her waist had hardly suffered at all, no doubt because she had not indulged in having children. It was still reasonably slim. But travelling upwards—ah, there was the problem! She had practically no bust to speak of, which was not something which could be said of Lucinda (as everyone, from the cut of her necklines, could see for themselves). How, Ursula thought sadly, could her own 34A cup compete with Lucinda's 38DD (at least!)? She had hitherto considered a small bust rather refined and an overlarge one vulgar, but men, she told herself—even her silly old Eric—clearly preferred vulgarity.

She was, by now, too depressed to look farther, though she made a mental note to do something about having her hair cut. Really, it was all too silly, except that Eric was worth fighting for, and fight she would.

'What shall I do?' She asked the question out loud to her reflection in the mirror. What she needed was a different shape, especially in the bust department.

She went downstairs and made another cup of coffee, her mind going around in circles until at last the bright idea came to her. What about one of those exercise videos which promised to give one a completely new body in no time at all, if only one stuck at it? Well, if that proved to be the answer,

225

stick at it she would. She had every incentive to do so.

Nor would she tell a soul. It was something she could do in the privacy of her own home. No way would she go to a gym and do it all in public, though that was all the fashion of course. You were not in the swim if you didn't spend a couple of hours every day 'working out'—whatever that was—but it was not her style, cavorting around, getting into a sweat in front of others. No, she would not even tell Eric. It would all take place while he was at the office. And she would specifically look for a regime which promised to firm the stomach and enhance the bust. All Eric would see of it would be the results.

Fifteen minutes later she was at the wheel of her BMW, driving towards Southfield.

CHAPTER FIFTEEN

Ursula had no difficulty in finding a suitable video. Indeed, she would have found it even sooner had she not, determined to leave no stone unturned, visited Boots, W. H. Smith, Virgin and at least two smaller shops before making a choice from a wide selection. Half the inhabitants of Southfield and surrounding areas must be seeking to improve their physique.

She chose one which promised to reshape the figure rather than simply to slim it down. A redistribution of her body's assets and liabilities was how she saw her needs.

That purchase made, she next sought and found

a sports shop, something until now beyond her ken. She had always prided herself on being an intellectual rather than a sporty type. However, the blurb on the video box strongly advised wearing the correct outfit for the exercises, and also recommended the use of weights, all to be found in a specialist shop. She bought a leotard—black—and some exercise shoes, the latter both ugly and expensive to her way of thinking but highly praised by the young salesman who, tall, muscular in all the right places (as far as she could see), glowing with health and fitness, was a living, speaking testimonial to his wares. He was also extremely attentive. In fact he could have persuaded her to part with her last penny. What a wonderful Demetrius *he* would have made!

These were all the purchases she would allow herself this morning. Even dear old Marks & Spencer must be given a miss today. Far more important things awaited her in Mindon. She walked briskly to the car-park, collected her car and drove above the limit all the way home.

Back in the house she marched straight up the stairs to her bedroom, pausing only to switch over to the ansaphone. No telephone call would be taken by her for the next hour.

She unpacked her purchases on to the bed and began to change into her new uniform. The leotard first! It fitted quite closely, as presumably it was supposed to, so that her shape was clearly defined.

I am not really too fat, she thought, viewing herself in the mirror through narrowed eyes. It is just that I am too plump—well *plumpish*—in some places and too skinny in others, and neither one nor the other in the right place. If by some magic

227

she could transfer the roll of flesh which had settled—almost unnoticed, when had it happened?—around her abdomen and transfer it to her breasts, which showed no more than a couple of minimal bulges under the leotard, then all would be well. And why didn't one's body do this of its own accord?

She put on her exercise shoes, tied back her hair as if she was about to train as a ballet dancer, and had picked up the video before she remembered that the machine was in the sitting room. She collected the weights—dear little things they were, so compact, so much more interesting than two bags of dried beans which the notes on the video box had suggested would do almost as well—and went downstairs.

For the very first time she regretted, as she walked into the room, the great sheet of glass which was the window, especially since today was the gardener's day, and right now there he was, walking up and down pushing the lawnmower. After that, it was his invariable pattern to work on the flower beds nearest the house. Too excited, she had not noticed him when she came back from shopping, and now she was in no state of dress, at least not for Arnold, to go out and suggest he should work in another part of the garden. Nor had she any choice as to where she would stand to do the exercises. She must be in close proximity to the sight and sound of the video. If she tried to move the machine she knew quite well that the wires would fall out, and that would be that. It had happened before. She was not into wires and plugs and suchlike mysteries.

No, she would have to draw the curtains, which

228

would seem quite odd to Arnold because it was a greyish day with no sun, but never mind. She crept up to the curtain and, hiding behind it as she moved, drew it halfway across the window. Then, with a quick intake of breath due to unaccustomed excitement, she inserted the video and switched on.

There was an immediate blast of loud music with a strong beat and then, seconds later, a woman emerged from the back of the scene and walked forward until she was now more or less right there in Ursula's sitting room. And dominating it. She had big hair, blond as the sunshine and not a lock out of place. Her large blue eyes looked straight into Ursula's and she opened her mouth in a yard-wide flash of perfect teeth. She was dressed in a leotard, though the name was all it had in common with Ursula's modest little black number. It was emblazoned with sequinned motifs over a pink base, legs cut high, front cut low, over a figure voluptuously perfect in every detail.

Are we to believe, Ursula wondered, that this figure has been achieved as a result of this woman following her own exercises?

'Hell-*o*!' the vision said. 'I'm Honey Lander! We're going to do great things together! I just know we are!'

Her voice did not match with her appearance. It was light, sing-song, rather nasal, with an accent which Ursula could only guess might be Scouse combined with West Midlands overlaid with transatlantic. Still, she sounded friendly.

'First, sit down and relax,' she invited, 'while I tell you about the programme!'

Ursula was happy to obey. Furthermore, she decided, she would watch quite a bit of the video, get some idea of what it was like before going back to the beginning and joining in. She chose a handy, exceedingly comfortable chair and leaned back.

Honey's voice triumphed over the insistent beat of the music as if someone had turned up a volume control knob in the middle of her back. She had now finished her introductory spiel and was starting the exercises, performing every movement, bending, stretching, turning, twisting, and all, it seemed to Ursula, without taking a breath, even though she talked unceasingly through every movement.

'And—one—two—three   and—bend—that—knee; and—arms—held—high, and—touch—the—sky. And—now—we—lunge   and—take—the—plunge, and—six—and—seven we—reach—to—heaven!'

It was amazingly soporific, almost like a lullaby. The chair was comfy. Ursula felt her eyelids droop.

It might not have been more than a minute or two later—would she ever know?—when she became aware that Honey was introducing another session.

'And now the bosom!' she was saying. 'A firm bosom is both fashionable and healthy. Firmness is all!'

'Oh no it's not!' Ursula cried, jumping out of the chair. 'Size is all!'

How could anyone fall asleep while taking part in an exercise routine? Annoyed with herself, she stood, feet apart as instructed, waiting for the take-off.

She began well enough, raising her arms, circling backwards, trying (unsuccessfully, but then could anyone *ever* do it?) to make her elbows meet in the middle of her back. The reason it all went to pieces was because she faltered on the rhythm and missed a few movements while Honey and the music forged inexorably ahead. There was no way, Ursula soon realized, she would ever catch up. The only thing was to call a halt, watch carefully, then slot in again. This might have worked well except that on the very instant she was about to take the plunge the telephone rang. Of course there was no way she would answer it, she had switched on the ansaphone, but the shrill interruption threw her and she was lost again. Well and truly this time. It was a whole new set of movements and there was no way she could break in.

She sat in the chair and watched the rest of the bust exercises which, she decided, she would try to memorize and do later on her own.

'Bottoms and thighs!' Honey announced presently. 'Which one of us doesn't need to do something about our bottoms and thighs?'

'Well, I'm not sure that I do,' Ursula said, 'but I'll give it a go!' She was already answering Honey out loud as if she was truly in the room with her. She felt guilty that she had fallen down on the previous set, as though at the end of the session Honey would give her marks out of ten.

Perversely, she did better with the bottom and thigh exercises, clenching and releasing her buttocks, running on the spot, high stepping with her legs like a well-bred carriage horse. She was well away, and would have gone through to the end had there not been a long, insistent ring on the front doorbell.

Who could it be? Not Arnold, who only ever used the back door. She was not expecting anyone.

Ignore it!

A disturbing thought came to her. Supposing, just supposing, that for some grave reason Eric had returned home in the middle of the day—and without his key? What should she do? If she didn't go to the door he might assume she was out, but what if it was something really serious? Then the bell rang again, longer this time, as if the person whose finger was on the bell-push knew perfectly well that the lady of the house was hiding in there.

Swiftly, Ursula switched off the recorder, extracted the video and replaced it in its box, which she hid at the back of a bookshelf, then she rushed to answer the door, not remembering her state of dress.

'I'm collecting the Red Cross envelopes, Ursula!' the woman at the door said pleasantly.

'Oh, Jane, it's you! I'm sorry! I can't find mine. In any case, I send a regular donation.'

Jane was not listening. Her gaze was fixed on Ursula, flushed of face, slightly sweating, clad in her leotard and exercise shoes.

I shall give her no explanation, Ursula decided. She can make of it what she will. She was just thankful it hadn't been Eric. She watched Jane retreat down the drive, then closed the door and went to check on the ansaphone. It was Amelia.

'I'm ever so sorry, Ursula, but little Emma has come out in a rash. I think it could be measles. It's going around and she has a runny nose and she's quite flushed, poor love. So I'm afraid she won't be able to come to rehearsals for the time being. Nor Teresa just in case. Nor me, of course. They'll need me. I'm ever so sorry. They were really enjoying being fairies.'

'Damn!' Ursula said. 'Damn and blast!'

She could rely on no-one. How could Amelia be so careless as to let her children catch measles at a time like this? She felt it as a personal insult.

She went upstairs to change her clothes. She was dispirited, tired, sweaty and still out of breath. And this had been only the first of several sessions with the video. If only, she thought, if only she'd chosen to produce J. B. Priestley instead of the *Dream* none of this would have happened. Eric would have fitted in perfectly as one of the husbands celebrating the wedding anniversary. He would have needed no make-over. Also she would not have had to cast Lucinda at all. I am a victim of my own ambition, she acknowledged. Except, of course, that she had done it not for herself, but for MADS. And, indeed, for Mindon.

*   *   *

The inquest on Moira had been fixed for Friday, George told Tina on the telephone, which meant that if all went well the funeral could take place on the following Monday.

'And there's no reason why it shouldn't go well,' he said. 'It's just a formality.'

All the same, Tina thought, she would be glad when it was over, and the funeral also, especially for George's sake.

As far as he knew, there would be no-one at the funeral. 'Unless any of the hospital staff attend,' he said. He thought it was unlikely. Moira had not been popular, not—as far as he knew—because of any wrongdoing, but because she had kept herself to herself to an extraordinary degree. She had, he believed, rebuffed any attempt at friendship. At home she had never talked about her colleagues and he knew none of them by name.

'In spite of everything, I do feel sorry,' Tina said. 'It must be awful, no-one at your funeral. But I can't very well come, can I? It wouldn't look right at all.' She didn't think she could even send flowers.

'Of course not,' George agreed.

Not a word had been said between them as to what might or might not happen after the funeral. While Moira was not yet buried, or in her case cremated, it seemed impossible to speak. It was too delicate. Indeed, they seemed at a greater distance from each other now than they had been when Moira was alive. Her death had separated them rather than brought them together.

'But I'm going back to work tomorrow,' George said. 'I can't just hang around and there's nothing more I can do. So I'll pick you up at half-past eight in the morning, as usual.'

Tina demurred. 'Are you sure?'

'Of course I'm sure,' George said. 'There's no reason whatever why I shouldn't give you your usual lift to work. *And* I'll come to rehearsals.'

'That will please Ursula,' Tina said.

But she wouldn't ask him back for coffee, not until after the funeral, perhaps not until a decent interval afterwards. Insofar as she could, she wanted to do the right thing. And she had Daniel to consider, perhaps more than ever now. She would need to talk to him.

'Very well, George,' she said. 'If you're sure. I'll be looking out for you.'

* * *

Ursula had decreed that Friday's rehearsal, the evening before Adam and Petra planned to go to London, was to be for everyone except the four lovers. They were the ones who were doing well; they had learnt their lines and they knew their moves. 'Which *cannot* be said for all of you!' she declared. 'Therefore I shall concentrate on licking the rest of you into shape.'

'I hope you are not including me in your remarks?' Giles said.

'Of course not, dear!' Ursula said. 'But I need you to be there for the others, to show them what *can* be done.'

'So we're free on Friday,' Adam said to Petra as they left the hall. 'I take it you don't have to show up?'

'No,' Petra said. 'In any case, I don't need to go to every rehearsal.' Sometimes she went simply because Adam would be there.

'Then why don't we do something nice?' Adam suggested. 'Why don't we drive out into the country and have a meal?'

They chose, or rather Adam did for Petra knew nothing of it, The George Inn, at Crowdean, a village just over the border into Sussex. The pub was an old-fashioned place, with a dark little bar, crowded on this summer Friday evening.

'Your table will be free in fifteen minutes,' the waiter said. 'We're a little behind, very busy as you can see. Perhaps you'd like to study the menu and have a drink while you wait?'

In the end, there were so many tempting dishes, Adam chose sea bass and Petra rack of lamb.

'It's the first time I've given you a meal,' Adam said as they sipped their drinks. 'You always do it for me. I'm sure I ought to ask you to my flat, and I will, but as I think I told you, I'm no cook.'

'We did very nicely from Marks & Spencer as I recall,' Petra said. 'But I'm happy either way.' The truth was she simply wanted to be with him.

They sat a long time over the meal. The waiter was attentive, but in no way did he hurry them, so that in the end they were the last to leave.

'What now?' Adam asked.

'Stay with me,' Petra said as they drove away. 'Don't go home. You don't want to, do you?'

'I don't,' Adam said. 'Are you sure?'

'Positive.'

They made an early start next morning, driving into Southfield to catch the London train.

'The last time I made this journey, though in reverse, I was coming to live in Mindon.'

'And what did you think?' Adam asked.

'I was very apprehensive.'

She had not, by any means, been sure that she was doing the right thing. On that occasion she had taken in very little of the landscape through which they'd passed. Her mind had been too full of other things. Would it work? Should she have stayed where she was, where everything was familiar—the people, the accent, the shape of the hills, the river—all the things which had always been with her. Now, it all seemed an age ago and another country.

'I'm glad I came!' she said suddenly. 'I don't mean this morning, I mean to Mindon.'

'And so am I,' Adam replied. 'I feel as if I have known you a long, long time.'

'Me too!' she said. 'And I'm looking forward to today. I expect you know London well?'

'Reasonably. I know the area where the gallery is, Duke Street, and so on.'

*　　　*　　　*

They took a cab from Victoria. 'Though we could well have walked,' Adam said as they were dropped at the door. 'It's not that far.'

They stood outside the gallery, looking in the window, which was small and held only three paintings on easels, all landscapes. But for a discreet card in the corner of the window, announcing the exhibition, Petra thought they might well have decided they'd come to the wrong place, and when they entered everything seemed equally low-key. Two or three people hovered at the far end of a long room, and quite close to the entrance an impeccably groomed young woman sat at a leather-topped desk, engaged in a telephone call. She paused briefly as Adam and Petra stood before her.

'Good morning,' she said pleasantly.

'We've come to see the portrait drawings,' Petra told her.

'Ah, yes! They're in the small gallery. Go through this one, and take the stairs at the end. I'll be with you when I've finished this call.'

'What will you do?' Adam asked Petra as they walked through the first gallery. 'What will you do if you decide that Eliot Frobisher is the artist you're looking for?'

'I don't quite know,' Petra admitted. 'I haven't thought that far ahead. I shall play it by ear.'

They climbed the stairs, steep, twisted and narrow and leading at the top, without any door, straight into a gallery which in turn led through a wide arch into a second room.

Petra, a yard or so away from the top of the stairs, stood still and looked.

'Damn!' she said. 'She didn't give us a catalogue or a list. How do we know what we're looking at?'

'Good point!' Adam said. 'I'll nip down and get one.'

He was forestalled by the woman from the front desk, now halfway up the stairs.

'I'm sorry to leave you to find your own way,' she said. 'It was quite an important telephone call. However, my relief has turned up, so I'm ready to help you if you wish. Are you looking for anything especially?'

'We'd like to have a general look around,' Petra said, 'but we're also interested in an artist by the name of Eliot Frobisher.'

'Eliot Frobisher's work is in the second gallery,' the woman said. 'Through the arch. Oh, and I've brought you the catalogue. It's not a large exhibition, as you will see, but there's some very nice work. So I'll leave you to it. And if you have any queries I have work to do up here, so I'll be on hand.' She took a seat at a desk in a corner of the first room.

'What she means,' Adam said quietly as they moved away, 'is that no way is she going to leave two strangers alone up here. And who can blame her?'

Petra made no reply. She was searching through the catalogue for Eliot Frobisher's name. As she turned the pages she realized that her hands were trembling.

'Here we are!' she said. 'Numbers twenty-three to twenty-six. Only four. I'd hoped there might have been more, but four will probably be enough.'

They found them quickly and stood in front of them. Two of female nudes, two of buildings with people standing in front of them, not especially posed, just caught almost in passing.

'I'd know the buildings,' Adam said, 'even if it didn't name them, which it does. Number twenty-five is the west front of Bath Abbey and number twenty-six is the entrance to the Pump Room in Bath.'

On the last, the entrance to the Pump Room, though beautifully drawn, was no more than a background which gave a setting to the chief character standing in front of it: a juggler, tall, slender, lithe, in fancy costume, five balls above him in the air. All the artist's attention was on the juggler. The group of spectators was sketchily drawn, no details.

Petra's attention was on the nudes. No names given, of course. The first had her back to the artist, the second faced him, though not much face since her head was turned away and a curtain of hair obscured what little there was of her features. It was that, as much as anything, which convinced Petra. An artist who drew women's bodies as if he revered, almost worshipped them, but who fell short of depicting their faces, their true identity remaining hidden.

'It is!' she said. 'I'm sure it is!' Her voice was almost a whisper as she stood there, staring at the drawings, drinking them in, absorbing every line. Nevertheless . . .

She had brought the drawing with her—the first one, which she had found in her parents' home, not the second, which she might have been obliged to show around while trying to establish an identity. It was too intimate for that. She had chosen to bring the largest handbag, short of her briefcase, so as not to damage the drawing in any way, and it was from this that she now extracted the drawing, and stepped closer to compare it with the ones on the wall.

If there had been any doubt before, there was none now. The nudes on the wall were two different bodies, and the drawing of her mother yet another, but there was no mistaking that the same eye had seen them and the same hand drawn them. Even to Adam, standing beside Petra now, knowing little of such things, it was apparent.

'Incredible!' he said. 'And there's no mistaking it. Even I can tell that!'

There was a low bench in the room and they sat down on it, facing the drawings. For a little while nothing more was said, then Adam spoke.

'What are you going to do?'

'I'm going to get in touch with Eliot Frobisher,' Petra said. 'I just want *his* confirmation and, if he'll tell me, when and where—in what circumstances he made the drawings. Where they fit in.'

'Have you thought that he might not want to tell you?' Adam said gently. 'You're asking him to tell you about something which he probably counts as private to himself.'

'I know,' Petra agreed. 'I have considered that. I realize I have to be tactful. Perhaps I'll tell him that my mother has died, and it seems to me he might have been one of her friends. If he's in London, or

240

I can go wherever he lives, we might meet for a few minutes.'

'Are you sure about all this?' Adam asked. 'Now that you're certain who did the drawings, is there anything more you need to know?'

'Perhaps not *need*, but want to desperately. And I can't tell you why because I don't know myself. In fact it is a need, though an emotional rather than a practical one.'

'Having come so far,' Adam suggested, 'having found out the most important thing you wanted to know, wouldn't it be best just to leave it at that?'

'No. It's having come so far that makes me want to go further,' Petra explained. 'If I'd come up against a blank wall then I suppose I'd have let it drop.'

'Then do think rather carefully about it.'

'I will, I am. I'm going to start by asking here if they know his address. That can't do any harm.'

At that moment the woman walked towards them.

'You've found what you were looking for, I see! They're rather nice, aren't they? Have you a special interest in them?'

'I have, actually,' Petra confessed. 'I have drawings of my late mother which I'm now quite sure were done by Eliot Frobisher. Look at this!' she handed the drawing over. The woman compared it carefully with the exhibits.

'Why, yes! I think you're right,' she agreed.

'For that reason I really would like to get in touch with him. I wonder if you could possibly give me his address?'

The woman shook her head.

'I'm afraid I couldn't do that. It's a strict rule we

241

don't divulge personal details. All his business with the gallery is done through his agent, and nor can I give you his address. In any case, as you will see from the catalogue, these drawings are not for sale.'

'Do you know Mr Frobisher?' Adam asked.

'Not really,' the woman replied. 'I've met him once, he's exhibited here before. He doesn't often come up to town.'

'He seems fond of drawing Bath,' Adam observed.

'Yes, he is rather,' the woman conceded.

Petra broke in quickly.

'Do you suppose he lives in Bath?'

The woman looked at her steadily before replying.

'As I've said, I can't tell you where he lives. You must draw your own conclusions.' She started to move away, then hesitated, and came back, moved by the disappointment in Petra's face.

'I suppose what I *could* do,' she said, though doubtfully, 'I suppose if you'd like to leave me your name and address I could pass it on to Eliot Frobisher through his agent. It would be up to him then. But if it's of any help . . .'

'Thank you,' Petra said. 'It might well be.'

She took a small sketch pad from her handbag, wrote down the necessary details and added, briefly, her reason for wishing to contact him.

'I'll do what I can,' the woman promised.

'And now shall we look at the rest of the exhibition?' Adam suggested.

'First, I'd like one more look at the drawings,' Petra said.

She stood in front of them for several minutes,

conscious that Adam wished to move on but not wanting to tear herself away.

In the end she moved. But I *will* find him, she told herself. She had little faith in the message she had left for the agent, but it hardly mattered. In any case it would take too long. She was impatient. She would find him of her own accord, she didn't know how or where, but she would do it.

CHAPTER SIXTEEN

They left the gallery soon afterwards. Petra could not concentrate on the other exhibits, she was too excited, her mind too full of other matters. What would she do next? Did she want to wait for Eliot Frobisher to get in touch with her—if indeed he would do so—or would she make the first move? Whatever that was.

'I think I shall go to Bath!' she said as they walked up to Jermyn Street and through to Piccadilly. 'And the sooner the better. I don't want to hang around. I don't want to wait for a reply which might never come.'

Adam protested. 'You don't even know that Bath is the place! All you're going on is a couple of drawings. For all we know the man might live in the North of Scotland or the South of France. There's simply no way of telling.'

'I have a feeling about it,' Petra said. 'Besides, if you were right about that I'm sure the woman in the gallery would have been kind enough to put me off Bath. In any case I have to start somewhere.'

'No you don't! You don't have to start at all. And

in the unlikely event that you track this man down, how do you know he'll see you? Why should he tell you anything?'

'Because he knew my mother,' Petra said obstinately.

'Which might be one very good reason why he *wouldn't* want to! Why not wait to hear from him?'

They were walking along Piccadilly, towards Hyde Park. Petra, who had never walked in London before, took no notice of her surroundings, saw nothing. She could have been in any city in the world, it would have made no difference.

Adam turned north, walked with familiarity through a series of streets then stopped outside a small Italian restaurant.

'I think we'll have lunch,' he said, taking her arm and marching her in.

'I'm not very hungry,' Petra demurred.

'Well I am. And so should you be. Did you have any breakfast?' he asked.

He sensed a slight distance between himself and Petra. It was not, he thought, that she had anything against him. It was rather that she had this bee in her bonnet about Eliot Frobisher. He saw no sign that he could talk her out of it, though he might try. She was an independently minded woman, it was one of the things he admired about her, and it was clear that in this she would have her own way.

'A bowl of cornflakes,' Petra said.

It was early for lunch. They had the choice of tables and settled for one in the window.

'I know this place,' Adam said. 'They do an excellent rigatoni, if you happen to like it, but there's lots of choice.' He handed her the menu.

'Then the rigatoni is what I'll have.' She handed

back the menu, unread.

While they waited for the meal to be served they drank a glass of wine.

'Are you really set on going to Bath on this wild-goose chase?' Adam asked.

'I'm sorry, I am,' Petra said. 'And even if it does turn out to be a wild-goose chase, at least I'll have made the effort.'

'Very well then,' Adam said. 'I'll go with you!'

'Oh, Adam!' Petra gave him the happiest of smiles. 'Will you really? You are kind. Are you sure?'

'I'm sure. I think you're mad, but I'll join you in your madness. When?'

'The first possible moment,' Petra said. She was all eagerness. 'Early next week!'

'Wait a minute,' Adam said. 'You know I can't make it next week. It's the Dublin Conference. I told you I'd be away for three days. Had you forgotten?'

'I'm sorry,' Petra said. 'I had, at least for the moment. Must you go?'

'Yes I must. You know how it is—no, I suppose you don't—the long vacation is always conference time. I'm lucky to have only this one, but no way can I duck it. I'm presenting a paper. But we can go to Bath the following week.'

'I don't want to wait so long,' Petra objected.

'But I've explained.'

'I know. And I quite see that, but I can go to Bath on my own, as I intended. Of course it would be much nicer if you were with me, but it can't be helped. I'll go to Bath while you're in Dublin. I daresay I'll drive there and back in a day, but if necessary I'll stay one night.'

'Why can't you wait?' Adam demanded. 'There's no set date for going to Bath.'

'There is for me,' Petra said firmly. 'In any case, what would Ursula say if you missed rehearsals two weeks in succession? Does she know about Dublin?'

'Damn Ursula! And yes, she does know. But Ursula doesn't run my life!'

'Oh yes she does!' Petra contradicted. 'She runs all our lives at the moment, but mine less than yours. Anyway, that's what we'll do. You go to Dublin and I'll go to Bath. I'll be there and back before you return.'

*   *   *

Having decided to go to Bath on Monday morning, Petra telephoned Ursula.

'. . . so I shan't be at Monday's rehearsal, and just possibly not Tuesday's,' she said. 'But I will be there for certain on Wednesday evening.'

Except for Saturdays and Sundays, which up to now were still sacrosanct, there were rehearsals almost every evening, and who knew how soon Sunday afternoons would be commandeered? It was only out of respect for the vicar that Sunday mornings and evenings had not been invaded. He had let it be known in what for him was a firm manner that he would view with great disfavour anything which might take place at the same time as the ten o'clock parish Eucharist and the six-thirty Evensong. Even so, Ursula had marked out in her mind Sunday evenings from seven-thirty onwards should it become necessary. As, she thought, the way things were going, it most certainly would.

By now the small fairies' measles were sweeping like a forest fire through the Brownie pack, knocking on the head any thought of replacements from that source. George had absented himself on the evening of his wife's funeral, saying it would be disrespectful not to do so, especially as his part in the play was a comic one. Cyril had totally lost his voice for several days and without the strength of Bottom the Mechanicals were no more than shadows of themselves. And though the vicar had attended punctiliously, she had had no success in getting him to speak in anything other than his usual cultured tones. She was stuck with an upper-class, public-school Mechanical.

And next week Adam, and now, it seemed, Petra. Sometimes it seemed to Ursula that the only one who could be relied upon to turn up regularly and in rude health—and 'rude' was the right word, though brazen would be even better—was Lucinda. I would not go quite so far, Ursula thought, as to fashion a wax image and stick pins in it in incapacitating (though of course not fatal) places, but if the tart were to sustain a minor injury which would render her unfit to play the Queen of the Fairies I would not grieve too much. I would simply play the part myself. But Titania went unscathed, not even catching measles from her attendant fairies.

Of course—Ursula faced the fact—if Lucinda were to break a leg she would play the part in crutches, thus attracting even more attention.

'Oh dear!' Ursula said tragically into the telephone.

'You don't really need me every rehearsal,' Petra

247

pointed out.

'We are *all* needed, every single minute of rehearsal time!' Ursula said. 'When one is missing, it weakens the whole!'

'But I don't even have a part,' Petra said.

'You are responsible for the sets—'

'Which are finished,' Petra interrupted.

'And for all the costumes! And now that Amelia, being careless enough to let her children catch measles, has fallen by the wayside . . .'

'Oh, don't worry about that!' Petra said. 'Amelia and I will see to them between us. I'll pop in and see her as soon as I'm back from Bath—'

'No! No, no!' Ursula cried. 'You must not go *near*! Amelia's house is totally out of bounds! Who knows what you might carry back with you, and give to the rest of us?'

'Oh, I don't think there's much danger,' Petra said. 'But I'll speak to you again when I get back.'

'Bath, did you say?' Ursula enquired.

'Yes.'

'I don't think you'll like it at this time of the year. It will be full of tourists. Americans.'

'I'll be fine!' Petra assured her.

'And Adam. Where's he off to?'

'Not Bath,' Petra said. 'Dublin. A conference. He said he told you.'

'I don't know why these academics are always going to conferences. What do they *do* there?'

'I don't know,' Petra said. 'Anyway, I must say goodbye. I think that was the doorbell.'

Ursula sighed as Petra's phone clicked into silence. She would have welcomed a nice long talk, she had several more woes to relate. Now she would have no further excuse not to switch on the

248

video and get on with her exercises. She had already been in her leotard when Petra rang.

Not that they were doing any good. There was no visible difference, at least not to her bust. Her thighs ached, her back ached and the pain in her shoulders was cruel. In addition she was stiff all over. She was undoubtedly using muscles which had been out of action for years and had no wish to be aroused.

Eric had noticed her stiffness. 'A touch of arthritis, dear?' he'd said sympathetically. 'Well, we're not getting any younger, are we? You should rest more!'

Most of all, she thought as she switched on the video and Honey bounded into the room, she hated this woman with her blond hair and sequinned leotard. She reminded her too much of Lucinda, especially in her abundant energy and her all-too-evident bust.

The visits to the Queen's Head after rehearsals were getting too regular. Not that they didn't all go, or most of them. They did. Jennie Austin was now a regular. Goodness knew what her mother thought. Actually, her acting had improved by leaps and bounds, she was now full of confidence. Indeed, she was one of the few players about whom Ursula had no qualms, none at all. As long as she kept well, of course. I made a good choice there, Ursula congratulated herself.

Hermia and Puck were as close as could be. Melvin was doing much better as Puck. She rather suspected that Vicky put him through his paces away from rehearsals. They were nice young things. Ursula felt quite pleased that she had brought them together.

The trouble was, the Queen's Head was just not her scene. Not that anyone drank too much, they didn't, but she preferred to go home, though there was no way she could leave Eric to Lucinda's wiles. Nor would she protest. The last thing she would think of doing would be to let Eric know she was the least bit worried.

She settled into the exercises. Mostly now she managed to keep up, not lose her place, but they bored her, they bored her and irritated her almost to screaming point. Knees bend, waist twist, shoulders back, arms raise. 'And now,' said Honey, 'I want you to take a cushion, a nice, firm cushion . . .'

Ursula picked up a cushion from the sofa and threw it with all her might at the television screen, right in the smiling face of Honey.

'Sod you!' she shouted. 'Sod you, you silly bitch! Get out of my room!'

She would like to have thrown one of the neat little weights which lay to hand on the floor beside her. And she would, she thought, if she could have explained to Eric when he came home why the television screen was smashed to pieces.

As it was the cushion hit the screen, doing no harm whatsoever before falling softly to the floor. Honey's voice continued. 'There! I'm sure we all feel better for that!'

'Sod you, we do not!' Ursula yelled—and ran out of the room, slamming the door behind her.

*   *   *

At the moment Petra wakened on Monday morning it felt like any other day, and then she

250

remembered it was not, and jumped out of bed. This was the day she was going to Bath where, if he was there at all, she would find Eliot Frobisher. And if he was not—well, she would meet that when she came to it. She had seen Adam yesterday. They had driven out into the country, then left the car and gone for a long walk over the Surrey hills. He had tried hard to persuade her not to go to Bath, or at least not to go yet.

'Wait until I come back from Dublin,' he'd said. 'Wait until I can go with you. Suddenly I don't like the thought of you going anywhere without me!'

She'd been touched by that.

'I don't know Bath,' she'd admitted, 'but it's always sounded safe and respectable to me. I'm going with one purpose in mind, as you well know.'

'And what will you do if you don't find this man, which is more than likely?' Adam had asked.

'If I haven't tried everything I shall book into a hotel for the night, and continue next day. I suppose there must be loads of hotels in Bath?'

'Oh yes!' Adam said. 'In fact my aunt used to go to Bath. She stayed at the Francis. If my aunt stayed there it must have been respectable.'

'Then if I have to stay over, I'll try for the Francis if it makes you feel better. Really, Adam, I'm truly sorry you're not going, but I can't wait another week. Do you understand?'

'Not really,' he'd said. 'But I'm trying to.'

On that note they had metaphorically parted company, or at least they had not talked about it for the rest of the afternoon, and apart from dropping her at the door he'd not gone home with her.

'I hope you enjoy Dublin,' she'd said. 'I should

251

be here when you get back. Will you come and have supper with me? I suppose it will have to be after rehearsal.'

'Try to stop me!' he'd said. 'I shall miss you.'

'And I shall miss you,' she'd told him.

*   *   *

It was true. It was Friday before she'd see him again. It was now only Monday morning and she was missing him already.

She showered and ate a quick breakfast. She would stop for coffee somewhere on the way. With Adam's help she had worked out the route on the map and calculated that it would take her rather more than three hours, so with an early start she should be there well before lunch.

The last thing she did before leaving home was to check, though there was no need to do so, she had done it at least twice, that she had the drawings with her. This time she was taking all of them, together with the photograph which had Eliot's name written on the back. She studied the snapshot again before replacing it in the folder. The three of them, Claire, her mother and Eliot looked so young, so happy, smiling, screwing up their eyes against the bright sun. Surely Eliot Frobisher would not be displeased to be reminded about such a time?

In spite of her early start the roads were busy and, surprisingly, mostly with heavy traffic. She wondered where it was all heading for. She knew nothing whatever of this part of the country, and it was so different from her native North Yorkshire. Much of it was beautiful, in its own special way, which was a softer and gentler way than the countryside she was used to. There were more trees, great oaks and beeches looking as though they had been there for ever, and although the hills were high they appeared less steep. Perhaps, she thought, because the valleys were wider.

In spite of the traffic she was making good progress, until nearing the journey's end—a signpost said 'Bath—17 miles'—when all that changed. The road narrowed and became a series of bends, one following quickly after another so that it was too dangerous to overtake. It was frustrating, but bearable. She could keep up a steady thirty-five to forty until, no more than a few yards ahead, a large farm vehicle pulled out from a narrow lane on the left and placed itself in front of her. It was wide enough to take up almost half of the road, and piled high with bales of hay, insecurely stacked, threatening to fall off at any moment.

She braked quickly and slowed down to a crawl. Her vision of the road ahead was now well and truly blocked and the driver in front was in no hurry whatsoever. Twenty miles an hour was his preferred speed, though if he went any faster, Petra realized, he would probably lose his shifting load.

Please God, she prayed, let him not be going all the way to Bath!

Six slow miles later, when he unexpectedly swerved into the middle of the road before making a left turn, her prayers were answered. The road was still narrow and twisting, with a steady stream of traffic coming towards her. Keep calm, she told herself. You are not in a race. You do not have to be in Bath at a certain time. The day is yours!

Self-counselling did not make her feel better. She was impatient to be there, intolerant of anything which delayed her the least bit. Also she was hungry. Wanting to save time she had not stopped for coffee. Now she felt around in the glove compartment for a square of chocolate, or a toffee, but without success.

When Bath finally came into view it took her by surprise. A city of stone, golden in the sunshine, small as cities go, the buildings set close together in a hollow then climbing the surrounding hills in orderly rows, terraces, crescents, to meet the green hilltops. It was easy to pick out the abbey, it rose above everything; and then the river, curling through the centre of the city. And within minutes she was driving down the hill to meet it all.

Her first discovery was that street parking was not on. When she had driven twice around the centre of the city, losing her way on each occasion, she opted for a large covered car-park which would clearly be expensive. Never mind.

She walked in the direction of the abbey, stopping at a bookshop to buy a street map and guide book. She would find somewhere for lunch and study them while she ate. She was close to the abbey now and it seemed natural to take the turning which led into the Abbey Yard, where she also found a restaurant with tables on the pavement. It was perfect weather for eating outside: sunny and warm, with no wind. She seated herself at a table and ordered a tuna salad, and while she waited for it to come she opened out the street map.

It was when she looked at the map that she realized, for the first time, the size of the task she had set herself. Standing in the London gallery, looking at the drawings, it had seemed to her quite certain that she would find Eliot Frobisher. Why wouldn't she? He was probably well-known in the art world. Someone must know where he lived, and Bath seemed as likely as anywhere, at least to start with. And if she didn't find him in Bath she would look elsewhere. Every hour which had passed since Saturday morning had strengthened her resolve. Adam had said she had a bee in her bonnet and she supposed that was true, but where was the harm in that?

Yet now, as she looked at the map—so many streets, so many buildings, so many, she was sure, thousands of houses and flats—she questioned for the first time whether she wasn't on a fool's errand. And was she even in the right city? Why not simply write to Eliot Frobisher via the gallery and his agent, sending him copies of the drawings, seeking confirmation that they were his (though about that she was already sure), asking him for anything he could tell her about her mother?

In fact, she challenged herself, did she really need to know that? As Adam had pointed out, whatever had taken place had done so many years ago, when those involved were quite young, in fact before she herself had been born. 'It has nothing whatever to do with you,' Adam had said.

She folded up the map and concentrated on her salad. Adam was right, of course. It was her mother's secret, if secret it was. The trouble was that she knew so little of her mother's early life. It had never been mentioned, her mother had not even talked about Claire, with whom she had clearly once been great friends. If it had not been for the accident, if she had not died so suddenly, so long before her time, perhaps I would have learnt more, Petra thought. Perhaps as my mother grew older she would, in the way older people did, have reminisced about her youth. She would not now have this burning curiosity to fill in the gaps, to want to know so much more about her mother.

She looked up now at the west front of the abbey, only a few yards from where she sat. Eliot's drawing of the gallery had been very true. She remembered how much she had liked the angels ascending the ladder to heaven, and here they were in the carved stone, and even lovelier.

Also, from where she sat she had only to turn her head to see the entrance to the Pump Room, the background to his other drawing of the juggler. Today, instead of the juggler, there was a group of dancers in eighteenth-century dress treading a gavotte. Eliot must have sat quite close to where she sat now, perhaps at this very café. The thought renewed her feeling that if she were to find him it would be in Bath. She would still, she decided, make every effort to do so but if it didn't work out perhaps she would take it as a sign that it wasn't meant to be. And she would think hard about what, if she were to find him, she would ask him.

When the waitress came with the bill Petra said, 'It looks from my map that the Tourist Information Office is quite near to here. Is that so?'

'Too right!' the waitress said in a ripe Australian accent. 'In Abbey Chambers.' She pointed a finger. 'That way!'

Petra paid her bill and left. The Information Office was busy and she stood in a queue of people mostly, as far as she could overhear, enquiring about accommodation, which appeared to be stretched to the utmost. Perhaps, if she intended staying overnight, and since it was after two o'clock and she'd not yet made a start, she should go and book into the Francis fairly soon.

Gradually, the people in front of her in the queue left, clutching street maps with hotels and guest houses marked.

'What can I do for you?' the elder of the two women behind the counter asked.

'I'm trying to trace a man named Eliot Frobisher,' Petra explained. 'He's an artist, probably quite well-known. I think he might live in Bath.'

'What do you mean, you're trying to trace him?' the woman asked.

'I want to know where he lives.'

'Well, we wouldn't give anyone's private address,' the woman said. 'Even if we knew it. You say he lives in Bath?'

'I think he might. I can't be sure.' What a lame story it sounded.

'I suppose it's a silly question,' the woman said, 'but have you looked in the telephone directory?'

Petra blushed.

'How stupid of me! No, I haven't.'

'We'll start there, then. How do you spell the name?' She took a directory from the shelf and checked it.

'There's no Eliot Frobisher,' she said. 'But that's not surprising. Lots of people are ex-directory. And if they are it's no use asking the telephone exchange because no way will they give it. They never do.'

The woman's colleague broke off a conversation

with a couple who wanted accommodation in the centre of the town, with a nice view, reasonably priced, quiet and preferably near the bus station.

'I've heard of the name,' she said. 'I think I've seen it in the *Bath Chronicle*. But that mightn't mean much. He could live anywhere from Warminster to Bristol. But I *have* read the name somewhere!'

Petra felt a leap of hope.

'Have you any idea where I might look next?' she asked.

'It'll be like looking for a needle in the haystack,' the older woman said. She felt quite curious as to why this respectable-looking woman wanted to find this man about whom she seemed to know next to nothing, but it was her job to answer questions, not to ask them.

'The only other thing I can think of,' she offered, 'is the voters' lists. You're allowed to look at those. They keep them in the Town Hall, and probably in the Reference Library. But they'll be in street order. You'd have to know the name of the street.'

'Which I don't!' Petra confessed.

'The library closes at six o'clock today,' the assistant said. 'Oh! I'd forgotten. There's the art gallery. It's quite close to the library. They might know something!'

'They might know more than we do, but they wouldn't give you an address,' the other assistant said.

'Thank you both, very much,' Petra said. 'I'm going to the Francis Hotel now to see if I can book in. According to the map it's quite close.'

'Five minutes. But you'll be lucky to get in at short notice. It's very popular.'

In fact, Petra thought as she walked out into the street, she would have preferred to have made straight for the art gallery, but it was in the opposite direction. Time was racing by and it seemed important that she should find a room.

'You're lucky,' the receptionist said. 'We've had a cancellation. A single room on the second floor.'

'Thank you,' Petra said. 'I'll pick up my car and bring it around later!' She didn't even wait to see the room. She had to get to the art gallery, of which she had the highest possible hopes. Surely they must know something?

They might have had, except that the assistant on duty had worked there only ten days and knew nothing of Eliot Frobisher. She was sure, however, that there was nothing of his on show in the gallery.

'My colleague will be back on Wednesday,' she said. 'She might be able to help you.'

'Thank you,' Petra said—and left for the library, which was no more than a minute or two away. There was at least one thing to be said for Bath, everything was close to everything else. Unfortunately it seemed that everywhere there were queues. She had to wait a long time before it was her turn to be attended to.

'Yes, we do have the electoral registers,' the librarian said. 'Which ward would you like to look at?'

'Ward? I've no idea!' Petra admitted.

'There are several wards,' the librarian explained. 'Depending on which ward you live in is where you vote in the elections.'

'Of course,' Petra said. 'I hadn't thought of that! I'm afraid I don't know which ward.'

'If you can tell me which street . . .'

259

'I'm afraid I can't do that either,' Petra said. 'I'm trying to trace an artist, Eliot Frobisher . . .'

'And he lives in Bath?'

'I don't even know that,' Petra confessed. 'I just think he might.' She felt an inch high. The librarian gave her a pitying look.

'There are literally hundreds of thousands of names on the roll. None of them in alphabetical order. All in street order.'

'And if this gentleman *does* live in Bath, will he be somewhere amongst the thousands?' Petra asked.

'Most people are,' the librarian said. 'I don't know how long it would take you to go through the lists. Quite a long time, I would think. Several days.'

'Perhaps Mr Frobisher is a member of the library?' Petra suggested.

'Perhaps he does use the lending library,' the librarian conceded. 'Even so, we wouldn't be able to give you his address. Such things are confidential.'

'Then I'm not sure what to do next,' Petra said, well and truly deflated. 'I guess what I will do is make a start on one ward list—any one, so why don't I take the most central—and see how I get on. I'll decide after that how far I can go.'

'Very well,' the librarian said. 'I suggest in that case you study the abbey ward list. But I'm afraid it's too late today. We close in ten minutes. Can you come back tomorrow? We open at half-past nine.' Perhaps when the lady had considered the enormity of the task, she wouldn't bother to return.

She was wrong. Petra was there next morning when the doors opened. In spite of a comfortable bed she had tossed and turned half the night, wondering what she should do. Was any of it worthwhile?

By the time she had eaten breakfast she had decided that perhaps it was. She could at least give the morning to it, there was nothing else she needed to do. She wished fervently that she had a number where she could telephone Adam. She needed him, even though she was pretty sure what he would say.

She collected the abbey ward list and sat at a desk. Less than half an hour later she gave a small cry, startling several students working assiduously and one old man who had already fallen asleep over his newspaper.

It was there! It was there in black and white. Frobisher, Eliot! She pulled herself together but her hands, as she took out her street map and opened it, were shaking. Great Pulteney Street. E3, F3. For a moment all the lines on the map merged into each other. Then they cleared, and she found it.

CHAPTER SEVENTEEN

Petra found the house without difficulty. It was one of an elegant terrace of stone houses in a wide street, obviously built in an earlier age for gracious living. Now the number of bell-pushes at most doors pointed to a multiplicity of flats. On the Frobisher house there were only two, neither of them marked with a name, so which bell to press was a matter of guesswork. She chose the top one.

261

Nothing happened. It was impossible to hear whether the bell had rung inside the house. The front door was solid, heavy. She rang again and waited. When still no-one answered, she pressed the bottom bell. Why was she so certain, she asked herself as she stood there, that someone, and in her mind it would be Eliot Frobisher himself, would answer? Because, she had decided, this was her lucky day.

The door opened and a young woman stood there. For two seconds—which felt like several minutes—they stared at each other. What Petra saw was like the image she looked at every morning in the mirror. Yet not exactly, by no means exactly. They would never be mistaken for each other. Taken separately, their features were not quite alike, but similar. High cheekbones, wide mouths. No, it was something in the putting together of the features which enhanced the similarities of the whole faces to each other.

Both had red hair, though the younger woman's—by the look of her she might have been five or six years younger—was lighter and brighter. Petra's was cut in a bob, with strands of fringe falling down willy-nilly over her forehead. The other woman's was drawn tightly back and caught in a pony tail. Both had the pale skin of a true redhead, dusted with summer freckles.

It was difficult to believe.

The other woman could believe it. She was surprised, and she was startled by the resemblance this woman on the doorstep bore to herself, even more so than the others had, but she was not disbelieving. It had happened before, and more than once, though some years ago now; and the

262

others had not actually turned up on the doorstep in the middle of a Tuesday morning.

Petra was the first to find her voice.

'I was hoping to see Eliot Frobisher. I didn't know which bell to ring.'

'Either would have done. I'm sorry, he's abroad. I'm his daughter, Tanya.'

'Oh! I see! Will he be . . . ?'

'I don't know when he'll be back. He's in Italy, painting.'

Neither of them were thinking about what they were saying. It was incidental to what was going on in their minds, what they saw in each other's appearance.

'The thing is,' Petra said, 'I have some drawings which I think are his. I mean, done by him.'

'You'd better come in,' Tanya said.

Petra followed her into a room on the ground floor, at the front of the house. It was large, and filled with books on shelves, on tables, on the floor. No sign, though, of easels or drawing boards or all the tools of the artist's trade.

'The house is divided into two flats,' Tanya explained. 'My father has the ground floor and the first floor. His studio is on the first floor. He needs a lot of room for his work. I have the top floor. I'm a writer. Writers don't need much room.'

'I see,' Petra said. 'I rang the top bell first.'

'I was downstairs,' Tanya said. 'I see to my father's post when he's away, chuck out all the junk mail.' They were neither of them saying what they were thinking. 'So you said you had some drawings?'

'Yes. Of my mother. I only discovered them after she'd died. They were done a long time ago, she

263

was clearly quite young. And there was a photograph with the name "Eliot" on the back. Eliot's not a common first name, is it?'

'I suppose not,' Tanya agreed.

'I might not have done anything about it, indeed I don't see what I could have done, but then I saw this notice in *The Times* about an exhibition of portrait drawings, and one of the artists mentioned was an Eliot Frobisher. It seemed worth taking a look.'

'I suppose so,' Tanya said. 'It must have seemed so.'

'What do you mean?'

Tanya shrugged.

'Once I saw his drawings,' Petra said, 'I felt certain they were by the same hand as the ones I had. If you were to look at them, would you be able to tell?'

'I expect so,' Tanya said. She didn't want to do it. She could see where it might lead, and she didn't want to go down that road. She went and picked up some books from the floor and added them to the pile on the table. It was simply something to do. 'Why do you want to know?' she asked.

Petra looked at her in surprise.

'Well, in the first place it would be nice to know for certain who did them. Your father is obviously a talented artist, and he must be reasonably well-known or he wouldn't be exhibited in the London gallery.'

'True!' Tanya agreed. 'He's both those things. And?'

'Well then, if he did these drawings he must have known my mother. I thought he might be kind enough to tell me something about her. I know so little—almost nothing—of her early life. She never talked about the past, nor did I ever know my grandparents. I suppose it's only since she died that I've been curious about it.'

'Not always a good idea,' Tanya said, 'but if you want me to, I'll look at the drawings.'

Petra handed them over. Tanya studied them, taking far longer than she needed to. It was clear to her that they were her father's work but she had no wish to continue the conversation. If this woman had eyes to see it was all there in the drawings, especially in the later ones. And in any case, Tanya thought, she has only to look at me.

'I noticed when I saw your father's drawings in the gallery,' Petra said, 'that he draws bodies so exquisitely, but the faces are half turned away. Has he always done that?'

'Quite often,' Tanya said. 'I think he didn't want to be reminded later who the model was.'

Petra said nothing, but the question showed in her face.

'One wouldn't,' Tanya answered. 'Not when you think of the circumstances. Yet he always drew my mother's face. *She* had a beautiful body too, when she was young. I've seen those drawings.' Her voice was hard and sharp.

'But I don't see—' Petra began.

'Don't you?' Tanya interrupted. 'Are you sure you don't? Then if not I think I shall tell you. I think perhaps it would be as well to get things clear in your mind. But first of all—'

She broke off, and in a swift movement she took hold of Petra's hand and pulled her across towards the mantelpiece, over which hung a large, gilt-framed mirror.

'Look!' Tanya commanded. 'Look in the mirror!'

Standing side by side the two women stared at their own reflections, and at each other's.

'Yes,' Petra whispered. 'Yes, you're right!'

'Yes you can,' Tanya said. 'It's there, in front of you! Now look again at the last of those drawings.'

'I don't need to,' Petra said. 'Not that one!'

It was not a drawing she would ever forget—not a line, not a highlight or shadow of it, though these were not what mattered. What she would never forget was the sexual power which emanated from the drawings. Seeing herself now in the mirror, side by side with Tanya, accepting what that meant—how could she not understand? She felt almost that she had been present at her own conception.

'You do see it, don't you?' Tanya pressed her.

'Yes, I do!'

She saw it. She understood it, knew what it meant, knew what Tanya was saying. This man is your father—and mine! But that was something she wanted neither to see nor understand. She wished with all her heart that she had never found the drawings, wished they had been destroyed before she could have done so. But she *had* found them, and it was her own obstinacy which had made her persist in tracing them. She had brought it on herself.

And then the moment of not wanting to know, not wishing to understand, passed. Suddenly she wanted to know more, she wanted to know everything.

They were still standing in front of the mirror.

'We are both very like him,' Tanya observed. 'His hair is no longer red, of course. He's sixty this year. It's white—and thick and beautiful, and he's

266

still the most handsome man you'll ever see, and he can still talk any woman out of her clothes and into his bed. And no doubt is doing so right now in Italy! In fact . . .'

She paused, seeing the pain in Petra's face.

'I'm sorry,' she said. 'It's all a bit much, isn't it? I suppose over the years I've got used to it, but as far as you're concerned I'm talking about your mother. Are you sure you want to hear? You don't have to.'

'I want to,' Petra said.

They sat side by side on the sofa.

'Where to begin?' Tanya said. 'I'd always thought it began with me, but you're older than I am. I'm thirty.'

'And I'm thirty-six.'

'Six years between us. So who knows what happened in those six years? Perhaps best not to, though I suppose my mother does. At any rate, I've always known my mother married to my father, and we always lived together, though not here in Bath. We've lived in various places. We were living in Brighton the first time.'

'The *first* time?'

'Yes. I liked Brighton. I liked collecting pebbles on the beach, going on the pier, watching the sea at high tide. I was eight when my father brought this lady home. She didn't actually come knocking on the door. He went up to London for something or other and brought her back with him, together with this little girl of five. The child was exactly like him to look at. He said it was a family likeness, she was my cousin Alice, and I was to call the lady Auntie Joan. They'd come to stay with us for a while until they found a place of their own, and he was sure we'd all get on well together, one big happy family!'

267

'And did you?' Petra asked.

'No. Certainly not for long. At first I enjoyed having another child around. I had no brothers and sisters. Well, that is to say—' She broke off, then started again.

'Anyway, at five years old she was too young for me to play with. And it was Alice herself who gave it away because within hours she stopped calling my father "Uncle" and simply called him "Daddy". My father explained to me, quite pleasantly, that really she was my half-sister, and wasn't that nice, and that it was quite possible for one father to have two children and both of them with different mothers. And wasn't it a good idea for them all to live together because that way they could look after each other. Even at eight I thought it was strange. None of my school friends lived in such a household.'

'And what about your mother?' Petra said.

'My mother hated it, I could see that. But she loved my father—he is a very lovable man. The competition between the two women was never who did he do most for, but who could do the most for him. And in any case, if she'd left where could my mother have gone? How could she support herself and me? In the end, however—and I think the other woman and her child stayed with us for almost a year—my mother put her foot down and they had to leave. I can tell you I was jolly pleased to have my own room back, and my parents to myself again.'

'It must have been quite difficult for you,' Petra said. 'Thank you for telling me. And now I arrive on the scene . . .'

'And lo and behold! I have another half-sister!

But I've not yet told you everything. There's more to come!

'It happened again. We'd left Brighton, we were living in Purley now. I was twelve and the little girl was eight. Monica. She was the spitting image of me. It's interesting how my father has daughters— three girls and not one of them like her mother!'

'Four daughters,' Petra said.

'Yes, of course. And you can't be like your mother.'

'No. People said I was more like my father . . .'

She was stabbed, swiftly and suddenly, by a pain which was almost physical. Her father! That kind and loving man who had been there, as far as she had known, since the moment she'd opened her eyes on the world; who had taught her to walk, to swim, to ride a bicycle. Teased her, comforted her, carried her on his shoulder when she was small and walked with her over the fells when she was grown up. How could anyone else in the world ever be her father?

'Her mother's name was Irene,' Tanya was saying. 'Whether my mother was consulted, or even warned, on these occasions I didn't know. By the time I saw these people it was a fait accompli, he just walked in the door with them. They suddenly had nowhere to live and our house, it seemed, was the perfect refuge. They left after a few months, months in which Irene and my mother had spent their time either in tears, or screaming at each other and Monica and I had quarrelled and fought. My father took himself off to his studio and buried himself in his work. Once he even took himself off for a week's painting holiday in Normandy. Then, as soon as Irene had packed their bags and she and

269

Monica had left, my mother packed *her* suitcase and mine, and so did we.'

'Where did you go?' Petra asked.

'To Charles. A friend of my mother's I hadn't known about. He had two children of his own. Later, my mother divorced my father and married Charles. He didn't like me, and I hated him and his children, so in the end I went back to my father. Actually, he's always loved me. He has a great capacity for love. Most of the time we get on well together.'

'You never married?'

'No thank you! I don't like what I've seen of marriage!'

Tanya stood up, and moved restlessly around the room, twitching a curtain, moving an ornament, plumping up a cushion.

'Anyway,' she said, 'there it is. I don't know how you feel at the moment, but I reckon we could both do with a cup of coffee—or would you prefer a stiff drink?'

'Coffee, please!'

'Come in the kitchen with me while I make it,' Tanya said.

They sat with their coffee at the kitchen table.

'This has been a shock for you,' Tanya said. 'I can see that. Perhaps I shouldn't have told you. I suppose I could have left it in the air.'

'No, you were quite right,' Petra assured her. 'After all, I did ask you to. But yes, it is a shock. I find I'm especially thinking of the man I'd always thought of as my father. Such a good man. I loved him very much.'

'Then don't let anyone displace him,' Tanya said. 'He was more of a father to you than Eliot

270

Frobisher could ever be.'

'No-one could have been better,' Petra said.

'I don't suppose my father even knew of your existence,' Tanya spoke with bitterness. 'It's possible that there are other red-haired, grey-eyed Frobishers around the world he's not aware of— nor they of him. As I said earlier, it's sometimes better not to know.'

'The thing is,' Petra said, 'it was my mother I wanted to know more about, and there are still questions to be answered. When did she know Eliot Frobisher, and where? When and where did he do the drawings?'

A sudden thought came to Tanya.

'I might, I just might be able to find out something about that!'

'You mean you'll write to him?'

'No. I've no idea where he'd be. When he goes off like this I never know a thing until he's back again. The house could burn down and I couldn't let him know!'

'So how . . . ?'

'In some ways,' Tanya said, 'my father is a very organized man, most particularly in relation to his work. He keeps all his sketch books, roughly in chronological order. You said the photograph was taken in nineteen-sixty, so let's go upstairs and see if we can find anything!'

It was true, Petra thought, following Tanya into Eliot's studio, as far as his work went he was an organized man. Never had she seen an artist's workplace so orderly, so tidy. Canvases were stacked neatly, according to size. Drawers were neatly marked with their contents; the floor was clear. I might have inherited something of this man's talent, Petra thought, but no way have I inherited his sense of order.

'His old sketch books and his records are in the far room,' Tanya said, leading the way. 'Nineteen-sixty will be almost at the beginning. He was obviously always an orderly man—except in his private life.'

It was a smaller room, shelved on three sides, the shelves holding boxed files, all labelled in date order.

Petra took the drawings out of her briefcase again.

'It might not help,' she said. 'These drawings have been extracted from a sketch book, either cut out, or torn out very neatly.'

'Ah, but that does *fit*!' Tanya said. 'I discovered, I can't remember why, that he had a habit of tearing some of his drawings out of the books. Perhaps, in the early days, so that my mother wouldn't see them. And it's possible, isn't it, that he gave them away? Tore them out and gave them to whoever was with him at the time?'

'Are you saying he was already married in nineteen-sixty?'

'I believe so,' Tanya said. 'They waited five years for me.'

From a box labelled with the year she extracted a sketch book. It was marked 'Petra'.

'Petra? I wasn't alive then. How could it be?'

Tanya opened the book and, standing together, they examined the contents.

'But it's Petra, the place! In Jordan!' Tanya exclaimed. 'Look! All the drawings are of the place. Different figures in the foreground, and to him they would be what was important, but the

272

background was Petra. Also,' she said slowly, 'it's quite easy to see where a group of pages has been torn out. Look!'

'And those are the pages I have,' Petra said, 'which proves that my mother was in that part of the world then. I'm amazed that she was there. She wasn't the kind of woman to go places. I wonder why she did? But apart from that, all this tells me nothing more.'

'Except what the last drawing tells you. And the fact that you exist, and your name is what it is.'

*   *   *

Petra set off to walk back to the Francis seeing almost nothing of her surroundings. She was aware that she crossed the Pulteney Bridge but otherwise she was deep in thought. Twice, she surfaced enough to wonder if she was heading in the right direction and then, deciding she probably was, she returned to the confusion of her thoughts until she found herself at the revolving door of the hotel. Inside, she went straight to reception.

'Could you make out my bill, please?' she asked. 'I have to leave quite soon.'

She would have a sandwich in the hotel and then be off. There was no further reason to stay in Bath. Tanya had offered to let her know when her father returned from Italy, but Petra was no longer sure that she wanted to meet him. What she had seen and heard pointed to the fact that Eliot was her father, but it was too early to accept it all rationally. In other circumstances she would have been proud to have known him, pleased that it was to her that he had passed on some of his talent, but the truth

273

was that he was a selfish bastard who had left a trail of scarred and unhappy women and children in his wake. And actually *I* am the bastard, she thought. Me and all those other kids he had so carelessly fathered.

Had he abandoned her mother, or had he never known she was pregnant? She might not have told him. In any case, if he was already married—as Tanya seemed to think was likely—he would not have been able to make an honest woman of her mother. And why was it always the woman who was to be made honest when as likely as not the fault was with the man?

She hoped that, at least, Eliot Frobisher had, if only fleetingly, loved her mother, and that she had loved him. I would like to have been born of love rather than of a casual encounter, she thought.

She ate her sandwich—not tasting it, forcing it down because she had a long drive before her and didn't want to stop on the way—paid her bill, and collected her car from the hotel car-park. For the next fifteen minutes she tried hard to concentrate on finding her way out of Bath, allowing herself no other thoughts until she was on the Warminster road and knew where she was going. Then all that she had pushed to the back of her mind leapt forward.

What about the man whom she would always think of as her father? Did he marry her mother when she was pregnant by another man in order to save her reputation, or was it possible that he had not known that she was pregnant by someone else and believed himself to be the father? Again, how would she ever know? She had thought until today that he was her father, so had *he* gone to his death believing that he was her father, or knowing that he was not? And in the latter case would he, or her mother, ever have told her? She thought not, or why would they have left it so long?

From time to time she was obliged to put these thoughts, and those of Eliot Frobisher, and of Tanya, her newly discovered half-sister, out of her mind again in order to cope with the traffic. There were roadworks, and between Bath and Warminster there was a complicated diversion on which she had to concentrate. She would be glad to be back home in Mindon—and she was interested and pleased to realize that she thought of Mindon as home.

She wished with all her heart that Adam could be there to meet her, but it was impossible. It would be twenty-four hours at least before she would see him, and there was no-one else she could talk to, not really talk. Nor was it just to talk that she wanted to see him. She wanted him to put his arms around her and hold her close: comfort her, sort her out.

Eventually, she turned off the major road on to the minor one which in a mile or so would find her in Mindon. When she passed the Queen's Head and the church, and then the village green—there were children still playing there—and turned into her own small drive, she had a tremendous feeling of having come home, of being where she belonged.

Two hours later she had attended to her post, there were no messages on her ansaphone and she had cooked herself some pasta. She had debated whether she would or would not go to rehearsal— and decided against it. She was tired, she was troubled and she hadn't definitely promised Ursula she would be there. In fact it all seemed trivial compared to what was on her mind.

An hour after that she had reason to be thankful she had stayed at home. The telephone rang. It was probably Ursula on her mobile, wanting to know where she was. Petra picked up the phone reluctantly, then cried out with delight as she listened.

'Adam! Oh, Adam, I can't tell you how much I want to see you!' she said. 'When will you be home?'

'Tomorrow. Around five,' he said. 'I've missed you!'

'Come straight here,' Petra said. 'I've missed you too!'

CHAPTER EIGHTEEN

It was four o'clock on Wednesday afternoon when Petra, looking out of the window—which she had been doing on and off for the last hour—saw Adam draw up in his car. She ran to the door to meet him. He came in and took her in his arms.

'I've missed you so much,' he said.

'And I've missed you,' Petra said. 'I thought you expected to be back by five.'

'I did. The traffic was good.'

They walked, arms around each other, through the hall into the kitchen. Adam sniffed the air.

'Nice! What's cooking?'

'Lamb casserole. It'll be ready by six. I thought we'd need to eat early because of rehearsal. I suppose we have to go?'

Adam pulled a face.

'I expect so. I don't want to.'

'Nor me,' Petra said. 'How was the conference?'

'Boring. Nothing new, nothing I hadn't heard before. I met one or two people I hadn't seen for a year or two. That was OK. But never mind me, what about you? You told me practically nothing on the phone.'

'I know.' She had switched the kettle on and was putting teabags in the pot. 'It wasn't something I wanted to talk about on the telephone. It's too complicated. It's also unbelievable, except that it's true!'

He looked at her intently, alerted by the sudden change in her voice. There was a deeply worried look on her face; her eyes were wide and anxious.

'Sit down. Tell me about it.'

She poured the tea and they sat down opposite each other at the table. She told him everything. How she had searched for and found the house, all that had been said there between herself and Tanya. How Tanya had dragged her to the mirror and what she had seen there. She told him about the discovery of the sketch book.

When she began her story it was in a level, matter-of-fact voice, but as she continued she lived it again, and when she came near to the end it was too much for her. She could no longer control her pent-up emotion. She had kept calm all day, not giving way, but now she could do so no longer. She covered her face with her hands and wept bitterly, the tears running through her fingers.

Adam rose to his feet and went to her, put his arms around her and held her close, stroking her hair.

'I'm sorry!' she sobbed.

'Please!' he said. 'You don't have to be sorry for crying. You've had a tremendous shock. *I'm* sorry that I wasn't with you. I should have chucked the conference.'

'You weren't to know.' She raised her head and took the handkerchief he offered her, mopped her tears. 'In any case, it would have been difficult for Tanya if you'd been there. I don't think she'd have told me all she did. In an odd way . . .' she hesitated '. . . well, I'm family. I don't feel it, except a little bit to her. Not to Eliot Frobisher. My father was Brian Banbury. He always will be. I'm crying for him as well as for myself.'

'I'm sorry you came home to an empty house, had to spend the night alone.'

'It doesn't matter. I'm all right now. You're here.'

'Do you want to talk about it any more—I mean just now?' Adam asked. 'I know you will want to talk about it sooner or later, to decide what you want to do. But remember, my love, that one of the options is to do nothing. You're perfectly entitled to do nothing if that's what you want.'

He couldn't imagine her doing nothing, it wasn't in her, but he hated the thought of her rushing into something which might hurt her still further.

'It isn't what I want to do. Nothing, I mean. I've thought and thought!' She'd spent most of the night thinking, reliving yesterday, reliving her years, especially the childhood ones, with her mother and father. 'There are things I'll want to do, but I'd sooner not discuss them now. They're too important. And we have to eat—I expect you're

278

starving—and then we have to go to rehearsal.'

'Whatever you say. You needn't go to rehearsal, and if it's what you want I'll stay here with you.'

'No!' Petra decided. 'We'll both go but will you come back with me afterwards? Then we can talk.'

'Of course I will,' Adam said.

*   *   *

Ursula was not in the best of moods, far from it, and it had started before she and Eric had set foot in the village hall. Immediately he had arrived from the office he had changed into a pair of dark-red jeans—he was now into Calvin Klein—and a blue tee-shirt bearing the words 'If you want it, I've got it!'

'And what is that supposed to mean?' Ursula had demanded.

'Ah! Whatever you want it to mean!' Eric replied.

'As far as I'm concerned,' Ursula said, 'it means nothing to me. It's rubbish!'

'You take life too seriously, love!' Eric said.

'Someone has to!' she retorted.

'But why you?' he asked.

He knew why, of course. It was because she regarded everything she did as important, everything had a purpose. He had thought, a few weeks ago, that she was loosening up a bit—look at the way she'd taken him into Southfield and chosen all those new clothes for him! He'd felt himself a changed man since then, and he'd thought she was a changed—well, partly changed—woman. Certainly she'd been better in bed than for years. But none of that had lasted long and now she was back to her old self—only worse. Very tetchy, she was. And when he got home she was always tired, almost as if she'd spent the day jogging, whereas he knew that Ursula did little that was physical. Never had. She prided herself on being the intellectual one. She was one of those people who if ever she had an exercise bicycle—which in itself was unthinkable—would have Shakespeare propped up on the handlebars to read as she pedalled.

'I shall have something to say to just about everyone this evening!' she warned him as she drove purposefully towards the village hall. 'There's too much laissez-faire, everyone's getting slack!'

'Don't be too hard on them,' Eric warned. 'When all's said and done, we do it for love! We're not hired hands!'

'And what do you think *I* do it for?' she demanded, rapidly swerving the car—she had espied a parking place outside the hall into which she might possibly fit, and did, with just inches to spare fore and aft. 'What *do* you think I do it for?'

Glory, he thought, but was wise enough not to say.

Precisely at half-past seven she stood in the middle of the stage, everyone else standing four feet below on the hall floor, and clapped her hands vigorously for silence. The response was half-hearted. Several people moved closer together in a desultory fashion; no-one stopped talking. She often wished, and never more so than at this moment, that she had an exceedingly shrill whistle which she could blow with all her might and main. As it was, she clapped her hands again, and called out, 'May I have your attention, please!

280

Everybody!'

She knew enough of drama not to say a single word until total silence reigned. She stood quite still, not moving a muscle, waiting until it happened.

'Thank you!' she said. 'Now what I have to say to you before we start this evening is for everyone, each and every one, *and that includes the children*!'

The children were something new, about eight of them, girls *and* boys, grouped together near the front, smirking and giggling. Ten or so days ago Ursula had cried in despair, 'What am I to do? Fairies, attendants, all either down with measles, or in contact with measles and likely to break out at any moment! What am I to do?'

It was the vicar's wife who had come up with the solution.

'The Sunday school doesn't seem to have been hit by measles. I can't think why, unless it's the Hand of God! Would you like me to see whom I can recruit? It might be boys and girls mixed.'

'Oh, Grace, would you? Boys are quite acceptable. They used boys in Shakespeare's day of course. But no very young children. I know they look sweet but they're always having to be taken to the lavatory!'

And so she had eight or nine children, depending on who turned up, and of an age to take themselves to the lavatory. Their chief drawback was that when they were not on stage they tended to clump together and carry on a low-volume conversation, but since it was seldom audible to anyone else Ursula could deal with it.

'First of all,' she said now, 'I hope everyone is here! I'm glad to see you back, Lysander, and you,

Petra. But I don't think I see the vicar, do I? Or the good doctor.' She looked to their respective wives for explanations.

'The vicar has a chapter meeting,' Grace Helmet said nervously.

'A chapter meeting. Is that something he *has* to attend?'

'Oh yes!' Grace said. 'He'd be in trouble with the archdeacon if he didn't!'

'Ah! So he's more afraid of the archdeacon than of me!' Ursula said, and waited for the small ripple of laughter.

'And the doctor had a full surgery,' his wife said. 'I left him still at it.'

'Some people rush to the doctor with every little thing!' Ursula said.

'Hear, hear,' the doctor's wife said, under her breath.

'However,' Ursula continued, 'to be serious! I'm not at all happy with the way the *Dream* is going at the moment! I'm sorry to say that too many of you don't know your lines, don't know your cues, don't know your entrances, don't know your moves.'

Giles Rowland took a nailfile from his pocket and began to file his nails. None of this applied to him, but she was right about the rest.

'There is *magic* in this play!' Ursula said. 'There is enchantment! There is poetry! Where are you giving me these things?'

'There's comedy!' Bottom said.

'That too,' Ursula agreed. 'And there's disorder and confusion! And I'm certainly getting that, though not in the right places! It's absolutely—'

She broke off at the sound of a peal of laughter from one of the children.

Ursula turned her head in the direction of the children.

'Have I said something funny?'

'No, miss!' the culprit said.

'Then why are you laughing?'

Suddenly, as if she had flicked a switch, all the children began to giggle, squirming about on the floor with mirth.

'Come!' Ursula said. 'I insist you share the joke with the rest of us! Speak up! You, Benjamin!'

'It's just that . . .' Benjamin's face was split by a wide smile, '. . . it's just that we invented nicknames for all the characters in the play. They were funny.'

'Then let's have them!' Ursula invited.

Benjamin looked around among his contemporaries for support—and got it. The answers came thick and fast, one after another.

'Lysander is Fibber!'

'Hermia is Hernia!'

'Snout is Nosey!'

'Bottom is Bum!' shouted a brave girl.

'Moonshine is Loony Mooney.'

'And Titania is Tits,' Benjamin said.

How very apt, Ursula thought. Out of the mouths of babes and sucklings!

'We have one for Puck,' a small boy piped up, 'but we can't say it because it's the F word!'

'Thank you,' Ursula said. 'On that note perhaps we can all get to work!'

Tits, she thought as she plunged into act one, scene one, minus the doctor, though as Philostrate he had nothing to say. She was having no success at all with her own tits. She had exercised every single day—though by now the mere sound of Honey's voice made her feel ready to throw up—with the result that she had gained not one millimetre on her bosom, and lost an inch and a half around her waist. Her skirts slipped down to her hips and there were days when she felt that her knickers would fall to the ground.

Nevertheless, she had not stopped exercising. Then because, on the front of a glossy monthly, she had seen the words, in large gold letters, 'Are you Happy with your Bust?', she had bought it. If the answer was, as in her case an emphatic 'No', then the remedy, it seemed, was a Balcony Bra. A Balcony Bra? Yes! And they were obtainable in all good stores, including Marks & Spencer!

She had bought one, in white polyester satin, taken it home and tried it on immediately. It was a sort of shelf—all right, a balcony—stoutly wired, thickly padded, the front curved upwards so that the goods, though abundantly on show and rising high, would not fall off the shelf. It was a bit like an épergne in which a couple of oranges could rest. (Or in her case, satsumas. And in Lucinda's case, water melons.) It was immensely strong and probably designed, nay engineered, by a man who built bridges. And where, she demanded of her reflection in the mirror, where was the cleavage, that dark, mysterious valley so beloved by photographers and which the magazine article had practically promised would be hers?

There was none. And even if she wore a neckline as low as her waist, there would be none. The very sight of the bloody balcony bra gave her an even worse inferiority complex in the bust section.

Such were her thoughts as Egeus and Hermia battled out their differences. She came to as

Helena entered. She had missed nearly six pages, she, who on this evening had intended that every phrase, every word, should be honed to perfection. Fortunately they were the pages with which she always found least fault, so her non-intervention was not noticeable. But now she must concentrate on the play. She was the producer, after all. The responsibility was hers. Everyone looked to her.

'Helena, dear!' she said. 'Shall we take your entrance again? I'm not quite sure . . .'

None too pleased, Jennie Austin walked off the stage and waited in the wings.

'You can come on now!' Ursula called.

'No I can't! I'm waiting for my cue.'

Ursula sighed. Sometimes these days Jennie could be quite awkward. No longer totally amenable. Answering back, arguing, not at all the shy little violet she had been. And it had all started on that awful evening in the Queen's Head. She was still going to the pub, after most rehearsals, and staying until the end, though to be fair she frequently drank nothing stronger than bitter lemon. She never touched sherry and she was not on speaking terms with Giles, though he appeared not to be the least bit upset about that. Dear Giles! Wedded to his art.

'Lysander!' Ursula said. 'Will you give Helena her cue?'

'Sure! "Keep promise, love—here comes Helena".'

'That's not the best cue!' Helena argued. 'It's too late to give me time to appeal. Can't I have Hermia's "Tomorrow truly will I meet with thee"?'

Just who, Ursula asked herself, was producing this play? Actually, though, the girl was right.

'Very well, then! Hermia!'

George and Tina sat side by side in the shadow at the side of the hall. These days Ursula kept all the light on the stage, dimming the rest, using a small torch to follow her script. The cast were no longer allowed to clutch their scripts.

'I wondered . . .' Tina said to George. 'Would you like to come to lunch on Saturday?'

'Well, I'm not . . .'

'I discussed it with Daniel. He was quite agreeable. He just wanted to make certain that he'd be able to go off not long afterwards to Southfield with his pals. It's Southfield carnival. I told him of course he could.'

'Then I'd love to come,' George said. 'If you're sure.'

'Quite sure!' Tina said.

*   *   *

'Well!' Petra said when she and Adam were back in Plum Tree House. 'That wasn't the happiest of rehearsals, was it?'

'It certainly wasn't,' Adam agreed. 'She was in a really bad mood. Which is unusual. Ursula is bossy, but not often bad-tempered.'

'Did you mind not going to the pub with the rest?' Petra asked.

'Don't be silly! Why would I want to be with the rest? I'd rather be with you.'

'I just had too much on my mind. I can't stop thinking about it, and I'll have to sort things out. Would you like a drink?'

'Not at the moment. So what are you going to do—if anything? Don't forget,' Adam reminded her, 'that you have the option of doing nothing. Write a nice, polite note to Tanya, and leave it at that.'

Petra shook her head.

'I can't. I can't leave it at that. Even if I never want to meet Eliot Frobisher, and I'm not sure of that either, I want to know more about my father—and I shall *always* refer to Brian Banbury as my father. I want to know how he came into it, how he met with my mother. Why did he marry her? I can only think that she already had me, or that she was pregnant with me at the time. And if you knew my father you'd think either of those things was an unlikely scenario.'

'He would have had to have been very much in love with her,' Adam said.

'Unless he thought *he* was the father,' Petra said. 'But it's difficult to fit it all together.'

They were sitting side by side on the sofa. Adam put his arm around her shoulders. 'Honestly, darling, I don't see how you can hope to find out. It's all so long ago. And the people who could tell you are no longer alive.'

'I must find out,' Petra persisted. 'I've not stopped thinking about it since Tanya told me!'

'And did you believe all she told you?'

'Why wouldn't I?' But should I have done? Petra asked herself. 'Why should she say it if it wasn't true? But if you'd seen her, if you'd seen us standing side by side you'd have known it was true, at any rate that Eliot Frobisher had fathered me.' Fathered me biologically, she thought. Not even remotely in any other way. She asked herself again whether he even knew of her existence.

'Tanya told me nothing about my mother,' she

287

said. 'How could she?'

'As far as I can see,' Adam said, 'Eliot Frobisher is the only one who can do that. And do you actually want to meet him?'

'I don't know about that,' Petra said. 'But I'm not sure he's the one who can tell me anything. I've thought about this. There might just be someone at the convent where my mother was at school who'll know something. In nineteen-sixty my mother would have left, though Claire might still have been there, or been on the point of leaving. In what circumstances did they go to Petra together? And where does Eliot fit in? If I take the photograph with me, which I shall, they might even recognize him.'

'Where *do* you think he might have fitted in?' Adam asked.

Petra shrugged.

'I really don't know! I suppose he could, for instance, have been a visiting art master to the school. When I was at school we had a man who came once a week and put us through our musical paces, mostly singing.' She remembered him well. Every Thursday the main corridor had echoed to snatches of 'Cherry Ripe' or jolly sea shanties.

'I don't know! It's all conjecture, nevertheless I might find some answers.'

'It's a long shot,' Adam said. 'It's not far short of forty years ago. They might well all have left.'

'Not necessarily,' Petra contradicted. 'Of course it's all conjecture, but remember they were nuns. Some will have died, of course; some might have been sent away to other houses in the order, they do get moved around, but it's quite likely some will still be there. Nuns, on the whole, don't change their jobs. It's a lifetime commitment.'

'I see what you mean,' Adam said. 'Some of them might have been quite young when your mother was there, but they could still be around.'

'That's right,' Petra agreed. 'That's why I think I've got to go to the convent.'

'You're determined?' Adam asked the question, though he already knew the answer.

'I am!'

He made one last effort.

'Couldn't you possibly let it all lie? Leave it where it is. Put it behind you?'

'I couldn't!' Petra said. 'It's not possible! Surely, Adam, you must see that?'

'I suppose I do,' he admitted reluctantly. 'Where is the convent?'

'In Bedfordshire. St Monica's. I came across the address amongst my mother's things.'

'Then I would want to go with you,' Adam said. 'But I don't see how I can. If we wait until the play is over, then I'll be back at work. A new academic year, new students and so on. I'll have a heavy workload. I won't be able to take the time.'

'In any case,' Petra said firmly, 'I don't want to wait so long. I want to go as soon as possible.'

'Then I still can't go! In all fairness I can't just miss rehearsals. It might take up to a week.'

'I know,' Petra said. 'It might take less, but I can't be sure. One never knows where things might lead. And of course you can't skip rehearsals, but I can. I'm well ahead with all my stuff. The scenery's done—or planned—and the costumes are almost ready. Ursula wants them to be worn quite soon now, so that people get used to moving in them.'

Adam sighed. 'I hardly seem to have known you

289

ten minutes before you're dashing off all over the place!'

'I know,' Petra said. 'But I must! You do see that? And honestly, Adam, I do think this is something better done on my own. In fact, the nuns might not talk to me if you were with me.'

'I know you won't rest until you do it,' Adam said. 'So I suppose you'd better go ahead.'

'I'll come back to you,' Petra said. 'I won't stay away a minute longer than I need to!'

'When will you go?' Adam asked.

'As soon as I can arrange it. I'll write to the convent tomorrow—I don't think it's something I can go into on the telephone. Or perhaps I can. I shall only say, to begin with, that since my mother died I've been trying to piece together parts of her early life, and so on. And will they allow me a visit? Preferably soon. I'll have to wait for the reply until I can make a definite date.'

'Right then,' Adam said. 'Then shall we try to stop thinking about it for now? Shall we listen to some music, and shall we have that drink you offered?'

And after that, Petra thought, we shall go to bed.

CHAPTER NINETEEN

Petra wrote to the convent immediately after breakfast the next morning, and took the letter to post at once. The reply came on the following Tuesday. Certainly she was welcome to visit. Yes, her mother was still remembered by Sister Gabriella, who had taught her French and would

290

Petra please telephone to arrange a mutually suitable date and time, and would she bear in mind that a fortnight hence they would be in retreat for a week and so could not welcome visitors then.

Petra telephoned Adam at once.

'I feel really hopeful,' she told him. 'I was right, wasn't I, in thinking there might be someone there who would remember my mother?'

'You were,' Adam agreed. 'I reckon it will be good for you to talk with this Sister Gabriella, but don't expect too much.'

'Why do you say that?' Petra demanded.

'Because she knew your mother as a schoolgirl. That's not to say she'll know anything at all of what happened after your mother left school.'

'She might. My mother might have kept in touch with her. Girls sometimes do with teachers they like.'

Adam could hear the stubbornness in her voice. Nothing he could say would put her off her cause and did he, in the end, want to do so? He simply didn't want her to be hurt further, or even deeply disappointed, but if that was to happen, if that was part of the story, then he couldn't prevent it. And given Petra's temperament wasn't it better for her to pursue the matter as far as it would go than to let it drop, and wonder about it ever afterwards?

'Of course they do!' he agreed. 'And you're right, your mother might well have kept in touch.'

'I shall call Reverend Mother as soon as you've rung off,' Petra said.

'Is that a hint?'

'No, but I would like to make the call. I want to go as soon as I can, especially as they have a retreat in the offing.'

'Very well,' Adam said. 'Let me know what happens.'

'I will,' Petra promised. 'In any case I'll see you at rehearsal this evening.'

Her conversation with Reverend Mother was short and to the point, though pleasant.

'When can you come?' Reverend Mother asked.

'Any time from tomorrow onward. The sooner the better!' Petra said.

'In that case make it tomorrow. How will you travel?'

'I'll drive up,' Petra said.

'Good! It's the best way. You can do most of it on the motorway. And now I'll hand you over to Sister Faith and she'll tell you exactly how to get here.'

Sister Faith did just that: road numbers, signposts, distances, landmarks.

'And I'll write it down and put it in the post,' she promised. 'You might just get it in the morning, before you leave.'

How businesslike they were, how orderly, Petra thought. But that shouldn't surprise her, theirs was a regimented life.

She called Adam again.

'I'm going tomorrow, first thing in the morning,' she told him.

'That's short notice,' Adam said.

'I know. But Reverend Mother said I could. And—oh!—it will be so much better than waiting!'

'When will you be back?' he asked.

'I'm not sure. I expect I'll stay the night, there must be somewhere I can book in. Or better still, they might let me stay in the convent. I'd quite like to spend a few hours where my mother used to be.

I'll phone you from wherever. And I think I shall skip this evening's rehearsal. I'll be far too busy.'

'Will you be too busy for me if I came round after rehearsal?' Adam asked.

'Never! I'd very much like you to do that. Oh, Adam, I'm so excited.'

'Shall I make your excuses to Ursula?'

'No. I'll call her. I think I ought to. I'll tell her I've had a sudden invitation to see an old friend of my mother—no other opportunity, etcetera. That's *all* I shall tell her, except I might say the friend is a nun. She might be less cross with me. People don't get cross with nuns, do they?'

'I don't know,' Adam said. 'I'm not acquainted with any.'

Nevertheless Petra thought, as, a little later, she tapped out Ursula's number, she *will* be cross. She didn't care. At the moment she didn't care about anything except what was to happen the next day.

'Ursula King!' a breathless voice said.

'Petra here. Are you all right?' There was some loud beat music in the background, so nothing was quite clear.

'I'm . . . yes, I'm perfectly all right. Wait a second, there's some stupid music on the radio. Let me switch it off.'

'Put a sock in it, you silly cow!' she hissed at Honey as she turned off the video.

'There!' she said, picking up the phone again. 'That's better! I don't know how I happened to light on that station. I usually listen to Classic FM, or Radio Three! Now what were you saying, Petra dear?'

'I was about to say . . .' Petra told her the rest.

'Going away!' Ursula shouted. 'But you've only

293

just come back from going away! A friend of your mother's? A *nun*? Is it important? Do you have to go?'

'I'm afraid I do!' Petra said. 'She's asked to see me.' She refrained from saying, in so many words, that the friend of her mother was at death's door, but the tone of her voice told the lie she wasn't prepared to utter.

'Oh! It's all very sudden!'

'It is, isn't it,' Petra agreed.

'We're at a rather critical part in the play, you know that, dear!'

'Yes, I do.' And so is what I'm about to do, Petra thought. 'But we don't have parts, and Amelia and I have just about finished the costumes, so you've no worry there.'

'I just don't like people being missing,' Ursula said petulantly. 'How long will you be away?'

'Not long. Two or three days at the most. Perhaps not even that. Look, Ursula, I'll have to ring off. I think there's someone at the door!'

There wasn't, but an hour later there was, and when Petra answered it, there stood Ursula.

'I had to come, dear,' she said. 'I thought you didn't sound quite yourself on the phone. I had to make sure you were all right!'

'How kind of you!' Petra said. She would have said 'do come in' but Ursula was already well into the hall. 'I'm fine, really.'

'I expect it's been something of a shock to you, suddenly being summoned by a friend of your late mother—and a nun at that. Do you know her?'

You are a nosey old boot, Petra thought, and I will tell you as much as I want you to know, and no more. And if I have to lie about the rest, then God forgive me. Perhaps Reverend Mother will put in a word for me there.

'They knew each other when my mother was at school,' Petra said.

'Ah! School friends! I never went in for school friends, but for those who do I believe it's quite a strong tie. Where does the friend live?'

'Bedfordshire. Somewhere north of Luton. Near Flitwick.'

Ursula dismissed Bedfordshire with a wave of her hand. 'I don't know that part of the world,' she said.

'Would you like to see the costumes for the play?' Petra offered. Anything to get Ursula on to a different subject. 'In fact you could take most of them in a week's time.' She led the way to what, for the moment, was designated the sewing room.

'Very nice!' Ursula acknowledged. 'Very nice indeed! I think perhaps Titania's is a wee bit too elaborate.'

'She *is* the Queen of the Fairies,' Petra pointed out.

Everyone, by now, knew of Ursula's dislike of Lucinda, and of the reason for it. It was a joke. No-one took it seriously except Ursula herself. Eric was just a nice, popular man, who liked to flirt with pretty women. Lucinda would make a pass at any man in sight, with the exception of Giles Rowland, which even if they had not hated each other would have been a waste of time since he was not into ladies. Melvin-alias-Puck was more in his line.

'Let's hope that everyone will perform better when they start moving around in the right clothes,' Ursula said. 'I must say, you've done a wonderful job here!'

'But not on my own,' Petra said. 'Amelia's been a great help. I couldn't have managed all this without her.'

'Good!' Ursula said. 'It's a pity about the measles.'

'They'll be over long before the production's date,' Petra said. 'You will let them back into the play, won't you?'

'Oh yes!' Ursula said. 'We can't have too many fairies and attendants, as long as they don't get under other people's feet on the stage. Lucinda, of course, would enjoy a train of a dozen if she could have them!'

'Would you like a cup of coffee?' Petra asked.

'That would be nice.'

Ursula used the coffee interval to sum up everyone in the cast, though she was not, Petra thought, really disparaging about anyone other than Lucinda.

'I think George is getting over his loss quite well,' she said. 'And of course Tina is helping him. She's just what he needs.'

'She's a nice woman,' Petra agreed.

'And have you noticed that Hermia and Puck seem to be making a go of it? So sweet! Between you and me, I didn't have much hope of Melvin as Puck, I simply couldn't find anyone else, but he's turning out quite well.' She nodded with satisfaction. 'It's wonderful, isn't it, how MADS brings people together. You'd be surprised—or perhaps you wouldn't—by the number of people over the years who have found their true loves in MADS. Doris and Norman Pritchard . . .'

'Really, I'd imagined Doris and Norman were married long before they joined MADS,' Petra said.

'Oh, they were!' Ursula admitted. 'But I do think that being stage manager and property mistress has brought them closer. Shared interests, you know! And that wonderful attic! And now George and Tina, and Melvin and Victoria. And I promise you I shall try hard to find someone for Jennie Austin. I'm sure it's what she needs. Really, sometimes I feel quite like Cupid!' She gave a trill of laughter. She could probably, she thought, run one of those dating agencies. They made a great deal of money for what she was doing for free! Out of the goodness of her heart.

'And now you and Adam!'

She smiled roguishly, looking for a word of acknowledgement, or even an up-date, neither of which came.

'Would you like to take a few of the costumes with you now?' Petra asked obtusely. 'Some of them are ready.'

'What? Oh, yes, why not?'

'I'll give you a hand with packing them into the car,' Petra offered.

'Are you quite *sure* you can't come this evening?' Ursula persisted. 'You'd be a great help with the dressing.' She got into the car and turned on the ignition.

'Absolutely sure,' Petra said firmly. 'I'll give you a call as soon as I get back.'

The post came early next morning. There on the mat, between two charity appeals, a fashion catalogue and an advertisement for a book club, was the letter from Sister Faith, though it was not a letter, simply a page of explicit instructions and a small, hand-drawn map. Who could go wrong?

Petra thought. M23, M1, turn on to the 5120. If the traffic wasn't heavy she should be there by lunchtime.

Like Ursula, she thought as she drove at a steady seventy up the motorway, Bedfordshire was not a county she knew. It was in sharp contrast to the hills of Surrey, and even more so to the fells and rivers of her own North Yorkshire, but it had its own particular grandeur in the breadth of its view and, even more, in its skyscape. The hills she was used to precluded such a great sweep of sky. On this summer's day it was blue and enormous, with high white cirrus clouds.

She was beginning to be hungry. She would, she decided, stop to eat before she left the motorway. St Monica's was out in the countryside, where there might be a shortage of restaurants. She wished to arrive there as fit and alert as possible. Being hungry would be no help at all. Besides, and she wondered if this wasn't at the bottom of it, pausing for a meal would give her one more chance to think about what she was doing, to make sure.

The car-park was busy, and inside the restaurant there was a long queue. When her turn came she made her choice, paid for it, and to her surprise found a small table unoccupied. The trouble was that as soon as she sat down to eat she was no longer hungry, not the slightest bit. She had chosen fish, and a side salad, but after two mouthfuls she put down her fork and gave up. The only thing she could stomach—she was very thirsty—was the can of coke. She drank that and left.

Following Sister Faith's instructions St Monica's was easy to find. Iron gates stood hospitably open at the entrance to a long drive. She stopped at the lodge in order to announce herself but it appeared to be uninhabited, so she drove forward to the house, of which she had a glimpse through a break in the trees lining the drive. It was a large, red-brick building, rather ugly, she thought, with a plethora of chimneys. She looked at her watch. It was a quarter to two. Had she arrived at a time when they were all taking an after-lunch rest? Did English nuns have a siesta?

She rang the bell, one of those bells which echoed as though through vast caverns, and was answered by a small, neat nun who looked far too lively to have been wakened from a nap.

'I have an appointment with Reverend Mother,' Petra explained. 'Well, not for a specific time, but for this afternoon. If it's not yet . . .' Convenient, she was about to say.

'Ah yes! Miss Banbury?'

'That's right.'

'Will you come in and sit yourself down here, and I'll let her know you've arrived!' She scuttled away like a small, grey animal, and in no time at all scuttled back again.

'Reverend Mother says, will you be so good as to wait ten minutes. She's occupied, but she won't keep you waiting longer than that.'

'That's fine!' Petra said.

In the next few minutes, since she had nothing to read, she observed her surroundings, the high, moulded ceiling, the large statue on a plinth, possibly, she thought, St Monica, and watched the nuns as they crossed and recrossed the hall, in ones and twos, on silent feet, purposely bound for somewhere or other. They all wore grey habits, though she had thought that nuns no longer did so.

299

Perhaps they had the choice, or perhaps they just wore the habit within their own convent?

Before the ten minutes was up the little nun reappeared.

'Reverend Mother's ready now. I'll take you to her.'

Petra, following the nun's quick footsteps down a long corridor, was shown into a surprisingly small room. The desk behind which Reverend Mother sat, and the visitor's chair in front of it, took up most of the space.

'Miss Banbury!' the little nun announced.

'Thank you, Sister Grace,' Reverend Mother said as she motioned Petra to the chair. 'Good afternoon, Miss Banbury. I'm sorry to have kept you waiting. May I call you Petra?'

'Please do!'

What struck Petra was how young Reverend Mother both looked and sounded. If she had thought of it at all she had expected an elderly, dignified lady with one foot in heaven. Well, this one sounded too friendly to be dignified. Possibly she had one foot in heaven, but elderly she was not. Petra judged her to be about her own age, and the simple habit enhanced her clear complexion and beautiful face.

'Do you want to know something about your mother?' Reverend Mother asked. 'Is it something specific you're looking for?'

Petra dodged the question. She was not, at this moment, prepared to tell what she knew and what more she needed to know, though she faced the fact that sooner or later it would have to come out.

'As I told you, my mother and father died as a result of a car crash . . .'

300

'Yes, I'm sorry about that.'

'I suppose I must have realized that my mother had never talked much about her early days, her childhood, her schooldays. In fact I hadn't thought that it mattered, there were years ahead in which she could do so. Perhaps when she was old she would enjoy looking back and talking about it, but she was not allowed to grow old.'

'So in fact you want to know anything you can about when she was young?'

'That's it! You see, there are hardly any relatives at all on either my father's or my mother's side. Some of the few there were emigrated to Australia. I've never seen them and now I've totally lost touch.'

'Well, as I told you,' Reverend Mother said, 'I wasn't here in your mother's time—indeed, I've only been here in the last year—and several who would have been here have moved on, but Sister Gabriella is still with us, and she remembers your mother.'

'That's wonderful!' Petra said.

'Though, I must remind you that Sister Gabriella is now quite elderly—she was middle-aged in your mother's time—and she's rather frail. She has to spend much of her time resting, so I must ask you not to tire her. However, you'll find her most interested in talking about the old days, though possibly she gets confused. I can't always judge that.'

'I also wonder,' Petra said, 'if you could tell me something else. I'm interested in finding out about a man named Eliot Frobisher. He's an artist. I know he was a friend of my mother's—and of Claire's—and I wondered how the three of them

301

first met. It seemed to me it might have been here. I wondered if perhaps he taught art in the school here, as a visiting teacher perhaps.'

'I think a male teacher would have been unusual, especially in those days,' Reverend Mother said. 'However, I will ask Sister Grace to examine the records. I'll take you to Sister Gabriella now and then you can come back to me, tell me what progress you've made.'

She led the way along yet another corridor—the house was a labyrinth—to a small, sunny room overlooking the garden, where Sister Gabriella sat propped up in bed against a pile of snowy white pillows. She was thin, and a yellowish sort of pale. Time had washed all the colour from her skin. Petra had not for one moment thought of Sister Gabriella being so old. It was a disappointment. What she must cling to now was the thought that old people often remembered the past more clearly than those who were not yet old.

'I've brought Petra Banbury to see you,' Reverend Mother said in a raised, clear voice. 'You told me you knew her mother, Marian.'

'I'm afraid I don't know any Marian Banbury,' Sister Gabriella said.

'She wouldn't have been then,' Petra said. 'She was Marian Greenwood.'

Sister Gabriella said nothing for a moment or two. It was as if her fingers were flicking through the card index of her mind. Suddenly, her face was lit by a smile of great sweetness.

'Marian Greenwood! Of course I remember her! She was very good at French. One of my star pupils! I hope she's kept it up?'

Why did I never know my mother was good at

French? Petra asked herself. She had never said a word about it.

'I don't suppose she had much time to do so,' she replied.

'I'll leave you for the moment,' Reverend Mother interrupted. 'Just ring the bell when you're ready, and someone will come.'

'I knew the other girl also,' Sister Gabriella said. 'The younger one. Marian's friend. What was her name?'

'Claire?' Petra suggested.

'Yes, I think it was. She was not so good at French.' Sister Gabriella dismissed Claire with a slight nod, after which she fell silent and looked as though she might fall asleep.

'Did you know my mother well?' Petra prompted. 'Did you keep in touch with her after she left St Monica's?'

'They were all such lovely girls!' Sister Gabriella said. 'Lovely girls!'

'And did you . . . ?'

'No, not at all. I was sorry to see her go. I always hated parting with the girls. I never kept in touch with any of them.'

Petra felt choked with disappointment. The visit had promised so much, and clearly there was nothing here. She'd been foolish to build her hopes so high.

'Well, thank you, Sister,' she said. 'It's nice to know that you remember my mother. I'll leave you in peace now. I hope I haven't tired you too much.'

Sister Gabriella did not hear her. She had closed her eyes and her chin had fallen to her chest. She was asleep. Petra pressed the bell at the side of the bed and waited to be collected. Petra watched her as she slept. She looked so frail, deep hollows in her cheeks, her eyelids, and the skin around her eyes, blue-shadowed.

There was a knock at the door and a nun entered. 'I'll take you to Reverend Mother,' she said.

At the sound of her voice, Sister Gabriella raised her head, opened her eyes and, as Petra was leaving the room, spoke.

'Sister Thomasina was the one who did that!'

And then she was immediately asleep again.

Petra stood still. She had a sudden, terrible impulse to stride back to the bed and shake Sister Gabriella, shake something out of her. Her impatience must have shown in her face. The nun shook her head, put a hand on Petra's arm.

'We mustn't disturb her any further. She really is unwell. Come,' she repeated, 'I'll take you to Reverend Mother.'

CHAPTER TWENTY

'Well,' Reverend Mother said, 'how did you get on?'

'I'm not quite sure,' Petra said doubtfully. 'Sister Gabriella *did* remember my mother, and it was nice to realize that she remembered her with affection, though she didn't recall many details, other than that my mother was good at French.' Indeed it was the only thing which had added anything to her knowledge, for what it was worth.

'And had you known that?'

'Not at all,' Petra said. 'I never heard my mother

speak a word of French, but why would I? We never went abroad. I think Sister Gabriella was too tired to say much.'

'Yes. Well, I did warn you of that.'

'There was one thing,' Petra said, 'just as I was leaving she mentioned a Sister Thomasina who, she said, had known my mother. Is Sister Thomasina here at St Monica's?'

'No, she isn't, but I do know where she is. She's at the Refuge.'

'The Refuge?'

'The Refuge for Abused Women,' Reverend Mother said. 'Sister Thomasina is in charge.'

'But that's . . .' Petra began.

Reverend Mother was still speaking.

'I don't know Sister Thomasina well, but of course I have met her. She's been at the Refuge a long time. Though she's now in charge, she was sent there as a young nun. Looking at the dates when your mother was here, I would have thought Sister Thomasina left St Monica's before your mother did. But of course I don't know for certain. I didn't have it in mind.'

'Perhaps they kept in touch,' Petra said. There must be a connection somewhere, it was to the Refuge that Claire had, according to Mr Craig, her solicitor, given so much money.

'Do you think I might be able to see Sister Thomasina?' she asked.

'Oh, I don't see why not,' Reverend Mother said briskly. 'The Refuge is near to Bedford—not many miles from here.'

'I'd be most grateful,' Petra said.

Reverend Mother picked up the telephone at once. Spoke, listened.

'Oh! I see!

'When . . . ? Would that be all right?'

It was a short, one-sided conversation. She put down the telephone.

'I'm sorry,' she said. 'Sister Thomasina is away. She had to go to her sister who's quite ill, in hospital.'

Petra felt the disappointment like a physical blow. But I shall come back, no way will I give up now, she decided even before Reverend Mother had finished speaking.

'She's expected back tonight, but quite late. Too late for her to see you, though it seems she could do so tomorrow morning.'

'Oh, but that would be wonderful!' Petra cried. 'Thank you so much, Reverend Mother. Then all I need now is to book into a bed and breakfast or an hotel for the night. Perhaps you could recommend one?'

'If you wish you may stay here overnight,' Reverend Mother said. 'We have guest rooms, and with the girls on holiday we're less busy.'

'That would be marvellous,' Petra said. She liked the thought of staying, even for one night, in a place where her mother had been.

'Nothing here is luxurious,' Reverend Mother warned her. 'Though I think you'll be comfortable! We shall be having a cup of tea in the common room at half-past three. Perhaps you'd like to join us?'

'Thank you, I would!' Petra said.

'Supper is at six-thirty. Rather early, I know, but we retire for the night immediately after Night Prayers. And now I'll ring for Sister Grace. We'll see what progress she's made on Mr Frobisher, and then she'll show you to your room.'

While she was speaking she had picked up her telephone and pressed a digit. 'Can you come now, Sister?' she said. It was not so much a request as a polite command, with the result that two minutes later Sister Grace tapped at the door and entered.

'Were you able to find out anything about Mr Frobisher?' Reverend Mother enquired.

'I'm sorry, nothing at all,' Sister Grace said. 'There's nothing in the records, actually there's no mention of any art master.'

'Thank you, Sister,' Reverend Mother said.

Another disappointment, Petra thought, but it had been a long shot.

'Petra Banbury is to stay the night with us,' Reverend Mother continued. 'Would you show her to one of the guest rooms? Which one will you choose?'

'Bethany,' Sister Grace said. 'It's ready and waiting. Also it overlooks the garden.'

'Good! And will you also give her a key to the side door.'

Reverend Mother turned to Petra. 'That way you can come and go as you please. We tend to keep the main door locked most of the time, but the lock is old and I daresay you would find the key difficult to turn. Then, Sister Grace, will you take Petra in to tea, and let Cook know we'll be an extra one for supper and breakfast?'

Without appearing the least bit impolite she made it clear that Petra could now leave. Was this how it felt to have an audience with the Queen? Petra asked herself as she followed Sister Grace out of the room.

'Bethany' was a tiny room with a narrow bed, a

small table beside it, a chest of drawers with a mirror on top, and a shelf of devotional books. Everything was spotless—the white counterpane, the polished wood floor with a mat patterned in grey and pink.

'Bethany is a lovely name,' Petra said.

'Yes. All our rooms are named after saints, or places in the Gospels. Much nicer than numbers.' She handed Petra two keys. The side door. One latchkey, the other for the mortice lock.'

'Thank you,' Petra said. 'I'm sure I shan't want to go out after supper but I might well do so between tea and supper. Will that be all right?'

'Of course! You must do as you please. I'll leave you now to settle in, and I'll knock on your door at twenty past three to take you down to tea.'

When Sister Grace had left, Petra moved across to the window and looked out. It was a beautiful garden: lawns, trees which looked as though they'd been there for centuries, shrubs and, closer to the house, flower beds. Beyond the garden were tennis courts and playing fields—a hockey pitch, she thought. She wondered if her mother had been good at games, as well as at French. Two nuns were on their knees beside a border, presumably weeding. What an impediment their full-skirted habits must be when it came to gardening! I would be wearing jeans, or in this weather shorts, Petra thought.

Tea was enjoyable. Almost everyone smiled at her—and there were Shrewsbury biscuits. When it was over she left the convent by the side door and walked along the road in the direction of the nearest village. It was good to be in the open air, stretching her legs, but the real reason for her walk was to find a public telephone from which she could call Adam.

She supposed she could have telephoned from the convent, probably she had only to ask, but she much preferred the privacy of a call-box to ringing from there, with the possibility of someone else in the room.

She had almost reached the village before she found a call-box, and mercifully it was unoccupied.

Adam answered at once.

'How's it going?'

'Not fantastically well up to now,' Petra said, 'but I have better hopes of tomorrow. No-one here knows anything of Eliot, and Sister Gabriella had little new to tell me about my mother except that she was good at French; but it seems that there's a Sister Thomasina at the Refuge for Abused Women, not too far from here, and that she perhaps knew my mother better . . .'

'The Refuge for Abused Women? Isn't that the place . . . ?'

'Yes. To which Claire left money. I don't know the connection there. Anyway, I'm to see Sister Thomasina tomorrow.'

'So you have to stay overnight? Where?'

'Here in the convent,' Petra told him. 'They've given me a nice little room—well, a cell really. It's called Bethany.'

'Don't let them keep you,' Adam warned. 'I want you here! I miss you too much!'

Petra laughed.

'They won't! They're very nice and very kind—and surprisingly businesslike and efficient at the same time as being holy—but it's not the life for me! Besides, I miss you too! Very much indeed. So

I won't stay a minute longer than I need to.'

'I wish I was with you,' Adam said.

'I wish you were—in a way,' Petra admitted. 'But it wouldn't have worked if you'd been with me. I was right about that. How was last night's rehearsal? You didn't tell me.'

'All right,' Adam said. 'Lucinda had a prima-donna fit—she wasn't happy with the fairies. All right in quantity now, but apparently lacking in quality!'

'Ursula can't have liked that!'

'She didn't! Sparks flew! I don't quite know what's wrong with Ursula these days. She's crochety, which isn't like her. Bossy, yes! Crochety, no!'

'It's getting perilously near the production,' Petra pointed out. 'I expect she's nervous.'

'Maybe,' Adam conceded. 'So you'll be back tomorrow evening?'

'I should be. I'll phone you if not. And I'd better ring off now, there's a young woman standing outside, looking anxious. I always think it might be an emergency.'

'Probably wanting to ring her lover!' Adam said.

'In that case I know just how she feels,' Petra said. 'Anyway, goodnight, my love!'

'And to you,' Adam said. ' "Goodnight, goodnight! parting is such sweet sorrow. That I shall say goodnight till it be morrow." '

'And if you do,' Petra warned, 'I think the woman outside will probably attack the phone box and me in a fit of passion! Anyway, I have to be back for supper.'

Supper was surprisingly good, not at all what she had expected. No stodge, no overcooked

310

vegetables, no tapioca pudding. I wonder if it was as good as this in my mother's day? she wondered. And why did my mother never mention any of it? she asked herself yet again. Perhaps because what happened afterwards was too painful. On the other hand, none of it had happened until after my mother had left school, not until two or three years later, so why blank out such a large slice of life? In any case, Petra thought, I was a daily reminder, and she was never anything other than loving and kind towards me.

'Would you like to come to Night Prayers?' Sister Faith asked when supper was over. 'It's quite short, but of course you don't have to.'

'I think I would,' Petra said.

She had no idea what it would be. As it turned out she sat, or knelt, in the small, peaceful chapel, listening to the nuns. Sister Faith was right, it was quite short.

'The Lord grant us a quiet night and a perfect end,' Reverend Mother concluded in her firm, clear voice, as if the Lord also was under her instruction.

The nuns rose to their feet and filed out silently, Petra following them.

She slept well. Perhaps it was the effect of Night Prayers, perhaps it was plain and simple fatigue after a long day. Also, she wakened early, and was pleased to remember that so did the nuns, and that if she wished to join them for breakfast it was at seven-thirty. Her appointment with Sister Thomasina was at half-past nine.

Reverend Mother gave her a cordial send-off.

'I hope all goes well,' she said, 'and that Sister Thomasina is able to help you. If there's anything more I can do, please let me know.'

'You've been very kind,' Petra said. 'I'm most grateful.'

'Then God go with you,' Reverend Mother said.

Sister Thomasina was quite different from Reverend Mother. She was much older, probably in her early sixties, Petra guessed. Her hair was thick, grey, cut in an untidy bob. She was plump, round-faced, pink-cheeked and smiling. It was a combination which seemed to have kept at bay the wrinkles. Also, she did not wear the habit, and that, at least in appearance, set her in another world from the sisters at St Monica's. She was dressed in a blue-and-white striped cotton dress, belted around an ample waist. Her office, too, was totally unlike Reverend Mother's: largish, shabby, untidy in a comfortable sort of way, as if it was on the verge of being sorted out but there was never enough time.

'Come in, come in!' she invited. 'Do sit down! That's a comfortable chair!' She indicated an armchair by the window and, instead of sitting behind her desk, took a chair close by Petra's. 'Did you find your way easily?'

'Oh yes!' Petra said. 'Sister Faith gave me precise instructions, I only had to follow them.'

'I don't know Sister Faith,' Sister Thomasina admitted, 'but that sounds entirely like St Monica's. It was like that when I was there, which is a long time ago. I was sent here when I was twenty.'

'I think you knew my mother,' Petra said.

'I did. I knew her when I was at St Monica's and she was a pupil there. I wasn't much older than she was. I was very fond of her.'

In fact, she had always thought that one of the

312

reasons why she had been sent to the Refuge—
though it wasn't called that then—was that she had
grown too fond of Marian, though none of that was
said.

'I was sorry to hear of Marian's death,' she said
to Petra. 'Claire wrote to tell me.'

'So you knew Claire?'

'Of course, Claire was two years younger than
Marian. When Claire first came to the school
Marian was chosen to keep an eye on her, to be a
sort of big sister. It was the usual practice in the
school and in this case particularly it worked so
well. Marian looked after her wonderfully. Of
course, Marian left school two years before Claire,
but they kept in close touch. Marian came to visit
several times when Claire was staying here.'

'Claire stayed *here*?' Petra said. 'This must have
been after she'd left school?'

'Oh yes! Some months afterwards.'

'So she came to work here?' That would explain,
Petra thought, why Claire had left money to this
place. She opened her handbag and took out the
photograph.

'This is my mother and Claire,' she said, handing
it to Sister Thomasina. 'According to the name on
the back the man's name is Eliot. In fact I know
now it's Eliot Frobisher. I wonder if you knew him.
I have a very good reason for asking.'

Sister Thomasina studied the photograph
carefully, taking more time than she needed
because she did not know what to say next. She
would have to say something. She sent up a swift
prayer: Lord, may the words of my mouth . . .

'Yes, it's lovely of Claire and Marian. I've never
met Eliot, but I knew of him,' she said.

313

The two women looked at each other. Petra spoke first.

'I believe Eliot Frobisher is my father. I don't want it to be true, but I believe it is.'

Sister Thomasina spoke with difficulty.

'Yes,' she said. 'He is your father.'

'And you knew about him? They didn't at the convent.'

'He was never in this part of the world. But I learnt about him.'

'Please tell me!' Petra said. 'Sister Thomasina, please tell me. I don't care about him. I want to know about my mother. How she met him, what happened. I need to know the truth!'

'Yes, I see that,' Sister Thomasina said. 'But the truth is not always easy, my child. Not always easy to bear.'

'I can bear it!' Petra interrupted. 'I can bear it as long as I know the truth! And I love my mother. Nothing you can tell me will change that! It's more as if . . . I want to share it with her. Can you understand that?'

Sister Thomasina nodded, without speaking. She had a story to tell, but it was difficult to know where to begin. Begin at the beginning, she told herself.

'Claire Harden,' she said, 'was an only child of Dr Harden and his wife. Mrs Harden was almost forty when their daughter was born—'

'But I don't want . . .' Petra interrupted.

'You don't want to hear about Claire I know. But you must let me tell the story in my own way,' Sister Thomasina said. 'It is not an easy story.'

'I'm sorry!' Petra said.

'Dr Harden and his wife had given up hope of a

314

family, they were not sure, at least Dr Harden wasn't, that they now wanted a child. Nevertheless they were conscientious parents and deeply religious. Claire had been brought up in the Church, so it was not surprising that when Claire left St Monica's, having done very well in her examinations, they rewarded her with a trip to the Holy Land. Since Dr Harden was too busy to go, and I think because both he and Mrs Harden were a little fearful of travelling abroad, they paid for Marian, Claire's "big sister" from school, to accompany her, which naturally delighted both girls.'

So that, Petra thought, is how my mother met Eliot.

'While they were on holiday,' Sister Thomasina continued, 'Claire fell in love with a young Englishman, resident in Jerusalem. He was an artist, but to earn more money he sometimes acted as a guide.'

'How do you . . .' Petra broke in.

'How do I know this? Because Marian and Claire told me. Everything I shall tell you is fact, none of it is conjecture. So . . . the friendship between the three of them developed, and as a result Claire returned home pregnant.'

'Claire?'

Sister Thomasina held up a hand to silence Petra.

'Claire! Dr Harden and his wife were deeply distressed. Claire refused to disclose the name of the father for fear her parents might pursue him. She knew by the time she left the Holy Land that he had no further interest in her and would never consider marrying her. She was devastated and she

315

was frightened, but Claire had a very strong, even wilful, core to her. She never told Eliot about the child.

'As a doctor, her father had the means to abort the child, and no-one would ever know, but his religion forbade this and, of course, in nineteen-sixty so did the law. It was also deeply ingrained in Claire that this would be wrong.

'He contacted St Monica's and asked the nuns if Claire could stay with them until she had her baby, at which time it would be put up for adoption. Their reply was that they did not have the facilities, but their order ran a home a few miles away for girls in such a situation. Claire would be well looked after there.'

'The Refuge for Abused Women!'

'It wasn't called that then. It was the Mary of Magdala Home, a home for unmarried mothers, as they were then called. But who can say that the girls who came here weren't abused?

'Marian, of course, was deeply distressed by her friend's plight. She felt herself partly to blame because it was she who had encouraged Claire to come out of her shell, to enjoy herself. Nor had she sensed that the guide—yes, his name was Eliot—was up to no good. But it wasn't wholly guilt and compassion which decided her to adopt Claire's baby. Marian was already engaged when she went to the Holy Land, but she had been told that, as a result of a childhood illness, she could never have a child. She and her fiancé put forward their wedding plans in order to be ready for the baby.

'When the baby was born, a girl, Claire insisted that her name should be "Petra". Everyone thought this was strange, except the very few of us in the know. Shouldn't she have a saint's name? the nuns said.

'Claire pointed out that Petra was the same as Peter, one of the great saints. In any case, it was the only condition on which she wouldn't move.'

There was a long silence, broken in the end by Petra.

'So I am . . .'

'You are that baby. Yes.'

'Claire was my mother! I never saw her!'

'She fed you for four weeks, bathed you, saw to your every need. Then she handed you over to her best friend.' There were tears in Sister Thomasina's eyes.

'But why didn't she keep me?'

'Of course I talked to her a great deal about that. But remember she was only eighteen, and single motherhood was not an acceptable lifestyle choice for a young woman in nineteen-sixty, especially in a small village like Mindon and with conservative and elderly parents like Dr and Mrs Harden.

'The condition of the adoption,' Sister Thomasina continued, 'was that you would be brought up entirely as the child of Marian and Brian Banbury, no connection at all with Claire. As Claire would go back to her home in Mindon, a long way away from North Yorkshire, this would not be physically difficult. One can only imagine what it did to Claire, but it was a case of what was best for you. It was at my suggestion that Marian promised she would send photographs of you occasionally, perhaps on your birthday. I don't know whether she did this.'

'I don't know either,' Petra said. 'I didn't find

any among Claire's belongings. But what I haven't told you,' she exclaimed, 'is that I now live in Claire's house! She left it to my mother and I inherited it.'

'I did know that from Mr Craig,' Sister Thomasina said. 'When he told me about the will he mentioned that Claire's house had passed to the daughter of an old school friend. I guessed it would be you, so I'm not entirely surprised by your appearance here.'

'But there is something I found, in a chest of drawers in Claire's house which, in view of what you've told me, puzzles me,' Petra said.

'Everything I've told you is the truth,' Sister Thomasina said. 'Don't forget, I was there at the time. I suppose you'd call me a mediator. Marian and Claire were pleased to have me, and so was Brian. And then, of course, I looked after Claire from the day she arrived here, three months pregnant, to the day she left. We became very close. She knew me from school, and that helped. So what is it that still puzzles you, Petra? What did you find?'

'I found some drawings,' Petra said. 'They were made by Eliot Frobisher. I've established that. May I show them to you? I have to say that you might be shocked.'

Sister Thomasina smiled.

'My dear child, I doubt it. Everyone thinks nuns and priests are easily shocked. The reverse is true. They see so much of human nature, in every situation and often at its lowest, that they're unshockable.'

Petra took the drawings from her holdall and handed them to Sister Thomasina, who looked at them closely.

'Beautiful drawings!' she observed. 'What puzzles you?'

'You can tell, can't you,' Petra said, 'what the circumstances were? Eliot had had sex with my mother. By which I mean with Marian. It's all there, isn't it?'

Sister Thomasina looked up, eyes wide with surprise.

'Petra, you've got it wrong! This isn't Marian, this is Claire!'

'But surely . . . ? Why do you say it's Claire? How do you know?'

'I just do! The face is turned away, so neither of us can go on that, but the rest of it is quite recognizable to me. Don't forget, I looked after Claire through her pregnancy, I was there at the birth—and I knew her as a schoolgirl. If I may say so, you didn't know Claire at all, nor did you know Marian at this stage in her life. Why did you assume it was Marian?'

'Because I'd found the earlier drawings in Marian's house and assumed they were of her. Why would she have nude drawings of Claire?'

'Why indeed?' Sister Thomasina agreed. 'Do you have them with you? May I see them?'

Petra extracted the other envelope and handed them over.

'I see what you mean,' Sister Thomasina said as she looked at them. 'And once again the face is turned away.'

'I found out that this was true of most of his nudes,' Petra said. 'I suppose he had his reasons.'

Sister Thomasina was holding both drawings, one in each hand, studying them carefully.

319

'Clearly, they're drawn by the same person. Every artist leaves his or her own stamp, even without knowing it. But though they have outward similarities—both bodies of nubile young women in similar poses—they *are* two different women. The hair, for instance, is different. It grows differently, it falls differently. But above all the atmosphere of the two sets is different. In the first set the artist is drawing a nude, beautiful, sensuous, but he is apart from it. In the second he is totally involved. It's a drawing by an artist who has a passionate, and sexual, involvement with the model. I would have thought that as an artist yourself you'd have seen that!'

'I think my eyes didn't see because my mind was intent on another aspect,' Petra said.

'Well, whatever!' Sister Thomasina said. 'But I am totally certain that the drawings you found in Claire's house are of Claire.'

'And what of the others?'

Sister Thomasina shrugged. 'I don't think there's any great significance. It must have been a very heady time for the three of them. They were young, away from home in an exciting, exotic part of the world. He was an artist, and by the look of this photograph, and from the account of Marian and Claire, Eliot was handsome, charming and very persuasive. So, Marian agreed to model on one occasion. We had life classes in the school. We were used to nudes in art. Convents are not nearly as prudish as people imagine.'

She handed the drawings back and Petra put them away.

'Did you keep in touch with Claire?' she asked.

'Only intermittently. More so in recent years

when this place became a refuge for abused women. She was very generous to us. I knew I could call on her to help, especially if we needed financial help for a specific woman who was going through a bad time. You see, she was grateful for the way she was looked after here.'

'I find it difficult to take in,' Petra said. 'At the moment I don't know where I am.'

'I know,' Sister Thomasina said. 'It will take time. But let us say this. You had two mothers, both of them infinitely loving, both of them making great sacrifices. Though they loved each other dearly, they sacrificed seeing each other, and Claire made the tremendous sacrifice of never again seeing her child. They did it out of love so that you would have a normal upbringing. And Claire obviously never forgot you. She has made you the gift of a new home and of a new life for yourself—even though she is not here to see you embark on it.'

Sister Thomasina allowed a short silence, then said, 'And now I'm going to give you a cup of coffee and pack you off. I have no end of things to attend to. But write, or telephone, or even come to see me whenever you feel the need.'

CHAPTER TWENTY-ONE

Stopping at a service station for petrol and coffee, Petra also looked for a telephone. She longed to speak to Adam.

'Petra! Where are you?'

'I'm on the M1. I've stopped for petrol.' It was so

good to hear him. 'I'll be home in a couple of hours. Could you be there? Are you too busy?'

'Of course I'll be there! Are you all right? You don't sound exactly yourself.'

'I'm all right. It'll be good to be home. I'll tell you everything then.'

She didn't *feel* herself. But who was herself? A stranger for a father, and now suddenly, no more than a matter of a few hours ago, a new mother; neither of them ever seen, and in her mother's case never to *be* seen. And would she ever see Eliot Frobisher? Did she, in fact, want to? No wonder she didn't feel herself!

'You know where the key is,' she said to Adam. 'Let yourself in.'

'I will,' Adam said. 'I'll be there when you arrive.' He could hear the strain in her voice but a public call-box wasn't the best place for questions, so he wouldn't ask them.

'Drive carefully!' he said.

'I will,' Petra promised.

True to his promise he was there, standing in the open doorway as she got out of her car and walked up the path. She looked pale and strained, devoid of her usual sparkle. When she stepped into the hall he closed the door behind her and took her in his arms.

'I'm glad you're back,' he said. 'It seemed so much longer than it was!'

'I know,' Petra said. It was less than two days since she had left him, and she felt as though she had lived through half a lifetime. In a few short hours what had been the solid, safe background of her life had dissolved. Nothing was the same, or ever would be, she thought bleakly.

She stepped back from Adam's embrace and looked at him hard and searchingly, as if she was checking he was the same man she had left behind so recently.

'What is it?' he asked. 'What is it you're looking at?'

'You,' she said. 'Oh, Adam, you won't change, will you?'

'Of course I won't!' he assured her. 'Not a chance! Now tell me what you want to do. Shall I make something to eat, or do you want to talk?'

'I'd rather eat later,' she said.

He took her hand and they went into the living room. Sitting side by side on the sofa she told him all that had happened. Her voice was quiet, lacking strength, but on the whole steady, except that once or twice she faltered as if she might break down. It was during the first of these pauses that Adam tried to break in, hoping to help her, to reassure her, but she shook her head, silencing him. After that he sat quietly until she had finished, and a little way beyond, leaving her to break the silence when she was ready.

'So there it is!' she said eventually in a wan voice.

'Oh, Petra love, I should have been with you!' Adam cried. 'You shouldn't have been alone!'

'No!' she contradicted him. 'It wouldn't have worked. I had to be there on my own. Those things couldn't have been said in front of a third person.'

'Yes, I see that,' Adam conceded. 'But I should have been there to drive you back. You were in shock and I suspect you still are. I would have been horrified if I'd known—I mean at the thought of you on that long drive. Why didn't you telephone

323

me? I'd have come to fetch you.'

'I didn't even think of it,' Petra confessed. 'You were the one I wanted most in the world to see but it didn't ever occur to me to ask you to collect me.'

'Well it should have,' Adam said. 'I'm surprised that Sister Thomasina let you set off!'

For the first time Petra gave a faint smile. 'Those nuns are tough!' she said. 'Loving, compassionate, but tough. I don't doubt if she'd been in similar circumstances she'd have driven to Land's End, let alone Surrey!'

'I'll take your word for it,' Adam said.

He took both her hands in his and gently pulled her around so that, though they were sitting side by side, they were looking directly at each other. He saw sadness.

'Tell me how you feel,' he said. 'You've told me the story, something I'd never have dreamt of, but you haven't said how you feel.'

'I haven't had time even to know that myself. All the way back I concentrated hard on the driving. The motorway was busy, I daren't let my thoughts stray. All I thought about was getting back to Mindon, and to you. It was interesting that every mile of the way I felt I was getting nearer to home. Not just Mindon. *Home*. Even though I've lived here such a short time.'

'That's good, isn't it?' Adam asked.

'Of course! But as to how I felt . . . well, I don't know, not quite, though aside from myself what's uppermost is still what I felt when Sister Thomasina first told me . . .'

'Which is?'

'Deep pity for Claire. She was so young! And she must have loved Eliot, in spite of what he'd done,

324

in spite of the fact that he'd thrown her over, or she wouldn't have been so insistent on calling me Petra. It would have been the last name she'd have given me if she'd hated him, if she hadn't been happy there.'

'That's true,' Adam said.

'And then, she'd not only lost him, which no doubt was inevitable, but she'd lost her baby. I was lost to her. As far as we know she never had another lover, and certainly not another child, or she'd have provided for it, wouldn't she? Can you imagine her, teaching children all those years, watching them grow up, knowing what she knew, what she was missing?'

Suddenly, it was all too much for Petra. She pulled away from Adam, covered her face with her hands and wept bitterly. It was the first moment she'd given herself time to weep. She was totally unable to stem her tears.

Adam watched her in silence. No way would he try to stop her.

Presently, she looked up, her face swollen, her eyes red-rimmed, held out her hand for the handkerchief Adam offered her, and dried her eyes. He had never, he realized, loved her so much.

'As for my mother—and I mean Marian,' she said, 'and I can never call her anything other than my mother, or think of her any other way, she was the first person I consciously knew and loved, and the next was my father. They were wonderful parents. No-one could possibly take their place. And now I have the dilemma of having no parents, yet four parents. Two mothers, two fathers!

'Not,' she added, 'that I can think of Eliot Frobisher as my father, even though I know he was.

I don't want to think of him at all. Not yet.'

'You don't have to,' Adam said. 'This isn't something you have to solve at once, or even at all. You can take whatever time you need, or if you wish you can walk away from it.'

'I shall write to Tanya,' Petra said. 'Tell her what I know. When you come to think of it, she's my blood relation!'

'That's up to you!' Adam said. 'I think you have Claire and your mother in their right places. The rest can wait, if necessary for ever.'

'If it hadn't been for my mother and father,' Petra said, 'if they hadn't adopted me, I'd have gone to strangers who wouldn't even have known Claire. I'd never have known who I was.'

'If your mother and father hadn't adopted you, you wouldn't be the person you are today, and, more important, you wouldn't be in Mindon and you and I wouldn't have met. So far as I'm concerned, whatever happened, happened for the best.'

Petra's eyes brimmed with tears again.

'And here I am, in Claire's house, which seems now more than ever precious, and more than ever my home. And I feel so close to Claire without being in any way more distant from my mother and father. And I'm here with you. How can I be so happy and so sad at the same time?'

There was a pause.

'I shan't tell anyone about Claire,' Petra said. 'She kept her own secret and it's not for me or anyone else to disclose it. What I do wonder, though . . .'

She hesitated.

'Yes?'

'I wonder if my mother was wise, as I grew up, to keep everything about me from Claire. Wouldn't it have been kinder to have kept her more in touch?'

Adam shook his head.

'You can't judge that. Not from this distance. It might or might not have been kinder to Claire, but would it have been better for you? I expect that's what your parents had in mind.'

'Well, whatever they did, I have to forgive it!' Petra said.

'Forgive?' Adam said sharply. 'My love, I don't think you have anyone to forgive. Three out of four people did everything they could for you. They sacrificed for you, and most of all they showered you with love. I can't see that those three did anything which needs forgiveness.'

Petra was surprised, slightly shocked, by the tone of his voice. She had never expected the slightest criticism from him. And yet, she thought almost before he had finished speaking, he was right, wasn't he? She had, through all this, seen herself as the poor victim, poor little girl, but she was not. All her life she had lived with love, more love than most people ever experienced. She was shaken now, she was probably, as Adam had said, in shock, but there was no way she wouldn't come out of it. That she now knew for certain.

'You are quite right!' she said to Adam. 'Of course you are!'

*   *   *

Ursula and Eric were still at the table, finishing breakfast. Ursula was deep into the easier crossword of *The Times 2* section of the newspaper,

Eric was feeling thwarted because *Times 2* also had the sports pages, which he wanted for himself and Ursula had once again beaten him to it. Never mind that the main section contained all the world's news, plus erudite, provocative and informative features by the *crème de la crème* of journalists, it was the cricket he wanted. He had thought often of writing to *The Times*, asking if they were aware of their contribution to a bad start to the day, probably in thousands of homes.

'Restless desire, four letters?' Ursula said.

'Itch!' Eric supplied. That was easy. It was what he had for the bit of the paper she was hogging.

'Of course!'

I should have known that one, Ursula thought. It was what Eric had for that slut Lucinda.

'I think we should take two copies of *The Times*,' Eric said.

'Don't be ridiculous,' Ursula murmured. 'That would be wildly extravagant—and totally unnecessary! Fed up—brackets—for the market. Six letters.'

'Fatten,' Eric said.

Ursula nodded. 'It fits.'

Did farmers have any difficulty when fattening cows for the market, in concentrating on certain bits of their anatomy? Did customers want fat legs and thin backs? The thought of her own anatomy was never very far from her mind. There was an itch if you like!

'I'd better be off,' Eric said. 'Busy day ahead.' He walked around the table and gave Ursula a quick kiss on the top of her head.

'Don't be late home,' she said. 'Rehearsal!'

'As if I could forget! But I won't be,' Eric

promised.

She heard him close the front door, start the car and zoom away down the drive. She gave one last glance at the crossword—four down, progress in reverse, (ship), eight letters, of which she had five in position, but the other three eluded her. She hated to leave it unfinished, and seldom did, but time was pressing, she also had a busy day ahead, and right now there were those sodding exercises to be done before, by then sweating freely, she would take her shower and dress for the day.

She left the kitchen, went upstairs, changed from her nightdress into her leotard, came down and switched on the video. Honey sprang to life in all her nauseating vitality.

*   *   *

Eric, on the way to the office, thought about the day ahead. Eleven o'clock meeting with the sales force . . . Great heavens he had left the file, all the figures, all the forecasts and projects and costings, at home! To the consternation of the queue of traffic behind him, he screeched to a halt, made a U-turn and headed back to Mindon.

*   *   *

Honey was in full and exuberant voice, cheerful and smiling as she flung herself around the screen, chanting to the heavy beat of the music.

'. . . and-one-and-two, and how-d'-you do! And three-and-four, and touch that floor! And five and six, now try these tricks, And seven and eight, we stand up straight, and nine and ten, do all again . . .'

Eric's key turned silently in the well-oiled lock. He opened the door. That was strange music for Ursula to be listening to. Her choice seldom veered from light classical, something tuneful. Perhaps, he thought as he crossed the hall, it was some modern opera?

Ursula was in the middle of arm-swinging exercises, those movements which promised so much and, in Ursula's case, delivered so little. She was into weights now, one grasped firmly in each hand as she flung her arms around to the beat. She did not hear Eric enter the room. One second she was alone with that cow, Honey, and the next second, as she raised her head, there was Eric, standing in the doorway, staring at her in astonishment.

Everything happened at once.

In a forward swing—she could not halt the momentum—her hand relaxed and the weight flew across the room, landing fair and square in Honey's shining white teeth. It was an action Ursula had longed to take for some time, but now was not the time to savour it since she was screaming at the sight and sound of the exploding television. Eric bounded across the room to her rescue, and as he took her in his arms the weight dropped from her other hand and landed on his foot. His bellow of pain blended with her now subsiding screams.

'What in God's name . . .?' Eric cried, hopping on one foot towards the sofa, on to which he fell.

It was impossible for Ursula to answer. She had burst into loud, wailing, uncontrollable sobs, which to Eric were even more inexplicable than the exploding television. In twenty-five years of marriage he had experienced nothing like it. Ursula

330

might, and did, raise her voice, criticize, carp and complain, but lose control? Never! Never, either, had he seen her shaken by sobs. A few tears, certainly, but no more than a gentle shower of rain against which this was a tropical storm.

With a mighty effort of will he put aside the pain in his foot, stood up and folded his scantily clad wife in his arms.

'I did it for you!' she cried hysterically. 'I did it all for you!'

'Did what, my darling?'

'All this! That stupid Honey!'

'Who is Honey?'

'That stupid woman on the exercise video! She's as bad as Lucinda! I can't be like Lucinda! I've tried. I can't! It doesn't work!'

'Lucinda?' he said. 'What has Lucinda to do with anything?'

'I hate her! I hate her hair and I hate her teeth and most of all I hate her bust! Her bloody, big, bouncy bust! I hate all women with big tits!'

'I don't understand any of this!' Eric said. 'Let's sit down quietly on the sofa and you can explain everything!' He would have to sit down. His foot was killing him.

She allowed herself to be led to the sofa and they sat there, his arm around her as he dried her tears and his foot throbbed.

'Now tell me what it's all about,' he said.

'I know she's attractive,' Ursula spoke through her subsiding sobs, little hiccups interrupting her words. 'But she's as common as dirt and as bold as brass but that's what men like, isn't it, but I thought you were different and you're not because you've fallen for her hook line and sinker.' She paused briefly to draw breath.

'And I can't be like Lucinda and if Lucinda's what you want then I'm sorry and if—'

He put a finger across her lips and stopped her in mid-speech.

'You've got it wrong!' he said. 'There's nothing at all between me and Lucinda. She's just a bit of fun. She's a joke. Everybody knows she's a joke, even Lucinda knows it. She's nice enough, but I don't love Lucinda. I never could. You're the one I love!'

Ursula stopped crying, blew her nose, looked up at him.

'Are you sure?

'Absolutely certain! Couldn't be more sure!'

Ursula gave a great sigh of relief. 'But you did chase after her! You must admit it!'

'We all chase after Lucinda. I never wanted to catch up with her.' He was not sure, even now, whether that was entirely true, but he was deeply impressed by Ursula's outburst. She must love him more than he'd realized. She was not, normally, a demonstrative woman.

'You are the only one for me,' he said. 'We're used to each other, aren't we?'

She snuggled closer. For a moment or two they sat in silence.

'With you,' Eric said presently, as one discovering an important truth, 'I don't have to try to hold my stomach in!'

'And with you,' Ursula told him, 'I don't have to pad my bra!'

They breathed twin sighs of satisfaction.

'Why are you here?' Ursula asked a minute or two later. 'Why aren't you at work?'

'I left my file at home. I came back for it. Anyway, I've decided I won't go in for the meeting. They must postpone it, or hold it without me. I shall ring in and tell them I've hurt my foot!'

'Let me do that for you,' Ursula offered. 'It will sound more convincing.'

*   *   *

'Well!' Ursula said, beaming. 'I don't know when we've had a rehearsal go so well. At long last you all seem to know your lines! So keep it up, don't let them go. Only a few more weeks now and it will be the real thing!'

She turned to Petra.

'Just one or two of the costumes need a nip and a tuck, now that we've tried them on. I'm sure you can easily deal with that.'

'Quite easily,' Petra confirmed. 'And the rest will be ready by this time next week. The scenery's all done, if you'd like to try some of it out.'

'Why not?' Ursula said. 'Atmosphere is so helpful! Did you enjoy your little trip to see your friend?'

'I did, thank you!'

'It's nice to be back, though.'

'I was only away one night,' Petra said. 'But it seemed longer. And yes, I'm very pleased to be back in Mindon.'

One or two mothers, and a big sister, came in to collect the fairies and see them safely home. Amelia rounded up Teresa and Emma, now completely measle-free.

'I thought the fairies were extra specially good this evening!' Ursula said kindly. 'Titania, you must

333

have been pleased with them?'

'Oh, I was!' Lucinda agreed. 'They were little angels!' What was all this sweetness and light? It was quite unnerving.

Ursula took a deep breath.

'And you, Titania! I think you gave your best performance to date. You were really most convincing!'

I can't be doing with this, Lucinda thought. It's unhealthy!

'And now that we've acquitted ourselves so well, who's for the Queen's Head? It sounds to me as if we've all earned a drink!'

'Me and George can't go tonight,' Tina said. 'We've promised Daniel we'd not be late.' The truth was, George had said he had something to tell Daniel, and so far he hadn't even told *her* what it was.

'It's to be a surprise,' he said.

'You can surely tell me, after all, I'm his mother,' Tina said as they gathered their things together, ready to leave the hall.

'Oh, all right!' George said. 'Only I want to be the one to tell Daniel. The thing is, I've got three tickets for the last test match at Headingly. You, me and Daniel. They came in the post this morning.'

'Oh, George! But Headingly? Isn't that in Leeds?'

'So what? It's not the North Pole! We can go on the coach, stay in a bed and breakfast. I've still got some holiday to come, and so have you. And it's school holidays for Daniel.'

'Oh he'll be so pleased!' Tina said. 'It's very generous of you, George!'

'I've saved a bit,' George said. 'I can afford it.'

'Will it be all right if I take my knitting? I mean, are you allowed to knit at a test match?'

'There's no law against it that I know of,' George said, 'though I can't imagine anyone wanting to do it!'

'Daniel will be over the moon!' Tina said happily. 'You couldn't have pleased him better. You're getting to be real friends, the two of you!'

The fairies had left, Tina and George left. The rest grouped loosely together, ready to depart.

'You're coming to the pub, Eric?' Lucinda asked.

Eric was standing next to Ursula. His foot was hurting like hell, he had limped through his part all evening.

'Not this evening,' he said. 'Ursula and I thought we'd have an early night.'

After only the briefest pause Lucinda said, 'Oh, you naughty things! So who's going to buy little me a drink?'

'I am!' Cyril said. 'It's only right that Bottom should buy Titania a drink.'

'Thank you, Bottom!' Lucinda said. She took his arm and led him out of the hall.

'What about you?' Adam asked Petra.

'Can we sneak away?' Petra said. 'Can we just go home?'

'Sure!' Adam said. 'I'd like that.'

CHAPTER TWENTY-TWO

It is Wednesday, the first night of Mindon's Amateur Dramatic Society's production of *A*

335

Midsummer Night's Dream by William Shakespeare. There will be a repeat performance on Thursday and another on Saturday, but not on Friday. No-one can remember the original reason for omitting Friday. It just is so.

The curtains are firmly drawn across the stage, which does not prevent Doris Pritchard contriving a very small opening between them, at her own eye level, so that she can observe what is happening in the body of the hall. Only she, as property mistress, her husband Norman as stage manager and Chalky White as carpenter (in case of sudden, desperate need) are allowed on the stage before the start of the performance. And Ursula, of course. She is allowed anywhere. She is fully in charge. On the other hand she is almost helpless. There is little she can do now beyond giving last-minute words of encouragement to all and sundry. It is too late for admonishments. She must now hope that all she has invested in time, talent and training (plus W. Shakespeare's provision of the lines) will bear fruit.

Ursula is on stage now, checking that Doris has done her job and everything needed is to hand. There is no need for this since Doris, though her job is a humble one, is perhaps the most reliable person in MADS.

'It's filling up nicely,' Doris reports. 'About half the seats taken so far. I can see the Ainsworths, and Minnie Porritt. I hope she lasts out the performance. Her baby's well overdue! And why does Archie Pickersgill sit at the back when everyone knows he's as deaf as a post?'

'So that he can grumble about people not speaking up,' Norman says.

'Let me just take a peep, dear,' Ursula says. It's

336

not a dignified thing to do, but she's curious.

Doris moves over and Ursula applies her eye to the narrow aperture.

'Oh yes!' she says with satisfaction. 'Angela has done a good job with her publicity. I hear the ticket sales were better than ever.'

'In spite of it being Shakespeare!' Norman says.

'Let's hope it goes better than it did at the dress rehearsal!' Chalky White says. 'That was diabolical.' He is a good carpenter but he would never make a diplomat.

'Come now, Chalky!' Ursula says, turning away from the curtain. 'It wasn't so very terrible. And in any case we all know that a bad dress rehearsal means a good first night!'

She is wrong about it not having been terrible. It was truly awful. Whatever could have gone wrong did so.

Players who had been word perfect from week one forgot their lines. Those who remembered their lines, forgot their cues. A few forgot lines, cues *and* moves. Hippolyta had a nosebleed. Peter Quince fell over a rope (what was a rope *doing* there?) and twisted his ankle. He would have a limp for the rest of the week, though rather a limping Quince than, say, a limping Lysander.

There had been several cases of childish tantrums, though not from the children. The children had been well-behaved, but unfortunately nerves had caused them to visit the lavatory one after the other.

The costumes, generally acclaimed, had needed several adjustments. Helena had complained that unless the hem of her skirt was turned up another two inches she knew she would trip over it and fall

337

flat on her face. Theseus's trouser zip jammed, which was unfortunate for so dignified a personage.

Demetrius complained that his artificial moustache irritated his upper lip, and wished out loud that he had not let Deidre at Cutting Edge shave off his very own one.

Ursula had come so near to losing her cool that she had been heard to say that this was probably the last play she would ever undertake and in future they would have to look elsewhere for a producer.

No-one had gone to the Queen's Head afterwards. It was past closing time when the rehearsal had ended. 'Everyone must get a good night's sleep,' Ursula had commanded, 'and be fighting fit for tomorrow!'

'What ever shall we do when all this is over?' Petra had asked Adam as they'd walked back to Plum Tree House. 'We shall have four spare evenings a week!'

'We could get married,' Adam suggested. 'The nights will be drawing in soon. We could sit by the fire and watch TV!'

'We can do all that without getting married,' Petra had replied.

'But it would be nicer to be married!'

She had written to Tanya, who had replied. Eliot was still in Italy, there was no news of when he might return. That's OK, Petra thought. She was in no mood to see him, and not sure that she ever would be.

Before she could answer Adam she had been called to fix Hippolyta's headdress.

Only Bottom had sailed through the dress rehearsal word perfect, cue perfect, confident, as

338

cool as a cucumber. He might at one point have been anxious had he known that a search was going on for the wreath of flowers which the fairies were to place on his ass's head, but that was kept from him. It was Doris who found it, exactly where it should be.

All that had been yesterday evening. Now it is the real thing. Real people are sitting in those uncomfortable chairs, people who have paid good money.

Ursula leaves the stage and makes for the dressing-rooms, which is what they are called for the week of the play. At other times they are two rooms shared between the Flower Club, the Badminton League, Brownies, Mothers and Toddlers, Senior Citizens, Keep Fit, Yoga and Miss Terry's Ballet Class, and both rooms—one for the men, the other for the women and children—bear something of the detritus of those other users.

'Now, girls!' Ursula calls out—she has to raise her voice to be heard above the wonderful sound of Mendelssohn's music to the *Dream*, which now swells and reverberates through the whole building. How fortuitous, she thinks, that he wrote this splendid music for the play they are about to perform!

'Now, girls!' she repeats in a cheerful voice. 'Is everyone ready to go?' She is as nervous as a cat, but trying not to show it. At this moment she knows they rely on her to give them confidence, and she will not let them down.

'Good!' she says, though no-one has actually replied. 'And do remember one thing. A small thing, but important! No-one, *no-one,* is to go into the hall, even after the performance is over, wearing stage make-up! It is *most* unprofessional!' Her tone of voice intimates that such a transgression is punishable by death, though everyone knows that there is no way she can prevent all those little fairies rushing out into the audience to show themselves off to parents, grandparents, aunts, uncles and admiring friends the minute the final curtain has closed.

Ursula's stern glance sweeps around the company, and rests for a moment on Titania who, with layers of make-up and wearing her ethereal white low-cut gown, plus the long golden wig she has insisted on hiring even at her own expense, is looking ravishingly beautiful. But Ursula is able to look at her now without a qualm. She is safe from Lucinda, and so, thank God, is Eric.

'So good luck, everyone!' she says. 'And now I shall go and wish the men the same!'

From the moment the curtain rises, the play is a great success. The scenery, thanks to Petra, is wonderful, so are the costumes. Theseus is majestic, as is Oberon. The lovers are passionate. Titania and her fairies are out of this world, and the Mechanicals draw many laughs. Indeed, it could be said that it is Bottom who is the star of the show—which comes as no surprise to him. He has always thought he would be.

' "So goodnight unto you all.

Give me your hands if we be friends

And Robin shall restore amends," ' says Puck.

But his final words are drowned by the tumultuous applause which breaks out even before the curtains close.

'Who says the MADS can't do Shakespeare?' Ursula asks the cast when the curtains close after three calls, and she has made a gracious little speech. 'Of course we can! And think what lies before us! *King Lear, Romeo and Juliet. Twelfth Night* would be suitable!'

'*All's Well that Ends Well,*' says Eric, easing off his false moustache.